THE RISE OF
AREDOR

THE RISE OF
AREDOR

Claire Banschbach (signature)

Claire M. Banschbach

TATE PUBLISHING
AND ENTERPRISES, LLC

The Rise of Aredor
Copyright © 2014 by Claire M. Banschbach. All rights reserved.

No part of this publication may be reproduced, stored in a retrieval system or transmitted in any way by any means, electronic, mechanical, photocopy, recording or otherwise without the prior permission of the author except as provided by USA copyright law.

The opinions expressed by the author are not necessarily those of Tate Publishing, LLC.

Published by Tate Publishing & Enterprises, LLC
127 E. Trade Center Terrace | Mustang, Oklahoma 73064 USA
1.888.361.9473 | www.tatepublishing.com

Tate Publishing is committed to excellence in the publishing industry. The company reflects the philosophy established by the founders, based on Psalm 68:11,
"The Lord gave the word and great was the company of those who published it."

Book design copyright © 2014 by Tate Publishing, LLC. All rights reserved.
Cover design by Allen Jomoc
Interior design by Caypeeline Casas

Published in the United States of America

ISBN: 978-1-62854-194-6
1. Fiction / Fantasy / General
2. Fiction / Coming of Age
13.12.06

DEDICATION

This book is dedicated to my sister of a thousand faces and a hundred names who irritated me until I finished this story. Some thanks are in order.

ACKNOWLEDGMENTS

Firstly, I would like to thank my sisters, who were the first readers of this story for their encouragement and for their pressure to finish it.

To my sister Sarah, who gave my final version a good once over before I decided to send it to the publisher, it was harsh, but necessary. You made me look good.

To my sister Jocelyn, who fell in love with Emeth and condescended to put her talent to use in illustrating this book—thank you. Your framed artwork will hang in our magical treehouse one day.

A brief thanks to my sister Catherine for working tirelessly with me on developing the pronunciation guide. I sincerely hope someone looks at it and finds it useful.

I want to thank Mary Kaylyn Miller for working patiently with me through e-mail and with my rough interpretations to produce the fully awesome map. It gave me chills to see my imagination on paper.

Many thanks to my parents, who, at first, didn't know I had written a book, much less sent it to a publisher. They have been very supportive, not just through this process but through my whole life. They are the ones who fulfilled my literary needs by supplying stacks of books for birthdays, Christmases, and just because. Thank you for everything that you have done for me. I know that they can't wait to actually read this story to be able to understand conversations around the dinner table.

I also want to thank the folks at Tate Publishing, who decided to give this story a chance.

PRONUNCIATION GUIDE

c: hard as in cat–e.g. Corin, Celyn, Cimbria, Cyndor, etc.
ae: long *a*–e.g. Braeton
ll: *l* rolled on the side of the tongue–e.g. Llewellyn, Lleu
í: long *e* as in *meet* when used in Calorin names–e.g. Hamíd. (sometimes *i* is long in last syllable as in Karif, Hosni, etc.)
j: sounded like soft *g* as in *gentle* when used in Calorin names– e.g. Jaffa, Janzori
g: hard as in *great*–e.g. Gavin, Gelion
I: pronounced as *e* for Aredorian names only–e.g. Iwan (Ewan) Ivor (Ee-vor)
y: sounded like short *i* when used as a vowel in Aredorian names–e.g. Colwyn, Celyn

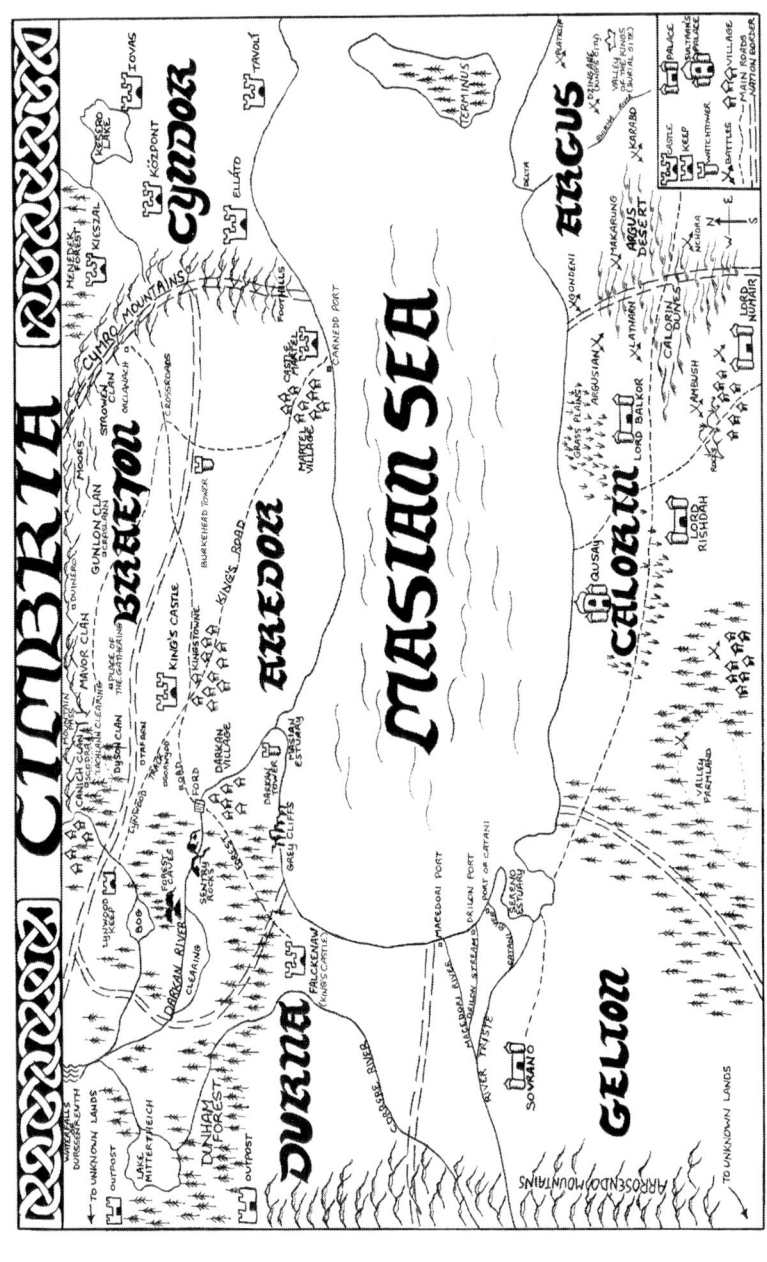

BOOK ONE

The Phoenix Guard

"I was twelve when it happened," he said to the dark-skinned man. "Twelve when I was ripped from my home and everything I knew."

"How did it happen, Corin?" the dark-skinned man asked. Corin looked up abruptly.

"You said that was your name."

Corin leaned back on the bed, wincing a little as firelight illuminated his features. "Yes, sir. I am Corin, second son of King Celyn and Queen Elain, Prince of Aredor."

CHAPTER 1

Thump…thump…thump. The boy's heel kicked the chair as he absentmindedly stared out the window. His paper and quill lay forgotten on the table in front of him along with the lesson he was supposed to be studying.

"Prince Corin!" The sound brought the boy back to earth with a jolt. "I do not think the proper declensions of those nouns lie outside," the old man said somewhat sternly. Corin glared at Bevan, his tutor, and gave one last rebellious kick to the chair. His older brother Darrin stifled a grin from his place across the room. Corin picked up his pen and began writing, threatening to break the quill pen in the process. Darrin could hear him muttering as he wrote the lesson. At twelve years of age, Corin hated the long afternoons full of grammar, history, science, language, and mathematics. Darrin was almost fifteen, but he could not resist a sudden temptation.

He tore off the corner of a piece of parchment. Dipping his quill into the ink, he began making sure strokes. A fat, grumpy image of the tutor slouching in his chair began to appear. Finished, Darrin rolled it into a ball and checked to make sure Bevan was absorbed in his book before flicking it expertly across the room to land on Corin's desk. Corin unrolled the parchment and barely stifled an explosive giggle. At the strangled noise, Bevan looked up, only to see his students writing industriously. As soon as his attention was returned to the book, Corin retaliated. His sketch was rougher than Darrin's but still brought out the desired effect. Bevan's attention was taken from his book again as Darrin became overtaken by a violent bout of coughing.

"Are you all right, Your Highness?" he asked, rising and walking over to Darrin's desk.

"Um...yes, sir. Something just caught in my throat, that's all," Darrin said. Quick as lightning, the tutor snatched up the paper from under Darrin's hand. Outrage covered his face. Crossing to Corin's desk, Bevan rifled through the papers until he found the second sketch.

"How dare you! I shall report this to your father! You shall both be punished!" Waving the papers madly, he strode from the room, slamming the door shut behind him. The boys slouched dejectedly in their seats.

"Sorry, Cor. Bevan looked really mad this time," Darrin said. Corin nodded glumly.

"Do you think Father will be very angry?" he asked. Darrin shrugged.

"I just hope he still lets us go to Lynwood with him," he said.

"That wouldn't be fair! He promised we could go!" Corin exclaimed. A gloomy silence prevailed in the room as the boys contemplated their punishment. They did not have long to wait before heavy footsteps announced the arrival of their father. The door swung open and King Celyn strode into the room followed by an agitated Bevan.

"It's outrageous, sire! This is not the first time that they have mocked me! I demand that they be severely punished!" Darrin and Corin could not help but exchange sly grins at their tutor's discomfort. Their father saw it and waved his hand to silence Bevan.

"Peace, Bevan! Leave us, and I will deal with my sons," he said. With a highly satisfied air, Bevan left the room, shooting one last murderous look at the boys before shutting the door. King Celyn crossed the room and sat down in the armchair. He held the sketches up in his hand.

"Have you anything to say for yourselves?" he asked quietly. The boys shook their heads. "Bevan is your tutor, and as such, you should give him proper respect. Although I do admit these are remarkable likenesses," he said. Startled, the boys looked up to see a twinkle in Celyn's deep blue eyes.

"You're not angry with us, Father?" Corin ventured. King Celyn laughed quietly.

"I suppose I should be, but Bevan takes himself very seriously sometimes."

"So…are you going to punish us?" Darrin asked.

"You are both to apologize to Bevan, and then you are excused from lessons for the rest of the day," the king said. The boys did not wait for him to change his mind. They dashed from the room, promising to find Bevan and apologize. King Celyn leaned back in the chair and sighed. Bevan would not be happy with the "punishment," but they were just boys after all. He could remember tormenting his own tutor when he was their age. He considered finding someone else to teach the boys. Bevan's complaining grated on his nerves, especially when he was dealing with more important affairs of Aredor. He would give more serious thought to it tonight. Maybe his wife would have some ideas. Reluctantly, he rose from the chair and strode from the room; the duty of kings called him back to work.

"C'mon, Martin!" Corin shouted. "Race you to the river!" A young boy about his own age ran beside him through the east gate of the castle and across fields until they came to the river. It was more like a stream that ran across the open plain. The boys frequented the stream to play in the shallow water or to cross over to reach the training grounds of the warbands. Corin and Martin arrived together, panting from their run. Their attention was soon taken by a frog that hopped out of the shallow water. After a few minutes, they gave up trying to catch the slippery creature. Corin sat on the bank and stared at the distant mountains.

"What do you think lives in the mountains?" he asked. Martin propped himself up on his elbows.

"I don't know," he said. "Someday, when we're both famous warriors, we can go explore. Father says they're too dangerous for young boys."

"Psh! They only tell you that so you don't ever go look," Corin said. He took strongly after his father, inheriting his blonde hair and the same piercing blue eyes. Corin was strong willed and impetuous, but held a battle sense that came from a long line of warriors. Martin was just as reckless as Corin. Martin was the son of King Celyn's most trusted general. The boys had been friends through thick and thin, getting each other in and out of trouble. When they reach the age of fourteen, they would begin their training together. That day was an event much longed for. Then they would be able to join the ranks of men that trained across the river. And one day they would each command a war band as a prince and as a captain.

"Did your father say you could go to Lynwood with us?" Corin asked.

"No, he said he's not going along this time. The king wants him to stay at the castle," Martin said. "But he said he'd make it up by taking me with him when he goes to Castle Martel in a few weeks."

"Lucky," Corin grumbled. "I hardly ever get to visit the coast. The only time we get to see Tristan and Trey is when they come here."

"They'll all come to the autumn festival though," Martin pointed out.

"Good, we can beat them at the races this year," Corin said. Every year at the festival, young boys raced their ponies bareback around the training grounds. And this year, Corin and Martin were determined to beat the two brothers from Castle Martel.

"It'll be our last year to race ponies. Next year we can finally race horses," Martin said. "Father is giving me the new colt from Braith. I get to train him all by myself."

Corin regarded him somewhat jealously. Training was a big responsibility; the colt would become Martin's first warhorse.

"Come on, I'll show him to you," Martin said. The boys hopped nimbly up from the bank and tore off in a full-out race back to the castle.

Corin sneaked up the stairs to his room. He had a few minutes before being called for dinner. He rounded a corner and encountered his mother.

"Corin! What happened? You're filthy!" Queen Elain asked. Corin shuffled his feet awkwardly.

"Well, Martin and I went down to the river and then to the stables. After that we met Bran outside, and we might have gotten into a fight," he said. Queen Elain sighed.

"What will I do with you when you insist on dirtying and tearing all your clothes?" she asked.

"I'll try to do better, really I will!" Corin promised her. The queen looked into his earnest blue eyes and sighed again. He was too much like his father. All too soon she would be worried about him fighting with weapons and hurting more than his clothes.

"All right, go change and clean up. Don't be late for dinner!" she said.

Corin arrived in the great hall just as the meal was beginning. He slipped into his place at the high table with his family, tugging on his younger sister's hair as he did so. Amaura made a face at him, and he stuck his tongue out in return.

"Father said he might get us a new tutor!" Darrin whispered to Corin.

"Really? Who?" Corin asked. Darrin passed him a plate of meat.

"I don't know. He said that Bevan might start teaching Amaura instead," Darrin said.

"I hope he does," Amaura said. "I like Bevan, and I don't see why you two are so mean to him." Corin looked aghast.

"You like him?? How is that even possible?" he exclaimed.

"He's always very nice to me," she said.

"That's 'cause you're just a little girl, and you don't see him all the time," Darrin said.

"I am not little!" Amaura exclaimed.

"You're ten," Corin pointed out.

"Yes, and you're only twelve," Amaura said. She stuck her nose in the air and began eating very primly. The boys rolled their eyes and tore hungrily into their food.

Queen Elain looked down at one of the lower tables and noticed Martin sitting with his family, looking freshly scrubbed and clean.

"Did you decide on a tutor yet?" she asked Celyn.

"I think so," the king replied. "I heard about the fight already. Don't worry. I'll see what Ivor can do for them," he said.

"Ivor? Are you sure, Celyn?" the queen asked.

"Yes, he can keep them in line. I think the boys will respond better to his teaching," the king said.

"Have you told them yet?" Elain asked. Celyn shook his head.

"No, they'll find out tomorrow. I confess I do want to be there to see their faces," he said.

The next day, the two young princes trudged unwillingly up to the school room. Opening the door, they stopped in shock. Instead of Bevan, another man stood at the window. He wore a leather tunic and vambraces over a blue-and-black uniform. Tall and muscular, he could easily carry the large broadsword that leaned against the wall. Darrin knew him from the training fields.

"Ivor?" he asked in astonishment. The warrior bowed.

"Your Highnesses," he said. Corin stared wide-eyed at Ivor as he sat at his desk.

"Where's Bevan?" Corin asked.

"Your father decided that Bevan's time would be better spent in the library and archives as well as teaching the Princess Amaura," Ivor replied. "He asked me to come teach you a few times a week. If you two are ready, we might as well get started."

From the very beginning, Ivor did not approve of the lessons Bevan had given them. He tossed aside the papers filled with math problems to be solved in terms of apples, sheep, and cattle and began asking the problems in numbers of supplies for armies, warhorses, and enemy soldiers. Problems that had proven difficult before were now solved easily by the boys. He took maps off the walls and spread them on the table and told them of the different countries in Cimbria, their people, and customs.

"Corin, what can you tell me about Gelion?" Ivor asked. Corin studied the map for a minute.

"They are a trade country," he said hesitantly.

"Yes, and what special privilege do they enjoy?" Ivor asked him again.

"They are at peace with every other country at all times because we all trade with them," Corin said more confidently. Ivor nodded.

"Gelion controls the Masian Sea with their merchant ships. Mostly they trade with the southern countries, Calorin and Argus. The southern lands are always trying to fight a war with someone or expand their territory, but they wouldn't dare attack Gelion because they depend too much on the trade," he said.

"Have you ever been to the south, Ivor?" Darrin asked.

"Once, a few years ago when the king visited the Calorin Sultaan," Ivor said.

"What was it like?" Corin asked curiously.

"Hot and flat," Ivor said. "I will say one thing for them: they breed the finest horses I've ever seen. Now, did you two know that there are two heroes with your names?" And so the lessons continued with the boys' attention completely captured by Ivor. The hours of lessons were no longer dreaded, and they learned quickly, much to the delight of their parents. Then finally, the much anticipated day finally came, and Corin and Darrin set out with their father to visit Lynwood Keep.

CHAPTER 2

Lynwood Keep was situated in the northwestern part of Dunham Forest. It sat close to the southern border of Braeton and the eastern border of Durna. Dunham Forest covered most of the western half of Aredor all the way to the Grey Cliffs by the Masian Sea and extended unbroken throughout much of Durna. A visual boundary had been cleared between the two countries, running seven yards wide and extending the length of Aredor from the cliffs to the northernmost corner between the two countries.

The garrison at Lynwood Keep was comprised mostly of foresters and rangers that patrolled through the forest, watching the boundary and keeping it cleared. A few times a year, King Celyn would visit his outlying forts to make sure all was in good order. He had decided to let his sons accompany him so that he might begin to show them how to keep an outpost organized. Besides that, they had been begging for months to go along on his next trip. The journey took almost two days from Kingscastle at the slow pace they kept.

On the third day at Lynwood, King Celyn gave Corin permission to ride out into the forest while he spent the day with Darrin, going over supply lists. The job sounded unutterably dull to Corin, so he jumped at the chance of exploring the forest by himself. After promising he would not stray too far from the known paths, he rode through the front gates of the keep and into the forest. After a time, he turned off the Lynwood Track and onto a well-worn path he knew would take him to the river. By lunchtime, he had reached the banks of the Darkan River. He ate and spent a lazy afternoon by the wide, flowing water.

The patterns of the sun through the leaves began to change, signaling the afternoon was moving toward evening. He gathered up his bag and slung it over the saddle. He needed to leave if he was to make it back to the keep in time for supper. As he prepared to mount his horse, the bushes parted, and four strange men stepped out. They seemed equally surprised to see him. Before he knew what was happening, they grabbed him and held him tight.

"Who are you?" he managed to say. Their leader gave a low laugh.

"Only poor dishonest tradesmen trying to find a profit in this blasted north land. And I think you'll add a nice bonus to our trip," the man said. Corin struggled, but the men were too strong for him.

"You can't take me! My father…," Corin began, but the man cut him off.

"I don't care who your father is, just as long as you fetch a fair price," he said. One of his men stopped.

"But, sir, look at how he's dressed. We could get a ransom out of him," the man said.

"No, I don't want to stay here any longer. Besides, they'd pay the ransom then come after us and kill us for kidnapping him. You underestimate these northerners, and I'd rather keep my head if it's all the same to you!" the captain snapped. "Tie him up and take him to the boat. If he starts talking, just gag him." He began issuing orders. "Get rid of that horse and cover the tracks so we don't leave any traces."

Corin's hands were tied tightly behind him, and one of the slavers shoved him roughly and led him down the river to where a small boat waited. The rest of the men joined them soon after, and the boat was cast off into the river. The slavers plied the oars expertly and sent the boat flying down the river. As the sun finally set, they turned down a side stream. Two days later, they boarded a ship anchored in a hidden bay by the Grey Cliffs. Corin was imprisoned in the hold and left to ponder his fate. He was still reeling from the abrupt abduction and told himself that he would be missed almost immediately and then his father would come looking for him. But that couldn't stop the sheer panic he felt at his helplessness.

After three weeks at sea, the slave ship docked at a bustling port town in the country of Calorin. Corin had been forced to exchange his fine clothes for the rougher garments of a slave. During the long voyage, he had hardly spoken a word, feeling any hope slipping away with each passing day. He was led up on the deck along with other unfortunate prisoners, blinking in the bright sunlight. The crew of the ship herded the slaves down the gangplank and into the busy town. Despite his predicament, Corin looked around curiously as they walked. The people around him were dark skinned and spoke a strange language. The marketplace was filled with bright spinning colors as people went about their daily business of buying and selling. The prisoners were given hardly a glance; slave ships were a common sight in the town. Corin found he was not to be sold in the market with the other prisoners; the slaver had something else in mind for him. A few days later, when the "business" in the city was completed, the slavers headed east toward their next destination. In desperation, he tried to run from his captors one night but was caught again and punished as harshly as the slaver dared. After that, his fear became very real.

"None of the others were suitable enough for your lordship," the slaver whined. Lord Balkor looked Corin up and down scornfully.

"A ragged northern brat? What am I supposed to do with him?" he asked the slaver. The man seized his chance.

"Why, a boy like this, he'll be quite a diversion. With a little training, he'd make a fine servant, take care of your worship-fullness's guests just fine." The slaver watched Lord Balkor carefully.

The Calorin lord was a hard, unpredictable man, but he always paid well for good slaves.

"I have enough house slaves right now, but I'll take him. Maybe as a stable boy, do you think?' he asked. The slaver nodded furiously.

"Yes, lord. He'd make a fine impression in your livery. I'm sure you won't regret it!" the slaver said, taking the money handed him by Lord Balkor, who then dismissed him with a wave of his hand. Corin had stood quietly by during the whole exchange, not understanding a word. He saw the money change hands and realized with a sick feeling that he had just been sold as a horse was sold in the market. Then to his surprise, Lord Balkor addressed him in the Northern language.

"You! What's your name?" he asked and then waved Corin off. "No, I don't care. It's probably something completely unpronounceable. Just know this, you belong to me now." With that, he strode off, leaving Corin with another servant.

"You…come…," the servant said haltingly. Corin nodded in understanding and followed the servant as he went outside. The servant left him with a woman who took him to the slave quarters and showed him where he would stay. That night, Corin lay huddled on the rough bed. The past few weeks had seemed like a bad dream from which he would awaken sooner or later. But the events of the day had struck home the bitter reality. He was in a strange country, his family knew nothing of his whereabouts, and he was a slave. He crossed his arms tightly over his chest as if to squeeze out the dull ache of homesickness and fright. Softly, he began to cry.

Corin wiped sweat from his face and rested a moment. The wide flat plains stretched on over the horizon. He missed acutely the green rolling hills and forests of his home. Lord Balkor had changed his mind about his newest slave, and Corin was sent to work in the fields. The overseer turned in Corin's direction, and he hurriedly bent and continued working. The months had dragged by since he first arrived. He learned quickly to keep his mouth shut and his eyes down. No one cared that he had never worked before, least of all the overseers. A young boy about his own age had befriended him and had begun teaching him the Calorin language. It was slow work at first; they made do with gestures and simple words until Corin began learning more. Corin would practice as they worked side by side in the fields while Hosni laughed at his accent. Hosni also gave him a new name, Hamíd. *A new name, a new life,* Corin thought. At first, he had wild plans of escaping back home, but he realized how impossible that would be. He had no idea where he was and wouldn't be able to make it back to the coast without being caught. So he worked, harder than he ever had in his entire life, and tried not to think about his family and home.

Corin was awake before dawn. He heard the sounds of the other slaves rising and making ready to spend another day in the fields. He lay still for a few more minutes. Today, he was fifteen. Three long years had passed since he first came there. Frightened, Corin realized that he had become resigned to this new life. Only a faint spark of his former spirit remained. Clenching his jaw, he silently resolved to find a way back home. He was no longer helpless here, and maybe he could make it. He was taller now and stronger and could speak the Calorin language fluently. *You may never go back,* a silent voice told him. He forced the thought away; he would find a way.

Footsteps sounded, and Hosni ran up.

"Tamir is looking for you," he said. Corin rose swiftly.

"Why?" he asked. Hosni shrugged.

"It can't be good though," he said as Corin pulled on his shoes. Tamir was the sadistic overseer who usually went out of his way to make Corin's life even more miserable. They slowly went outside where Tamir waited.

"You," he said, pointing at Corin. "You're to help Fikri in the forge from now on. Get to it!"

"Yes, sir," Corin mumbled, making his way to the smithy by the stables. Inside, the blacksmith had begun to light his fires. He turned and sized Corin up as he came in.

"So you're the one they sent?" he said. Corin nodded silently. "You'll have to do, I suppose," the blacksmith grumbled. He kept Corin busier than ever before: fetching wood, keeping the fires hot, and leading horses to and from the stables. In his spare time, Fikri began to teach him how to work the metal and shape it into horseshoes or weapon blades, or how to repair chain mail shirts.

His close proximity to the main house brought him into more frequent contact with Lord Balkor. Each time he saw the lord, fresh anger would flare up in Corin's heart. Lord Balkor sensed it and had him soundly beaten for his "rebellious nature." The night of the punishment, Corin lay on his bunk, fighting back tears. But the pain radiating from the cuts on his back was no match for the shame of the mark now branded into the palm of his hand. It showed the world that he was nothing more than a slave. Corin took a strip of cloth and wound it about his hand, hiding the brand. *I will not break,* he vowed silently.

The only comfort he ever found was in the quiet of the stables, surrounded by the horses that reminded him of home. The years passed slowly as Corin grew quiet and withdrawn. He grew stronger with his work at the forge. Lord Balkor became angry at the cool defiance shining in Corin's blue eyes. He would devise punishments in an attempt to break Corin's spirit, but Corin refused to become intimidated, taking the beatings without a sound. Fikri looked out for Corin as best he could, keeping him out of Lord Balkor's way as much as possible. But as the years passed, Corin's memories of Aredor faded. He had only vague pictures of his family left. *They will have all changed so much. Do they remember me? I wonder,* he thought. *One day, I will escape this place and I will return,* he vowed.

CHAPTER 3

Hamíd placed the shoe over the gelding's hind foot and hammered it into place. Hosni handed him a file, and he smoothed the edge of the hoof. He slowly lowered the gelding's hoof down and straightened up trying not to grimace. It didn't work.

"How's your back doing?" Hosni asked. Hamíd leaned against the horse's back and sighed. It was no good trying to lie.

"Horrible. I feel like I'm going to be sick," he replied. Hosni was worried; Hamíd had been beaten again recently, and the wounds were bleeding, leaving red streaks across his shirt.

"You need to rest, Hamíd," Hosni said. Hamíd laughed bitterly.

"Try telling the high and mighty Lord Balkor that. See how far you get," he said, giving the gelding a pat as the groom led it away. "Here he comes now, and I don't think it's to inquire about my health." He and Hosni stood with heads bowed as Balkor came up.

"You," he said to Hamíd. "Get over here now!"

Hosni gave Hamíd an encouraging look as he made his way over to the irate lord.

"Yes, my lord?" Hamíd asked, bowing stiffly. Balkor gestured to the man standing by him.

"Slave, this is the Lord Rishdah. His horse needs looking after. See to it now!" Balkor ordered.

"Yes, sir," Hamíd said with another bow.

"This way, young man," Lord Rishdah said. He led Hamíd back across the courtyard to where several men stood holding horses. Two were dressed as guards in the livery of the Lord Rishdah. They wore deep-red shirts under jet-black tunics with a red phoenix emblazoned on the front. White pants were tucked into sturdy leather boots. Bright mail shirts peeked out from under their tunics. Thick leather belts were buckled around their waists, holding their weapons. One carried a scimitar while the other carried two blades across his back, the twin handles sticking up above his shoulders. Each carried several knives as well as a bow and a stocked quiver. The guards' companion was dressed more richly than they and carried himself with an easy confidence that suggested he was the Lord Rishdah's son.

"Emeth, bring the stallion!" Lord Rishdah called. The guard with the double swords took the reins from the son and led the horse over. Hamíd saw the stallion was limping badly on his right front foot, and as it came closer, he saw the ragged edge of the hoof as well as some small cuts on its leg.

"His shoe was loose, and he went and tore it off. Fell and cut his leg up a bit too," Emeth said to him. Hamíd nodded briefly as he went up to the horse to better examine it. As he felt down its leg, the stallion shied away. Hamíd caught at its bridle and stroked its forehead reassuringly.

"Hey now, easy boy. You're in no shape to be dancing around like that," he said quietly in his own tongue. The stallion snorted gently and settled down as he continued to talk gently to it.

"He likes you. He usually doesn't settle down that easily," said Emeth laughingly. Hamíd looked at him in surprise. He had spoken Rhyddan, the northern tongue. He saw now that Emeth was fair skinned like him and had wavy black hair and sparkling green eyes.

"You are far from home," Hamíd said.

"I could say the same for you," Emeth replied. Hamíd risked a glance at Balkor. He was looking angrily at him. Hamíd turned back to the horse and said in Calorin, "If you'll bring him to the forge, sir, I'll take care of him there."

Emeth nodded, and they went over to the smithy. Once the stallion was settled in the cross ties, Hamíd went to work. He gently trimmed the ragged edge from the hoof and then measured a shoe and shaped it to size. As he finished putting in the last nail and straightened up a wave of dizziness swept over him. He swayed and grabbed at the anvil to steady himself. Emeth instinctively reached out to help him, but Hamíd pushed his hand away.

"Don't! He is watching!" he said. Emeth looked over to see Balkor watching darkly as he stood by Lord Rishdah. Emeth shot a glance at his master and then turned to see what he was staring at. It was then that he saw the blood seeping through the young man's shirt.

What has he done to him? Emeth thought. *He won't last much longer like this!* It seemed Rishdah had the same thoughts. He turned to Balkor and began walking towards the main house. Emeth then turned to Hamíd and helped him sit down.

"Here, drink this," he commanded and held his waterskin to Hamíd's lips. He took a few slow sips then pushed it away and tried to get up. Emeth pushed him back down.

"You're in no condition to be working! What did he do to you?" he asked.

"Twenty-five lashes. I got blamed after his son ruined another horse," Hamíd replied. "Let me up. I need to finish with those cuts, and if he sees me like this, I'll get worse."

Emeth pinned him back down.

"My master will keep him occupied for a while," Emeth said. "Just sit. Here, tell me what to do for the cuts on Rais's leg." He had just finished wrapping a light bandage around the stallion's leg and was helping Hamíd to his feet when Lord Rishdah came up.

"Finished?" he asked.

"Yes, sir," Emeth replied.

"Good. Take the stallion. And you're coming with us," he said pointing at Hamíd.

"What?" Hamíd asked in surprise.

"I struck a deal with Lord Balkor. You belong with me now." Emeth led Hamíd over to where the others still stood accompanied by Lord Rishdah.

"Come, we leave now," Rishdah said. "Nicar, take the stallion. Ismail, you ride behind me, and, Emeth, take the boy behind you."

Nicar, the second guard, mounted his horse and took the stallion's reins from Emeth. Hamíd looked around for Hosni. He stood by the forge, watching them prepare to leave. He caught Hamíd's gaze and gave him a small smile. Hamíd raised a hand in farewell, then Emeth pulled Hamíd up behind him, and they rode through the gates.

The stallion was moving slowly, and they had to match its pace. The miles crept slowly by as they rode out of the farmlands and through the grassy plain. Nicar rode close to Rishdah.

"Sir, that young man won't make it much farther, especially in this heat. I suggest we make camp and let me look after him," he said. Rishdah nodded his agreement.

"Very well. Find a camping place where we can spend the night. We'll wait here," he said. Ismail took hold of the stallion from his place behind his father as Nicar cantered off.

"Why did you take him?" Ismail asked his father.

"He's been overworked and mistreated, but there's more to that young man than meets the eye," Rishdah said. "He was made for a sword and not a blacksmith's hammer." He glanced over to Emeth's horse standing a few feet away. Emeth had an arm wrapped back around Hamíd to keep him from falling off the horse. They waited only a few minutes before Nicar came back.

"There's a small oasis of sorts up ahead, sir. Trees and plenty of water," Nicar reported. Lord Rishdah gave his approval, and Nicar led them forward to the chosen campground. Once they reached the cool shelter of the trees, Nicar dismounted and quickly spread some blankets on the ground. He helped Hamíd down from the horse and made him lie down on the blankets. Hamíd instinctively obeyed, still confused by the sudden turn his life had taken.

Emeth and Ismail also dismounted and began setting up camp. Lord Rishdah tethered the horses nearby and began building a fire. Nicar scooped water from the pond and set it on the fire to heat. Then he took his knife and cut Hamíd's shirt off. His back was covered with deep, ugly gashes. Some of them were beginning to fester. He caught Hamíd looking at him warily.

"Easy, lad, I'm just going to clean up your back," Nicar said, calling for his pack. Emeth tossed it to him, and he took out a pouch of herbs and some bandages. He handed Hamíd a cup of liquid.

"Here, drink this. It'll help a little," he said. Hamíd raised himself up on an elbow and took a few sips, almost choking as he swallowed. Nicar forced him to finish, and then he lay back down on the blankets. Nicar took the hot water from the fire and began washing the cuts. Hamíd stiffened and tried to twist away. Nicar held him down and continued relentlessly. When he finished washing, he took out a needle and thread and began stitching the worst cuts. He then spread ointment on Hamíd's back and placed bandages over it. Once Nicar finished, Hamíd relaxed and soon fell asleep, his head pillowed on his arms. Nicar gently placed his cloak over Hamíd and moved quietly over to the fire.

"How's he doing?" Emeth asked him.

"He'll be all right with some rest and proper food," Nicar answered.

"Speaking of which, Emeth, you're on cooking duty," Rishdah said. Emeth groaned.

"I don't suppose there's any way to appeal, is there, sir?" he asked.

"No," Rishdah replied.

"Didn't think so," Emeth said as he picked up the food packs and took the fish Ismail had caught.

Hamíd slept all that night and most of the next day. Nicar woke him only to take some food. On the second day, he awoke feeling stronger and well rested. Emeth tossed him a fresh shirt he had rummaged from his pack. Hamíd pulled it gently over the bandages and stood slowly. He found he could move easily and with almost no pain, thanks to Nicar's ministrations. He watched in silence as the men began packing and saddling their horses. He was bewildered by the strange turn of events that had taken him away from Lord Balkor. The two guards were friendly enough, but he dreaded to think what might happen to him when they finally reached their destination. Within an hour, they had broken camp and were on their way home. Hamíd was once more mounted behind Emeth. They rode quietly for a few hours, and then Emeth broke the silence.

"So where are you from, Hamíd?" he asked in Rhyddan.

"Aredor, sir," Hamíd answered. Emeth laughed.

"You don't have to 'sir' me. We're about the same age. Just call me Emeth," he said.

"All right then, where are we going, Emeth, and what exactly am I in for?" Hamíd asked.

"Don't be so gloomy, Hamíd. We're headed home to Lord Rishdah's castle. We should get there just after dark," Emeth said. "He's a good man, treats everyone fairly, soldiers and servants alike. As a result, he's one of the richest men in Calorin and one of the Sultaan's chief advisors."

Hamíd found this hard to believe as the only other Calorin lords he had encountered were as cruel as Balkor.

"So what's your story then, Emeth? How'd you come to be in his service?" Hamíd asked.

"Ran away from home in Braeton when I was sixteen, too much like my father to get along with him. I'm his third son, so I figured he wouldn't miss me much. Picked up a ship in Aredor and went to Gelion. That's where I learned to use these," he said, gesturing to his double swords. "Two years ago, I made my way to Calorin. Lord Rishdah found me, and I fought my way up to his personal bodyguard, and here I am. What about you?" Emeth asked.

"I was taken from my home about eight years ago and sold to Lord Balkor, and I've survived ever since," Hamíd answered.

"I never thought I'd run into another northerner here. Makes me think of home again," Emeth said. "What happened to your family?" he asked.

"They probably think I'm dead," Hamíd answered shortly. Nicar dropped back to ride with them.

"How are you holding up, lad?" he asked Hamíd.

"I'm fine, sir," came the short reply.

"Good. I've been talking to Lord Rishdah. He'll give you a week to get your full strength up, and then your training will begin," Nicar told him.

"What training?" Hamíd asked apprehensively.

"You're to be a soldier, and if you're good enough, you'll become one of us, the Phoenix Guard," Nicar said.

"Why? I've never used a weapon before in my life, and why should he trust me? How does he know I won't run away the first chance I get?" Hamíd asked.

"Something tells me you won't," Nicar said. "Lord Rishdah saw something in you. He thinks you can make it."

Emeth thought for a moment.

"Who'll be training him?" he asked.

"Azrahil mostly," Nicar answered. Emeth whistled softly.

"He's the captain of the Phoenix Guards," Emeth told Hamíd. "I hope you're not easily intimidated. He still has some unexplainable grudge against me after two years!"

"He hates those double swords of yours. He's dedicated himself to studying to try and beat you," Nicar said. Emeth laughed.

"I'm not about to tell him how either!" he said.

"How many are there in this guard?" Hamíd asked.

"Four, including Azrahil. You'll meet Ahmed tonight. Be warned, he's a little hard to get along with at first," Nicar said. Hamíd spent the rest of the journey in silence, listening as Emeth and Nicar told him what he would need to know about life at the castle and Lord Rishdah and his family. He watched Lord Rishdah riding some distance ahead of them. In a way, the lord reminded Hamíd of his father—stern, shrewd, and commanding, but with a kindness hidden not too far under the rough exterior. Hamíd didn't know what would happen in the days to come, but he resolved to do his best for the man who had just saved his life.

Hamíd rose early several days later. He had been quartered in a small room in the Guard's barracks where Nicar kept a close eye on him. He had spent the past few days getting to know the castle and surrounding lands. Emeth had been a willing guide on his off-duty hours. Hamíd had taken an instant liking to the cheerful young guard. The night before, Nicar had declared him healed and ready to start training. Azrahil, the fierce captain of the Guards, had ordered Hamíd to meet him in the training court outside the barracks. Hamíd dressed in fresh clothes and stepped out into the cool morning to meet the captain.

Emeth had also risen early that morning to go about his duties. He saw Hamíd crossing the courtyard and was struck at the change in him. Hamíd walked more confidently now with head held high. His thick blonde hair had been trimmed, and he had filled out. Looking at him, Emeth would never have guessed that only a few short days ago, he had been a captive. Only his eyes had stayed the same. Bright, piercing blue, they were cold still, masking something deeper. Hamíd remained quiet, never smiling or laughing, speaking only when he had to. Emeth greeted him and wished him luck before continuing on to relieve Ahmed on guard. With Emeth's encouragement still ringing in his ears, Hamíd walked through the courtyard and into the practice ring where Azrahil waited.

Azrahil studied the young man in front of him. He liked what he saw. His new student was tall and lean, with the build of a swordsman. Strong too, Azrahil mused, but that comes from the hard work the boy is used to. Initially, he had been surprised when Lord Rishdah asked him, the captain of the guard, to train the former slave. But he found that he now looked forward in anticipation to discovering the young man's capacities.

Hamíd stood unmoving, hands clasped behind his back, eyes downcast. His gut twisted with nervousness, but many a harsh lesson had taught him how to keep his face expressionless. He had experience with men in Azrahil's position, none of which had been good. He wasn't expecting the burly captain to be any different.

"You ever handled a weapon before?" Azrahil asked suddenly.

"No, sir, other than for repairs at the forge," Hamíd said.

"Do you know why you're here?" Azrahil asked.

"I was told that I was to be trained, sir," Hamíd replied.

"It doesn't sound like you believe that," Azrahil commented.

"No, sir," Hamíd said truthfully.

"Hamíd," Azrahil said, and the young man's eyes flashed up in surprise as the captain used his name. Azrahil saw for a brief second the pain, hurt, hate, and uncertainty in Hamíd's eyes. The look reminded him of a wild horse that had been beaten to try and break its spirit.

"Let me see your hand," Azrahil said. Hamíd felt another surge of apprehension as he slowly brought his right hand forward and unwound the strip of cloth he always kept around his palm. Azrahil took a sudden step forward, and Hamíd tensed involuntarily.

"It's all right," Azrahil said. Hamíd looked up again in surprise at the softness in the captain's voice. Azrahil gently opened Hamíd's hand to reveal the brand. Pushing up Hamíd's sleeve, he saw a scar encircling his wrist. Azrahil sighed interiorly; he had a similar scar around his wrist. Once, a long time ago, he had been like Hamíd.

He saw Hamíd's gaze was averted from the brand as he tried to hide the shame he felt as it was exposed.

"We'll get you a proper glove for this," Azrahil said, releasing his hand. Hamíd met his gaze. *He knows,* he thought. *He knows at least part of what I've been through.*

"How long?" he asked quietly.

"Two years, after an ambush went wrong," Azrahil answered. He was surprised at himself. He never told anyone about his past life. But he had a sudden urge to help the young man in front of him, just as someone else had once helped him.

"Are you ready to begin?" Azrahil asked. Hamíd took a deep breath and squared his shoulders, preparing to meet the challenges of his new life.

"Yes, sir," he replied.

Azrahil entered the guard's barracks that night. Emeth sat in the common room, cleaning his saddle. Azrahil joined him, slinging his own saddle on to a rack.

"Anything wrong, Captain?" Emeth asked casually, noting the pensive expression on his captain's face.

"You've spent some time with Hamíd, haven't you?" Azrahil asked. Emeth refolded his cloth and began to polish the leather.

"Yes, sir," he said.

"What do you think of him?" the captain asked.

"I don't know yet. He doesn't say much," he replied.

"So I've noticed," Azrahil commented wryly. "You talk to him much?"

"Not much more than what he needs to know to get around. I figure he'll open up when he's ready. He's just not ready to trust anyone yet," Emeth said.

"After what he's been through, I'm not surprised," Azrahil said. "We'll see how he copes with the training."

"He notices small details, like any good warrior or commander should. It wouldn't surprise me if he's in the Guard before the year is out. And then I'd hate to be his enemy," Emeth said. Azrahil remembered Hamíd's expression as he first held the scimitar, and he couldn't agree more with Emeth.

CHAPTER 4

"Block! Now strike! Move your feet! Watch my sword. Parry! Good!" Azrahil said as Hamíd finished the exercise. "Now we'll try it with the scimitar," he said. Hamíd handed him the wooden practice sword he had been using and accepted the scimitar Azrahil handed him in return.

"Remember to watch my blade. This'll go quicker with the swords. Ready?" Azrahil asked. Hamíd nodded and took up his stance. Azrahil lunged, and Hamíd brought up his scimitar to block. Swords flashed in the sunlight as they sparred. When they drew apart, they were both breathing heavily. Hamíd had been training for three months and was slowly mastering the Calorin scimitar. Azrahil found him an able and willing student and had proceeded to teach him all he knew. Besides training with Azrahil, Hamíd spent two days a week with Jaffa, captain of Lord Rishdah's small army. Jaffa taught him how to use the light javelin and to fight from the back of a horse. Surprised at how well Hamíd could already ride, Jaffa showed him various battle maneuvers and techniques for overpowering an enemy on the ground.

He learned how to engage more than one enemy at a time, to move silently, and to use his surroundings to disappear. Another warrior taught him to fight without weapons, honing his reflexes in the intense and aggressive style of hand-to-hand combat. Emeth, a highly skilled tracker, showed him how to read the tracks left by animals or, more importantly, the signs left by any enemy they might have to follow. His days were filled with fighting and riding from dawn to dusk, and he would tumble into his bed, exhausted, but strangely content.

"Come, Hamíd," Azrahil said. "I told Jaffa we'd meet him down on the training grounds. More archery practice."

Hamíd couldn't help but grimace. Archery was the one thing he couldn't seem to master. It didn't help that Jaffa was now having him shoot from the back of a moving horse. Reluctantly, he sheathed the sword and followed the captain out of the courtyard. They walked out of the castle and down into the open training grounds.

"You bring it down?" Azrahil asked Jaffa as they approached.

"Yes, I sent one of my men for it. He will be back shortly," Jaffa said.

"Bring what, sir?" Hamíd couldn't help but ask. Azrahil smiled.

"You'll see soon enough," he replied.

Jaffa handed Hamíd the archer brace, and he buckled it on. He had just finished when a soldier came up, carrying a long object covered in a cloth. Jaffa took it from the soldier, unwrapped the object, and handed it to Hamíd. He ran his hand down the smooth curve of the longbow, and a shiver of recognition ran through him.

"An Aredorian war bow. Where did you get it, sir?" Hamíd asked.

"A merchant from Gelion had it. Lord Rishdah was intrigued by it and bought it. No one has been able to use it effectively yet, so we thought you might give it a try," Jaffa said. Hamíd bent the bow and smoothly strung it and tested its draw. The longer, more powerful weapon fit more easily into his hands than the light Calorin bow. Azrahil handed him the quiver, and Hamíd slung it over his shoulder. Drawing an arrow, he knocked it to the string. Stepping forward, he took aim at the target and let fly. The arrow hit almost dead center. Jaffa whistled softly. Hamíd fired four more arrows before Jaffa called a halt.

"Well, I think we've finally found you a bow," he said. "All right, you can stop smiling now. I'll have Inzi brought in for you."

A fiery, restless chestnut mare was led up. Unhesitatingly, Hamíd mounted her.

"I thought you said no one could ride that horse," Azrahil said quietly to Jaffa.

"That's what I thought. Just watch," Jaffa told him. Hamíd moved the mare in a small circle, and then suddenly, she stopped and reared. Hamíd leaned forward, adjusting easily. As they landed, he pushed her into a trot, moving out on the circle. Again she reared, and again he rode it and resumed the circle. Finally, the mare quieted, and he nudged her into an easy canter. Slowing, Hamíd rode over to the two captains and halted.

"We're ready, Captain," he said. Azrahil watched the mare. She was standing quietly, sides heaving as she licked and chewed at the bit.

"The usual targets, Hamíd, and watch her over the ditch!" Jaffa said.

"Yes, sir," Hamíd replied and rode off. The "targets" were stuffed sacks mounted on poles and scattered all over the field. Hamíd pushed Inzi into a canter and headed toward the first target. Dropping the reins, he fitted a shaft and fired before quickly grabbing the reins and heading to the second target placed to the left. Again nocking an arrow, he turned and fired. He shot at two more targets and then went for the last. It was placed to the right of a long ditch, which forced the rider to jump the ditch after firing. Hamíd loosed his last arrow then prepared for the ditch.

The mare jumped cleanly over but stumbled as she landed. Hamíd was knocked off balance as she stumbled, and then the mare bucked, sending him flying to the ground. He lay still for a moment, trying to regain his breath. He sat up as Inzi came walking up to nose at him. Laughing at her, he gently smacked her nose, sending her shying away. He stood slowly and picked up the bow, undamaged by the fall. Catching the mare, he walked over to where the captains stood. Azrahil's face was a mixture of concern and amusement as they came up slowly.

"I told you to be careful over that ditch!" Jaffa said to Hamíd.

"Yes, sir, I know," Hamíd said. "I'm fine by the way."

"Does that happen often?" Azrahil asked.

"Yes, sir. She gets me almost every time. Yesterday was a bit more spectacular," Hamíd said with a rare smile. Azrahil couldn't help but laugh at this.

"Retrieve your arrows, Hamíd, and then you can have the rest of the day off," Azrahil said.

"Thank you, sir," Hamíd said as he mounted again and rode off. Azrahil watched him go then turned to Jaffa.

"You know, I've never seen him smile like that before," he said.

"He's always happier around the animals. I swear sometimes it's like he can understand what they're thinking," Jaffa said. "I don't know his bloodline, but he's got such a natural instinct for weapons and fighting, it's unbelievable."

"I know," Azrahil said. "He's learning quickly. If I'm not careful, he'll be able to beat me pretty soon."

Jaffa laughed.

"When that happens, you can always have him fight Emeth. Maybe he can beat those double swords for you," he said. Azrahil laughed with him. A lone rider cantered up behind them.

"He's retrieving arrows, Emeth," Jaffa said.

"Thank you, sir," Emeth said. "Captain." He threw a salute to Azrahil before riding toward Hamíd while raising a shout in Rhyddan. Hamíd gave an answering wave. The two captains watched them talk to each other in their own language as Emeth said something that made Hamíd smile. He threw an answer back at Emeth then spurred his horse into a gallop. Emeth laughed and chased after him.

"Emeth usually come down here?" Azrahil asked.

"Yes, sometimes Ahmed comes with him. They've struck up quite a friendship with Hamíd," Jaffa answered.

"Good, that's what he needs most of all: friendship and trust," Azrahil said. "I should get back to the castle now. Lord Rishdah will want a full report on today. A pleasure as always, Captain." Jaffa returned the salute.

A few short months later, Hamíd stood before Lord Rishdah in a large chamber. The lord had witnessed the final trials that Azrahil and Jaffa had put Hamíd through and was now ready to give his verdict.

"You have repaid my trust and became what I saw in you. Hamíd, you have earned your place in the Guard," Lord Rishdah said. He drew his scimitar and held it out. Hamíd knelt and laid his hand on the hilt, and in the presence of the other four members of the Phoenix Guard, he swore the oath.

"I, Hamíd, do swear to protect the Lord Rishdah and his possessions with my life. I swear to stand by him and serve honestly and faithfully until I am so released or until my death."

"And I, Lord Rishdah, do accept and take you into my service," Lord Rishdah replied, sheathing his sword as Hamíd rose. Nicar stopped to congratulate Hamíd before accompanying Lord Rishdah from the chamber. Emeth and Ahmed stayed for a few minutes until they had to return to their various duties. Azrahil then took Hamíd to the Guard's armory. He handed Hamíd the black-and-red uniform of the Phoenix Guard. Reaching onto a shelf, he pulled down two leather arm bracers.

"There's a thin sheet of steel inside each. It's been forged such that it does not bend or break unless under severe circumstances. It's the best thing for blocking a blow. You'll soon get used to the added weight," Azrahil said, handing them to Hamíd. He took them and saw a rising phoenix etched into the leather on one of the bracers. He set them aside as Azrahil took a scimitar down from the wall.

"Tell me what you think," the captain said as he handed it to Hamíd. The razor-sharp edge of the blade glittered brightly in the light of the torches. The handle was tightly bound in black leather all the way to the carved pommel. Hamíd felt the balance of the blade as he hefted it. The scimitar seemed to fit perfectly into his hand. It was not an elaborate blade, but it was perfect for a warrior. He sheathed it and offered it back to Azrahil.

"It's beautiful, one of the best I've ever seen," he said. Azrahil made no move to take it.

"It's yours," he said. "I had it made for you a few months ago after I saw how talented you were. It suits you well, and I know you'll put it to good use. Jaffa had Inzi brought up to the stables for you. She's quartered next to our horses. You did me proud, lad, you're one of the best I've ever trained."

"Thank you, sir. For everything," Hamíd said.

"Time for that later," Azrahil said gruffly. He added two daggers to the pile of weapons along with a coat of chain mail and a sturdy leather tunic. Once he was finished, Azrahil sent Hamíd to change into the uniform.

Hamíd settled easily into the routine of the Guards. One to two of the Guards always stayed with Lord Rishdah night and day; sometimes a guard would be assigned to either of Rishdah's sons. Every six hours, the guard would change with Azrahil overseeing the changes in guards. The Phoenix Guard was comprised of the best men under Lord Rishdah's command. Hamíd soon learned that they did more than protect Lord Rishdah; the lord also relied on them to undertake difficult missions and tasks.

A few weeks had passed since Hamíd took the oath when some startling news came. He was on duty with Lord Rishdah when an errand rider dressed in the livery of the Sultaan was brought before Lord Rishdah. After reading the dispatch, Lord Rishdah summoned his captains.

"I received word an hour ago that the Sultaan and the king of Argus have declared war on each other. The Sultaan has ordered me to take command of his troops and march to the border to engage the Argusians. We are to meet with the main army in three days' time. Jaffa, mobilize your men. Assign a force to remain here and protect the castle. Hamíd, you are dismissed for now. Tell the others to prepare to leave tomorrow morning," Lord Rishdah said.

"Yes, sir," Hamíd replied and left the council room while Rishdah and his captains began discussing the intricate details of providing for their forces.

Emeth was off duty and cleaning his weapons when Hamíd found him.

"I saw the rider come in. What's the news?" he asked.

"The Sultaan declared war on Argus. Lord Rishdah was given command of the army. We leave tomorrow morning," Hamíd told him.

"Finally! It's been unutterably boring around here for the last five months. We'll see some action at last!" Emeth exclaimed. Hamíd couldn't help thinking that his and Emeth's definition of "boring" was very different.

Together, they went to alert Nicar and Ahmed. The Guards spent the rest of the day packing their belongings and provisions and inspecting their horses to make sure they would hold up for the longs months of campaign that were coming. The next morning, Lord Rishdah rode out with half of his force to meet with the Sultaan's army. Jaffa would join him with the other half as soon as they could. Rishdah's oldest son, Ismail, rode with them. The captain of the Sultaan's army was a stern man named Murad. He and Lord Rishdah knew each other well, having fought together on many previous campaigns for the Sultaan.

Hamíd was a bit overwhelmed at the sight of the army awaiting them. Thousands of men were encamped on the plains around the road. It took a few days to get the troops in position and ready to continue the march to the border. Once there, Rishdah divided the army into three smaller forces, taking command of one and assigning Murad to the second. Another general by the name of Tahmid took charge of the third force. Murad was the first to encounter the enemy as he fought for and took control of an Argusian town just east of the border.

The afternoon sun shone down brilliantly on Lord Rishdah's army. Hamíd squinted against the light reflected off the sand. They had entered into the Argusian Desert on their way to attack the city of Makurung. So far, the going had been miserable. The army did not just have to contend with the overwhelming heat of the desert but also with attacks made by the Argusians. The enemy knew the desert well and used it to their advantage. They would spring suddenly from the sands or come thundering from the desert in their light chariots, strike, and disappear. Lord Rishdah viewed Makurung as a strategic opportunity. The city lay two days from the coast and the city of Gondeni and a day's journey from the southern town of Ncorha, now occupied by Murad. If the Calorins controlled the western cities of Argus, then they would be able to march unhindered across the desert and take Dzingahe, the city of the king. By all reckoning, the army lay ten miles west of Makurung. Rishdah pushed his men as hard as he could in the heat in order to reach the city by the next day.

By means of unseen scouts, the Argusians became aware of their plans and moved to cut off Rishdah and his army. The towers of Makurung came into view the next day, and in front of the city stood the battlelines of the Argusians. Lord Rishdah quickly moved his men into position, placing his cavalry in front to counter the enemy's chariots. Drums pounded and horns blared as the two armies closed. The cavalry wove in between the chariots while attempting to cut the lines or take down the archers and spearmen that stood on the swaying platforms.

Hamíd found himself in the thick of the fight alongside the rest of the Phoenix Guard. Out of the corner of his eye, he saw

Emeth leap from his stallion into a chariot, knocking the driver and spearman to the ground before disabling it. Again, he made a dangerous leap from the chariot to the back of the galloping horse that pulled it. Cutting the tracers, he left the light vehicle to tumble into ruin. Wheeling his new mount, Emeth joined Ahmed, who fought alongside Ismail. Hamíd saw an Argusian with a spear raised to kill a soldier, and spurring Inzi forward, he grabbed the spear and moved alongside a chariot. Dodging an arrow, he leaned over and rammed the spear into the spinning wheel of the chariot thereby jamming the wheel and smashing the chariot. Hamíd then turned and began to fight his way back to Lord Rishdah.

A mounted Argusian pulled alongside him. Lunging, the man knocked Hamíd from his horse. Without time to think, Hamíd drew his sword and moved into the familiar motions of hand-to-hand combat. A young Calorin soldier was hemmed in by a fallen chariot. Hamíd fought over to his side and helped him drive away the deadly Argusian spearmen. The soldier's helmet had come off, and Hamíd recognized him.

"Castimir! What are you doing here?" he yelled. Castimir, the youngest son of Lord Rishdah, answered as he parried a sword blow.

"Fighting. Father wouldn't let me come, so I ran away!"

Hamíd grabbed a thrusting spear and killed its carrier. Gaining a temporary respite, Hamíd turned to him.

"What are you going to do if your father finds out?" he asked.

"I'll make sure he doesn't," Castimir answered.

"What about me?' Hamíd asked. "You going to get rid of me so I don't tell him? What happens when we find your dead body on the battlefield?"

"I can take care of myself!" Castimir retorted angrily. "I've been waiting for a chance to fight! Ismail has been in scores of battles even before he was my age. You would have done the same!" He grabbed his helmet and pulled it back on. "Thanks, and good-bye!" He ran off before Hamíd could stop him. Nicar rode up, leading Inzi.

"You all right, Hamíd?" he asked.

"Yes, sir, I'm fine," Hamíd replied. Nicar tossed the reins to him.

"Mount up. The Argusians are regrouping, and Lord Rishdah has ordered a retreat," he said. Hamíd cast a last glance around for Castimir, but he had disappeared into the tumult. They rejoined the rest of the Guard as trumpets rang out, signaling a retreat. The Argusians were content to let them withdraw, sending small groups of soldiers out to watch their progress and cause small skirmishes. By the end of the day, Hamíd was exhausted, having ridden out on more than one sortie to drive away the Argusians. The enemy was unlike anything he had ever seen. The Argusians were tall, savage men, and their skin was jet-black. They wore loose, flowing robes to withstand the heat of the desert. Masters of horses and of the chariot, they wielded fearsome double-pointed spears with great efficiency. Those on foot carried axes or heavy curved blades along with rectangular wooden shields covered in cowhide.

With a large army still between him and Makurung, Lord Rishdah decided to join Murad at Ncorha and combine forces. They arrived at the town two days later, slowed by the wounded and by sandstorms. Lord Rishdah quartered his forces outside the walls of the town while he met in council with Murad. Lord Rishdah still wanted to take Makurung, but he did not have enough men to besiege the city. Murad split his army in half, giving more men to Rishdah but still leaving Ncorha well guarded.

Hamíd walked down out of the town. He was off duty and had a few spare hours. As he passed through the gate, he heard his name called. He was surprised to see Castimir hurrying after him.

"Hamíd, what news?" he asked

"Why are you asking me, sir?" Hamíd asked him. Castimir grinned.

"Well, since Father hasn't torn the camp apart looking for me yet, I assumed you didn't tell anyone. So I partly came to thank you I guess. And I still want to know what's going on," he said. Hamíd shook his head.

"You should wait to hear that from your commanding officer," he said.

"Oh, come on!" Castimir groaned in frustration. Hamíd grinned maliciously.

"What if I don't tell you?" he asked.

"I take it all back, I hate you!" Castimir said. He pleaded for a few more minutes and Hamíd finally relented.

"All right, we're going back to Makurung in a few days," he said.

"Is that all?" Castimir asked suspiciously.

"Yes, it is," Hamíd replied.

"No, I don't think it is," a stern voice said. Hamíd and Castimir suddenly found themselves looking into the piercing eyes of Azrahil. "You both have some serious explaining to do," he said.

CHAPTER 5

Lord Rishdah was furious when he found out that Castimir had joined the army against his orders. Castimir stood quietly during the lecture his father delivered that contained threats of numerous different punishments.

"Do you have anything to say for yourself?" Lord Rishdah finally asked.

"No, sir. Just please don't punish Hamíd. He tried to get me to go back," Castimir said.

"I'm leaving his punishment to Azrahil. He has failed in his duties," Lord Rishdah said.

"No, he didn't," Castimir said. "He stopped me from getting killed down at Makurung. Please, Father!" he pleaded. Lord Rishdah frowned.

"Leave now, Castimir, while I determine your fate," he ordered. Castimir left the room and sat dejectedly on a bench in the hallway. Azrahil stormed through the hallway followed by Hamíd and knocked on the door to Lord Rishdah's chamber.

"Stay here," he ordered as he entered the chamber. Hamíd slumped against the wall. They waited for a few minutes before Castimir broke the silence.

"What's going to happen to you?" he asked. Hamíd shrugged.

"Don't know. I heard just about every punishment imaginable within the space of a few minutes," he said.

"Same here. I'm really sorry I got you into this," Castimir said.

"Thanks, I'm going to need that thought here in a few minutes," Hamíd said with a wry grin. They didn't have to wait long before being called back into the chamber together.

"Well, it seems that neither of you think that the other should be punished," Lord Rishdah began. "Therefore you will share the punishment." He gestured for Azrahil to continue.

"Hamíd, you will escort Castimir home, and you will remain there until sent for, which will be my decision. I do not have to tell you what will happen if you fail to obey orders this time."

"Yes, sir," Hamíd replied somberly.

"Is everything understood?" Lord Rishdah asked.

"Yes, sir," came the reply from both young men.

"Good, supplies will be made ready. You'll have to go on foot until the border. You can get horses there. Pack your things. You will leave in an hour," Lord Rishdah announced. Captain Jaffa escorted Castimir to his tent; Azrahil did the same for Hamíd. The captain told the other Guards what had happened while Hamíd made ready to leave. Only Emeth dared to speak to him as he came out of the tent.

"Idiot," he whispered. "Good luck!" Hamíd gave him a slight smile in response. Castimir, still escorted by Jaffa, walked up, carrying the packs.

"You shouldn't run into any Argusians, but keep a sharp lookout," Azrahil warned.

"Yes, sir," Hamíd replied while shouldering a pack.

From Ncorha, Hamíd and Castimir turned northwest towards the Calorin border. They walked in silence through the hot sand. As the sun fell over the horizon, they made camp in the shelter of some dunes.

"I'll take first watch," Hamíd said, wrapping his cloak around him against the cool breeze that had sprung up.

"You didn't think I should be punished?" Castimir asked curiously.

"I just pointed out several people who would have done the same in your place. That led to a rather heated argument between the captain and me. Which is why he's going to make me stay at home for a while," Hamíd replied. Castimir whistled softly.

"You aren't short on nerve, that's for sure. I don't think even Emeth would say anything like that," he said.

"It wasn't the smartest idea in the world," Hamíd admitted. "We'd better turn in. We still have a ways to go tomorrow. I'll wake you in a few hours." Castimir nodded in agreement. Using his pack as a pillow, he wrapped his cloak around him and fell asleep.

The night passed quickly, and Hamíd and Castimir were on the move as the sun first peered over the edge of the desert. They trudged wearily through the day, stopping only to drink water and take a few bites of food. The sun seemed to move slowly across the sky. They halted at midday and took shelter from the blazing sun under an awning. They took off their heavy chain mail and tunics in a further effort to keep cool. A few hours later, they resumed their journey in silence. Castimir drew his shirt sleeve wearily across his face and looked hopefully for any change in the landscape. Disappointed, he kept walking as the desert stretched on into the distance.

Night fell again, and they made camp. A restless night passed, and they arose to face another day in the desert. By late afternoon, the land began changing. The desert rose up into dunes and fell away into ragged grasslands. They had reached the border. In a few miles, they would reach the Calorin city of Latharn. This knowledge raised their spirits significantly, and they walked with renewed energy. Their hopes were soon dashed at the sight that greeted their eyes. Hamíd first heard the sounds of marching feet, creaking wheels, and horses on the move. Castimir and Hamíd worked their way around several dunes and looked out over an army.

"Argusians," Hamíd whispered grimly.

"They're headed for Latharn," Castimir said. "It's virtually undefended."

"The nearest army is in Ncorha. Tahmid left to attack Gondeni last week," Hamíd said. Rank after rank of the Argusian army passed with the end seemingly nowhere in sight.

"If the Argusians take Latharn, then Makurung will be of no use to us," Castimir said. "We have to go back and tell Father."

"You do know what will happen if we show our faces back there again without orders?" Hamíd asked. Castimir nodded.

"Yes, but we can't just leave. Tahmid is long gone. We can cut across the desert and meet Father at Makurung," he said.

"All right, but remember to talk fast once we get there and preferably before we see Azrahil," Hamíd said. Castimir grinned. They worked their way backward until they were out of sight of the Argusians. Finding a small well, they replenished their water supply and headed back toward the desert. Three days later, Makurung came into view with the banner of the Sultaan flying from its walls. Castimir and Hamíd were slowly approaching the main gate when hoof beats sounded behind them. The two riders approaching the gate slowed when they saw Hamíd and Castimir. Before he knew it, a spear was leveled at Hamíd's chest.

"You've got a lot of nerve showing up here," Ahmed said.

"We have to talk to Lord Rishdah now," Hamíd said pushing the spear away.

"You think you're even going to have a chance to talk?" Emeth asked. Nevertheless, the two Phoenix Guards escorted Hamíd and Castimir to the citadel. Lord Rishdah was in the great hall, listening to reports from his scouts. The Argusians that they had defeated in the city were gathering together again in the surrounding desert. He barely took his eyes from the maps on the table when Ahmed announced their arrival. Castimir took a deep breath and stepped forward.

"Father," he said. Lord Rishdah glanced up sharply.

"I thought I had made myself perfectly clear, Castimir!" he said.

"Yes, sir, you did," Castimir began again. "We had every intention of going back home until we saw an Argusian army marching on Latharn," he said. At this news the whole room fell silent.

"Is this true?" Lord Rishdah asked Hamíd.

"Yes, sir. I knew General Tahmid had already left, so we came back to tell you," Hamíd replied.

"How many?" Azrahil barked at him.

"Five thousand at least, sir," Hamíd said. Lord Rishdah looked at them carefully, seeing in their faces that they told the truth.

"Commander Jaffa, I want three thousand men ready to march tonight. The rest, stay here to guard the city," Lord Rishdah said. "You two!" he pointed at Hamíd and Castimir. "You will come with us, only to make sure you don't get into any more trouble. Consider this a temporary suspension of your punishments." Lord Rishdah then indicated that they were dismissed. Ismail accompanied his brother from the hall as Azrahil approached Hamíd.

"As Lord Rishdah said, you are temporarily suspended from punishment. Don't think I'll let you off though. Get some rest and clean yourself up and get presentable. You look horrible," Azrahil told him. Hamíd bit back a grin.

"Yes, sir," he replied.

It was true; he and Castimir were coated in sweat and dust from crossing the desert. Most of his uniform was still in his pack, and he'd hardly slept in two days. Ahmed took Hamíd to the Guard's quarters where he washed and dressed in clean clothes. After eating a quick meal, Hamíd went to visit Inzi in the stables. The mare whinnied softly when she saw him. He talked quietly to her in Rhyddan while he gently rubbed her forehead. Hamíd did not stay long as Azrahil had ordered him to report for duty.

Shortly before midnight, the Calorin army left Makurung. The city was left in the charge of Jaffa and two thousand Calorin soldiers as the main army hastened to the aid of Latharn. Lord Rishdah drove his men hard and crossed the desert in two days. As the army neared the border, they began sending out advance scouts. Azrahil often ordered Hamíd out on a patrol. Small mobile groups of Argusians became more frequent, and the scouting trips became more dangerous. Emeth rode beside Castimir after orders not to let the young man out of his sight. Ismail rode with them behind Lord Rishdah and his captains.

"Why does Azrahil keep sending Hamíd off like that?" Castimir asked Emeth after watching an exchange between the captain and Hamíd.

"Captain is testing him. Hate to say this, sir, but he got into a lot of trouble over that incident," Emeth replied.

"Will Azrahil let him stay in the Phoenix Guard?" Ismail asked.

"That's what he's trying to decide. If Hamíd doesn't drop of exhaustion first," Emeth replied a little anxiously. Nicar was having some of the same thoughts as he dropped back to ride next to them.

"I've tried to reason with Azrahil, but he won't budge. See if you can do anything, Emeth," Nicar said. Emeth shot him a look as if to say, *I don't know what good that will do, but I'll try.* Emeth urged his horse forward until he rode even with Azrahil.

"Captain, let me take the next patrol and let Hamíd take a break," Emeth said.

"Aren't you supposed to be with Castimir?" Azrahil asked somewhat disapprovingly.

"Yes, sir, but truthfully, I'm worried about Hamíd," Emeth replied. Azrahil continued scanning the horizon in silence. Emeth was about to speak again when Azrahil cut him off.

"He's coming back now. Emeth, ride ahead to the city and find out what we're up against," Azrahil ordered.

"Yes, sir," Emeth replied gratefully.

Hamíd rode back to the army. As the front ranks came into sight, he tried desperately to straighten up in the saddle. A brief encounter with three Argusians had left him with a cut to his arm and hand. After making sure no report of their presence would reach the Argusian army, he had turned back in order to report to Azrahíl once again. Concern shadowed Azrahíl's face when he saw the blood covering Hamíd's sleeve.

"Hamíd, I'm relieving you. Emeth has volunteered to take your place as a scout. Dismissed," he said. Then leaning closer to Hamíd, he said, "Have Nicar look at that. You've done well, Hamíd. You're off duty until tomorrow morning."

"Thank you, sir," Hamíd said a little hoarsely. He joined Nicar, who immediately drew bandages out of his bags.

"What'd the captain say?" he asked Hamíd.

"I'm off duty until tomorrow," Hamíd replied, drinking sparingly from his waterskin. Nicar sighed in relief.

"It's about bloody time!" he muttered, leaning over to wrap a bandage around Hamíd's arm. "Once we finally make camp, I'll take a proper look at that," Nicar said.

"So what happened?" Castimir asked, ignoring disapproving stares from Ismail and Nicar.

"We're almost to the border, Argusian patrols are getting bigger, it won't be long before they find out we're here. I ran into three of them about half a mile out. Luckily, they were just as surprised as I was and didn't get away in time," Hamíd replied, not bothered by Castimir's curiosity. More scouts began returning, some bringing news on Argusian movements and others having found a suitable camping place for the host. The place chosen was several miles from Latharn, next to a small river. Grateful to be out of the desert, the men rested as well as they could and prepared for the upcoming conflict. Emeth rode into camp as the sun set.

"The Argusians are in the city, but they haven't completely taken it. The defenders have retreated into the inner two circles. The Argusians still have plenty of men outside the city as well," he reported.

"How close did you get?" Azrahíl asked.

"Up to the outer wall, sir," Emeth said. "I was able to hear that they're going to stage a big attack on the second circle tomorrow and that they're not expecting any reinforcements to help our boys, sir."

"Excellent," Lord Rishdah said. "Tomorrow, we'll attack and draw off as much of the main army as we can. Ismail, once the Argusians are diverted, you and Captain Ghalib will take a force into the city to strengthen the defenders." As he finished giving orders, he looked to his other son, who stood quietly by. "Castimir, you will accompany me with the main force. Azrahil, assign an appropriate Guard."

The next morning, after all plans had been made, Lord Rishdah moved his army into position. Flanked by Azrahil and Hamíd, he led his cavalry into sight of the city. Alarmed at the sight, the Argusian commander ordered over half his army to engage the Calorins. As the Argusians neared, Lord Rishdah began an ordered retreat to draw the enemy away from the city and into the hills where the rest of his army waited. The Argusians crested the hill and thundered down to engage the smaller Calorin force.

With the enemy sufficiently distracted, Ismail and Ghalib led their force to the city. Fighting their way through the guards left behind, they made it to the gates of the second circle and were welcomed joyously by the defenders. Ismail saw that the city was largely undefended, and he led a small force back to the main gates and then closed and blockaded them. Once the gates were secure, the Calorins engaged the remaining Argusians in the city. A few escaped and ran to alert the main army.

Out in the hills, the two forces were battling furiously when suddenly the harsh, blaring horns of the Argusians rang out, and they began to retreat. Finding the gates of Latharn locked against them and Lord Rishdah's army closing in again, the commander ordered a full withdrawal from the city. Lord Rishdah sent out scouts to follow the Argusians while he led his army into Latharn. The scouts returned quickly with dire news. The Argusian army had been strengthened by a fresh army that had just come out of the desert. They had turned and were marching toward Latharn again. The defenders quickly manned the walls and watched as the enemy slowly surrounded the city. But the Argusians made no attack that day or the next. The week stretched on, the enemy seemingly content to lay siege to the city. Provisions began to run low in the city, and Lord Rishdah began forming a desperate plan to break the siege.

CHAPTER 6

"What we need is a distraction," Lord Rishdah said. "They outnumber us, so we'll have to strike whenever we can and weaken them. Any force we send out right now would be quickly overrun. A night attack will be best. Someone will go into their camp and create a diversion by firing the supply lines and so forth then two forces, led by myself and Azrahil, will ride out of both gates and engage the enemy while we can. Their chariots will be useless in the camp, and they will be forced to go on foot against our horses. It's incredibly risky, and I want only the best men," he finished. "Who is willing to create the diversion?" he asked his Guards. They all hesitated; going out alone into the midst of the enemy who numbered almost four thousand strong was a daunting prospect. Finally, Hamíd spoke up.

"I'll do it, sir," he said.

Lord Rishdah nodded. "Very well. We'll move tonight," he said. After they were dismissed, Emeth found Hamíd.

"I'll go with you," he said. Hamíd shook his head.

"No, if I don't make it back, then there's only one man lost. We need everyone right now. Besides, Captain wants you out on the sortie," Hamíd said.

"You're the bravest fool I've ever met," Emeth said.

Hamíd only laughed. "It runs in my family, I'm afraid," he said.

"You'll make it back," Emeth asserted. "If you don't, I'll find you and kill you again."

"Thanks for those encouraging words," Hamíd said. "I'm betting I'll be the first one back then."

"We'll see about that," Emeth replied. They then parted ways to prepare for the night.

The night was only a few hours old when Hamíd stood on the battlements. He had dressed all in black for the task at hand. He checked his weapons for what seemed the hundredth time while a soldier threw a rope over the wall and made it secure. Nicar climbed the wall steps and came over to him.

"I'll be waiting for you here," he said. "Be careful and good luck."

Hamíd nodded his thanks before grabbing hold of the rope and slipping over the wall. Keeping his feet against the wall, he quickly rappelled down to the ground. The darkness was overwhelming at the base of the walls. As he cautiously made his way forward to the Argusian camp, the rope was hauled back up onto the battlements behind him. The only noise in the camp was the quiet pacing of sentries, the movements of horses, and the crackling of fires. Hamíd dodged two sentries and made his way slowly into the camp.

Keeping well into the shadows, he looked for the best place to start his work. He saw a long line of picketed horses. Slipping among them, he began to cut the lines. When most of the ropes had been severed, he moved on to the next line.

Jumping on to the broad, bare back of one of the horses, he knotted his hand in its mane and grabbed a torch. Wheeling the horse, he began firing the tents surrounding them. The horses began to mill about nervously as the flames took hold of the tents. Aroused by the fire, sentries came running, and men stumbled out of their tents. Hamíd threw the torch into a wagon and drew his sword. Laying about with the flat of his blade, he drove the horses through the camp. The flames leapt higher as they spread from tent to tent. The panicked horses thundered through camp, trampling everything in their path. Inside Latharn, the lookouts saw the flames and heard the commotion in the camp and opened the gates. From the east gate rode Lord Rishdah at the head of five hundred men; from the west gate came Azrahil leading three hundred soldiers. The startled Argusians turned to see this new foe and met the points of Calorin spears.

Hamíd was hotly pursued by a few Argusians who had mounted horses once they saw what was happening. Still driving the herd before him, he looked for a way to escape as the sounds of battle broke out. A sudden idea struck him. Dodging tents and men, he managed to turn the horses toward the edge of the camp. The Argusians following him saw him change direction and began to call out panicked orders. As soon as he neared the edge, Hamíd turned his horse around and headed back toward Latharn as horns rang out, recalling the sorties. Two Argusians gave chase while the rest attempted to stop their horses from scattering on the open plains.

Hamíd wove frantically around tents and scattered groups of men trying to put out the fires. In the dancing light of the flames, he saw spearmen, heeding the shouts of his pursuers, blocking his path. The blades gleamed viciously as he came closer and closer. He saw one of the soldiers waver slightly, and whipping his horse to a greater speed, Hamíd charged directly at the Argusian. The man gave way before his furious charge, and Hamíd rode on as his pursuers became entangled with the remaining spearmen. Reaching the walls of Latharn, he rode along them until he came to the place where Nicar waited. Cries rang out behind him as the Argusians continued with their pursuit.

Hamíd gave a frantic whistle, and the rope was thrown over the battlements. Sheathing his scimitar, he grabbed hold of the rope, slid from the back of the horse, and began climbing. As he reached the top, Nicar leaned over and helped him on to the walls. Hamíd collapsed against the battlements. The excitement of the chase was wearing off, leaving him exhausted. Nicar handed him a flask. He took it and drank. The fiery liquid burned as he swallowed it.

"What is that?" he asked, coughing.

"Well, you don't think I drink water all the time, do you?" Nicar asked, grinning. "You looked like you could use some." Hamíd took another drink and handed it back to Nicar.

"Everyone else got back all right?" he asked.

"Aye, from what I heard, we only lost a few men," Nicar said. "We'll find out once we check in with Azrahil." Descending from the walls, the two Guards made their way back to the citadel. Azrahil met them in the hall. The captain was covered in blood and grime and had a rough bandage on his leg.

"You all right, Captain?" Nicar asked.

"Yes," Azrahil answered. "Hamíd, glad to see you're in one piece. Good work," the captain complimented him.

"Thank you, sir," Hamíd replied. "How did the sortie do?" he asked.

"Very well. We broke through their lines in several places. Easy in and out, they didn't know what was happening. Can't say I like that kind of business. I prefer to get a straight fight from my enemy," Azrahil said. "You both are dismissed for a few hours."

Nicar and Hamíd left the hall and went to the Guard's chambers. Ahmed was already there, cleaning up. He greeted them with a slight nod. By now, Hamíd was used to the quiet, young guard. Ahmed had lived on Lord Rishdah's lands all his life since his father tended to the lord's herds. Ahmed was tall and well built from a life of hard labor. Under his reserved exterior lay a staunch, unflinching character. Over the course of the past few months, Hamíd had come to know his companions better and learned that no matter what, they would stand beside each other until death.

"Where's Emeth?" Nicar asked.

"Stables," Ahmed replied. "Narak got hurt. Emeth's taking care of him."

"Any chance that animal will die?" Nicar asked, somewhat hopefully.

"I heard that, and I'm severely hurt that you would say such a thing about Narak," Emeth said as he entered the room. His companions chuckled. Narak was a temperamental young stallion and not very friendly with people, particularly grooms. He and Emeth had taken an instant liking to each other.

"How bad is it?" Ahmed asked.

"I'll have to take another horse out. He'll be lame for a few days," Emeth said.

"You think Lord Rishdah will send out another sortie?" Hamíd asked. Nicar shrugged.

"Depends on how much damage we did and how much longer we'll last," he said. With that sobering thought, the guards turned in to get what sleep they could.

The next day was darkened by smoke still rising from the Argusian's camp, which cast a haze over the city. Large swathes had been cut through the once orderly tent lines, wagons and chariots lay overturned, and horses wandered through the encampment. The defenders did not have much time to view the handiwork of the previous night's sortie as drums began pounding outside the walls and the Argusians made ready to attack. Lord Rishdah hurried to the walls to order the defenses.

Hamíd slumped against the wall beside Nicar. Fighting had been raging incessantly for two days with the enemy repeatedly scaling the walls and being repelled by the Calorin defenders.

"How you holding up?" Nicar asked him.

"I'm fine," Hamíd replied. "You?" he asked.

"I'm not having my best day," Nicar said. Hamíd chuckled as he began to sharpen his scimitar. Nicar looked up at the sky, judging the position of the sun.

"You think they'll attack again tonight?" Hamíd asked him. Nicar shrugged.

"Hopefully not," Nicar said stifling a yawn. "But right now, I'm going to get some sleep. Wake me only when they're coming over the walls." He leaned back against the wall and shut his eyes. Hamíd continued sharpening his blade, trying to occupy his mind. He hadn't been able to forget the men he had killed in battle. The cold steel felt heavy in his hands as he polished it.

"You all right?" A voice startled Hamíd out of his reverie. He looked up to see Emeth crouched beside him.

"I'm just tired," Hamíd replied. Emeth seemed to accept this answer.

"Captain wants us," he said. "Lord Rishdah is planning something."

Hamíd shook Nicar awake. Crouching low, they made their way to the wall steps. As they descended, Emeth spoke to Hamíd.

"You'll learn to live with it," he said.

"Have you?" Hamíd asked.

"Somewhat. It gets a little easier with time. Believe me, I was sick for a week after my first battle," he said.

Lord Rishdah and the other guards were gathered in the council hall of the citadel.

"I'm sending out another sortie," Lord Rishdah announced. "Captain Azrahil, you will lead it. Pick two guards and two hundred men to accompany you."

"Yes, my Lord. When do we leave?" Azrahil asked.

"After sunset," Lord Rishdah replied.

Three hours passed quickly, and Hamíd moved Inzi into position beside Ahmed at the west gate of Latharn. On Azrahil's signal, the gates swung out, and the sortie rode out. The camp in front of them seemed deserted. The gates clanged shut behind them, heightening the guards' sudden feelings of foreboding. Nevertheless, Azrahil ordered the men forward.

"Sweep through as fast as you can. If there's nothing here, we continue around the east side," he ordered. Horses were urged into a canter, and they entered the camp. Men reigned up sharply as a heavy barricade suddenly came into view. Torches flared, and Argusians let loose a flurry of arrows into their midst. Surrounded on three sides by the barrier and with more Argusians advancing, the Calorins sought to escape. Azrahil marshaled those still mounted, and they charged the line of Argusians advancing behind them. Once they broke through the enemy's ranks, the Calorins wheeled their horses and tore back through the lines. Meanwhile, those on foot were now fighting the Argusians that had come over the barricades.

"Captain! We need to get out of here! They're gaining reinforcements!" Ahmed yelled over the battle. At Azrahil's signal, one of the men sounded his horn, and the Calorins began to retreat. Hamíd and four other men formed a rearguard. A riderless horse careened after them. Recognizing it as Ahmed's, he looked around for the guard. Ahmed was nowhere in sight. Spurring Inzi forward, Hamíd raced back toward the barricades. Ahmed was fighting desperately, backed up against the walls. Hamíd plunged through the Argusians until he reached Ahmed. Startled Argusians backed away, allowing Ahmed to swing up behind Hamíd. Still surrounded, Hamíd looked for an escape.

"Hang on!" he warned and drove Inzi toward the opposite wall of the barricade. Men dodged away as they tore across the ring. Inzi gathered herself and jumped the wall; then Hamíd wheeled her around and galloped back to Latharn. The gates had begun to swing closed as they rode through and into the courtyard. Ahmed slid off from behind Hamíd and slumped against a nearby wall. Hamíd leaned forward over Inzi's neck as they tried to catch their breath. He dismounted shakily, and Inzi was led away by a groom.

"Thanks," Ahmed said.

"Well, I figured you didn't want to stay back there," Hamíd said.

"Not exactly," Ahmed replied with a laugh.

"All right boys, come with me, we've got a problem," Azrahil said. They hurried after him as he strode up to the citadel.

"My Lord, may I speak with you in private?" Azrahil said after giving a report. Lord Rishdah dismissed his other generals and attendants. Only the Phoenix Guard remained.

"Sir, they knew we were coming. I'm afraid we have a traitor among us," Azrahil said.

"Are you sure of this?" Lord Rishdah asked him.

"Yes, sir. They were waiting for us. There's no other explanation," Azrahil answered.

"There are nearly four thousand men here, it could be anyone. It was no secret where and when the sortie would leave," Nicar said.

"That does present a problem," Emeth whispered to Hamíd.

"Keep this to yourselves," Lord Rishdah commanded. "We have enough trouble without everyone mistrusting each other." The guards voiced their assent. Their attention was suddenly arrested by the blaring of horns from the walls. Drawing his scimitar, Lord Rishdah ran from the hall closely followed by the guards.

The enemy had begun an assault on the southern wall. Ladders were placed against the wall as catapults hurled fiery missiles into Latharn. Emeth was halfway up the wall steps when he chanced to look over at the north wall. It was deserted. Panicked, he saw that Lord Rishdah was already engaged in the fighting on the walls. Hamíd and Ahmed were still behind him. Turning to them, he yelled over the noise of the battle, "Get to the north wall!" Other men heard him and followed him as they raced along the walls around to the north gate.

They arrived barely in time as Argusians began to climb over the battlements with the aid of ropes and grappling hooks. The small force attacked the Argusians already over the walls and cut ropes whenever they could. Hamíd saw an enemy soldier standing on the battlement, waving his arms and gesturing at the gate. Hamíd knocked him from the wall and saw a new force charging the gates. He leapt down the wall steps to the gates. They stood wide open; he was now the only thing that stood between the city and the oncoming Argusians. Dropping his scimitar, he threw himself against one of the doors and began to push it closed. The massive gate moved a fraction as a chariot thundered toward him. Frantically, he threw all his weight behind the door, and it began to close.

On the walls, Ahmed saw the chariot charging the gate. Hefting his spear, he threw it straight at the horse, causing the chariot to crash. Turning to go down to the gate, he found his path blocked by an Argusian wielding a massive battle axe. Hamíd saw the chariot tumble into ruin and block most of the gate. He managed to swing the door shut. Picking up his scimitar, he prepared to defend the remaining opening. Ahmed fought desperately against his opponent, striving to overcome him, but the Argusian repelled his every attack. Emeth saw another Calorin soldier killed. A ladder bumped against the wall. He pushed it down, but three more sprang up in its place. Sickening recognition settled over him as he realized they would soon be overrun and the city would be lost.

Ahmed stumbled backward, and the Argusian pressed in for the kill only to be halted as Ahmed's knife plunged into his stomach. Free at last, Ahmed raced down to the gate. The enemy thronged the walls, and Emeth and his small force were about to be overwhelmed when a new battle cry sounded, and Castimir led a fresh force into the fray.

A pile of bodies choked the gateway. Hamíd still fought on, bleeding from multiple wounds. The enemy could only come a few at a time around the fallen chariot. Then they parted, and one man stepped forward to face Hamíd. A champion of the Argusians, the man stood a head taller than he and wielded a fearsome sabre. Hamíd recognized the challenge and, mustering his strength, stepped out to meet him. They circled each other, swords flickering as they struck and parried. The ground was slick with blood, causing them to slip more than once. They fought on and on, neither gaining the upper hand until Hamíd stumbled over a corpse. The Argusian caught him and threw him against the gates. Stunned, he fell defenseless to the ground.

The Argusian kicked him over and placed a foot on his chest. Raising his sword, the Argusian prepared to plunge it through Hamíd. But then he staggered and crumpled to the ground. Ahmed helped Hamíd up, and they retreated as a new wave of Argusians charged the gate. They fought side by side, barely holding back the fresh onslaught. Hamíd saw a line of Argusians level bows at them, but the line fell under a hail of arrows from the walls. The enemy halted uncertainly at this turn of events.

"Get out of there!" a voice yelled behind them. Ahmed and Hamíd retreated through the gate and into the city. Calorin soldiers quickly closed and barred the doors. All was quiet; the northern walls had been held by the Calorins. Hamíd leaned wearily against the stone walls.

"Thanks for the help," he said to Ahmed.

"You're one of us, and I look after my brother," Ahmed replied. Emeth came down the steps.

"The fighting is still bad on the south walls. We should get over there," he said.

"Stay here, Hamíd, you've done enough tonight," Ahmed said. Hamíd made no argument, and his two companions hurried off. One of the soldiers helped him bandage his wounds, and he slowly made his way back up the wall stairs to stand with Castimir.

The fighting continued long into the night as the enemy hurled their might against the walls. Dawn brought a respite for the defenders as the enemy withdrew to regroup and count their losses. The Calorins devoted their remaining energy to extinguishing the fires still burning within the city and caring for the wounded. The Argusians made no further attacks that day, which allowed Lord Rishdah to reorganize his troops.

That night, Hamíd was returning from the walls with Ismail when they heard the clash of steel coming from Lord Rishdah's chamber. Breaking into a run, they arrived at the doors at the same time as the rest of the guards. The door was partially opened, and they rushed in. Lord Rishdah leaned against the table, clutching his arm, and Emeth struggled with a man he had pinned against the wall. Nicar and Ismail rushed to help Lord Rishdah while the others turned their attention to the attacker. Emeth now had his knife at the man's throat and was unleashing a tirade of Rhyddan at the assassin. Thoroughly aroused and angry, the thick brogue of the Clans of Braeton came out in full force as he spoke. The man's face was a picture of terror, and he made no resistance as Azrahil and Ahmed took firm hold of him. Hamíd's shoulders shook with suppressed laughter as Emeth continued to mutter in Rhyddan as he tried to staunch blood dripping from a cut on his forehead.

"Emeth!" Azrahil said sharply. Emeth snapped to attention.

"Yes, sir!" he said in Calorin.

"Care to explain this?" Azrahil asked.

"He was waiting in the room and caught me by surprise as we came in. He knocked me over the head and went after Lord Rishdah, sir," Emeth said.

"Not to worry, Captain, it's only a shallow cut. He didn't get a chance to finish the job," Lord Rishdah assured Azrahil.

"With your permission, my Lord, I will question him. He might tell us who our informant is. Ahmed, stay with Castimir. Nicar, look after Emeth, then accompany Ismail. Hamíd, stay with Lord Rishdah," Azrahil gave his orders to the Phoenix Guard.

"What about me, sir?' Emeth asked.

"Lie down for a few hours," Azrahil said, his tone stifling any arguments from Emeth. The guard took up their assigned stations, and Lord Rishdah's chambers were quiet once again.

"Do I even want to know what Emeth was saying?" Lord Rishdah asked Hamíd.

"It loses something in translation, sir," Hamíd answered, repressing fresh laughter. Lord Rishdah chuckled.

"So, tell me, Hamíd, you are from a different country than Emeth, correct?" he asked. Hamíd was taken off guard by the question but replied, "Yes, sir. He comes from Braeton, farther north than Aredor."

"Do you miss Aredor?' Lord Rishdah asked.

"I can barely remember it now, sir, but part of me still longs to return and see my family again," Hamíd answered.

"Do you have many siblings?" Rishdah asked.

"A brother and a sister, sir," Hamíd said, surprised at how easily he was talking about his family. Lord Rishdah began to ask another question but stopped, turning instead to other matters.

"I heard how you fought at the north gate last night," he said. "But I also hear you wish no praise for it." Hamíd colored slightly.

"Anyone would have done the same in my place, sir," he said.

"I think you underestimate yourself, Hamíd," Lord Rishdah said. "You should be honored by all for what you did."

"I've spent years trying to remain unnoticed, sir, and I'd rather stay that way," Hamíd said.

"Very well, but just know that you have earned my respect, Hamíd," Lord Rishdah said.

CHAPTER 7

The next day, when the enemy saw that the attempt on Lord Rishdah's life had failed and that Latharn would not fall easily, they began to withdraw. Scouts were sent out to monitor the Argusian's retreat. With the enemy safely gone, Lord Rishdah sent out riders to the rest of his army. News came back that Ncorha had been retaken by the Argusians and Makurung was again under siege. The remnants of Murad's army joined Lord Rishdah at the border. There, the war turned to small skirmishes up and down the border with neither side gaining a clear advantage. Lord Rishdah again sent Castimir home, and this time, the young man obeyed and returned safely home.

Four months passed and found Hamíd mounted on Inzi beside Lord Rishdah. The two main armies had found each other and had drawn into battle lines. Emeth and Nicar were stationed with Ismail some way down the line of cavalry. Inzi shifted nervously beneath Hamid, and he stroked her neck soothingly. Beside him, Ahmed was doing the same as they waited for the signal. Azrahil galloped towards them.

"Everyone is in position my lord!" he said.

Lord Rishdah nodded and raised his hand. A trumpet blared, and the cavalry began to move. Picking up speed, they flew toward the waiting Argusians. Closer and closer they thundered. Suddenly, the enemy seemed to spring up from under their hooves. Spears were raised against the oncoming charge. Hamíd threw his javelin at the soldier in front of Lord Rishdah, clearing a path. Inzi came closer to the glistening spear in front of her. Hamíd pulled heavily on the reins, which caused her to rear and strike with her front hooves, killing the Argusian spearman. Hamíd drew his scimitar and spurred Inzi to where Lord Rishdah and his guards were fighting. Ahmed and Azrahil had made it safely through the line and were hardpressed in the fighting.

The battle raged unceasingly around him for hours, and he was trapped in the bloody sea. Then the battle slowed around him, and he saw that the day was almost gone.

"Hamíd!" shouted Azrahil. He looked to where the captain was pointing and saw Ismail and Emeth unhorsed and pressed against a rocky outcropping. Hamíd urged Inzi toward them and came from behind to surprise the Argusians. He quickly dismounted and helped drive off the enemy. Nicar was sitting against the rocks with part of a spear protruding from his leg. Ismail leaned on his bloody sword as Emeth pulled the spear from Nicar's leg and began bandaging the wound.

"Bloody spear! Never liked those things anyway," Nicar muttered, groaning a little as the bandage was tightened. Hamíd and Ismail stood side by side, gazing out over the field. The fighting had stopped, and the Calorins looked to be victorious. The sun sank lower in the glowing western sky, tinting the battlefield a deeper shade of red.

"Strange, isn't it? We've lived to see the sun set, and there are so many that won't," Ismail said. Hamíd nodded silently, feeling sick as he watched the carrion begin to gather.

"We should find your father," he said. Nicar's horse had been killed, so they helped him on to Inzi. Emeth found his and Ismail's horses wandering nearby. They slowly made their way over to the crowd forming at the center of the field.

Lord Rishdah watched the retreating Argusian army.

"We will see them again all too soon," he said to Azrahil. "But a more welcome sight!" he boomed as he caught sight of his son coming toward them. "It seems we have all survived this day. For that, I am very grateful." He embraced Ismail.

"I am well, Father. You?" Ismail asked.

"Better now that you are safe," Lord Rishdah replied. Then he began to give orders for the transportation of the wounded and any prisoners and the clearing of the battlefield. Azrahil looked Emeth and Hamíd up and down and was satisfied they were not seriously injured.

"Take Nicar back to camp and get him to a healer. Hamíd, take care of the horses," he ordered them.

"Yes, sir," they replied, throwing him a tired salute. Emeth saw Nicar taken care of by a healer and made him as comfortable as possible on his cot.

"I'll be back later," he promised. Nicar grunted softly and closed his eyes. Emeth left the tent and found Hamíd outside. He had unsaddled and picketed the horses. Drawing fresh water, he began to rub the horses down as they drank thirstily. He just finished caring for an ugly gash down Narak's leg when Emeth came up. Emeth laughed as Hamíd turned to him. His face and clothes were smeared in blood and dirt. Emeth was in slightly better condition.

"You look terrible," he said.

"Thanks," Hamíd replied. "You don't look half bad yourself."

Emeth glanced down at his clothes.

"You're right, I should probably try and clean up before the captain gets back," he said. Hamíd saw a rough bandage around Emeth's arm.

"You do that yourself?" he asked gesturing to his arm.

"Now you're going to start on me?" he asked indignantly. "It's fine, I think."

"Let me look at it. I'll at least make it look neater," Hamíd said grinning.

"Only after you take care of yourself," Emeth retaliated.

"Well, if you're going to be that way, I'll wait until Azrahil comes back so he can hold you down," Hamíd replied.

"Cheater!" Emeth muttered good-naturedly. "Between Nicar, Ahmed, and now you, it's a wonder I haven't been killed with concern!"

Hamíd laughed, freely and happily for the first time in years. As he did, a tension eased inside of him.

They went inside the guards' tent to clean up as best they could. They washed and cared for the other cuts and scrapes they had sustained, and Hamíd rebandaged the long wound on Emeth's arm. After dressing in clean uniforms, they began cleaning their weapons and chain mail. Once completely dressed and outfitted, they clasped fresh black cloaks around their shoulders and went out to meet the returning Lord Rishdah.

After the battle, the war turned back to small skirmishes until one day, news came from the Sultaan ordering Lord Rishdah to reach a peace treaty with the Argusians. Two weeks later, the Sultaan and the king of Argus met on the border five miles south of Latharn. Lord Rishdah stood by the Sultaan, flanked by Nicar and Azrahil. The remainder of the Phoenix Guard stood slightly apart with Ismail to watch the proceedings. The king of Argus was a tall, powerfully built man, dressed in the finest clothes, flanked by his best warriors. Gold bracelets decorated his bare arms, and an ornate battle-axe hung at his side. He towered over the Sultaan, a short, rotund man, but with an unmistakable aura of power about him.

"How much do you want to bet he's never fought before in his life?" Emeth whispered out of the side of his mouth to Ahmed, glancing at the finery of the Sultaan and the small dagger he carried. In contrast, the Argusian king was covered in scars of numerous battles.

"That's not a fair bet considering the answer's obvious," Ahmed whispered back. "Just look at the jewels he wears. The smallest one is worth more gold than I'd ever make in a lifetime."

"That's not hard to believe, considering the way both of you lose to Nicar at cards," Ismail murmured. This brought a slight smirk from Hamíd and muffled indignant expressions from Emeth and Ahmed. They lapsed back into silence when Azrahil half turned and looked at them with a withering expression. The hours dragged on as the two rulers debated. As the sun rose higher in the sky, they moved into the welcome shade of a pavilion. Finally, two documents were written out and the king and Sultaan affixed their seals to the papers. Cheers rang through both armies as the treaty was signed. Each with a document in his possession, the two rulers bowed formally to each other and withdrew. Gondeni and Makurung were surrendered back to the Argusians, and provisions were made for prisoner exchange. Two days later, the armies departed, and the borderlands were left in peace.

CHAPTER 8

Two months passed quietly after Lord Rishdah returned to his small domain. Hamíd, now proven in battle, settled down into his second year in the Phoenix Guard. Then news came from the Sultaan that filled him with horror.

Hamíd stood on guard at the doorway to Lord Rishdah's study as he received the messenger.

"The Sultaan is pleased to announce that his armies have successfully invaded Aredor," the man said. Hamíd felt like he had been stabbed in the stomach as the man continued. "Our men caught the northerners completely off guard, and their pathetic warbands were swiftly overcome. The Sultaan's general has taken care of the king and his family and now sits in the royal palace."

"This is somewhat surprising news. I did not know the Sultaan was planning such a campaign," Lord Rishdah said.

"He kept it secret from all but a few. Why do you think he made peace with Argus? He needed the soldiers to help expand his domains," the messenger said.

"What happens if a rebellion stirs in Aredor? Or worse, in our own country? The southern lords are always restless," Lord Rishdah said.

"The Sultaan is assured that there is no resistance left in the north. And if he needed more men, the alliance with the king of Argus will give the Sultaan mercenaries to use as he wills," the man said. "If I did not know you better, Rishdah, I would say that you do not support our illustrious ruler."

"Well then, it is good that you know me," Lord Rishdah said. Pouring two cups of wine, he handed one to the messenger. "May our great Sultaan be blessed with health, prosperity, and victory in battle," he said.

"Always. In Zayd's blessed name!" the man replied. Draining his goblet, he bowed to Lord Rishdah and left the room.

Lord Rishdah cursed as he saw Hamíd standing still in shock at the door.

"Hamíd, I knew nothing of this news. You should not have heard it like that," Lord Rishdah said.

"How would you mean to tell me that your bloody Sultaan invaded my homeland? Or did you mean to tell me at all?" Hamíd spat angrily.

"Yes, I would have. But understand that I can do nothing about this," Lord Rishdah said.

"What does this mean for me then? Do you turn me in or kill me? Or perhaps you will just enslave me again as you just did my people?" Hamíd asked heatedly. Lord Rishdah rose.

"None of those," he said sharply. "I took you because I saw the courage and honor you have. Do not do anything that will make me change that view. I make it very clear that even though I serve the Sultaan, I do not agree with everything he does. You swore an oath to me and as such are still bound to me. I trust you and I ask you to do the same."

"Yes, sir," Hamíd gritted out.

"You are dismissed for now. I will speak to Azrahil," Lord Rishdah said. Hamíd bowed and left the room.

Emeth found Hamíd sitting against the north wall of the castle.

"Figured I might find you here. You can't see much, but at least it faces north," Emeth said.

"You heard the news?" Hamíd asked in Rhyddan. Emeth nodded.

"Aye, just now," he replied. "I'm sorry."

"Doesn't make much difference, does it?" Hamíd asked bitterly.

"Don't think I don't know what this means. How long do you think it will be until they turn to Braeton? A day doesn't go by that I don't think of my own family," Emeth said.

"At least you know your family is still alive," Hamíd returned. "I should have been there. Leading a warband alongside my father and brother."

"What did you say?" Emeth asked a little incredulously.

"Does it matter?" Hamíd asked. He took off the leather glove covering his palm, revealing the brand. "A slave. That's all I am."

"No, no you're not. You're a prince?" Emeth asked trying to grasp the implications of what Hamíd had said.

"Not anymore," Hamíd said. "There's nothing left." He turned again and faced north. Somewhere, over the trackless plains and ocean, was his home. Suddenly Emeth spoke again.

"Aiden."

"What?" Hamíd asked, confused.

"You didn't think my name was really Emeth, did you?" he asked with a grin.

"Fair enough. My name's Corin," Hamíd replied with a slight smile.

"Does Rishdah know?" Emeth asked. Hamíd shook his head.

"No one does, except for you. And that's how it'll stay," he said. They sat in silence for a long moment and then Emeth spoke.

"So what was it like?" he asked.

"What?" Hamíd returned.

"I'm just trying to imagine you as a prince, strutting around," Emeth said. Hamíd grinned.

"Well, I admit I was a little spoiled. Running everywhere, usually in trouble. I planned most of our escapades, dragging my friend Martin, and my brother Darrin, along with me. And after I got us all in trouble, Darrin would get me out of it," Hamíd said.

"Sounds like my older brothers," Emeth commented.

"I was so impulsive and reckless and wouldn't let Darrin talk me out of anything. He would actually stop to think about what might happen if we got caught," Hamíd said.

"What was one of the worst things you ever did?" Emeth asked. Hamíd thought for a moment.

"I actually stole my father's crown for some reason and lost it for about a day and a half before I found it again. I don't think I sat down for a week," Hamíd admitted as Emeth laughed. "Funny thing is, afterwards, I don't think my father was very angry with me. You could always tell when he was really mad if you watched his eyes. Most of the time, you could see the laughter in them, so we always knew we wouldn't be punished too badly," he said.

"What about your friend, Martin?" Emeth asked curiously.

"He was just like me. We both dreamed of growing up to be famous warriors. I hope he's still out there alive somewhere," Hamíd said pensively.

"Well, if he's still anything like you, he probably is. And don't worry, your secret's safe with me, Corin," Emeth said. Hamíd suddenly laughed.

"I haven't been called that in so many years," he said. "Thanks... Aiden."

Emeth made a low bow. "Anything for Your—"

"Don't say it," Hamíd warned as he rose. "I will hurt you if you ever call me that."

"Really? How badly?" Emeth asked, grinning.

"You're about to find out," Hamíd said.

Despite his best efforts, Hamíd found himself thinking more and more about Aredor. His companions never mentioned the invasion, but it remained at the forefront of his mind for days. Castimir, having formed a strong friendship with Hamíd since the Argusian war, tried to find some way to distract him. He and Hamíd would go on frequent hunting trips, often joined by

Emeth or Ahmed. Grasping light javelins, they would race their horses against the fleet gazelles that roamed the plains. Castimir was finally rewarded one day by the return of the cocky grin to Hamíd's face. Watching Hamíd's angular features, Castimir was reminded of the solitary gray hawks that traveled the sky. He began to call Hamíd simply "Hawk," to the quiet amusement of his companions.

CHAPTER 9

Several months later Emeth, Castimir, and Hamíd raced each other along the road. Bending low over the necks of their horses, they urged them on, quickly outdistancing the rest of the company. Lord Rishdah smiled as he watched them go. It had been a long and tedious journey. The Sultaan had sent him to gain the support of the southern lords in order to supply the Sultaan with more troops. Lord Rishdah had brought Castimir along to begin to educate his youngest son in the intricacies of diplomacy. But long talks and councils did not sit well with Castimir's wild spirit.

"Come!" he said. "We'd best hurry if we don't wish to be left behind." The soldiers smiled as they spurred their horses on to a quicker pace.

The three of them flew down the road for more than a mile until they pulled their horses to a stop. Castimir whooped in excitement.

"I never thought we'd leave!" he gasped.

"That boy Castimir is too wild and reckless for his own good!" Emeth said in a deep voice. His companions doubled over with laughter.

"That old lord, ha! Too pompous for *his* own good!" Castimir said. "I don't know how Father stands it!"

"He doesn't! You should see him after days like that," Hamíd said. Castimir flashed a grin.

"Come on, we'll wait for them by those rocks up ahead," he said. The rocks in question were huge stones piled on either side of the road about a quarter mile away. Dark eyes watched their progress carefully.

"That's not Rishdah," one man said. "That's the son."

"He'll do just as well," the leader said.

"He's got a few of those bloody guards with him," the first man said.

"Don't worry. They won't be so lively with arrows sticking through them. Once they're out of the way, the boy'll be easy enough to take down. They're coming on fast. Tell the others to get ready!" his leader said.

They were almost to the rocks when an arrow flashed from the rocks, narrowly missing Hamíd's shoulder. Another followed, striking Inzi. She reared up, screaming in pain as two more thudded into her. She fell, throwing Hamíd clear. He lay still for a moment, trying to regain his breath. Castimir and Emeth strove to control their mounts as arrows whizzed by. Emeth cried out as a shaft hit him in the leg. He fell from Narak, and the frightened horse bolted back up the road. Hamíd helped him up as Castimir quickly dismounted.

"You able to stand?" Castimir asked.

"Looks like I'll have to," Emeth gritted, nodding at the men who now surrounded them. They unsheathed their swords.

"Back to back!" Hamíd ordered. He looked at the men. They all wore masks covering their noses and mouths.

"Forty against three. Sounds fair," Castimir said as the men drew their swords.

"We don't have to hold them off long. Your father should be here soon," Hamíd said.

"Let's hope its sooner rather than later," Emeth said as he struggled to keep his balance.

The first wave attacked, and a few minutes later, they struggled back, leaving four dead and two wounded. Their leader hissed in frustration and ordered all the men forward. In the battle, the three companions were driven apart. Emeth was forced against a rock, battling furiously; his double swords glinting in the sunlight became stained with blood. Then a sabre cut across his hand.

Reflexively, he dropped the sword. His assailant swung out with his shield, sending it crashing against his arm. He cried out as his arm broke against the force of the blow. Hamíd heard the cry and turned to see the bandit looming over Emeth. Drawing a knife, he threw it into the man's back. As Emeth huddled against the rock cradling his arm, he looked up to see Hamíd racing to help Castimir. He screamed with Hamíd when he saw a bandit plunge his sabre through Castimir.

Hamíd ran towards Castimir as he fought off the bandit. Hamíd dimly heard his own cry as Castimir fell, and then he was on the bandit. They fought fiercely, and Hamíd cried out again as a dagger was plunged into his side. He whipped his scimitar up into the bandit and then grabbed hold of the dagger and crumpled to the ground. Emeth saw what was left of the band running away, and he crawled to where Castimir and Hamíd lay. Tears streaked his face as he knelt by Castimir's body. Castimir opened his eyes and gave Emeth one last smile, then his breath grew ragged, and pain flashed across his face. Emeth grabbed his hand as he trembled and grew still.

"No!" he whispered. "No!" Then he felt arms around him, and Lord Rishdah was kneeling by his son. Emeth dimly saw Nicar bending over Hamíd, and then all went black.

Ahmed held Emeth as he lapsed into unconsciousness. He staunched the blood still flowing from the arrow wound in Emeth's leg. Ahmed gazed around at the carnage surrounding them. Fifteen bodies lay on the road. Azrahil made his way among them, looking them over. Most were Calorins but a few were Argusian soldiers.

"My lord, there's one still alive over here!" he called. Lord Rishdah looked up from his place by Castimir's body. He took off his cloak and gently spread it over his son. Azrahil grabbed hold of the wounded man and shoved him against a rock. He stripped the mask off the man's face, revealing the features of a Calorin soldier. Lord Rishdah joined him.

"Who are you?" he demanded.

"My name is Raja. We were given orders to meet with several Argusians. We were to ambush and kill you," the man said, looking at Lord Rishdah.

"Why?" Lord Rishdah asked.

"I don't know. But it wasn't going to stop with you. Your family is going to be hunted down and slain as well," Raja said.

"Who ordered the ambush?" Lord Rishdah demanded.

"None of us knew except the commander, and he's dead now," Raja answered.

"Azrahil, make sure he doesn't die yet. I might have a use for him," Lord Rishdah commanded. Azrahil set two soldiers to guard the man as Lord Rishdah strode off to order a bier made for Castimir's body.

Nicar knelt by Hamíd. He was lying on his side, both hands clutched around the hilt of the dagger protruding from his side. He was still conscious, his face ashen white, and he trembled uncontrollably. Nicar moved him gently on to his back. Hamíd moaned, his eyes looking pleadingly at Nicar.

"Hold on, lad!" Nicar whispered. "Jaffa, get over here!" he shouted. The captain hurried over and knelt by them. "Hold him up and make sure he doesn't move," Nicar ordered. Jaffa propped Hamíd's head and shoulders against his knees and wrapped his arms around Hamíd's chest. Nicar moved Hamíd's hands from the dagger, took hold of the handle, and pulled. Hamíd cried out as it moved a fraction. Nicar felt around the wound.

"It hit a rib. Hold tight," he said as he pulled again. Jaffa held Hamíd down as he convulsed in pain. He gave another great cry as Nicar pulled once more and the blade came free. Nicar ripped open his shirt and tunic and pushed up the mail coat, exposing the wound. He frantically reached for needle and thread and began to stitch the wound closed. Jaffa lifted Hamíd slightly as Nicar wrapped a bandage around him. He had lost consciousness when Nicar pulled the dagger out. He lay limp in Jaffa's arms as

Nicar felt his pulse. It was weak but steady. Jaffa and another soldier carried Hamíd to the place Azrahil had chosen as a campsite and laid him on some blankets. They then spread Hamíd's cloak over him and left.

Nicar moved over to where Ahmed still sat, holding Emeth. Emeth awoke as Nicar knelt by them. Nicar laid his hand on the broken arrow shaft sticking from his leg.

"You ready?" Nicar asked. Emeth nodded weakly. Ahmed winced as Emeth crushed his hand against the pain.

"Sorry," Emeth said as Nicar bandaged the wound.

"That's all right. I think," Ahmed replied. He placed his dagger between Emeth's teeth as Nicar moved to his arm. Nicar glanced at Emeth. He nodded then screamed against the dagger as Nicar wrenched the bones back into place. Ahmed helped him stand and limp to the camp where Nicar fashioned a splint from pieces of wood. He placed Emeth's arm in a sling made from a torn blanket as Lord Rishdah came up. Ahmed helped Emeth sit against a rock and handed him a waterskin then left him alone with Lord Rishdah.

Lord Rishdah sat beside him. Emeth couldn't meet his gaze.

"I'm sorry," he said, tears filling his eyes again. "I'm sorry I didn't protect him. I failed you."

"You did not kill him, Emeth. It was them. From the looks of things, you did all you could," Lord Rishdah said. Emeth nodded miserably.

"What happened?" Lord Rishdah asked. Emeth began to recount the events of the ambush.

"There were too many of them, and we got separated. I went down halfway through, and Hamíd stopped me from getting killed. Then he fought over to where Castimir was. He got there just as…it happened. Then the bandit stabbed him, and the rest fled. I guess you know the rest," he finished. He scrubbed a sleeve across his face and drew a shaky breath. "It's my fault. If Hamíd hadn't stopped to help me, Castimir would be alive right now," he said. Lord Rishdah laid a hand on his shoulder.

"We will never know that, Emeth. But it seems as if you boys took care of almost half their force. Forty against three," he marveled.

"Castimir said it was fair, sir," Emeth said with a small smile. Rishdah smiled. Then he rose and made his way from the campsite. Emeth cursed his carelessness as he watched Lord Rishdah leave.

Rishdah stopped a short way from the camp where they had laid Castimir's body. He would spend the night there watching over his son's body. He sat down and looked at Castimir's face then softly began to weep.

Hamíd woke suddenly, his wound aching horribly. Azrahil came and knelt by him.

"Are you all right, Hamíd?" he asked, concern covering his features.

"No," Hamíd said miserably. "Captain…I failed. If only I had been faster, Castimir might be alive right now."

"Hamíd, telling yourself that won't change anything. Years ago, I watched my brother and my friend die right in front of me. I relived it every day, thinking that if I had taken another path, I would have been there beside them, to save them. Some things are meant to happen, and you can't stop them," Azrahil said.

"But how do you live with it? How do I face Lord Rishdah or his family?" Hamíd asked.

"He'll understand," Azrahil said.

"How can you be so sure?" Hamíd asked.

"Because I have failed him before," Azrahil replied somberly. Despite the captain's words, Hamíd knew it would be a long time before he could forgive himself.

Azrahil and the five other soldiers stood watch over the camp all night while Ahmed and Nicar took turns caring for Emeth and

Hamíd. They slept fitfully, plagued by nightmares of the ambush. They stayed one more day at the camp and then moved on, leaving behind a burning pile of corpses. Hamíd rode Castimir's stallion, staring straight ahead. Emeth rode beside him, both trying not to think about the body stretched on the bier behind them. It took another day to reach Lord Rishdah's castle; they all dreaded what would happen once they arrived.

The sun was low in the western sky as they rode slowly through the gates. Ismail came out to greet them followed by Lord Rishdah's wife. The smile of welcome died on their lips as they took in the somber company. Then the soldiers came forward, carrying the bier. Ismail gently held his mother as she fell to her knees, mourning her lost son.

Hamíd slid from the horse, leaning against the saddle, as he waited for the pain in his side to subside. He preferred the pain to the hollow feeling of loss and failure inside him. He pressed his hand against his side as he choked back new tears. He had grown close to Castimir. The young man had reminded him of Martin, and that thought brought home fresh sorrow.

Ismail stepped back as Lord Rishdah came to comfort his wife. He felt a tear trickle down his cheek. He couldn't believe that his brother was dead. He looked over to see Nicar putting an arm around Hamíd to help him walk. Hamíd briefly met Ismail's gaze as Nicar helped him to the barracks. As if in a dream, Ismail made his way back inside the castle.

They buried Castimir the next day. Emeth watched from the window in the barracks. The company was dressed in black, and the guards stood at attention. As they lowered the body into the tomb, Emeth turned away. He limped over to his bed and lay down. Hamíd lay in the bunk beside Emeth with his face turned to the wall.

"Do you think we could have done any more?" he asked Emeth quietly. "I mean, do you think if we had tried harder, we could have saved him?"

"Rishdah thinks we did all we could," Emeth said by way of an answer.

"I just keep seeing it, and know I'm too late. I don't know how to live with that," Hamíd said.

"I don't know either," Emeth said. He adjusted his arm in the sling. "But for now, I'm wounded and need to get some proper rest," he said mimicking Nicar. Hamíd smiled faintly.

"You know," he said. "I could get used to lying in bed all day, being waited on."

Emeth laughed, "They'd have to roll you off the bed you'd be so fat!" he said. Hamíd winced as he laughed.

"Don't make me laugh, it hurts," he said. Emeth waved a hand.

"Silence now, I need my beauty sleep. Just wake me up when the food comes," he said.

"Yes, master," Hamíd replied with another laugh.

That night, Hamíd had a dream.

He was standing in a strange forest. He sensed that the trees were very old and that he was not the first to ever pass through them. As he glanced around, he caught sight of someone coming towards him. It was Castimir.

"Don't worry about me, Hawk. My time had come," he said. "Look after my brother for me and keep him safe. Don't hesitate, and you can save him."

"What do you mean? What's going to happen?" Hamíd demanded.

"It is not for me to tell you. Keep him safe, please!"

With that, Hamíd awoke. He could see the faint rays of the rising sun coming through the windows. Troubled by the dream, he was unable to rest. He slowly sat up and swung his legs over the edge of the bed. Wincing, he found his boots and pulled them on then slipped a tunic over his shirt. He took up his cloak and threw it about his shoulders and quietly made his way outside. He moved slowly across the empty courtyard and into the stables. They were quiet and deserted as he walked past horses until he came to a stall. Hamíd leaned on the door and looked at its inhabitant.

A big black stallion stood in the darkness; its white stockings and blaze glimmered dimly through the blackness. He sighed as he looked at Castimir's horse. It looked lost without its former master. The stallion saw Hamíd and came slowly toward him and snorted softly as Hamíd reached out and began stroking its nose.

"Shouldn't you be in bed?" Lord Rishdah asked, coming up quietly behind him.

"Yes, sir, I should be I guess. But I couldn't sleep and wanted to get out for a minute," Hamíd replied.

"I understand," Lord Rishdah said. "How are you feeling, Hamíd?" he asked.

"Better, sir. Hopefully not much longer, and I'll be good as new," Hamíd replied.

"I'm glad to hear it. You seem to be getting along with Zephyr," Lord Rishdah said.

"Yes, sir. He doesn't seem to mind the attention," Hamíd answered. He rubbed the stallion's broad forehead and then he said, "My lord, I never told you how sorry I am. I dishonored my oath to you." He met Lord Rishdah's steady gaze. "If there was any way I could, I would exchange places with him right now."

Lord Rishdah nodded his thanks as he fought against the raw sorrow over his son's death. They stood in silence a moment more then he spoke.

"I want you to take Zephyr," he said.

"What?! Sir, I can't!" Hamíd exclaimed.

"Yes, you need a new horse, and he will serve you well. Take him, that's an order," Lord Rishdah said.

"Well then, I'll gladly take him, sir," Hamíd replied.

"Good man. Don't stay out to much longer or Nicar will have your head," Lord Rishdah said with a smile.

"Yes, sir," Hamíd said, returning the smile. As Rishdah left the stables, Hamíd turned back to Zephyr. "I guess it is you and me now, boy," he said. Zephyr snorted and gently butted Hamíd with his nose. Hamíd gave him one last pat and made his way slowly back to the barracks. He felt tired as he lay down on the bed. The short walk was harder on him than he thought. Sighing, he resigned himself to another day of bed rest.

CHAPTER 10

"Well, it's healed nicely. You're now fit for duty. Congratulations. Maybe I'll get some extra sleep now," Nicar said a few weeks later as he finished picking the stitches out of Hamíd's side. Hamíd laughed as he slipped his shirt back on and donned the rest of his uniform. Buckling on his weapons, he made his way to the stables to meet Lord Rishdah as ordered. On the way, he met Emeth, his arm freshly out of the sling. He was buckling his swords into place across his shoulders. He fastened a quiver about his waist as he fell into step beside Hamíd.

"How's your arm?" Hamíd asked.

"A little stiff, but Azrahil will get it loose in a hurry. He said something about whipping me back into shape. Not sure what all that entails, but it can't be good," Emeth replied.

"It's not. He wore me out yesterday," Hamíd replied. Emeth grimaced.

"That's not what I wanted to hear," he said as he turned to go to the training courtyard to meet the captain. Hamíd tacked up Zephyr as the stallion pranced in excitement.

"Too much energy, just like me," Hamíd said, leading him out into the courtyard where Lord Rishdah waited. Hamíd mounted, and Zephyr strained forward eagerly. He pulled the stallion to a halt, focusing on keeping him still. Lord Rishdah watched carefully.

"Ready? Now we'll see what kind of a horseman you really are," he said. Hamíd felt Zephyr respond immediately to his signals, and a surge of exhilaration ran through him.

"Lead the way, sir," he said.

The remainder of the year passed quietly. The bandit they had captured could provide no more information for Lord Rishdah. No further attacks were made on Lord Rishdah or Ismail, but the Phoenix Guard remained watchful and prepared. There was hardly any more news of Aredor; no real resistance was left in that country. Hamíd tried to forget his home. While he fervently wished to go back, he knew that there was now nothing left for him to return to. Their life in Calorin moved on and, during the summer, Ismail became betrothed to a neighboring lord's daughter. The wedding was set to take place at the New Year.

Lord Rishdah and his family rode out accompanied by his guards and a company of soldiers. Lord Jamal was a close friend of Lord Rishdah's. His lands lay two days' ride away to the southwest of Calorin, close to the Gelion border where the grass plains gave way to a small scrub forest. Lord Jamal's castle lay in a small valley well inside the forest.

The journey passed uneventfully, but Hamíd could not shake a feeling of foreboding. He had dreamed of Castimir's warning twice in the past few days. He was not the only who felt on edge; Azrahil also seemed nervous especially as they entered the forest. They spent a few days at the castle and were to go hunting the next morning. Hamíd slept fitfully that night before rising at dawn. After a light meal, the hunting party assembled in the courtyard. Hamíd rode close to Ismail, not wanting to let him out of his sight. They rode all morning and brought down several small deer. By midafternoon, they turned back to the castle. As they passed through a small dell, Hamíd reigned up sharply, causing those behind him to stop.

"Hamíd? What's wrong?" Ismail asked

"I don't know yet, sir," Hamíd replied. Zephyr snorted suddenly and began to rear and move nervously. Ismail pushed his horse a few steps ahead of Hamíd. A rustle in the bushes to his left caused Hamíd's head to turn sharply. A young lion burst out of the undergrowth and headed straight for Ismail. Hamíd yelled a warning as he spurred Zephyr forward between Ismail and the lion.

The lion jumped as Hamíd turned to face it. It knocked him off the horse, and he tumbled to the ground. Hamíd's arm went up as the lion went for his throat; its powerful jaws locked around his vambrace. They rolled over and over, and Hamíd screamed as its claws cut into him. His hand found a dagger, and he drew it out. He plunged it again and again into the lion's side. Then all grew still. The lion lay on top of him with its jaws still clamped around his arm. His hand slipped from the bloody dagger handle as he began to lose consciousness.

The rest of the hunting party had watched in horror during the fight and were unable to shoot for fear of hitting Hamíd. Emeth and Ahmed ran forward as it ended. Emeth pushed the carcass off Hamíd as Ahmed began trying to staunch the blood. Their movements galvanized the others into action. Nicar went to join Emeth and Ahmed. Lord Rishdah looked up at where the lion had come from. He froze as he saw two men with bows pointed down into the dell. He cried a warning as they fired. He ducked one arrow as it flew towards him; the other hit Ismail in the arm as he moved. Lord Jamal ordered men to pursue as the assassins fled. Lord Rishdah ran to Ismail, helping him from his horse as Ismail tried to stop the bleeding. Azrahil ordered the remaining men to guard the perimeter.

Nicar tore his cloak into strips to bind Hamíd's wounds. The lion's claws had raked down his upper left arm and his right thigh to the knee. Its jaws had gouged the underside of his arm unprotected by the vambraces. His mail coat had prevented any other serious injuries. Emeth and Ahmed held him down as Nicar finished tying the crude bandages.

"Where's Ismail?" Hamíd rasped.

"He's fine. But what were you thinking, idiot?" Emeth asked. His question went unanswered as Hamíd lapsed into unconsciousness.

"Emeth, stay with him. Ahmed, come with me. We'll need a stretcher. He needs proper care quickly if he's to live," Nicar said.

Lord Rishdah looked up as Nicar came running over. He finished tying a bandage on Ismail's arm then turned to Nicar.

"How is he?" he asked, looking at the limp form of Hamíd.

"Not so good, my lord. We need to get him out of here fast. I don't have what I need for him with me." He looked at Ismail's arm.

"I'll be fine," Ismail said. "Take care of him first." Nicar gave a nod and then hurried over to where Azrahil and Emeth were placing Hamíd on a makeshift stretcher made of spears and cloaks. As Ahmed covered him with a cloak, Nicar could see blood already seeping through the bandages.

"Azrahil, how long until we make it back?" Nicar asked worriedly.

"It's almost a mile back to the castle, but I'm afraid that might be too long," Azrahil answered grimly as he ordered men over to carry the stretcher.

The journey seemed to take forever. Hamíd moaned in his sleep, and sweat beaded his forehead. When they reached the castle, they took Hamíd to a secluded room and laid him on the bed. Nicar found his pouch as hot water was brought to the room. He quickly washed his hands and began removing Hamíd's tunic. Nicar called Emeth over to help him. Emeth removed his cloak and weapons and helped Nicar take off Hamíd's mail coat and shirt. Emeth handed Nicar hot water and cloths, and he began washing the ragged wounds on Hamíd's arm. The edges of the cuts were bright red and hot to the touch. Hamíd flinched as Nicar bathed them. Nicar swore as he saw that the wounds were already becoming infected. Emeth watched worriedly as he prepared a salve, which he spread on the wounds and wrapped in fresh bandages.

"It's swelling, so I can't stitch it yet," Nicar explained as he bandaged Hamíd's leg, ripping open the pant leg. The wounds on his forearm seemed uninfected, so he washed and stitched them. Emeth laid his hand on Hamíd's forehead.

"He's too hot," he said. Nicar leaned over and felt Hamíd's pulse. It was weak and irregular.

"Will he die?" Emeth asked, his voice shaking a little.

"I don't know yet, lad, but I'm not giving up without a fight," Nicar replied and then sent him for more water and cloths. After Emeth left, Lord Rishdah came in quietly.

"Any change?" he asked.

"No, sir," Nicar replied. "I don't know what was on that lion's claws, but it's making the wounds worse." He drew blankets over Hamíd. "Forgive me, sir, but how is Ismail?" he asked.

"He'll be all right. The healer saw to his arm, but I'm afraid he's still in shock over what happened. We all are. The whole place is in an uproar," Lord Rishdah said. "Lord Jamal just made it back. I'm on my way to see him. Nicar, do your best please." Nicar nodded gravely.

Emeth came back accompanied by a servant carrying more water and herbs. Nicar made a potion and, as Emeth held Hamíd up, poured a little into Hamíd's mouth. His eyes, clouded in pain, flickered open for a moment. Nicar dampened a cloth and began bathing Hamíd's forehead. Emeth stood by, looking a little lost.

"Go and get cleaned up, Emeth. You can come and relieve me in a few hours. It's going to be a long night," Nicar said grimly.

Lord Rishdah went out into the courtyard to meet Lord Jamal.

"We got both of them," Lord Jamal said. "But not before they talked. I know who's after you now." He led Lord Rishdah inside to a private chamber.

"It's Numair," Lord Jamal said.

"You are sure of this?" Lord Rishdah asked.

"Yes, I know he's your brother—" Lord Jamal began.

"Half brother!" Lord Rishdah interrupted.

"Well, it seems that he's tired of living on the eastern border. I must say, he's done a good job of trying to make your death seem accidental," Lord Jamal said.

"He always was a small, scheming man," Lord Rishdah said. "I'm sure the Argusians were only too happy to take the chance for revenge by killing me. But Numair has gone too far now!"

"What do you plan?" Lord Jamal asked.

"There was always little love lost between us, so he'll understand when I take my army to put him in his place," Lord Rishdah said furiously.

"Well, this attack took place on my lands and against my future son-in-law, so naturally, my men and I are coming with you," Lord Jamal said.

"Thank you, my friend," Lord Rishdah.

"How is your young guard? You know, in all my life, I've never seen anything like that," Lord Jamal said.

"He's not doing well," Lord Rishdah said.

"Let me know if he needs anything. My best healers are at your disposal," Lord Jamal said.

"Thank you, my men are looking after him now. If you'll excuse me, I should go explain things to my family," Lord Rishdah said. Lord Jamal laughed shortly.

"Aye, I'm sure I have some guests that want an explanation as well," he said.

Nicar stayed with Hamíd all night as his fever raged on. Nicar placed cold compresses on him and changed poultices on his wounds, trying to draw out the infection. Emeth came in just after dawn. Nicar was sitting half asleep in a chair. He jumped slightly when Emeth came up.

"Any change?" Emeth asked. Nicar shook his head. Hamíd lay still on the bed as he labored to breathe.

"I'll stay with him. You're exhausted," Emeth said.

"All right. I'll be back in a few hours. He needs water. See if you can get him to take any," Nicar said. Emeth nodded. As Nicar left, he sat down in the chair by the bed. He poured a cup of water and moved over to the bed.

"Hamíd," he said. Hamíd's eyes flew open. "Here, drink this," Emeth coaxed as he propped Hamíd up. He poured some of the water into Hamíd's mouth. He swallowed and then closed his eyes again. Emeth felt his forehead; he was still burning up. The hours stretched on as Emeth, unable to do anything, sat by, listening to Hamíd's ragged breathing.

Nicar came back later as he promised and began checking the bandages. He breathed a sigh of relief. The infection seemed to have passed. He crushed some herbs into a cup of water and handed it to Emeth.

"Get that down him. I can start stitching now," he said. Emeth turned to Hamíd again. He called his name, but no response came from Hamíd. Emeth glanced at Nicar preparing his things.

"Come on, don't do this to me, mate," Emeth whispered. "Corin! Corin, come on, wake up!"

His eyes opened again.

"Aiden, it hurts," he said hoarsely.

"I know, Cor. Drink this, it'll help." He drew Hamíd up and held the cup to his lips. He swallowed some and winced as he coughed.

"Come on," Emeth prompted. "All of it. Nicar's going to start sticking you here in a minute."

He drank the rest slowly and then fell back into a restless sleep.

"Emeth, hold him steady," Nicar said. Emeth held Hamíd's arm gently as Nicar began to stitch the wounds shut.

"So is that his real name?" Nicar asked.

"What?" Emeth asked in return.

"Corin," Nicar said. Emeth looked up sharply. "I might be older than you, but I'm not deaf," Nicar said with a smile. "It's a good name. Just like Aiden is a good name for you."

"You know I changed it for a reason," Emeth replied. Nicar nodded in understanding. Emeth wiped fresh blood away as Nicar finished stitching. Nicar spread ointment on and rebandaged the wound. They repeated the process on Hamíd's leg and then turned to the small gashes and cuts he had also sustained. Hours later, they finished. Nicar grimaced as he straightened up and felt Hamíd's pulse. It was no different from the previous night. They covered him warmly with blankets as Ahmed came to relieve them. Nicar met Lord Rishdah in the hallway.

"He's not doing well, Lord," he said in response to Lord Rishdah's question. "If the fever doesn't break by tonight, he might not make it."

"Have you told Emeth or Ahmed this?" Lord Rishdah asked. Nicar shook his head. Around the corner, Emeth moved quietly away and then made his way outside.

CHAPTER 11

Lord Rishdah saw Emeth run outside and followed. He found Emeth leaning against the back wall of the stables.

"You heard?" Lord Rishdah asked. Emeth nodded dejectedly, crossing his arms tightly across his chest.

"I feel so useless. He's dying, and I can't do anything to stop it," Emeth said. "I guess he knew it might happen though."

"What do you mean?" Lord Rishdah asked curiously.

"He asked Azrahil about his dream, and I figured you knew too," Emeth said. "The night you buried Castimir, he first had it. Castimir came and told him something would happen to Ismail, and to protect him. He's had it several times," Emeth explained. Lord Rishdah leaned against the wall, shaking his head in disbelief.

"Emeth, what do you know about him?" Lord Rishdah asked. Emeth hesitated.

"Not much, other than his real name and that he's from Aredor, sir," he replied cautiously.

"But it seems that you know more than you tell," Lord Rishdah said.

"It's not my place, my lord," Emeth replied.

"Well then, pray to Zayd or to your god that he makes it through this," Lord Rishdah said before he left.

He lay still, surrounded by darkness and pain. His last memory was lion jumping at him and then after that came the pain.

Around him in the black, he could sense something prowling, waiting to strike. He yearned to break free and to fly away, but he was pinned down. He tried to fight against it, but he couldn't move. He was trapped!

Late in the afternoon, Emeth went to the stables and began brushing Narak while trying to clear his head. As he finished, he heard a disturbance a few stalls down. He moved over to see Zephyr prancing restlessly in the stall, throwing his head and neighing thunderously. Emeth went up to the door.

"Careful, sir," a groom said. "That one's half crazy. He fought the whole way back that day of the hunt. Almost hurt the soldier leading him."

Emeth cautiously reached a hand out. Zephyr snorted as he drew in Emeth's scent. He stood still and stretched his head toward Emeth.

"That's it. Come on, you know me," Emeth murmured. The stallion took a tremulous step forward. Emeth gently stroked its nose and felt in his pouch for an apple slice. Zephyr came forward to take the apple, snorting as he chomped the treat. Emeth rubbed Zephyr's forehead.

"You were worried about him, weren't you, boy? He means a lot to you, doesn't he?" he whispered softly. The stallion relaxed and nosed Emeth's tunic, looking for more treats. Emeth laughed as he slipped inside the stall and began rubbing Zephyr down. He was feeding the horse the remainder of the apple when Ahmed ran up.

"The fever broke. He's awake!"

Hamíd still lay in the darkness, exhausted and burning with pain. Suddenly, a light broke through overhead. He strained toward it, and broke free, flying toward it. He opened his eyes to see Nicar standing over him. Nicar grinned in relief.

"Welcome back," he said. He gently propped Hamíd up and held a cup of water for him to drink. He drained the cup, and Nicar helped him settle back down on the pillows as Ahmed and Emeth burst in.

"You made it through! How do you feel?" Emeth asked, breathlessly.

"Pretty terrible," Hamíd said hoarsely.

"Well, you still look terrible," Emeth said. Hamíd flashed a tired grin.

"I'll take that as a compliment," he said. Ahmed laughed.

"You should. We're just glad to see you alive," he said.

"All right, you two. He's hurt and needs to rest," Nicar said. Ahmed and Emeth stifled grins.

"For once, I'm not going to argue," Hamíd said.

"Good. I don't suppose either of you told Lord Rishdah anything?" he asked, turning to Emeth and Ahmed. They both shook their heads a little sheepishly.

"Must I do everything myself?" Nicar asked. Emeth made a face at him.

"All right, all right, we're going!" Ahmed said. As they went out, Hamíd looked at Nicar.

"How bad is it?" he asked.

"You got ripped up pretty badly," Nicar said. "But it should all start to heal now. I'm warning you though. It'll take a long time. You need some proper rest. No arguments!"

"Yes, sir," Hamíd replied, and within minutes, he was asleep.

Emeth and Ahmed went off in search of Lord Rishdah. They found Azrahil standing outside the council room.

"Lord Rishdah is inside with Lord Jamal. They are not to be disturbed," Azrahil told them.

"What are they doing?" Ahmed asked.

"Lord Rishdah plans to move against Lord Numair after the wedding. They are planning their campaign," the captain said.

"Good!" Emeth said in grim satisfaction. "That treacherous dog doesn't deserve to live."

"You'll get your chance soon enough, Emeth," Lord Rishdah said as he emerged from the council chamber. "We leave after the wedding, two days from now. We still have a little time to continue planning. Now, any news?" he asked.

"It looks as if our hawk will fly again, sir," Ahmed said.

"Good," Lord Rishdah said with a smile. "You two will stay with me for the rest of the day. Captain, make a list of the soldiers and supplies we have with us then send someone back home to alert Captain Jaffa to have my army ready to march in five days' time!"

Hamíd slept soundly for the rest of the day and through the night. Nicar woke him to take some water and drink some broth. Nicar again felt his pulse. It was strong and steady. He nodded in satisfaction. The young warrior was on his way to recovery. He checked to make sure Hamíd was warmly covered before leaving the room. Then he headed to relieve Emeth on guard duty. Ahmed had been sent to attend to Ismail some hours earlier. As he took up his position, Lord Rishdah inquired about his young guard.

"He's sleeping now, sir. He's still a bit weak from the infection, but he'll soon get his strength back," Nicar answered.

"How long until he's up?" Lord Rishdah asked.

"Those wounds will take a while to fully heal. He'll limp badly on that leg, if he's lucky to walk at all, sir. But I'd say at least two months before he's able to resume duties, sir," Nicar said. Lord Rishdah frowned. Two months was long, and he needed every available soldier.

"Thank you, Nicar," he replied.

The next day, Ismail went to visit Hamíd. Nicar had helped him into a fresh shirt, and he leaned against the pillows with his arm in a sling.

"I wanted to thank you properly for saving my life," Ismail said quietly. "But why did you do it? You didn't have to." Hamíd toyed with the blanket's edge before looking up and meeting Ismail's gaze.

"This may sound strange, but your brother told me to," he said. Ismail looked confused.

"My brother?" he asked. Hamíd nodded and related his dream.

"I'm not sure if jumping in front of the lion was the smartest idea, but it seemed like the only thing to do at the time. I couldn't save him, but I could try and protect you," Hamíd said.

"Well, I thank you again. I am deeply indebted to you now. I hope a day comes when I'll be able to pay you back in like manner," Ismail said. He extended his hand to Hamíd, who hesitated a moment before clasping it firmly.

Hamíd's four companions also visited throughout the day as their duties allowed. They brought news of the upcoming campaign. In addition, Emeth brought news of Zephyr. Hamíd was relieved to hear Emeth was caring for the stallion.

"You seem to care more about that animal than you do about us," Emeth complained with a grin.

"That's because he doesn't talk back like you do," Hamíd shot back. Emeth barely managed to put on a wounded expression.

"I thought you cared. I suppose not. Not a friend in the world! That's me!" Emeth said mournfully. Hamíd threw a pillow at him. Emeth caught it deftly.

"How long do you have to stay here?" Emeth asked.

"Nicar told me two months. Says he'll tie me down if I even think about trying to get up before then," Hamíd answered. Emeth gave a low whistle.

"Two months! Well, I hope you enjoy lazing away in a comfy bed while I'm off fighting," he said.

"Don't remind me!" Hamíd exclaimed. "I'd give anything to be able to go fight!"

"Don't worry, mate, I'll try and save some for you," Emeth laughed.

"I don't know how to thank you," Hamíd said with a grin.

"Let's see, a castle would be fine, half your lands, you could even find me a princess…," Emeth began.

"Shut up! What'd I tell you?" Hamíd exclaimed.

"A thousand pardons, Your Highness!" Emeth bowed with a flourish. Hamíd half rose threateningly from the bed. "Ah, you're not supposed to move, remember?" Emeth said.

"For you, I might make an exception," Hamíd said.

"Are you bothering my patient, Emeth?" Nicar asked as he came into the room.

"Me? No," Emeth said.

"Actually, he mentioned he wasn't feeling too well and was looking for you," Hamíd said straight faced.

"Really? What's wrong?" Nicar asked.

"What? Nothing," Emeth answered.

"You call overtiredness and a slight fever nothing?" Hamíd asked, grinning maliciously at Emeth.

"You're right. He's does look a little pale," Nicar replied. "I have just the thing for you."

"Touch that, and you might lose a hand!" Emeth threatened as Nicar reached for a beaker of medicine. Nicar laughed.

"All right, all right! I can't argue with that," he said.

"Good. I shudder at the very thought of your 'medicine.' I'm sure you tried to poison me last time," Emeth said.

"I did what was necessary to keep you alive," Nicar said seriously.

"He keeps telling me that," Emeth said to Hamíd. "I'd just be very careful from now on."

Nicar tried to hide a smile.

"Enough, before you ruin my reputation for good! Oh, Azrahil wants you, by the way," he said to Emeth. A look of horror crossed Emeth's face.

"Now you tell me! He's probably ready to kill me by now! Don't drink anything!" he yelled to Hamíd as he ran from the room. Nicar shook his head as he began to change Hamíd's bandages.

"What were you two talking about just now?" Hamíd asked curiously.

"Before he joined the Guard, he served in Lord Rishdah's army. He was good friends with another young man about his age then. They were both so wild and reckless in battle, like berserkers. Azrahil and Jaffa couldn't stop them. One day, we stormed a fortress, and afterward we found both of them. Emeth was holding his friend. He was dead, and Emeth was nearly there himself. We almost lost him, and it took days before he finally regained consciousness. Even after that, I wasn't sure what he would do. He was so quiet and depressed. Azrahil took care of him and trained him. He would make Emeth so angry, trying to bring back his old fire. He finally succeeded, and that's when Emeth joined the Guard," Nicar finished.

"But something changed? He's not like that anymore," Hamíd said.

"Aye, he finally learned to control himself. It was a hard lesson for him though. Do me a favor, Hamíd. Don't tell him I told you that story. He too keeps a lot of memories to himself," Nicar said. Hamíd nodded.

"One more thing," Hamíd said before Nicar left the room. "What was his friend's name?" he asked.

"Emeth," Nicar answered.

Late that night, Lord Rishdah came to visit him. He sat down in the chair by the bed.

"Are all warriors in the north as reckless as you?" Lord Rishdah asked.

"It seems to run in my family as I remember, sir," Hamíd answered. He could recall wild tales of his father and grandfathers in battle.

"Do you remember much of your family?" Lord Rishdah asked.

"Only vague memories, sir. But I'm dead to them. This is the only life I have now," Hamíd said.

"How old were you, Corin?" Lord Rishdah inquired.

He looked up in shock. "How…?"

"Emeth told me your name when I asked," Lord Rishdah replied. Hamíd pushed himself upright, wincing a little.

"I was twelve when the slaver ripped me away from my country, my family, and everything I knew," he said.

"Would you go back?" Lord Rishdah asked curiously.

"To what, sir? No, there is nothing for me to go back to anymore. You couldn't let me go anyway," Hamíd said.

"What do you mean? Who are you?" Lord Rishdah pressed. Hamíd hesitated for a long moment before answering softly,

"I am Corin, second son of King Celyn and Queen Elain, prince of Aredor."

Lord Rishdah sat alone in his chambers, thinking over what Hamíd had told him. For once he was at a loss. What do you do with a prince whose country you have just invaded? *A prince who hasn't seen his country in twelve years? he thought. He's given me two and a half years of service, saved my son's life, fought by my side many times, and protected me. How do I reward him?* He stared into the fire for a long time. "I'm dead to them. This is the only life I have now," Hamíd's words echoed in his mind.

A dead man. Lord Rishdah mused. *No one knows who he is. He'll be safe enough. After the campaign is finished, I will give him his freedom.*

CHAPTER 12

The wedding took place the very next night, and at first light of the following morning, Lord Rishdah departed. Lord Jamal and Ismail would follow later with a large force. Nicar left Hamíd in the charge of Lord Jamal's healers after making him swear to stay until properly healed.

The days passed slowly for Hamíd as he gradually felt his strength coming back. His leg had been placed in a splint to ensure it healed as best as it could. The news that messengers brought of the campaign only increased his restlessness. It seemed Lord Rishdah was successful in most of the engagements. One afternoon, the garrison captain came to see him.

"The healers say you are restless," he said.

"Yes, sir," Hamíd answered. "It's frustrating to just sit here while everyone is off fighting. I feel so useless!"

"I know how it is, lad," Captain Hatim said. "They say you can get up and move around a little."

"Somewhat, sir," Hamíd replied.

"Well, get down to the armory if you can. There's always plenty to do down there," the captain ordered. Shortly thereafter, Hamíd sat in the armory, refletching arrows with his leg stretched out on a chair in front of him. Hampered a little by the heavy bandage still on his left arm, the task took all of his concentration. The armory was quiet and deserted. Only a small number of soldiers had remained behind to guard the castle and surrounding lands.

"Whatcha doin'?" a small voice asked. Startled, Hamíd looked up to see a small boy watching him curiously.

"I'm fixing these arrows so they can fly," he answered.

"Like a bird?" the little boy asked hopefully. Hamíd laughed.

"No, not exactly like a bird," he answered. "What's your name?"

"Me be's Makin, and I'm five. What's your name?" he asked.

"Hamíd," he answered.

"Can I help, Ahmid?' the boy asked. Hamíd was a bit taken aback at the request.

"I suppose, Makin," he said to the delight of the little boy. He set Makin to sorting out feathers and handing them to him as he needed. They worked together as Makin chattered away.

"Did you get hurted, Ahmid?" Makin asked, looking at the bandage on Hamíd's arm.

"Yes, I did," Hamíd answered.

"I remember. I saw you," the boy said. "You were sick, and everyone was worried. You were like my mother before she went away," Makin sat quietly, messing with a feather. Hamíd felt sorry for the boy and quickly changed the subject.

"Do you like animals?" he asked and soon had Makin happily talking about different animals.

As Hamíd finished the last of the shafts, the captain came in.

"There you are, Maki! I've been looking for you," he said.

"I helped Ahmid make arrows fly like birds, Da," Makin said importantly. Hamíd fought back a smile at this.

"Yes, sir. He was a big help," he said, making the little boy beam in delight. The captain lifted Makin into his arms.

"Thank you for looking after him. He doesn't have much to do here, and I can't properly look after him all the time," Captain Hatim said with a hint of sadness in his voice.

"Can I come tomorrow and help?" Makin asked Hamíd.

"That's up to your father," Hamíd answered. "I don't mind, sir," he reassured the captain. The little boy turned to his father.

"Please, Da, please!" he begged.

"Yes, I suppose you can," the captain consented as Makin yelled in excitement.

Every afternoon from then on, Makin would sit with Hamíd as he sharpened blades, fletched arrows, or repaired chain mail coats. Hamíd would tell him stories of the heroes of Aredor or Calorin or of great battles. Time now passed quickly; his arm healed enough to be taken from the bandage and the splint to be taken from his leg. He could move slowly but without the aid of crutch. It would still be sometime before he could take up his weapons again. Makin shadowed Hamíd everywhere. They now visited the stables regularly to take care of Zephyr. The big stallion was overjoyed to see Hamíd again. Makin was a bit frightened of the stallion at first but was soon won over. He would sit on the stall door, feeding apples and carrots to Zephyr as Hamíd brushed and cleaned him.

The afternoon sun shone down brightly on Hamíd as he stood in the center of the arena behind the stables. He held on to a long line, the other end of which was fastened to Zephyr. He urged the stallion up into a trot and moved in circles around him. The stallion moved easily as Hamíd put him through the different paces. As he slowed to a walk again, Hamíd led him over to the side of the stables and threw the saddle on. As he tightened the buckles, he wondered how well his leg would hold up. It had healed but he now walked with a pronounced limp.

"Oh well, we might as well give it a try, right, mate?" he said softly to the stallion as he put his foot in the stirrup iron and climbed into the saddle. He eased Zephyr into a trot again then to a canter and then began putting him through various maneuvers. When he was satisfied, Zephyr was coated in sweat. As he rubbed Zephyr down inside the stables, the captain found him.

"I just received word from Lord Jamal. They expect to be here in a week. You will be able to rejoin Lord Rishdah then," he told Hamíd.

"Thank you, sir," Hamíd said.

"I see you've taken up your weapons again," Captain Hatim commented.

"Yes, sir. It's slow right now. Hopefully, I'll be back up to speed by the time Lord Rishdah arrives," Hamíd replied.

"Good. From what I've seen and heard, they can use you out there," Hatim said,

"Aye, sir. I'm anxious to do my part," Hamíd said. As Captain Hatim left, Hamíd heard a rustling over in a corner. Curious, he went to investigate. One of the stable cats had cornered a large bird. The cat hissed and moved in, only to retreat from the talons of the bird. The cat tried again, jabbing out with its claws. The bird retaliated, slashing with its beak. Hamíd took pity on the bird and chased the cat away. He crouched in front of the bird as it retreated into the corner again. Hamíd looked up as Makin came up behind him.

"Whatcha got there, Ahmid?" he asked peering over his shoulder.

"I think it's a hawk of some sort, Maki," Hamíd said.

"Ooh! A birdie! Is it hurted?" Makin asked.

"Yes, something's wrong with its wing, see?" Hamíd pointed. One of the hawk's gray wings hung awkwardly beside it. "You remember that big windstorm two days ago?" he asked. Makin nodded. "It must've gotten trapped in here then."

"What are you gonna do with it?" Makin asked. Hamíd shrugged.

"I don't know. I don't think I can fix real live birds," he said. Makin brightened at that.

"We can ask Nasim!" he said and ran out the door.

"I guess that means I'm staying here," Hamíd said as he watched Makin run off. A short time later, Makin was back, dragging another man with him.

"See! See! The birdie hurted!" Makin bounced excitedly, pointing at the bird.

"Hmm. It looks like it's dislocated," Nasim said, looking at the wing. "If you can catch it, young man, I'll fix that wing up," he said to Hamíd.

Nasim stood back with Makin as Hamíd began to edge quietly toward the bird, talking soothingly all the while. The hawk eyed him warily but remained motionless. Hamíd quickly bundled it up in an old saddle blanket. The young hawk struggled for a few moments then subsided in exhaustion. They took it to Nasim's rooms where he pushed the wing back into place and bound it with strips of cloth to hold the wing against the bird's body. Filling a dish with water, he placed it in front of the bird. It drank thirstily as Nasim sent Makin off to the kitchens to get some meat.

"It wasn't out of place too badly, so I'll be able to take the bandage off in a few days," Nasim said. "Meanwhile, you boys can keep it fed." Hamíd grinned.

"Thank you, sir. You're too kind," he said. After the bird had eaten, Hamíd and Makin took it to Hamíd's chamber where it perched on the windowsill.

Over the next few days, the hawk came to accept Hamíd as part of its surroundings. It would even perch on his arm as he and Makin fed it. The morning of the fourth day, Nasim removed the bandages, and they took the hawk outside. It perched on Hamíd's arm and spread its wings. Makin watched breathlessly as Hamíd threw it in the air, and it flew away, screeching wildly. They watched it until it was out of sight.

A commotion at the front gate caught Hamíd's attention. He made his way over to where Captain Hatim was anxiously questioning a soldier.

"How many were there?" Hatim asked.

"About two hundred, Captain. They were flying a blue standard with a black panther, sir," the soldier replied.

"Are you sure, Imran?" Hatim demanded. Imran nodded. "It's Lord Numair. How long do we have?" Hatim asked.

"Not long. An hour maybe," Imran replied.

"Take two men with you. Tell everyone out in the fields to gather supplies and the livestock and get behind the walls now. Alim, I want those battlements well stocked with arrows and javelins. Kadir, I want everyone not fighting inside the keep. Now!" Captain Hatim began issuing orders, and the garrison sprang into action.

"Captain, what are my orders?" Hamíd asked. Hatim looked at him.

"Get yourself ready for a fight. We're going to need you on the walls," he said. Hamíd threw him a quick salute and hurried off.

Hamíd went to his chamber and donned his battle uniform and pulled on his short-sleeved mail coat that reached almost to his knees. Then he fastened on a long, red leather tunic, emblazoned with a phoenix, overall. A thick black belt completed the uniform into which he thrust his scimitar and knives. He took another smaller knife and put it in his boot. Hamíd took up his bow and quiver and pulled them over his shoulder. Finally, he picked up the heavy vambraces and buckled them over his arms. He was ready—a Phoenix Guard once again.

Hamíd found Captain Hatim on the wall above the gates, watching the last of the refugees stream in. the gates swung shut with a dull thud as the soldiers bolted them securely. The captain watched the distant tree line anxiously. He did not have long to wait. The first ranks of the enemy force broke through and advanced.

"You think we can hold out for three days?" Captain Hatim asked Hamíd. "Fifty men against so many?"

"Fifty-two, Captain," a voice said behind them. Hamíd and Hatim turned to see Ismail's young wife Nadirah and Nasim coming up the steps to join them. Both wore mail coats and bore scimitars as well as bows and full quivers.

"You shouldn't be up here, m'lady!" Hatim protested.

"Captain, you know my father had me trained well," Nadirah said.

"Yes, ma'am, but this is different than bouts in the practice ring. It's my duty to protect you, and I can't do that if you're up here trying to get killed!" Hatim exclaimed.

"I know very well how dangerous it is, Captain. But I would be ashamed if I did nothing to protect my home. I stay!" she said authoritatively.

"All right, but you will follow my orders. I still command here," Hatim said sternly.

"Yes, Captain," Nadirah answered. Hatim strode off, ordering the defense of the walls and keeping an eye on the advancing force. He concentrated his men on the front and west walls, which faced the open valley. The rear and east walls were protected by the forest.

Nadirah moved to stand by Hamíd. "How many?" she asked looking out over the walls.

"About three hundred now. They must've picked up some more men just outside the border," Hamíd answered.

"If they're here, then do you think anything happened to Ismail and my father?" she asked worriedly. Hamíd thought for a moment.

"I don't know, ma'am," he admitted. "The last we heard, our army was headed back here. My guess is Numair sent this force to try and cut them off by capturing this castle. Besides," he said, "Ismail's not going to let anything stop him from getting back to you."

Nadirah blushed. "You really think so?" she asked.

"Of course I do. It's my duty to look after Lord Rishdah and his family. That includes you now. Stay close to me, and I'll make sure you're at the front gate to meet Ismail when he comes back," Hamíd said. Nadirah nodded gratefully.

"Everyone at the ready! Here they come!" Hatim shouted. Hamíd laid a shaft on the string of his longbow as a group of soldiers approached the walls.

"I am General Sa'id of Lord Numair's army," their leader announced dramatically. "I know you have only a small force. You can never hope to hold out. Surrender now and your lives will be spared."

"Not likely," Hatim shouted back. "I command here, and my soldiers will not surrender."

"Brave words," General Sa'id sneered, "but your last!" He took a quick step back as an archer stepped forward and took aim. The arrow struck Hatim high in the shoulder. He staggered but remained on his feet. Hamíd quickly drew on his bow and fired an answering shot, taking out the archer below. Hatim gritted his teeth as he pulled the arrow out of his shoulder. Snapping it in half, he threw it defiantly over the wall. The battle had begun.

The afternoon stretched on, but no attack came from Sai'd's men. The defenders shifted restlessly at their posts.

"What are they waiting for?" a young soldier asked nervously.

"They're trying to make us anxious and frightened," Captain Hatim told him as he adjusted the bandage around his arm. "We won't have to wait much longer. They'll attack at dark."

As dusk fell, fires were lit in the valley. Hatim ordered torches set up on the walls as darkness set in. Suddenly, an arrow whizzed by Nadirah. She cried out a warning and pointed to dark shapes moving along the ground towards the walls. Nasim bent his bow and fired off an arrow, hitting one of the advancing soldiers who fell with a cry. Seeing they were discovered, the rest of the soldiers broke cover and advanced at a run. The defenders followed Nasim's example, firing arrows as quickly as they could. A ladder hit the wall beside Hamíd. He dropped his bow and grabbed a javelin from a nearby stack. The first soldier to make it to the top of the ladder was met by a vicious thrust from Hamíd. As he fell, more ladders were set against the walls. Soon, bows were dropped in favor of swords and javelins.

Hamíd fought two soldiers, parrying and thrusting with the javelin. He lashed out with the spear, knocking one over the parapet. The javelin shattered under the impact. He tossed it away and locked blades with the second attacker. The fighting was heavy all along the walls, the defenders battling desperately. Nasim killed the soldier in front of him and ran to the nearest ladder and began pushing it. It fell backwards, crashing to the ground. He then fought his way over to where Hamíd and Nadirah were surrounded by Numair's men. Nasim came crashing in from the side, surprising the enemy. Aided by Nasim, Hamíd and Nadirah drove them off.

"We've got to get the ladders down!" Nasim shouted above the noise of battle. Hamíd nodded and tossed them both a javelin. Sheathing his sword, he also armed himself with a fresh javelin.

"Come on!" he yelled and, giving voice to a savage war cry, led them into the fray. He cut a path to the nearest ladder and fought off attackers as Nasim and Nadirah used their spears to lever the ladder away from the wall. Farther away, Hatim and two soldiers were doing the same.

"There's two more left!" Nadirah cried as Hatim ran to join them.

"No time to lose!" he yelled. "Hamíd, you and Nadirah take one. Nasim, you come with me!" Hamíd and Nadirah struck toward the nearest ladder. Knocking off the uppermost men on the ladder, they jammed their javelins under the top rung and began pushing. Creaking and groaning, the ladder began moving and fell to ruin on the ground below. Suddenly, the battle was over. The weary defenders raised a cheer. The first victory was theirs!

Captain Hatim ordered the removal of the dead and wounded and posted guards. They had been strangely fortunate. Only five of his men lay dead; however, many more were wounded. But almost two score of the enemy had fallen. He paired the guards together; one would sleep while the other kept watch, switching every few hours.

Shaking slightly, Nadirah stood on the wall top. She gazed numbly at the carnage around her and then retched violently. As she straightened up, she felt an arm steadying her.

"You all right, ma'am?" Hamíd asked. Nadirah drew her hand wearily across her face and nodded.

"Why don't you go get cleaned up and get some sleep, m'lady? There's still a few hours till dawn. I don't think they'll attack again tonight," he said.

"What about you, Hamíd?' she asked. He smiled.

"I'll be up here. Don't worry about me, ma'am, I'll be fine," he said. Hatim came up a few minutes later.

"How'd we do, Captain?" Hamíd asked.

"Only a few seriously wounded. Most everyone else is hurt in some way, but we can't afford to bring them off the walls," Hatim answered. "Where's Nadirah?" he asked.

"I sent her inside, sir. I figured it would be better for her to rest than to stand guard duty," Hamíd replied.

"Thank you for taking care of her, Hamíd," Hatim said.

"Yes, sir. There's too many people that would kill me if I didn't," Hamíd rejoined.

Hatim chuckled. "Make sure you get some rest yourself, Hamíd," he said.

"Yes, sir," Hamíd saluted.

Hamíd stood guard with the young soldier named Imran. Slaves came up to the walls, passing out blankets and hot soup with bread. Hamíd noticed the young man's hands shaking as he took the food. Imran sat staring numbly at the food. Hamíd draped the blanket around the soldier's shoulders and crouched beside him.

"Hey, you need to eat and keep your strength up," he told him softly. Imran looked at him.

"I can't. I just…I keep seeing it all over again," he said.

"I know. It's hard the first time. Just trust me. Eat then get some sleep. I'll take first watch," Hamíd said.

He took the first watch and the second as well, letting Imran sleep. Hamíd leaned on the battlements, watching the sun rise over the trees. Nasim came to stand beside him.

"You get any sleep?" Nasim asked. Hamíd shook his head. They both stiffened as drums began to pound and the enemy began to advance.

CHAPTER 13

Emeth woke at dawn. He quickly dressed and went to relieve Nicar on guard duty. He felt strangely restless, as if something was amiss. But nothing seemed out of place in the quiet camp.

We've been gone three months now. I'm just ready to rest for a while, he told himself. *Well, maybe I'm not the only one.* he thought as Lord Jamal, a frown crossing his face, came hurrying toward Lord Rishdah's tent. Lord Rishdah met him outside the tent.

"One of my scouts reported a large force passed this way two days ago heading west. They were flying a blue banner with a panther," Lord Jamal said.

"Numair," Lord Rishdah said grimly. "Sounds like they're headed your way. How many?"

"Three hundred strong," Lord Jamal answered. "There is only a small force at the castle."

"Emeth, I want my cavalry ready to leave in an hour. Alert the rest of the Phoenix Guard," Lord Rishdah ordered.

"My men will be ready as well. If we ride without stopping, we can get there tomorrow morning," Lord Jamal said.

General Sa'id had ordered a battering ram into action. His men pounded at the gates all morning while his archers keeping the defenders' heads down. The ram would keep them occupied while a separate force would sneak through the woods and over the back walls.

Hamíd lay behind the battlements. All around, Hatim's men did the same, unable to move or fire back for fear of getting hit. So far, the doors had held strong, but it was only a matter of time before they began to weaken. Hamíd moved over to where Hatim was.

"What if they try and come around back?" he asked the captain. Hatim smiled grimly.

"There's a small force on the back wall watching for that. But the woods around the walls are so full of traps and snares, Sa'id's men would be lucky to get through alive," he said.

The day stretched on as the sun beat down mercilessly. A sentry reported a group of Sa'id's men had been seen in the forest but had quickly retreated. Meanwhile, Imran had come up with a solution. Thick wooden shields were brought up to the battlements. Hatim selected the best archers and instructed the rest to hold the shields. Sheltered from enemy fire, the defenders were now able to retaliate.

General Sa'id was furious. Not only had the raiding party come back unable to reach the walls, but the defenders were now driving off the battering ram crew. He was running out of time. He should already be in the castle. Calling his captain over, he gave orders.

"Gather plenty of wood and brush. We'll burn them out tonight."

Hamíd drew his bowstring taut. "Now!" he yelled. The shield bearers in front of him stepped apart, allowing him to shoot. Taking quick aim, he fired, killing one of the ram carriers. The shields snapped back in place just in time as answering arrows thudded into them. He nocked another arrow to the string, gritting his teeth as his left arm quivered under the strain. It wouldn't hold out much longer. He drew on the string again. "Now!" he called.

They rode hard all day, stopping only to rest the horses. Emeth wiped the sweat from his face and stared at the flat plains surrounding them. It seemed they had made hardly any progress. He watched the sun sink lower into the western sky. *At least it'll get cooler now*, he thought as he spurred Narak on.

Twilight brought a short respite for the defenders. Nadirah found Hamíd sitting against the wall, sharpening his daggers. She handed him a beaker of water. Sheathing his blades, he took it gratefully.

"Captain Hatim ordered a barricade set up in the courtyard. What's going to happen?" she asked anxiously. Hamíd hesitated before answering.

"Sa'id's going to order another attack tonight. We're all exhausted and stand a good chance of being overrun. The gates won't hold up much longer, so we're going to need something to fall back to. I'm afraid that's the truth, but keep quiet please, ma'am. There's plenty of young soldiers who are frightened enough by now," he said.

"When do you think General Sa'id will make his move?" she asked. Hamíd glanced at the sky. Night was falling quickly.

"It won't be long now. We'd best get ready, m'lady," he said.

Everything was quiet on the walls; hands gripped javelins and bows nervously. Hatim strode up and down the lines, whispering encouragement as he went. Nadirah chanced a glance at Hamíd standing beside her. He was standing quietly leaning on his bow.

"You don't look scared at all," she said with a nervous laugh. He smiled.

"My stomach's been doing somersaults for the past hour. It's not too fond of waiting," he said. Nadirah giggled.

"I hope something happens soon then, because I think my hands are frozen to this javelin," she said.

A soldier pointed to a bobbing light in the valley below. It suddenly sprang into the air and flew toward them. They watched as it flew over the walls hitting the roof of a building and blossomed into flame.

"Fire arrows!" Hatim yelled a warning as more came pouring over the walls. Servants rushed to put out the spreading flames as storehouses, barracks, and the armory were hit. Then all went quiet. Hamíd heard a hissing sound.

"Get down!" he yelled as a hail of arrows fell, invisible in the darkness. He jumped at Nadirah, knocking her flat and shielding her from the incoming arrows. The air was filled with the screams of those who were hit. Two more deadly flights followed, and then the fire arrows began again. Hamíd helped Nadirah sit up, and then chanced a glance over the walls.

"Captain!" he cried urgently. "They're headed for the gates!"

Hatim cursed as he saw soldiers carrying torches toward the battered gates.

"Pick them off if you can!" he ordered. Hamíd and a few other soldiers stood and began firing at the advancing soldiers. An answering volley of arrows came back, killing two men and wounding more. Hamíd looked over the walls again. The enemy had successfully set fire to the gates. Hamíd found Hatim.

"It's no use. The gates will be down in a few minutes and the barricade isn't finished. We need everyone off the walls now. I can hold them at the gates until it's finished and everyone is behind it," Hamíd said.

"No, I won't let you!" Hatim said.

"Sir, it's our only chance. Otherwise, we'll be caught out in the open and be slaughtered," Hamíd argued as they heard the ram pounding at the burning gates.

"Very well. But once it's done, you retreat, understood?" Hatim asked sharply.

"Yes, sir." Hamíd saluted and grabbed a javelin. He pushed past Nadirah and hurried down the steps. The courtyard was a scene of chaos. Soldiers scrambled between burning buildings, making for the safety of the barricade. Hamíd arrived at the gates as they fell. A blast of heat drove him back a few steps. He readied the javelin as the first of the enemy soldiers leapt through the burning doorway. As more men poured through the gates, he threw the javelin, felling a soldier, and then he drew his scimitar. Yelling a war cry, he threw himself into the fray. Taken aback by the ferocity of his attack, the invaders wavered for a moment. Then a piercing whistle rang out behind him. Still fighting, he retreated toward the barricade. As he turned to run, a soldier tripped him with a spear. Hamíd fell heavily to the ground. He twisted to see the spear raised for the kill when a shriek cut the air and a dark object flew into the soldier's face. Hamíd got up and ran to the barricade where Nasim and Imran helped him over. As they helped him sit down against an overturned wagon, Nasim saw a broken shaft protruding from his shoulder.

"Hamíd, when did this happen?" he asked worriedly. Hamíd winced as he answered,

"Tonight. Don't worry, it's not too deep. I'll be fine." The harsh shriek rang out again as a hawk swooped down and landed unsteadily near them as it tried to see through the darkness and flame.

"Is that…?" Nasim asked incredulously. Hamíd slowly reached his hand toward the bird. It flapped its wings and perched on his arm.

"Never thought to see you again," Hamíd said as he softly ran a finger down the hawk's feathered breast. Nasim shook his head in disbelief.

"Well," he said. "It looks like we have another soldier."

They were distracted by an outbreak of fighting farther along the barricade. Wearily, Hamíd rose and accepted a new javelin from Nadirah and turned to face the oncoming foe. After what seemed an age, they drove off the first wave of attackers. The burning buildings still flamed brightly, illuminating the courtyard as the enemy regrouped. The hawk came and perched on Hamíd's arm as he watched for the next attack. Nasim ran up.

"Hamíd, Hatim's been severely wounded. We have no one to lead us now!" he said. Nadirah gasped.

'We'll be overrun!" she cried. "Take his place!" she begged Hamíd.

"I can't! I've never commanded before!" Hamíd exclaimed.

"You're the only one with enough battle experience. Please, you have to!" Nasim pleaded. Hamíd glanced at the soldiers along the barricade, regarding him anxiously.

"All right, I'll do my best," Hamíd said. He moved along the barrier issuing fresh orders.

"Bows and arrows everyone. When they charge, we can catch them in the open. Imran!" he called to the young man.

"Yes, sir?" the young soldier asked.

"I want you to stay by Nadirah. Do not let her get hurt, understand?" Hamíd asked.

"Yes, sir!" Imran saluted.

"Good man. Get ready, they're coming again!" Hamíd called as the enemy began advancing. Bows were raised and leveled at the oncoming foe.

"Fire!" he ordered. The first rank went down under the deadly burst of arrows. "Ready? Fire!" he gave the order again. The enemy pushed forward. "Javelins ready!" he called. Along the line, bows were dropped and spears thrust through holes in the barricade. More soldiers met their death on the sharpened points. Movement along the wall top caught Hamíd's attention. On both sides, small forces were creeping along to try and outflank them.

"Nasim!" Hamíd cried urgently. "Take five bowmen and drive them off!" he ordered pointing to the east wall. "Kadir, take the west wall. Take them down!"

The troops on the walls were forced to retreat under the barrage of arrows from Nasim and Kadir's bowmen. Along the barricade, the battle raged on. Wave after wave of the enemy broke against the barriers, and each time the defenders barely managed to drive them back. Hamíd strode relentlessly down the line with the hawk perched on his shoulder and joined in wherever the fighting was heaviest.

Then all went quiet. Hamíd looked at the brightening sky. Dawn had come.

They had finally reached the trees marking the border of Lord Jamal's land. Emeth looked at the sky; dawn was fast approaching. It was still almost a mile to the valley and the castle. As the sun first peeked over the horizon, they came to the edge of the trees. The castle seemed deserted. Smoke billowed from inside the walls, and there were no signs of life. Lord Jamal stared at the bodies lying outside the walls and the ruined siege ladders.

"You think any are left alive?" Lord Jamal asked. Lord Rishdah took in the burnt, smashed gates.

"It seems deserted. Emeth, go in and see what you can find. Azrahil, you and Jaffa see if any of Numair's force is left or if any of Lord Jamal's people survived," Lord Rishdah ordered. Emeth slid down from Narak and tossed the reigns to Ahmed. Unsheathing a sword, he quietly slipped inside the walls.

Silence reigned inside the walls. Sa'id's men seemed to have retreated outside the walls. Hamíd glanced around at the small force remaining.

"Sir, listen," a soldier said. "I think they have some sort of reinforcements!" Hamíd listened to the faint voices outside the walls and saw men on horseback moving through the thick screen of smoke.

"Keep ready for anything," he ordered. A sick feeling settled over him. If the enemy had gained reinforcements, then it was all over.

Emeth made his way into the courtyard, viewing the destruction around him. None of the bodies looked to be Lord Jamal's men. He peered through the smoke swirling from the ruined buildings. The main keep was still intact.

"Anyone here?" he called, halting in the middle of the courtyard.

Hamíd watched the lone figure coming towards them. "Anyone here?" a voice called. His heart leaped at the familiar voice. He climbed over the barricade and made his way toward Emeth.

Emeth saw a movement and readied his sword. He stared at the figure limping slowly toward him.

"Hamíd?" he said in disbelief.

"It's about time you showed up," Hamíd said with a grin. Emeth sheathed his sword and wrapped Hamíd in a fierce embrace.

"You all right?" Emeth asked.

"For the most part," Hamíd replied. "Who's here with you?"

"Rishdah and Jamal and about a hundred and fifty men. We got here as fast as we could," Emeth replied. Hamíd turned and gave a sharp whistle. The small body of defenders came out from behind the barricade.

Lord Rishdah looked up as Emeth came back through the gates.

"I found a few people you might want to see, sir," Emeth said casually as Hamíd and Nadirah came through followed by the rest of the soldiers. Nadirah ran to Ismail and was swept up into his embrace. Hamíd saluted Lord Rishdah and Lord Jamal.

"We lost about twenty-five men, sir. Captain Hatim was wounded badly last night, and the rest of your people are safe inside the castle, my lord," he said.

"Who took command then?" Lord Jamal asked.

"I'm afraid that would be me, sir" came the reply. Lord Rishdah looked his bedraggled guard up and down. "You seem to have done a good job," he said.

"I did my best, sir," Hamíd replied.

"How many of Numair's men attacked?" Lord Rishdah asked.

"Three hundred, sir. I'd say they lost almost half of their force, but where are the rest?" Hamíd asked.

"They were gone by the time we got here," Lord Rishdah answered. "Captain Azrahil is looking for the remainder."

"Thank you for defending my home," Lord Jamal said. "How badly are you hurt?"

"Nothing too bad, sir, I don't think," Hamíd answered, not looking at Nicar.

"Which means I'll have to patch you up in a dozen different places as usual," Nicar said drily.

Azrahil came back with his report.

"About a hundred and fifty men left, sir. They've taken shelter in the village at the end of the valley for now," he said. Lord Jamal gave orders for part of the force to keep watch on the village and the rest to remain at the castle. As the soldiers went about their duties, Lord Rishdah and Lord Jamal went inside, leaving the guards together.

"I see you're still in one piece," Azrahil said to Hamíd.

"Good to see you too, Captain," Hamíd replied. Ahmed started as the hawk swooped in and landed on Hamíd's shoulder.

"Meet Karif," Hamíd said, gesturing at the hawk.

"Well, someone's got to look after you when we're gone," Nicar said. "Come on, let me look at you. You're about to drop of exhaustion." He would brook no arguments and went with Hamíd back inside. After digging the arrowhead out of his shoulder and inspecting the lion wounds that had now healed into scars, Nicar ordered Hamíd to rest. Wearily, Hamíd complied and was soon fast asleep.

A few hours later, he awoke, washed and dressed in a clean uniform, and reported to Azrahil.

"Nicar tells me that you're healed," Azrahil said.

"Yes, sir," Hamíd replied.

"I will say that I almost didn't expect you to recover," Azrahil said. "And that leads me to a point of disagreement between Nicar and myself." He paused before continuing. "I said that you should not be allowed back to the Guard."

Hamíd tried to hide the sudden panic he felt at the Captain's statement.

"What do you mean, sir?" he stammered.

"Your wounds may have healed, but you won't be as strong as you were before," Azrahil said.

"I will be," Hamíd asserted. "I'm getting better every day. My leg—"

"Exactly, your leg," Azrahil interrupted. "I've seen just enough to know that it will slow you down. You could endanger yourself and the rest of us."

"No, I just need some more time…," Hamíd said.

"We don't have that," Azrahil said. "We leave here within a short time. You won't be coming," Azrahil said.

"Sir, you can't—" Hamíd said desperately before Azrahil interrupted again.

"You think I enjoy this?" he asked. Hamíd's head snapped up and Azrahil was caught in his gaze.

"I'm not staying behind. I can still ride and fight, and I'm good enough to take on any of Numair's men. This is all I have. Don't take it away from me….please," he said. Azrahil regarded him for a long moment. He had almost anxiously interrogated the soldiers that had defended the castle about how well Hamíd had fought, even presuming to question Nadirah. Their near-glowing response had done little to help him. But there was one sure way to make sure. He drew his scimitar.

"You think you are still capable of being a Phoenix Guard? Prove it to me."

For the next hour, he drove Hamíd relentlessly through weapon drills and maneuvers and Hamíd pushed back just as hard. He had been given a second life, and he would not lose it. In the end, Azrahil was not completely satisfied, but he knew Hamíd spoke the truth—he would not be left behind.

"You may yet prove me wrong," he told him and he knew that Hamíd would not rest until he did.

The captain sent him down the valley to replace Ahmed, who was stationed with Ismail.

A long day passed outside the village. Hamíd was still with Ismail when a solider came up to report.

"They're moving out. What do you want to do, sir?" the soldier asked.

"We can follow in the morning. They'll lead us back to Numair's main army. Have two scouts follow them. I want full reports on their movements," Ismail said. The soldier saluted and rode off. Ismail and Hamíd rode back to the castle to report. Lord Rishdah approved of his son's decision and welcomed the chance to let his men rest. He then dismissed his guards for the night, ordering them to rejoin him in the morning.

At dawn, Hamíd, Ahmed, and Emeth shouldered packs and weapons and went down to the stables. On the way out, Hamíd heard someone call his name. He turned and saw Makin.

"Where you goin', Ahmid?" he asked. Hamíd crouched down so he was eye level with the boy.

"I have to leave now. I have to go wherever Lord Rishdah goes," Hamíd explained.

"Do you have to fight more?" Makin asked.

"Yes, I will," Hamíd replied.

"I was scared from all the fighting here," the boy admitted.

"It wasn't fun, was it?' Hamíd said. "Why don't you come say good-bye to Zephyr? He'll miss you."

Makin nodded enthusiastically. Hamíd handed the boy his big war bow to carry as they walked to where Emeth and Ahmed were waiting. They both smiled at the sight of the small boy struggling with the weapon.

The stables were teeming with life as men hurried to prepare their horses to leave. Makin watched as Hamíd tacked Zephyr up and buckled on his weapons. Reaching out, Makin gently stroked Zephyr's nose one more time and then he turned and hugged Hamíd.

"Don't get hurted again, Ahmid," Makin said.

"All right. Take care of everyone here, Maki," Hamíd said. He handed Makin one of the hawk's gray feathers. Giving a last pat to Zephyr, Makin ran out of the barn. Settling his bow across his shoulder, Hamíd led Zephyr out into the courtyard followed by Emeth and Ahmed. They were joined soon after by Azrahil and Nicar, who held Lord Rishdah and Ismail's horses as well as their own. When the lords came into the courtyard, everyone mounted. A small force was remaining behind to reinforce the castle. A pair of riders was sent to bring the main army to meet them as the rest of the force rode out of the gate and onto the trail of Numair's men.

CHAPTER 14

They rode east for two days before meeting with the main army. They were encamped at the rocks around the road. Hamíd shifted uncomfortably as he recognized the scene of the ambush where Castimir had died. They stayed there one day before continuing eastward. In his spare time, Hamíd began to train the hawk, teaching it to respond to his signals. It learned quickly, adapting its previously solitary life to follow him. The rest of the Guard became used to seeing the gray hawk with him, fitting perfectly with the quiet mystery of Hamíd.

Some days later, they came within sight of a town a few miles from Numair's castle. Lord Rishdah sent Hamíd, Ahmed, and Emeth into the town to gather information on Lord Numair's movements. Laying aside the uniforms of the Phoenix Guard, they dressed in plain clothes to avoid attracting too much attention.

"I don't see any of Numair's men," Hamíd said quietly to Ahmed as they leaned against the wall of a house in the main square of the town.

"We're still a day's journey from his castle," Ahmed replied. "But you'd still expect to see some soldiers here." Then he laughed softly. "Watch this. Emeth's about to get caught."

They watched as Emeth made his way across the square towards them only to be stopped by several young women by the well in the center of the square. Obligingly, he helped them draw water from the well but was stopped from leaving. Successfully cornered, he plastered a smile on his face and began talking with the eager girls. Every word he spoke sent them tittering and laughing coyly. Hamíd and Ahmed forced down bouts of laughter at the scene and the trapped look growing on Emeth's face. Emeth shot a desperate look toward them, and Ahmed waved back at him. Finally, he managed to excuse himself and escape. He stalked across the square, glaring at them.

"Oh, sir! Would you help me? I can't seem to lift this bucket half full of water!" Ahmed said in a high voice. Hamíd snickered as he took the part of Emeth.

"Why, certainly ladies. Is there anything else I can help with?" Emeth began walking between the houses out of the town. His companions followed, haranguing him mercilessly.

"How strong you are! And just look at those dreadfully sharp knife things you carry!" Ahmed continued in a high falsetto voice. Emeth turned suddenly.

"You two done yet? 'Cause you're about to make the list as casualties of war," he threatened. Ahmed gave a low moan and fell backward into Hamíd's arms. Despite himself, a smile spread across Emeth's face.

"You two are just jealous," he asserted.

"No, not really," Hamíd replied. "I'll leave the role of heart-breaker to you."

"I don't know what you're laughing about, Ahmed," Emeth said slyly. "I've seen you two meeting when you're off duty. What's her name again?"

Ahmed shoved Emeth. "You know very well that's my sister," he said. Emeth looked to Hamíd.

"Do you believe that?" he asked mischievously.

"It is hard to believe that anyone that pretty could be his sister," Hamíd said, grinning.

"I agree," Emeth said as they arrived at where they had left their horses. Mounting, they reverted to the serious business for which they had been sent to the village and exchanged information as they rode back to the army to report to Lord Rishdah.

"Numair's army passed through two days ago, sir. They headed southeast," Ahmed reported.

"Villagers figured about three hundred men, sir," Emeth continued.

"His lands lie about a day's ride away. I was told he still had a sizeable force there, which would bring his strength up to almost five hundred men, sir," Hamíd concluded the report.

"Anything else?" Captain Azrahil asked. Emeth shifted uncomfortably, and Ahmed shot him a sly glance.

"Well, sir, how useful does it need to be?" he asked. Emeth kicked him.

"No, sir, that's all," Emeth said hurriedly. Azrahil's eyes narrowed as Hamíd began coughing uncontrollably.

"Sorry, sir," Hamíd said, trying to regain his composure.

"Emeth, you're on duty. You two are dismissed," Azrahil said.

"Come on, Hamíd, let's get you some fresh air," Ahmed said. They both staggered out of the tent, stifling fresh laughter. Emeth glared after them.

"For your sake, I'm not going to ask," Azrahil said.

"Thank you, sir," Emeth replied frostily.

The next day, the army began marching and skirted the village before they continued southeast after the retreating army. Finally, they encountered the enemy. They had gathered in a large village some distance from Numair's castle. It was decided a small force would attack and occupy the village and then the rest of the army would have a straight path to Numair's fortress.

In the half light of the morning, Lord Rishdah put his troops in position. Ismail, flanked by Hamíd and Emeth, would lead the first charge. They would attack from the front as Lord Jamal led a second assault from the southern side. The horses shifted restlessly as they waited for the signal. Ismail urged his horse forward; on either side, Hamíd and Emeth did the same, and slowly the line moved forward. Riders crouched low in the saddle to avoid oncoming arrows, and then they were sweeping through the village. The first line of archers had fled as they charged, leaving the village empty. Ismail sent scouts out; they returned reporting the houses were empty and there was no sign of life anywhere. Lord Jamal came galloping up at the head of his force.

"Where are they?" he demanded.

"There!" Emeth pointed. Numair's entire army was marching towards them. As they watched, it split and moved to surrounded them.

"We're outnumbered, sir," Hamíd said as Karif flew in to perch on his arm. "We won't last long without reinforcements."

"The rest of the army is a mile away," Ismail said. "We'll cut through the left flank and retreat."

"Two hundred against four hundred. Think we'll make it?" Emeth asked Hamíd.

"I knew someone who would've thought they were good odds," Hamíd replied as he sent Karif flying off again. Emeth grinned. War horns blared as a line was formed. Ismail sounded the charge. Soldiers dashed spurs into the sides of their steeds. Hamíd and Emeth rode beside Ismail as they charged the enclosing flank. Weapons clashed, horses screamed, men shouted as the lines clashed. The force of the charge carried them well into Numair's ranks. Ismail's band fought through and retreated back to the camp. It was only after the army had reached the camp safely that Hamíd realized that Emeth was missing.

"Our losses were few. By my reckoning, Numair has his full force out on the plain," Ismail told his father. Lord Jamal voiced his agreement.

"He looks to have the same numbers as we do. He probably wants to keep the battle away from his castle," he said. Lord Rishdah stroked his chin thoughtfully. Hamíd shifted restlessly by his place at the tent entrance. Darkness was falling and still no sign of Emeth. Lord Rishdah turned to his captains.

"Prepare the army to fight tomorrow. I think this will be the final battle," he said.

As soon as he was off duty, Hamíd went to find Azrahil. They met outside the Guards' tent.

"Still nothing," Azrahil said. "I talked to a few soldiers. One said he saw Emeth go down." He held up his hand forestalling Hamíd. "I don't know if he's alive or not."

"Well, sir, it seems there's only one way to find out," Hamíd said.

"Requesting permission to go along, sir," Ahmed said as he stepped up beside Hamíd. Azrahil gave a grim smile.

"All right. Be back by dawn, with or without him," he said. Hamíd and Ahmed saluted as Azrahil strode off.

"Ahmed, I feel like an idiot. I should've realized he was missing sooner," Hamíd said.

"Instead of agreeing with you and making you feel worse, let's get going. We've got a lot of ground to cover by dawn." Ahmed said.

Emeth came awake slowly. He tried moving his hands, but they were tightly bound behind his back. He took stock of his position. He was sitting in a richly decorated tent tied to the tent pole. His weapons had been taken from him and, on top of everything, his head ached horribly.

"Lovely. Just lovely," he muttered to himself. The tent flap swirled aside, and two men swept in. Emeth sized them up as they stood in front of him. One was obviously a Calorin, the other was tall and powerfully built with the black skin of the Argusians.

"I am Lord Numair," the Calorin said. "Since you were careless enough to get captured, you will tell me of Rishdah's plans, his forces, everything!"

"Not likely," Emeth laughed.

"I think you will come around soon," Numair said. He gave a nod to the Argusian who dealt a punishing blow across Emeth's face.

"I know you are of the Phoenix Guard, so you have access to Rishdah's plans. Tell me what I want to know," Numair said.

"What makes you think I would tell you anything?" Emeth said, spitting out blood. "You've tried to kill my master and his family several times. That doesn't exactly make you my friend."

"Why do you serve him? You aren't even a Calorin. You are a northerner, a barbarian from the north," Numair said.

"You almost got me there, except for the barbarian part," Emeth said. Numair's lips tightened.

"Why don't you leave you pathetic master? Surely you could be someone important in your homeland?" Numair asked.

"My! Full of questions tonight, aren't we?' Emeth replied. He was rewarded with a series of brutal blows from the Argusian. Numair crouched in front of him.

"I will give you a few minutes to decide whether or not to help me. Believe me, I can make your death long and slow." With that, he stood and walked out of the tent. With a last kick at Emeth, the Argusian followed.

As soon as he was sure he was alone, Emeth went to work. Maneuvering himself up on to his knees, he moved his right leg to where his bound hands could reach inside his boot. His arms and shoulders protested at the movement, but gritting his teeth, he continued, moving his hands along the inside of the boot until they found the handle of a small dagger. Slowly, carefully, he withdrew it and sat back down. Twisting the dagger, he set its edge against the ropes. The keen blade sliced through his bonds, and he was free.

Standing, he wiped blood from his face and considered his next move. His swords were not in the pile with the rest of his weapons. Slipping the small knife into his vambrace, he took another dagger and thrust it into his belt. Picking up his black cloak, he threw it over his shoulders, drew the hood over his head, and slipped out of the tent. Keeping away from the torchlight in the shadows, he moved slowly away. Suddenly, an outcry rose behind him. Numair had discovered his escape. Shouts rose around him; orders were given, and the hunt was on!

Emeth moved quietly out of the shadow of the tent and behind a supply wagon as a patrol hurried by. He saw a lone soldier walk by and he gave a low whistle. The soldier came to investigate the noise. When he got close enough, Emeth grabbed him and hit the soldier's head hard against the wagon. The man collapsed against the force of the blow. Emeth quickly donned the soldier's helmet and thrust the scimitar into his belt. Picking up the spear, he moved out cautiously. Keeping out of the torchlight as much as he could, Emeth walked toward the camp boundaries. Passing groups of soldiers paid him no heed. He could see the camp edge and sighed in relief. Too late. He came face-to-face with one of Numair's men. Caught in the full glare of the torches, the soldier could see his face through the openings in the helmet.

"You're not one of us!" he cried. Emeth swung the spear, felling the soldier and ran as Numair's men gave chase. Another soldier stepped into his path. Ripping off the helmet, Emeth brought it crashing down over the soldier's head, clearing his path. He saw a group of soldiers closing in on his left. He dodged right to avoid them only to see another squad coming from that direction. Putting on a burst of speed, he ran straight for the camp boundary only to be confronted by a tall barrier. He turned to see himself surrounded.

Drawing the scimitar and readying the spear, he placed his back against the wooden barrier. Captains urged their men forward to try and recapture him. Emeth fought with devastating efficiency, but he knew he couldn't fight forever. A sword raked his arm, causing blood to flow. A spear cut his leg, and still he fought on. He had lost the sword but battered on with the spear. A sword blade hit him hard against the ribs, knocking the breath from him. He staggered and was brought down by more soldiers. They held him down as Numair stood over him.

"Bind his wounds and make sure he is securely restrained and guarded. I want him alive for now."

Hamíd and Ahmed returned an hour before dawn.

"Any sign of him?" Lord Rishdah asked. Ahmed shook his head.

"Nothing, sir. All we found were these," he said as Hamíd placed Emeth's swords on the low table in front of Lord Rishdah. Azrahil looked at the two young men who were clearly worried about Emeth.

"Well, he might be alive yet. Probably bothering Numair in some way or another," he said. Everyone smiled at the rather apt description.

"Hamíd, hold on to those swords for now. You two are dismissed," Lord Rishdah said. Hamíd and Ahmed saluted and left the tent.

"You believe what you said?" Lord Rishdah asked Azrahil.

"I hope it's true," Azrahil replied.

"If it's not, those two will take on Numair's entire army to avenge him," Nicar observed.

"That's what I'm afraid of," Lord Rishdah said. "Numair will have much to answer for in a few hours."

CHAPTER 15

At midmorning, the armies met out on the open plains. Ahmed first saw the small group advancing toward them bearing a white flag. Lord Rishdah signaled to his guards as he and Lord Jamal went forward to meet Numair.

"Hello, brother, at last we meet again," Numair said smoothly.

"What do you want, Numair?' Lord Rishdah asked bluntly.

"I think you know very well what I want," Numair said. "I was always second to you, and now I'm tired of it. I want power and position, and you will give it to me."

"You know very well I will never give you anything now," Lord Rishdah replied.

"Yes, but I have something that might change your mind," Numair said as he signaled to his soldiers. Two men came forward holding Emeth between them. A severe look from Azrahil kept Hamíd and Ahmed in check. Numair surveyed the emotionless faces of Lord Rishdah and his men.

"Oh, come now. I know he means something to you. Surely you wouldn't want to see a son and one of your guards dead out of all this, Rishdah?" Numair asked.

"No, you are right. What terms do you bring?" Lord Rishdah asked.

Emeth stood quietly by during the exchange, working away at his bonds. Soon he was rewarded by a faint loosening in the ropes. It was just enough for him to fish out the small knife still hidden in his vambrace. Looking to either side, he checked to make sure his guards hadn't noticed anything. They weren't pay-ing any attention to him. He sawed frantically away at the ropes when he heard Lord Rishdah ask for Numair's terms.

"Half your lands and herds, a place in the Sultaan's council, as well as tribute from any who followed you," Numair stated, looking at Jamal who shifted angrily and laid a hand on his scimitar hilt. Lord Rishdah raised a hand to forestall any objections from Jamal.

"Many demands for just one prisoner. And if I refuse?" Lord Rishdah asked. Numair signaled again, and Emeth suddenly found himself with a knife to his throat.

"He will die as will you and your whole army," Numair said.

Emeth pulled his hands apart and the ropes parted with a snap. Moving quickly, he knocked the blade from his throat and drove his elbow into the surprised guard's stomach. As the soldier stumbled, Emeth grabbed the scimitar from the guard's belt. There was a rattle as swords were drawn, and the Phoenix Guards stood ready.

"Hate to break up the party, sir, but it looks like we should get moving," Emeth said to Lord Rishdah as Numair and his guards fled toward his oncoming army.

"Azrahil, give the signal," Lord Rishdah ordered. The captain turned and waved his scimitar in a great flashing arc. From the front of the army, Ismail saw it and ordered the cavalry to charge. Two hundred men and horses flew toward the advancing foe. As the cavalry passed around them, Emeth took hold of the scimitar in his left hand and stabilized his wounded arm by pushing it into his cross belts.

"You know how to use that thing?" Ahmed asked him jokingly.

"It'll have to do, I suppose. Don't know how you use the great clumsy things," Emeth replied lightly. The remainder of the army had come up behind them. Flanked by his guards, Lord Rishdah led the three hundred foot soldiers into the fray.

Ismail and his soldiers had cut deep into Numair's lines, but now they were facing superior numbers, and only the arrival of

Lord Rishdah and his soldiers saved them from being cut to pieces. Hamíd mounted a stray horse and joined Ismail, who was still fighting at the center of the battlefield. Close by Hamíd, Karif swooped down from the sky, clawing at the enemy. Emeth and Ahmed stood back to back, wreaking havoc with their flashing blades. A short distance off, Nicar and Azrahil fought by Lord Rishdah.

Ismail gathered a small group of horsemen around him, and joined by Hamíd, they charged again and again and cut through the packed ranks of the enemy. As the battle raged on, Emeth stumbled more than once, his rough treatment telling on his body. Then he saw Azrahil surrounded by three of Numair's men. He and Ahmed ran to help. As Azrahil fought off the men, a fourth crept behind him and raised his sword. In desperation, Emeth threw the scimitar like a spear. The man looked down in surprise at the sword piercing his stomach and fell. Ahmed helped the captain fight off the remaining soldiers as Emeth, now weaponless, found himself confronted by the Argusian.

He dodged as the Argusian's sword flashed toward him. Again and again he moved. Hampered by his wounded arm, Emeth knew he was helpless. Grinning savagely, the Argusian moved in for the kill. Readying himself, Emeth ducked the blade again then lashed out strongly with his unwounded left arm, hitting the Argusian's forearm, and causing him to drop the sword. The Argusian retaliated by punching his wounded arm. As Emeth staggered back, the Argusian drew his dagger and stabbed. Emeth cried out as the blade bit deep into his shoulder, and he fell. The Argusian's smile of triumph died with him as Ahmed thrust a spear through him.

Hamíd and Ismail reigned in their horses, watching what was left of Numair's army retreat. Both sides had suffered heavy losses. Less than half of their cavalry remained; stray horses roamed the battlefield as the survivors regrouped. Karif swooped down to land on Hamíd's shoulder as they picked their way over to where

Lord Rishdah. They found him leaning heavily on Lord Jamal as Nicar bandaged a wound on his leg. They both dismounted, and Ismail reported his losses.

"But it seems we are victorious after all," he said.

"Aye, son. Numair will trouble us no more," Lord Rishdah said, looking at the crumpled body of his half brother lying nearby. "Your brother is avenged."

Ahmed came running up.

"Pardon, my lord! Nicar, we need you quick!" he said, gasping for breath. At a nod from Lord Rishdah, Nicar and Ahmed hurried off. Hamíd led the horses as Lord Jamal followed, still supporting Lord Rishdah.

Azrahil was holding Emeth up in a sitting position. Emeth had drawn out the dagger and was trying to staunch the blood pouring from his shoulder. He felt himself getting weaker by the second.

"Hold on, I see Nicar coming," Azrahil said as he listened to Emeth's ragged breathing. He managed a small nod, struggling to remain awake. Lord Rishdah and the others came up as Nicar finished putting a rough bandage on Emeth's shoulder. Gray-faced and half conscious, Emeth still managed a crooked smile when he saw Hamíd.

"With your permission, my lord, I'd like to get him back to camp and properly taken care of," Nicar said.

"Ahmed can go with you," Lord Rishdah said. Spare horses were brought up as Hamíd helped Emeth to stand. Hamíd held him firmly as he swayed and almost fell.

"I'll be fine, don't worry," Emeth said in Rhyddan in response to the worried look on Hamíd's face. Hamíd helped him mount and then handed the reins to Ahmed as they rode back to camp.

Hours later, Azrahil and Hamíd prepared to leave the battlefield. Lord Rishdah had left some time earlier since his wound was troubling him. Ismail and Lord Jamal had remained, directing the clearing of the battlefield. The dead were buried, weapons collected, and wounded were taken back to camp in wagons. Azrahil passed him a waterskin, and he drank gratefully. He was exhausted, as was everyone else. The battle and its aftermath had taken its toll on the survivors. A soldier led up horses for them. Murmuring their thanks, Azrahil and Hamíd mounted and fell in place behind Lord Jamal and Ismail.

Back at the camp, Hamíd unbuckled his weapons, shrugged off his mail coat, and tumbled on to his cot, falling immediately into a deep slumber. He was awakened shortly before dawn. He opened his eyes to see Karif perched on the edge of the cot, looking at him. The hawk butted him gently on the chin again and flew off. He landed over by Emeth and cocked his head as he looked again at Hamíd. Quietly, Hamíd rose and moved past the sleeping forms of Azrahil and Ahmed. As he came up to Emeth's cot, Hamíd saw he was awake.

"How are you feeling?" Hamíd asked in their tongue.

"Not so good," Emeth admitted. His right shoulder and arm had been firmly bandaged. Hamíd took down the waterskin hanging nearby as Emeth half levered himself up on his left arm. As Hamíd helped him drink, he noticed strange markings on Emeth's left arm.

"These your clan markings?" Hamíd asked.

"Aye, every member of the clan has the same sign on their left forearm," Emeth said. Outlined in intricate knot-work was a four pointed star with a circle in the middle. Inscribed within the circle was a *C*.

"It stands for Clan Canich," Emeth explained. Hamíd looked again at the tattoo that took up most of his upper arm. It depicted a wildcat standing on its hind paws, claws and teeth bared savagely. He realized that it was the first time he had ever seen them.

"I got that when I was fifteen. It's the clan emblem," Emeth told him.

Hamíd's eyes widened in surprise as he remembered a lesson from long ago.

"The chieftain and his sons are the only ones to have it marked on their arms," he said.

"So now you know who I am," Emeth said, falling back into the thick brogue of the Braeton Clans.

"Why didn't you ever tell me?" Hamíd asked.

"For the same reason I've kept it hidden for all these years. I don't want tae be reminded of who I am, but it's engraved intae me. Someday I might go back and face it," Emeth replied bitterly. "My father and I weren't exactly on the best of terms, that's why I left. I've got a few scars of my own."

"I'm sorry" was all Hamíd could find to say.

"Och, both my father and I are tae blame. I inherited his quick temper, and he seemed tae find fault with everything I did. It didn't take much for him and me tae let fly at each other. And it didn't help that I did things that were forbidden. I do miss my family, and even though it may not sound like it, I do miss my father. I regret a lot of things now," Emeth said, a note of sadness creeping into his voice.

"Maybe time will have changed things," Hamíd said.

"Maybe…," Emeth said pensively.

Nicar walked into the tent.

"Good, you're awake, Hamíd. You have the next shift," he said. Pulling a wry face, Hamíd moved away. Washing and dressing quickly, he buckled his weapons back on and whistled softly. Karif flew over to take up his perch on Hamíd's shoulder. On his way out, Hamíd laid something on the table by Emeth's bed.

"Ahmed and I found these. I figured you might want them back," he said, before he ducked out of the tent. Emeth smiled when he saw his swords.

It was midmorning when the first signs of the sickness appeared. Hamíd and Azrahil stood behind Lord Rishdah. He was discussing a peace offer just received from Numair's son with Lord Jamal and his captains. The son, it seemed, had not completely agreed with his father on the campaign against Lord Rishdah. It had left his new forces severely depleted. He offered peace and a sizeable tribute to Lord Rishdah. After a lengthy debate, the messenger was called back into the tent.

"I agree to your new master's proposals for peace. I too have had enough of this war," Lord Rishdah said.

"Yes, sir. My lord only wants to be left alone," the envoy said.

"If he will swear allegiance to me, I will give him peace as well as protection in time of need," Lord Rishdah said. There were some slight murmurs from his captains at the last statement.

"You are most forgiving, my lord, but you would understand if my master refused? It would not sit well with his people or yours, I think," the man said. Lord Rishdah nodded.

"He tries to do what is best for his people. He shows wisdom. Then tell him that I accept the treaty," Lord Rishdah said.

"Thank you, my lord," the envoy said.

"We will withdraw soon, but know this: if anything ever goes awry, no treaty or family bond will stop me from raising my armies and utterly destroying him," Lord Rishdah declared. The messenger bowed once more and made his way from the tent. As the captains stood to be dismissed, one suddenly swayed and collapsed. Hamíd knelt by the man and felt his pulse.

"He's burning up, my lord!" he said.

"Jaffa, fetch a healer quickly!" Lord Rishdah ordered. "Captain Taysir, find out what you can. I want to know if this is poison."

Captain Taysir saluted and left the tent. Captain Jibril held up the fallen Captain Ghalib as Hamíd tried to give him some water. Ghalib drank some and then began coughing violently. As he stopped, the healer entered. After examining the captain, the healer reported to Lord Rishdah.

"It looks to be a camp sickness, my lord. I'll do what I can, which is not much, I'm sorry to say," he said. Captain Taysir came back with his report.

"It doesn't look to be poison, sir. I saw two of his men that were stricken down with it last night. No one else has caught it yet, and the animals seem healthy enough. We give them water from our supply," the captain said.

"Alert everyone. This needs to be prevented," Lord Rishdah ordered. Two soldiers came and carried Captain Ghalib to his tent under the supervision of the healer. As the day passed, more reports came in of fresh cases. As darkness fell, Nicar came in to report that Emeth had fallen sick. A long night passed with dawn bringing no relief. Almost half of the army had fallen victim to the raging fever. A scout brought news that men in Numair's camp were suffering from the same illness. Hamíd found Ismail by the horses.

"Sir, your father would speak with you," Hamíd said. Ismail made no answer, suddenly overtaken by a violent fit of coughing. Hamíd helped him walk to the tent where Nicar was caring for Emeth. He helped Ismail on to the cot, laying his weapons to one side.

"Nicar, you've got one more," Hamíd said. "Nicar?" Receiving no answer, he turned to see the guard leaning heavily on the camp table. Hamíd ran over to him. His skin was hot to the touch. Hamíd made Nicar as comfortable as he could on the cot and went to report to Lord Rishdah.

"Where is Ismail?" Lord Rishdah asked sharply.

"He just fell sick, sir. So did Nicar," Hamíd said. Lord Rishdah took the news in silence and then he spoke.

"Captain Jaffa, take everyone who is still healthy and move a safe distance away. We have to stop this sickness from spreading."

"What about you, my lord?" Jaffa asked.

"I will remain here with my son" came the reply.

"Then I stay as well," Azrahil said. Ahmed and Hamíd voiced their agreement. Lord Rishdah nodded his consent. "Jaffa, prepare to move out," he said.

A few hours later, the camp appeared deserted. All but a few healthy soldiers had withdrawn and took with them supplies and most of the horses. Those who remained dedicated themselves to nursing the sick. The air was filled with the violent coughs and groans of the wounded and sick men. Azrahil, Hamíd, and Ahmed worked in shifts caring for their sick comrades. Lord Rishdah helped as he could, still hampered by his wounded leg. Days dragged by slowly, only a few men recovering at first.

Hamíd sat at the tent entrance watching Azrahil come slowly toward him.

"Where's Ahmed?" he asked.

"Asleep," Hamíd replied, gesturing inside the tent.

"Any change?' Azrahil asked. Hamíd shook his head.

"Don't know how much more of this I can take," Azrahil said hoarsely. "It's your turn to sleep. Leave Ahmed for a while longer, it'll do him good."

"Yes, sir," Hamíd complied wearily, stumbling over to his bunk.

When he awoke, it was dark. The tent was strangely quiet. Ahmed was still fast asleep nearby and Azrahil had dozed off in the chair. Hamíd moved softly by him and opened the tent flap. A cool breeze had sprung up. Hamíd gazed at the bright moon and stars and let the wind bathe his face. A shiver ran through him. A change was coming!

He pulled the flap aside and tied it open, allowing the fresh air to seep inside the tent. As he went back inside, he saw Ismail stir. His skin was cool to the touch. When Ismail opened his eyes, they were clear and bright. Hamíd helped him drink some water and covered him warmly. Ismail settled back down and fell asleep. Hamíd heard a movement nearby and looked up to see Ahmed.

"Why didn't you wake me earlier?" he whispered reproachfully.

"I only just awoke myself," Hamíd answered. "We all overslept a little. Ismail's fever broke." Ahmed sighed in relief and went to check on Emeth and Nicar. They were both sleeping peacefully, their fever gone. Azrahil woke as they moved.

"Take my bunk, Captain. I'll take over here," Ahmed offered. Accompanied by Karif, Hamíd left to stand watch at Lord Rishdah's tent.

CHAPTER 16

Almost a week later, the army made ready to leave. The sickness had finally abated but not before claiming the lives of the most weak and wounded. So it was a severely depleted army that made its way back to Lord Rishdah's small realm. A month of peace followed their return and life returned to normal. Then one afternoon, Lord Rishdah called Hamíd before him.

"Hamíd, before I left on the campaign against Numair, I made myself a promise," Lord Rishdah said. "It is one that I will fulfill now. I am giving you your freedom."

"What?" Hamíd said in disbelief.

"You have done many great services for me, and this is how I choose to reward you," Lord Rishdah said.

"But sir, you—" Hamíd began, but Lord Rishdah interrupted.

"I know what you would say, but it doesn't matter who or what you are, I have made my decision," Lord Rishdah said. "You can go wherever you wish, or you can remain here if you desire."

"Thank you, my lord," Hamíd said. He couldn't believe the words that Lord Rishdah had just spoken. He was free after twelve long years.

"It will be some time before my forces are back to their former strength, but when they are, the Sultaan will most likely order me to Aredor. If we meet again, it will be on opposite ends of the sword," Lord Rishdah warned.

"I never forget those who saved my life," Hamíd said. Rishdah extended his hand, and Hamíd grasped it firmly.

"Good luck, Corin," Rishdah said.

"Thank you, sir," he replied.

Emeth found his friend standing outside the castle walls looking north. They stood in silence for a few minutes before Corin spoke.

"I'm free," he said.

"Where will you go?" Emeth asked. Corin spoke a single word.

"Home."

"What will you do?' Emeth asked.

"I don't know yet. I know things have changed so much there, but I need to find my family," Corin said. "What will you do?" he asked.

"Stay here," Emeth replied. "I'm happy enough right now. It won't be the same without you around here, mate. But I do have one favor tae ask."

"Name it," Corin said.

"If you meet any of my Clan, would you let them know I'm all right?" Emeth said. Corin nodded.

"Look after yourself, Aiden," he said.

"You too, Corin," Emeth replied and wrapped him in a tight embrace.

Corin left early the next morning after bidding farewell to his companions. The parting was hard as he had become close with all of them, particularly Emeth and Ahmed, but he was overtaken with a longing to see his own country again. He turned Zephyr west toward Gelion, where he would find a ship to take him to Aredor. Karif soared above him as he spurred Zephyr onward, toward home.

BOOK TWO

Hawk Uprising

CHAPTER 1

Ship timbers creaked in the darkness as Corin led Zephyr down the gangplank and on to the pier. The Gelion merchant ship had docked at the port town of Carreg in Aredor. Castle Martel sat above on the cliffs that overshadowed the town. Below the castle lay Martel Village. To the north and west, fertile farmlands stretched on for miles interrupted by small villages. Corin drew on a pair of gloves and pulled the hood of his cloak well over his face. He was taking no chances, even in the dark. He led Zephyr down the pier and into the town, passing groups of Calorin soldiers on patrol.

He was able to reply to any challenge the sentries gave and passed through the town unhindered. Once safely outside the town, he mounted Zephyr and rode until the port was well behind him. Turning off the road, he made camp in a sheltered dell.

When Corin awoke the next morning, the sun was well up into the sky. Zephyr stood nearby, tearing hungrily at the fresh sweet grass. Unrolling from his cloak, Corin sat up and took a deep breath of the clear air. He was home.

He stood and looked about him with his eyes almost aching at the quiet beauty of the morning and feeling, not for the first time, that this was a dream from which he should surely awaken. After breakfasting on what was left of his supplies, he saddled Zephyr, whistled Karif to his shoulder, and rode out of the dell.

Skirting Martel Village, he traveled northwest toward Kingscastle. Corin stayed off the roads as much as possible to avoid the frequent Calorin patrols. It was late afternoon when he came upon a small village consisting of a dozen houses. He hesitated for a few minutes, but no Calorins were to be seen. Dismounting, he led Zephyr into the village. Corin had not gone far when he was confronted by an old man carrying a pitchfork.

"Who are you?" the man asked gruffly. Corin spread his hands to show he meant to harm.

"I'm just passing through, and I need water for my horse," Corin said.

"Are you mad?" the man exclaimed. "No one just travels around anymore, unless you're one of them!" His tone became menacing, and he leveled the pitchfork at Corin.

"No, I'm as Northern as you are," Corin said. This seemed to placate the man somewhat.

"What's your name?" the man asked.

"Corin," he replied.

"All right, Corin. You look honest enough. The water trough's over there. Don't try anything funny though," the man said. Corin refilled his waterskin as Zephyr drank thirstily.

"I've been away for a few years. Perhaps you could tell me what's happened?" Corin asked the man.

"There's not much to tell," the man said. "Two years ago, we were overrun by the Calorins. The king was away across the mountains in Cyndor with most of his warband helping to clear up a bit of trouble over there. Castle Martel was taken completely by surprise, and then Prince Darrin had his hands full trying to hold the Calorins back. But without the main warband, they were driven back. Once the king returned, they tried again but were heavily outnumbered. The warriors not slain were imprisoned or pressed into slavery under the Calorins.

"They come and go as they please, taking what they want or burning and destroying it. We live off what we can save. Half the men of the village were taken last year. The women and boys work the fields as best they can. It's the same story all over Aredor," he finished sadly.

"What happened to the prince and the king?" Corin asked.

"There's rumors that Darrin is imprisoned at Kingscastle. Of the king, there's been no word or sign of him since the Calorins ambushed him near the mountains. And as far as anyone knows, the queen and Princess Amaura are in hiding somewhere. Lord Balkor hasn't got his filthy hands on them yet," the man said.

"Balkor!" Corin exclaimed.

"You know him?" the man asked.

"I have a score to settle with him!" Corin replied angrily.

Panicked screams rent the air. The old man ran off toward the sounds. Stopping only to grab his bow from the saddle, Corin ran after him. They rounded the corner to see a small troop of Calorins. They had grabbed a small boy and girl and were carrying them toward their horses. A frantic young woman tried to stop them, but she was flung roughly aside. Laying a shaft on his bow, Corin shouted out in Calorin, "Drop them now!"

Surprised, the soldiers stopped and turned around. Seeing that he was alone, the leader called out mockingly. "You're outnumbered. Drop your weapons, and we might let you live!"

Corin smiled thinly.

"I said drop them," he repeated.

The Calorin drew his scimitar and held it at the girl's throat.

"Drop it or she dies," he threatened.

Corin carefully took aim and fired. The arrow slew the soldier holding the girl. He quickly nocked another arrow to the string. The girl scrambled away as the soldier fell. The Calorins began backing away as two fitted arrows to their bows. One mounted and held the boy in front of him. Menacing Corin with their bows, the others mounted and galloped away.

Corin ran to where Zephyr still stood. Leaping into the saddle, he let out a piercing whistle as he galloped after the soldiers. Villagers scattered as he tore out of the village. Karif dove from the sky to join him. Zephyr stretched forward eagerly, bringing them in range of the soldiers. Dropping the reins, Corin drew his bow and picked off a soldier. Then he slung the bow over his shoulder and drew his scimitar. Putting on an extra burst of speed, Zephyr drew even with the soldiers. One drew his sword and crossed blades with Corin. He swept the soldier's blade aside and brought his scimitar slashing down. The terrified riderless horse careened sideways, crashing into the horse running next to it. Both animals stumbled, and the soldier holding the boy fell to the ground. The remaining soldier lashed his horse to a greater speed and drew away from Corin.

Knowing he couldn't catch him, Corin reined in Zephyr and turned back. The soldier who had fallen lay on the ground, moaning and nursing a broken leg. The boy had landed unhurt and was sitting nearby, still in shock. Ignoring the soldier, Corin dismounted and went over to the boy.

"You all right?" he asked. The boy nodded numbly. Corin picked him up and took him over to Zephyr. "Come on, let's get you home," he said. As he helped the boy onto Zephyr, Karif landed on his shoulder.

"We'll find you and make you suffer for what you did today!" the soldier spat. Turning to him, Corin answered, "Then you'll have to outfly the west wind to catch me." He mounted behind the boy and rode away.

As they came back, they were surrounded by anxious villagers. The boy slid down into his mother's arms. Corin dismounted and was thanked by the tearful woman. He stood awkwardly, unsure of what to do. The men of the village came forward to talk to him.

"We can't thank you enough for what you've done," the old man said.

"What were they taking them for?" Corin asked.

"Servants or to work in the fields," another man answered. "They took most of our young men already. No one can stop them."

"I plan to change that!" Corin said, his blue eyes flashing.

"And how do you plan to do that, Your Highness?" someone asked from behind the crowd. The villagers parted, and a man limped forward.

"Who are you?" Corin asked. "And how...?" The man stopped and looked him up and down.

"So you're alive after all. By Lleu, I can't believe it!" he said.

"Who are you?" Corin demanded again.

"You were a good student—for the short time I had with you," the man said.

"Ivor?" Corin asked in astonishment. The man nodded.

"You look just like your father, lad," he said.

"What happened? Where is he?" Corin asked. Ivor shrugged unhappily.

"I don't know, sir. I was with Prince Darrin and was badly hurt in the last battle. I barely made it here," Ivor said. "And before you ask, I don't know where your brother is either. I'm sorry."

"Were there any others that escaped?" Corin asked.

"If any survived that last fight, they would have gone to Dunham Forest. There are plenty of places to hide in there," Ivor replied.

"That's where I'll go then. Will you come with me?" Corin asked Ivor. The warrior shook his head.

"I would, sir, but I'm afraid I'll only slow you down. My leg is such that I cannot ride," he said ashamed. Corin looked him in the eyes.

"If you can still wield a sword or draw a bow, then come looking for me. You know where I'll be," he said.

"Yes, my lord," Ivor said, a fresh light shining in his eyes.

"I should go before the Calorins come back looking for me. I hope they'll not punish you worse for helping me," Corin said.

"We'll take it gladly," the old man said. "You gave us fresh hope today."

As Corin mounted, a woman handed him a bag of food.

"It's not much, lord, but it will keep you until you reach the forest," she said.

"Thank you, ma'am," Corin said, taking the bag. The sun was setting as he rode from the village. He rode all night, skirting other towns and garrison outposts. At dawn, he could see the dark line of Dunham Forest in the distance.

CHAPTER 2

Corin rested well away from the road. Opening his pack, he drew out some bread and cheese and dried meat. It was plain, but filling. Also in the bag were some round cakes made from oats and dried fruit and sweetened with honey. Memories came flooding back as he ate: journeys to the coast, picnics by the river, he and Darrin racing their ponies across the plain. His father laughing, his mother singing, Amaura teasing the cats that roamed the castle. She would be a young woman of twenty-one now. Darrin showing him a move with the broadsword…what was he like now? The brothers had been close as they were only separated by three years. Amaura and Darrin were dark haired like their mother, but all three siblings had inherited the same piercing blue eyes of their father.

Amaura was gentle, ready with a laugh but deep down possessed a resolve the equal of her brothers. Darrin had always been a little more serious and cautious and was quietly confident though patient with his headstrong, mischievous brother. Corin had known how to get him to laugh with head thrown back and eyes sparkling. He was always helping Corin out of trouble or getting drawn into another wild idea of Corin's that would get them both in trouble, but they would laugh helplessly about it later. He seemed so close to seeing them all again but knew it might take years before he found them, if they were still alive at all. His gaze turned again to the distant forest, and he wondered if there was any hope of ever overthrowing the Calorin rule.

Corin dozed all morning, letting Zephyr rest. It was relatively quiet and peaceful. When Karif returned from hunting, Corin rode out again. As he traveled closer to the forest, the road became more heavily traveled by patrols. Keeping away from the roads, he was able to slip by until he came to the Darkan River.

The river flowed by to his left, and in front of him stretched the road guarded by an outpost. The river was too deep for him to cross, and the bridge was heavily guarded as was the town on the opposite bank. He had to cross the road in order to reach the forest, which still lay a half mile away. During the day, the patrols were too frequent for him to make it across unseen. And he didn't want to spend another night out in the open. His luck had held so far, but he knew how quickly that could change. He decided the only way to cross was to bluff his way.

Corin tethered Zephyr in the trees by the river where he wouldn't be seen, and then he slipped over to view the outpost. A familiar and much hated standard fluttered in the breeze above the outpost—Balkor's emblem of a leopard prowling across a purple field. He lay hidden in a ditch by the roadside while watching the soldiers carefully.

"What are we watching for this time?" a soldier asked.

"Some rebel escaped and was giving some trouble in a village. General Kadar brought orders from Kingscastle that all roads are to be watched. He wants him caught alive if possible," his companion replied.

"Maybe he'll come this way and give us some excitement," the first soldier said. The other snorted.

"You weren't here when we invaded. You didn't fight these Northerners. He won't want to be caught. You'd get more excitement than you want," he said.

Corin had heard enough. He slid quietly back to Zephyr. Seeing the banner had brought back all his anger against Balkor. Corin now knew what he would do. He had training, and he would fight against the Calorins any way possible in the hopes of exacting retribution against Balkor. He had first felt it in the village. His past life here was too far gone to reclaim, and now away from Calorin, he was no longer Hamíd. It was time to find out who he really was. He sent Karif flying off and rode toward the road.

The soldiers guarding the road watched the horse and rider coming toward them. The rider pulled his stallion to a halt, his face partially obscured by his hood.

"Where are you going?" the soldier in command asked.

"I'm to deliver a message in the town," the rider replied.

"Who sent you?" the commander asked.

"General Kadar" came the reply.

The soldier waved the messenger through. Throwing a salute, the rider spurred his horse through the barricade. The commander watched him ride slowly off. Something wasn't right. Then he saw it: the Aredorian war bow draped across the man's back.

"Stop him!" he shouted. Corin turned to see a dozen Calorins galloping toward him. He turned Zephyr off the road and headed toward the forest.

Zephyr thundered across the open plain, and Corin fumbled for his bow as arrows flew around him. Two cloaked figures watched from the safety of the forest.

"You think he'll make it?" one asked.

"He might. He's got a few arrows off now," the other replied.

"Should we help?" the first asked.

"You know, that's what I like about you, Liam. Always ready to help," his companion said, nocking an arrow to his bow. Liam smiled, "Just as long as it involves shooting some of these blasted Calorins," he said, firing a shaft.

The Calorins fell back in surprise at the arrows coming from the forest, allowing Corin time to disappear into the trees. Zephyr reared in surprise when a dark figure appeared in front of him and nearly unseated his rider. Corin unsheathed his scimitar, ready to fight. The man held up his hands placatingly, throwing back his hood.

"I'm a friend. I thought you might like to get away before they decide to come in looking for you," he said. Corin sheathed his blade and slid down from Zephyr.

"Thanks for your help," he said as Karif flew in to perch on his shoulder.

"Shall we hold the pleasantries? I hear them coming," the man said. After a brief moment's hesitation, Corin followed him.

He led Corin through the trees and on to a narrow forest track. He walked quickly, taking them deeper into the forest. Corin sized up his guide as they walked. He was tall, well built, and carried a broadsword and a bow complete with a well-stocked quiver. He wore dark clothes to blend with the forest. Corin noticed most of it was made up of an old uniform as a wolf insignia adorned the front of his tunic. Corin recognized the wolf as the crest of Aredor. The man wasn't much older than Corin was and had dark brown hair and serious brown eyes.

His guide stopped suddenly.

"Before we go any farther, I have to know if I can trust you," he said. "You look too much like one of them for me to bring you to our camp."

"I'd do the same in your place," Corin replied. "I've been in the South for a few years and just now been able to return. I came in at Carreg and have been traveling overland since. I heard from some villagers that the forest is the safest place to be. My name's Corin," he said. The man studied him carefully for a moment.

"You look to be telling the truth," he said. "But one false move and I'll run you through. Now that's out of the way, I'm Liam," the man said. Corin grinned and extended his hand. Liam shook it firmly, and they continued on. Suddenly, they came upon an open dell. A small fire was burning, which was tended by another young man.

"Trey, we've got some company!" Liam called. Trey rose and walked over. He was dressed and armed just like Liam. Lithe and muscular, he looked as dangerous as the longsword he carried at his side. Steely gray eyes looked Corin up and down.

"I'm Trey," he said, extending a hand. Corin grasped it firmly and introduced himself, albeit to an old friend.

"There's only one person I ever knew by that name," Trey said. "But I haven't seen him in a long time."

"Almost twelve years at last count," Corin replied. A smile crossed Trey's face.

"You made it back. But there's someone you'll want to see more than me in a few minutes," he said.

A low whistle announced the arrival of a third outlaw. A cheerful-looking young man with black hair and green eyes bounded into the clearing.

"What happened to the Calorins?" Liam asked.

"They'll be going in circles for a while. I wouldn't worry too much about them," Martin laughed. He stopped as he caught sight of Corin.

"Lleu's hands," he whispered. "Corin, is that you?" he asked in disbelief, and in turn, Corin could hardly believe his own eyes.

"Aye, Martin. It's me," Corin replied. Martin wrapped him in a wild embrace.

"What happened? We thought you were dead! They looked everywhere for you!" Martin said.

"I stumbled upon some slavers. They took me to Calorin. I lived under Balkor for eight years and then another lord took me and trained me to fight. After three years, I won my freedom and made my back way here," Corin explained quickly, pouring out a story for his oldest friend.

"Cor, I'm sorry," Martin said. Corin shrugged.

"None of that matters anymore. What happened here? How'd you three escape?" he asked, tethering Zephyr nearby. The four men moved around the fire as Trey began to cook fresh deer meat.

"I was with the king in one of the last battles. I got knocked out after a Calorin took a swing at me with his shield. When I came to, the battlefield was deserted," Martin began. "As soon as I could, I made my way here to the forest where I met up with them."

"I led the last of the coastal warbands under Darrin. We were cut off with our backs to the forest. We tried to retreat inside but couldn't make it. Darrin made me run for it while he fought them off. I was the only one who made it in safely. Last I saw, he was still alive," Trey said. "If I hadn't run, we could've made it in together."

Corin saw the anger and frustration in Trey's eyes and knew all too well how he felt.

"What about Tristan?" Corin asked. There was a frozen agony in Trey's voice as he spoke about his brother.

"I don't know. Most likely dead."

"Lynwood Keep was the last to fall. That's where I was stationed," Liam said. "They were taking me to Darkan Village when Trey rescued me. As far as we know, we're the only ones still free."

"You've stayed in the forest this whole time then?" Corin asked.

"Aye, there's plenty of food, with caves and valleys to hide in, and blessedly free of Calorins. They hate this place," Martin answered.

"You ever try to free anyone else?" Corin asked. Trey shook his head.

"Prisoners and slaves are too heavily guarded. I know a bit of Calorin. It might be enough to bluff my way out, but we never tried," he said.

Corin contributed the food in his pack, and they ate in silence. He tossed meat to Karif as the faint beginnings of an idea began to nag at the back of his mind. Martin watched him closely.

"I remember that look," he said. "You've got some sort of crazy plan, don't you?"

"Maybe. I'll have to get to know this forest better first though," Corin said.

Corin and Martin walked down a forest path. Martin was showing him the main paths and trails that the outlaws usually followed through the forest. Martin surreptitiously watched Corin from the corner of his eye. He still couldn't believe that his friend was alive. He was quieter and more reserved than Martin remembered, but he showed flashes of the same roguish boy of twelve years ago. Martin took another glance. Corin was moving quietly despite his limp with his weapons within easy reach; and Karif, as always, flew nearby.

"You ever make it to the mountains?" Corin asked, breaking the silence. Martin smiled as he remembered their childhood dream.

"No, I didn't want to after you disappeared," he said. Corin glanced at him. They had done everything together. Martin had never backed down from anything, always ready for the next adventure.

"Truth is, I went a little crazy after that," Martin continued. "Father wouldn't let me go along with the search parties, and after they told me that you were probably dead..." He shrugged. "There seemed to be no point in anything. Father sent me to Castle Martel to start training the next summer. I was a lieutenant in the king's warband by seventeen," he finished.

"You must have gotten plenty of fighting on the coast," Corin said.

"Aye, two years of fighting off the Raiders will prepare you for anything," Martin said. "Trey was always of the opinion that we needed our own fleet. That way, we could follow them back and attack Terminus, but he was always looking to start a fight somewhere. Having our own warships might have given us a warning of the Calorins."

"What happened in the attacks? In Calorin, I heard it from the Sultaan's messenger. He said it was a massacre," Corin said.

"He wasn't exaggerating much," Martin said. "We had almost no warning. Martel wasn't ready to withstand the assaults and by the time we were able to make it to the coast, the Calorins had taken the castle and were pouring inland. We tried to send to the Clans for help, but our messengers never made it."

"What happened to your father?" Corin asked.

"He was captured with his men when they were out scouting. Trey and I and some of my men tried to rescue him, but the Calorins had killed them all by the time we got there," Martin said.

"Martin, I'm sorry," Corin said. He knew how Calorins treated prisoners of war. Martin gave him a sad smile.

"Your father gave me his position. That was about the time things really started to get bad. When I regained consciousness on that field, I saw more than half my men were dead. We had been the last big threat to the Calorins. The last person I saw was my sister. I was trying to make it here and ran into a Calorin patrol. Ended up half dead on the side of the road outside Gorwydd village. She was there taking care of the wounded soldiers. The villagers hid me until I could travel again," Martin said. "But I'm sure you don't want to hear any more of this. I've been doing all the talking so far, what about you? You said you fought for them in Calorin?"

"I was almost twenty when I met Lord Rishdah. He was so different than anyone else I knew. He was stern, but not cruel. All his people respected him, and so do I. He wanted me in his personal guard, so I trained hard for months until the captain thought I was ready. After that, there were wars to fight. We went to Argus on a campaign, survived the desert, and came out victorious," Corin said. "In between wars, there was never really peace. Bandits roam the roads, lords fight over boundaries or any reason they can think of. One month, Lord Rishdah had an alliance with another lord. The next month, they were fighting each other after a southern lord started an uprising."

"Is that all they do? Fight each other?" Martin asked, somewhat disbelievingly.

"Pretty much," Corin said. "I've done a little bit of everything: scouting, getting captured, professing allegiance to another lord in order to get information, been on both sides of a siege."

"So everything you always wanted to do?" Martin asked, grinning. Corin laughed.

"What kind of training did you go through?" Martin asked curiously.

"My friend called it assassin training," Corin said.

"That explains everything then," Martin said as they both laughed. "We'll see how good you are with that blade later," he challenged.

"I think you might be pleasantly surprised," Corin replied, grinning in anticipation. Anyone who made lieutenant at seventeen had to be an expert swordsman.

"This should be good," Trey said, leaning back against a log and crossing his arms as Corin and Martin prepared to spar. Liam joined him.

"Who do you think will win?" Liam asked.

"I'm rather hoping Corin will," Trey replied.

"You're just jealous because I won our last bout," Martin called to him. Liam smirked.

"You can fight the winner, Liam," Corin said. Trey looked at the identical grins on Martin's and Corin's faces and suppressed his own smile.

"The terrible duo has returned, I see," he said.

Martin and Corin began to circle each other, handling their blades with apparent carelessness. One would flicker forward and be tossed away by the other. Liam and Trey watched closely.

"You ladies going to dance all day? We're dying of boredom over here!" Trey called. As if that were a signal they were waiting for, Corin and Martin clashed together. Their swords wove spinning, flashing arcs as they exchanged blows. Finally, they drew apart and conceded a draw.

"Not bad," Martin said.

"He probably didn't tell you that after he beat our sword master, he went back to Kingscastle and began terrorizing the warband as the newest blademaster," Trey said.

"An expert swordsman, eh? I could've killed you twice," Corin said to Martin. "You leave your left side open."

Trey and Liam chortled at Martin's indignant expression.

"Show me!" he demanded. Corin drove him into a sequence and halted suddenly. Martin looked down. Their swords were locked, but a knife had appeared in Corin's hand and was pressed against his side.

"Well, if you're going to cheat like that," Martin said. He disengaged his sword and lunged at Corin. Seconds later, Corin's scimitar was pinned across his body, and a knife hovered above his chest.

"Very nice, but…" Corin prodded Martin's side with his knife.

"Neither one of you is going to win this," Liam warned as they withdrew. A smile gradually broke over Martin's face as he sheathed his sword.

"It's been a while since someone stayed with me that long," he said.

"You're one of the best I've ever encountered," Corin said. "You'll have to show me that last trick."

Martin was about to reply when Liam held up his hand.

"Did you hear that?" he asked. In the silence, the others could hear the sound of horses and creaking wheels. Corin grabbed his bow and quiver and slung it over his shoulder. The others guessed his intent and grabbed their own weapons. Corin looked questioningly to Liam, who nodded and led them toward the sounds.

It was a large wagon laden with barrels and sacks of provisions. A Calorin soldier drove it accompanied by five mounted soldiers. They travelled down the path and, a few moments later, were lost to sight.

"Where did they come from?" Corin asked.

"It looked like some of the Blaen garrison," Liam said. "They have the storehouses there."

"How far away is Blaen?" Corin queried.

"A few miles northwest of here," Trey replied.

"And how are you proposing we get in and out without being seen?" Martin asked, guessing the reason behind Corin's questions.

"We could go at night, and if we were dressed as Calorins..." Corin let the thought hang.

"I think I might have something to help us look even more like them," Liam put in. Since they had first met, Corin had discovered that besides being a lieutenant in Lynwood Keep, Liam had also been the healer and, as such, had a wide knowledge of herbs and plants and their uses.

Trey shrugged. "Let's go get some uniforms then," he said. They set off in quick pursuit of the Calorins and their wagon.

CHAPTER 3

"I got the keys," Martin said, joining his companions at their hidden campsite just outside of the town. "The next guard isn't due for almost four hours," he said.

The outlaws had spent the past two days learning the guard rotation on the storehouses. The large buildings were built close to the edge of town, making them an easier target. They were dressed in the uniforms of the Blaen garrison, and Liam had come up with a fine powder that turned their skin the dark brown of the Calorins.

"Just be careful, it rubs off easily," he warned. Corin led the horse that had been harnessed to the wagon, and the others led the horses that had been taken from the unfortunate troop in the forest. They halted, unchallenged, by the doors of the first storehouse. Martin produced the keys and swung open the doors.

"Would you look at that!" he whistled. Racks of longbows lined the walls, interspersed with swords. Piles of spears were stacked in the corners, and mail coats lay on tables.

"Aredorian weapons!" Liam said.

"Let's load as much of this as we can in the wagon and then we can cover it with food sacks," Corin said.

They worked as quickly and quietly as they could. When they had loaded the wagon as much as they dared, they closed and locked the storeroom and moved to the next one. The sun had almost set, and Corin lit a torch to help them see as they brought out bags of provisions to cover the weapons. They halted as footsteps sounded behind them. Liam turned and saw two soldiers coming towards them.

"What's going on here?" one asked.

"Corin, there's someone out there!" Trey whispered.

"Who's in charge here?" the other asked. From inside the storeroom, Corin's heart lifted as he heard the slurred speech of the men. *They're drunk!* he realized. He grabbed a flagon off the shelf.

"I hate this stuff," he muttered and took a deep draft. Spluttering, he took another drink.

"Corin, what are you doing?" Trey hissed.

"Keep working. I'll be back as soon as I can," Corin said. Liam and Martin watched bewildered as he staggered past them toward the soldiers.

"That'd be me," he slurred the words. "Lieutenant Hamíd, at your service, boys!"

The soldiers looked at him through slightly unfocused eyes.

"I'm Lieutenant Zafir and this is Lieutenant Hamzah," one said. "What are you doing out here so late, Hamíd?" he asked.

"We were supposed to leave earlier, but they didn't get the wagon loaded in time," He jerked a thumb back at his companions. "You know how lazy those cavalry soldiers can be." He took another pull at the flagon as Zafir and Hamzah voiced their agreement loudly.

"We were just going to the tavern. You should join us, Hamíd!" Zafir said. When Corin hesitated, Hamzah clapped him on the shoulder.

"Come on! You'll have plenty of time before these buffoons get the wagon loaded," he said, taking the flagon from Corin and drinking.

"You're right!" Corin said. "There's no reason I should have to stand out here in the dark while they work!"

"Aye, you look like you work too hard already!" Zafir said. The three of them roared with laughter.

"Don't send someone after me when you're done. You'll probably take all night!" Corin raised his voice as he gave the order to the other "Calorins." Trey's salute told him that he understood. Relieved, Corin draped a friendly arm around Hamzah's shoulder as they made their way toward the tavern.

"*What* is he doing?" Martin asked Trey.

"I hope he knows. Come on, let's hurry with these." Trey slung another bag up to Liam.

An hour passed and there was no sign of Corin. Liam scanned the street anxiously. They had finished filling the wagon almost half an hour ago.

"The sentry will be along any minute," Martin whispered to Trey. "What do we do?"

"Wait," Trey replied, equally uneasy.

As Martin feared, the new guard came on duty and saw them standing by the wagons in the torchlight.

"What are you doing?" he asked suspiciously.

"Waiting for the lieutenant," Trey replied. "He's been down at the tavern all afternoon. The guard just left. We're supposed to give you these." He tossed the keys to the soldier.

"You're not the first. These lieutenants think they can just leave anyone waiting for them. I don't know how many wagons have been held up here," the soldier said. "How long have you lot been waiting?" he asked Liam.

Liam glanced helplessly at Trey. Just then, Trey saw Corin coming towards them.

"Here he is now!" he said, relief too evident in his voice. "Everything's ready, sir," he said to Corin.

"Good, let's get going. Taysir needs these supplies," Corin said. Trey nodded to Martin and Liam and they took up their positions. The guard shook his head in disgust at the "drunk" lieutenant and his carelessness before walking away. Trey watched Corin walk a little unsteadily to the wagon, not so sure he was still acting. Corin mounted a horse as Martin took up the wagon lines.

The journey back to the forest took longer with the heavy wagon. They spent the morning unloading the supplies and carrying them to a hidden cave deeper in the forest.

"So what happened to you?" Liam asked when they made it back to their campsite.

"Well, after having more drinks than I wanted with our friends, they weren't going to let me leave. So I managed to get Zafir to start a fight. I've found that sergeants get pretty touchy after a drink or two. I had to knock a few heads before I finally got out. And Hamzah unknowingly donated the money for this," Corin produced an oversized flask. "I figured we should have something to celebrate with. The tavern's finest and infinitely better than what the Calorins insist on trying to destroy their mouths with."

His companions laughed. Martin took the flask.

"I'll drink to that," he said.

"So what now?" Trey asked. Corin grinned conspiratorially.

"I managed to overhear some interesting information at the tavern. How do you feel about stealing horses?" he asked.

CHAPTER 4

A month passed quickly after Corin entered the forest. He used the stolen Aredorian livery to adopt a uniform similar to his companions while retaining his weapons, vambraces, and sturdy boots. The three others in their small band began looking to Corin as their leader. Under his command, they held several more daring raids, carrying off more weapons and uniforms taken from Aredorian soldiers as well as food supplies. Using the cave as their base, the four outlaws planned their next raid.

"Most of the men working on the tower were part of the warband," Martin said, reporting after a scouting expedition.

"How many did you see?" Corin asked.

"I counted fifteen," Martin replied.

"At night, they're chained together out in the open by the walls with no more than four guards," said Liam, taking up the report. "There's a small fort not too far away. It's held by about two score Calorins."

"You think we can get them all out, Cor?" Trey asked. Corin nodded grimly. As he had traveled farther into Aredor, slaves working the fields had become a common sight. Anger flared inside him every time he had seen a whip raised, and he was now determined to end as much of it as he could.

"We're going to do our best," he said. "Let's break camp and head out. We can be there by dark."

They packed the necessary supplies on the horses that they had "honestly liberated," according to Martin, and headed south and east toward Darkan Village.

The village lay a short distance from the forest's edge. The tower was situated farther downriver. The fort housing the garrison had been built on the outskirts of the village. It was well in sight of the tower under construction. From the forest's edge, the outlaws watched the work progress on the tower.

"Most of them don't even look strong enough to make it back to camp," Trey said watching the slaves. Corin gritted his teeth as he saw the overseer lash out with a whip on the unprotected back of a young boy. Liam slid in beside them.

"We found a good place farther west from here. We should be able to hole up there for a few days without being found," he said. Liam led them back to the campsite. It was a small hollow protected by huge rocks that thrust from the ground. A small stream trickled nearby. Martin had unpacked the horses and lit a small fire. Corin glanced briefly at the sky. The sun would set in a few hours, and then they would begin.

Corin and Trey dressed in dark clothes. Corin strapped his scimitar to his back and buckled on his vambraces. Nearby, Trey was putting a finishing edge on his favorite weapon, a long dirk. He thrust the weapon in the back of his belt and buckled his longsword across his back. Nodding to Martin, the three of them moved out as Liam saw them off. He would remain at camp.

They set off, threading their way quickly and quietly through the forest. At the edge, Martin halted and wished them luck before melting back into the shadows. Corin and Trey drew their hoods over their heads and set off toward the tower, passing like ghosts across the open field and halting behind a low wall. The half-built tower loomed above them in the darkness. Crouching by the wall, they listened to the tramping of a guard as he made the rounds and the softer sounds of men breathing and chains clinking as they moved.

Trey picked up a small stone and tossed it over the wall. One of the prisoners sat up as the rock struck him. An owl hooted softly nearby. Shaking slightly, he sent back a dove call. In answer, a wolf howled, long and lonely. Trembling now in excitement, the prisoner turned to the man beside him and shook him gently. Seeing the look in his eyes, the man came fully awake. Within minutes, the whole line had been quietly aroused. Taking a glance at the guards dozing around the fire, the first man sent off another dove call. Seconds later, a dark figure dropped soundlessly over the wall next to him. A second figure followed shortly after.

"How many guards?" Corin asked the prisoner quietly.

"Three tonight," the man replied. Corin nodded to Trey, and they slid off into the darkness. A sudden noise from behind the tower alerted the guards. Two soldiers ran to investigate, carrying torches. The third came to check the prisoners. A shadow loomed behind him, and he fell without a sound. Corin dragged the unconscious guard over to the tower and bound him with rope. Gagging the soldier, Corin slipped something between the man's hands. Trey rejoined Corin, wiping off his long dagger. Motioning the prisoners to remain quiet, Trey produced a set of keys and began unlocking the chains. Rubbing his raw wrists, the older prisoner addressed Corin.

"Thank you, sir," he said.

"Time for that later," Corin said. "We've got to get all of you out of here by dawn."

Trey counted fourteen prisoners. *Martin must have miscounted,* he thought.

"Trey, take seven men back to Martin and then come back," Corin said. Trey nodded and, keeping a wary eye on the nearby fort, led the small band across the plain to the forest. Martin greeted them anxiously.

"Get them to the camp. Corin and I will follow with the rest," Trey said. Martin nodded and ushered the freed prisoners down the forest track.

Corin crouched with the remaining men as he waited for Trey to return. He found himself next to a young boy of seventeen. Corin recognized him from earlier that day. The boy was doing his best not to look anxious or frightened. Corin gave him an encouraging smile.

"It'll all be over soon," he whispered. "How's your back?"

"It really hurts," the boy admitted. His voice carried a strange accent. In the faint light cast by the fire, Corin could see a star-shaped tattoo on the boy's forearm under his tattered shirt. *He's a Braeton!* Corin realized.

"They seem to pay more attention to him because he's young," a man beside them said.

"Then Tristan stopped them one day, and they took him away. He's probably dead and it's all because of me," the boy said miserably.

"Where did they take him?" Corin asked.

"To those barracks," the man said. "They have some horrible prison down there."

"What's the easiest way to get inside?" Corin asked.

"You're going in there?" the man exclaimed. Corin nodded.

"I'm not leaving a man behind in captivity if I can help it. If Tristan's alive, I'll get him out," he said.

"The walls aren't very high, and they weren't built well, so you should be able to climb over. I don't know where the prisons are once you get inside though," the man said. "When are you going in?"

"Now," Corin said as Trey came around the wall. "They have a prisoner inside those barracks," he told Trey. "I'm going in to get him."

"It's too dangerous, Corin. Wait for a while," Trey argued.

"Your brother may not have much more time," Corin said. Trey turned pale.

"Tristan? He's alive?"

"Take them back to camp and I'll rejoin you as soon as I can," Corin said, his tone brooking no arguments.

"What if you're caught?" Trey asked.

"Give me four hours. If I'm not back by then, you can come looking for me," Corin said.

"I'm holding you to that," Trey promised. "Good luck."

"You too. Make sure to cover the tracks well. The whole garrison will be after us by dawn," Corin warned. He waited until Trey led the rest of the prisoners out on to the plain before he headed toward the barracks.

He circled around to the north wall. It stretched upward a few feet above his head. Two sentries patrolled the walls. Corin waited until the sentry above him passed and turned down the west wall, and then he began to climb. The rough stones gave him plenty of hand- and footholds. The sentry paused to talk with the other soldier at the western corner, allowing Corin to slip over the wall and on to the parapet below. Footsteps announced the return of the sentry. Corin rolled off the parapet, landing lightly on the ground. The sentry continued on overhead, ignorant of the intruder.

Keeping against the wall, Corin made his way around to the main building. The doors were unguarded, and he stepped cautiously inside. The only movement in the sleeping garrison was the torches flickering along the walls. Corin walked quietly along until the corridor branched to the right and left. He decided to take the right hallway first. His search proved fruitless, and he returned to go down the second corridor, at the end of which was a flight of stairs. Taking a torch from the walls, he descended into the dungeon. He found Tristan in the very last cell.

He was sitting hunched over, his arms around his knees. Tristan blinked at the sudden light.

"Who are you?" he asked hoarsely.

"A friend of your brother," Corin replied. Tristan's grey eyes flashed at the mention of Trey.

"Where is he?" Tristan asked.

"Once we get out of here, I'll take you to him," Corin replied. He found the keys hanging on a peg by the entrance. Taking them down from the wall, he unlocked the cell door and knelt by Tristan. Corin released the chain that shackled Tristan to the wall and helped him stand.

"Do I know you?" Tristan asked.

"It's been a few years. I'll explain everything once we're quit of this place," Corin replied. "Ah, it sounds like they've discovered some prisoners are missing," he said as a commotion broke out upstairs.

Orders were shouted as men ran to collect weapons and search parties were formed. Corin and Tristan remained hidden until the noise subsided. As they prepared to venture up the stairs, they heard footsteps coming toward them. Corin drew his scimitar. The guard saw a dark, hooded figure waiting at the bottom of the stairs and turned and ran. Corin sprang after him, felling him with a quick stroke. Tristan joined him and grabbed the guard's scimitar. Cautiously, they continued on. Voices alerted them to more soldiers coming down the hallway toward them. They quickly ducked into an adjacent passage as the soldiers hurried by.

Corin and Tristan made their way to the main doors as fast as they could. Cracking the doors open, Corin glanced outside. The courtyard was deserted, and the gates wide open. He looked at Tristan. His captivity was telling on him as he breathed heavily.

"Ready?" Corin asked. Tristan nodded, and they stepped outside into to the early morning sunlight and ran to the stables. A cry went up as they crossed the courtyard. They had been seen! Bursting into the stables, Tristan grabbed a bridle and put it on the nearest horse. Corin did the same, and then leaping onto the horses' bare backs, they clattered out of the stables. Surprised soldiers dodged out of the way as they charged through the courtyard and out of the gates. Horns sounded behind them. A signal was being sent to the other patrols. It wouldn't be long before the enemy was on their trail.

Back at the camp Trey paced restlessly. Liam and Martin exchanged helpless glances as they tended to the rescued prisoners.

"I'm going to look for them," Trey said as he picked up his bow and quiver.

"Take a horse, they might need one," Martin said. Trey grabbed the reins of one of their horses and rode out of the camp.

"He's still as stubborn as ever, isn't he?" one man said.

"Aye, Iwan. Only I think he might have gotten worse," Martin said. Iwan laughed.

"Who was the other man with him at the tower?" he asked.

"Our Captain," Liam answered, tying off a bandage on the young boy. "How's that, Kieran?" he asked.

"Better, sir, thanks," Kieran replied. "Do you think he got out with Tristan?"

"Most likely," Liam said. "He's not one to get caught easily."

"But who is he?" a man named Gavin asked.

"It'll be easier for him to explain when he gets back," Martin said. "It's been several years, and he's changed a little."

The captain in question was running into some difficulties. They had managed to dodge one patrol by sending the horses down one track and taking another. But Tristan had slowed considerably. He stopped and leaned against a tree, breathing hard and clutching his side. Corin helped him sit down for a moment. He saw a dark stain on Tristan's ragged shirt under his hand. Corin lifted the shirt, revealing a long, ugly wound along Tristan's ribs.

Angry red welts covered his back—punishment for interfering with the boy, Corin guessed.

"We need to keep moving. You think you can make it?" Corin asked.

"I'll try," Tristan replied. Corin helped him up and put an arm around Tristan to support him, and they started off again. They hadn't gone very far when a chilling sound rose behind them—the howling of hounds. The hunters were on the trail once more.

Trey heard the distant sound, and sickening realization hit him. He spurred his horse toward it. Corin and Tristan fled as quickly as they could as the sounds of the pursuit grew closer. Corin knew it wouldn't be much longer until they were caught. Relentlessly, he pushed on. Suddenly, a familiar cry rent the air, and Karif swooped down. Hope flared in Corin as the hawk was followed shortly by Trey.

He jumped from the saddle and ran toward them. Tristan fell into his brother's arms.

"I'll hold them off while you get him out of here," Corin said as the Calorins came into view on the path behind them. Trey didn't argue as he saw the battle light in Corin's eyes. He turned and half carried Tristan off the track and farther into the forest.

Karif perched on Corin's arm as he faced the oncoming soldiers. Corin drew his scimitar and prepared to fight. The two foremost soldiers were mounted. Leveling their spears, they charged. Karif launched himself in the air and flew at a horse, raking its face with his talons. The horse reared and screamed in pain as blood flowed from its nose. Corin threw a knife at the second horse, killing it and sending its rider tumbling to the ground. The foot soldiers hesitated a moment before charging him. Yelling a war cry, Corin plunged into the battle. Karif struck from the sky, and Corin dealt deadly blows. Then it was over. The few survivors fled and left the rest of the patrol wounded or dead. He watched them disappear, and then he cleaned and sheathed his sword. Whistling to Karif, he caught Trey's horse and headed wearily back to camp.

Trey and Tristan had fled with the sounds of battle ringing in their ears. Not long after, they stumbled into camp. Trey left his brother with Liam and ran to find Corin. He met up with Corin as he was leaving the forest path. Trey stared momentarily at the bloody path.

"Leave it," Corin said. "The other patrols will find them. It will be a warning to the Calorins. Aredor is rising. This is just the beginning."

The camp was quiet. Most of the men—having been cared for, fed, and dressed in clean clothes—had fallen asleep. Liam was bandaging Tristan's side as he sat wearily by the fire. Trey joined his older brother as they entered the dell.

"You hurt?" Liam asked, taking in Corin's bloodstained clothes.

"No, just tired," Corin replied. "Where's Martin?"

"He took Kieran out hunting. What happened with you?" Liam asked.

"He took on a whole Calorin patrol by himself, that's what happened," Trey said. "Eight dead. The rest fled."

"I wasn't completely alone. I had Karif with me," Corin said, sitting down and leaning against a log.

"Did you train him to fight, sir?' Gavin asked.

"No, I found him when he was hurt, and he's followed me ever since," Corin replied.

"Corin, this is Gavin, the best forester and tracker you'll ever find," Liam said. Gavin blushed slightly.

"I was raised at Lynwood Keep. I know almost every inch of this forest," he said.

"Well, I'm glad you're with us," Corin replied. Liam introduced him to the older warrior, Iwan.

"Prince Corin," Iwan said as he recognized Corin's name and his resemblance to the king.

"I haven't gone by that title in years," Corin said. "As far as I'm concerned, my brother can keep it."

"Fair enough, sir," Iwan said. "Young Liam here says you have a plan?"

"Aye, but it'll take more than twenty of us to drive the Calorins out," Corin said. "We'll free as many as we can and build an army in the forest. It might take years, but I won't rest until every last Calorin is gone from these shores and my father is restored to the throne."

"Give us weapons, my lord, and every last one of us is with you to the death!" Iwan replied, and his eyes shone with a fierce light.

CHAPTER

5

Three days later, they broke camp and left no trace that they had ever been there. Back at the cave, Trey and Martin handed out weapons. Martin picked up a large ornate war bow and quiver.

"Here, Flynn, miss these at all?" he asked. Flynn, tall and brawny with flaming red hair, took his bow.

"More than a little," he said. Inspecting it closely, he pronounced himself satisfied. Trey tossed him a long dirk, similar to the one he carried. Martin found a lighter broadsword, which he gave to Kieran. He also gave him the smaller Calorin bow.

"I don't think you'll struggle as much with these," Martin told him. Tristan found his sword. A large two-handed broadsword that he lifted with ease. Buckling it across his back, he thrust a dirk into his belt.

Outside the cave in a large open meadow Corin and Liam had fashioned a target. Flynn was the first to shoot. Carefully stringing his bow, he laid an arrow to the string and loosed. It hit dead center. Two more followed in quick succession with the same result.

"He's the best archer in the warband. I've never seen him miss," Trey told Corin. Flynn retrieved his arrows, and Gavin stood to shoot. Two of his arrows hit the center while the third missed by almost an inch. Grimacing in disgust, he drew his arrows from the target. And so it went on, each man firing three arrows with most hitting the target's center and the rest going just wide. Then the warriors moved to swordplay. Corin was satisfied with what he saw. They were well-trained warriors and were solid, trustworthy, and loyal. Martin stood with him watching the men spar.

"So what now, Captain?" Martin asked. A shiver of excitement ran down his spine as he saw a familiar gleam in Corin's eyes.

"I think it's time we planned our next raid," Corin said.

Lord Balkor was furious. Over the past month prisoners, weapons, horses, and supplies had gone missing. They would vanish into the forest without a trace. He paced the great hall of Kingscastle heaping scorn on his captains.

"Ten horses! How do ten horses disappear without leaving a hoof print?" His captains stood stoically, silent as he raged. "Just last week, five prisoners vanished, leaving only this." He held up a gray hawk feather. "Where do you think they are going, hmm?" One man shrugged.

"You idiot!" Lord Balkor screamed. "They are forming a rebellion in that blasted forest. Find them! Flood that forest and bring me those rebels and their leader in chains!"

Corin watched his opponent's blade. Suddenly, he lunged and gave a twist with his scimitar. His opponent's sword flew out of his grasp. The young man groaned in frustration as he retrieved his scimitar.

"Don't worry, Ian. You'll get it," Corin said encouragingly. Ian sheathed the blade.

"I don't know, Captain. That's the third time you've done that today," Ian said. Corin laughed.

"I'll show you how I do it tomorrow," he promised.

Liam and Gavin hurried toward them across the clearing. Men gathered unobtrusively as they reported to Corin.

"We went into Kingstown. Balkor's pretty upset with the way things are going," Liam said.

"He's ordered his generals out with a large force in order to get rid of us," Gavin continued.

"When?" Corin asked.

"They're to start tomorrow," Liam said. Corin glanced around the clearing. Over the past month, their numbers had swelled to two score men.

"We have most of today and all night to get something ready for them then," he said. "Martin, Tristan, Trey, pick nine men each. Liam, you're with me. Now here's what we'll do."

CHAPTER 6

The young Captain Farid rode out of Kingstown at the head of three score Calorins with orders to find and crush the outlaws in Dunham Forest. They rode down the Lynwood Track. Once in the forest, they would turn south and comb the woods. As soon as the troops were out of sight, two peasants left the town. Mounting horses, they circled well around the town and galloped off cross-country to the forest. They would arrive well before the Calorins.

"They've taken the Lynwood Track, Captain," Ian said. "We counted about sixty men."

"Trey, take your group and watch where they come in then send Kieran to report," Corin said. Trey saluted and headed off with his nine men.

Trey watched the Calorins ride slowly into the forest. They halted, and Farid ordered his men into position. Three abreast, they turned off the main road and on to a smaller path that led deeper into the forest. Trey signaled to Kieran, and the boy sped off through the forest. Halting by a pine tree riven by lightning, he gave a sharp whistle. Corin and his men stepped out.

"They turned south, Captain," Kieran said.

"Perfect. Tell Trey to follow behind them. Martin, cover to the east. Tristan, take the other side of the path. We'll split them three ways," Corin ordered. "I'll take my men and keep them coming south." Kieran saluted and ran off again.

The forest sheltered quiet animosity against the Calorins. Farid was nervous, feeling that they were being watched. The feeling grew the farther they rode into the forest. As they came around a bend in the path, Farid reined up sharply in surprise. A dark figure, hooded and cloaked, stood in the middle of the road. As Farid stared, a gray hawk swooped down to land on the man's shoulder.

"It's him! The Hawk. Get him!" Farid ordered.

Three men spurred forward. Corin stood motionless as they thundered toward him. Suddenly, the soldiers collapsed, pierced by arrows. A soldier behind Farid took aim, but before he could shoot, an arrow came whistling from the trees and wounded him. Farid ducked as the arrow shot by. When he straightened, the path was empty. A wolf howled somewhere to the right of the path.

"That's them! Follow the sound," Farid shouted.

Two dozen men rode off the path. Another howl sounded to the left. Farid sent twenty men after it. He continued cautiously down the path with the rest of his men. When they were out of sight, Trey and his men emerged on to the path. Taking the weapons and armor from the slain Calorins, they dragged them off the path to be buried later. Then they hurried off after the larger group of Calorins.

Farid and his men soon found their path blocked by a fallen tree.

"Shields up, weapons ready!" he ordered just in time as arrows flew out of the surrounding trees. Some arrows hit several horses and caused them to panic. Men dropped shields to control their steeds. More arrows flew. Seeing his men fall around him, Farid called a retreat.

The twenty men that had gone left from the path had picked up fresh tracks. They followed the footprints until they came to a river. They halted at the bank. A cry went up from one of the soldiers. A dark figure stood watching them from the opposite bank. A Calorin raised his bow. His companion knocked it away.

"Don't, you'll get us all killed!" he said. As they watched, the figure turned and melted into the woods.

"We can cross down here," another soldier called. Downstream, a large tree trunk spanned the river. Dismounting, half the soldiers ventured cautiously out on to the rough bridge. They had almost reached the opposite bank when it suddenly collapsed. Arrows zipped viciously out from the bushes to add to the confusion. Finally, the soldiers were pulled out of the water by their companions.

A Calorin sent an arrow flying over the river. An answering shot made him duck. Mocking laughter rang out as rustling in the underbrush marked the outlaws' departure. The Calorins tried to find their tracks to return to the path, but they were gone—completely erased.

The outlaws gathered back at their camp, exchanging stories. The Calorins that had followed Tristan's group had decided to fight back. Aided by Trey and his men, none of the Calorins left the forest alive. Corin pulled Martin, Trey, and Tristan aside.

"I think we should start a regular patrol. Each of us will keep the men we had today," Corin said.

"Where exactly would we be patrolling?" Tristan asked. Corin pulled out a rough map of the forest.

"Gavin and I worked this out. We marked three different routes, which means three patrols out and one at camp at all times. We'll circle through, spend about a week in each position, before moving on. Watch for Calorin patrols, keep an eye on the villages nearby, and there's always movement on the Lynwood Track," Corin said.

"So we're generally harassing the Calorins any way we can?" Martin asked.

"Exactly," Corin replied.

"Perfect. When do we start?" Trey asked.

"Tomorrow," Corin said.

They drew lots to see who would remain at camp first. Martin took the short straw. Tristan took his patrol by Darkan Village and Sentry Rocks. Trey took his band from the river to Lynwood Track, and Corin patrolled from the track to the border. In an effort to keep young Kieran out of the fighting, Corin made him a message runner between the patrols and camp. Gradually, life in the forest settled into a routine: patrols going in and out regularly, engaging the Calorins, aiding the villages, and raiding supply trains in or near the forest. They were only able to free a few more men before it became too dangerous. Lord Balkor was furious with the increasing resistance. He sent messengers back to Calorin, asking for more soldiers to "exterminate the outlaws."

CHAPTER 7

A lone rider crossed the border from Braeton into Aredor. A day later, the rider came to a large village. Dismounting, the stranger led its horse into the village while trying to keep behind houses and out of sight as much as possible. Halting by a large water trough that was sheltered by the stables, the rider pushed back its hood, revealing the features of a young girl no more than seventeen. She wore pants, tall riding boots, and a white shirt under a soft leather tunic. Light leather vambraces were buckled about her arms. A rapier was belted about her waist. Keeping in the shelter of the wall, she watched the townspeople go about their daily business while trying to ignore the Calorins lounging around the market square.

A woman walked past with a basket laden with ripe apples. A Calorin soldier stopped her rudely. Taking an apple, he bit into it and stepped aside to let the woman pass. As she did, he tripped her. The woman fell, spilling the contents of her basket everywhere. Laughing, the Calorin kicked the basket out of her reach. Seething with anger at this, the girl stepped out and began helping the woman. The Calorin knocked fruit from her hands.

"Who are you?" he demanded in broken Rhyddan.

"What's it tae you?" she replied. The soldier strained to understand her accented speech.

"How dare you address me like that! I am one of Lord Balkor's captains!" he said.

"I don't care who you are! You're just a big bully!" the girl snapped back. The captain raised a hand to strike her, but to his surprise, she knocked it away. Outraged, the Calorin drew his scimitar, and she drew her rapier in answer.

"Well, well, what have we here?" a new voice asked. They whirled to see a cloaked and hooded figure leaning casually on his long bow. All activity in the square had ceased at his appearance. Soldiers now jumped up, reaching for weapons.

"You!" the captain said.

"Well who else were you expecting?" the man laughed. "I can't let the girl beat you, now can I?"

"You will pay for that!" the soldier raged.

"Not today, I'm afraid. My men are everywhere, you'd be cut down instantly. Now, miss, if you'd be so kind as to come with me," he said. The girl grabbed her horse and joined the stranger.

"Start walking away. They'll figure out I've only got five men with me pretty soon," the man said in an undertone. Obediently, she began walking out of the village. A few seconds later, she was joined by the man. The Calorins watched them leave. The captain saw them break into a run and realized he had been tricked.

"After them!" he shouted.

Corin heard the shout and, slowing down, he gave a whistle. Five men galloped up leading his horse. The young girl mounted and they raced off to the forest.

"My name's Kara," said the girl, introducing herself. They had easily given the Calorins the slip and halted on a hidden track. "Thanks for helping me out of that mess." She spoke with the soft brogue unique to the Clans of Braeton.

"You're welcome," Corin said as he introduced himself. "Tell me though, Kara, why were you in the village?"

"I'm looking for my brother," she said. "I haven't seen him in three years."

"Where are you from?" Liam asked.

"Braeton. I crossed the border yesterday," Kara said.

"Can you prove it?" Corin asked. Kara unbuckled the brace on her left arm and pushed up her sleeve, revealing a six-pointed star with a *G* inscribed in the center tattooed on her forearm.

"I'm of Clan Gunlon," she said proudly. "As is my brother. My father was Aredorian. Our mother died when we young, and our father brought us up in Braeton."

"Why is your brother here?" Liam asked.

"Every year, my father would bring us here tae visit his family. Three years ago, I stayed home with my aunt tae help her with her baby. My father and brother went and never returned. We heard about the invasion and thought them dead. I convinced an old warrior tae train me so that I could come looking for them. And I...um..." here, Kara hesitated. "I ran away from my aunt three days ago, and now I'm here."

"Your brother," Corin said. "How old would he be now?"

"Seventeen," Kara replied. "We're twins."

"I think we might be able to help you then," Corin said.

"Really?" Kara said hopefully.

"Aye, but we have to finish our patrol first. We head back to the main camp in two days so you can tag along. Ian, take Kara to the crossed pines. The rest of us will continue on and be back tonight," Corin said.

"Yes, sir," Ian said. He led Kara off the path and farther into the forest. They rode in silence, each quietly sizing the other up. Ian had pushed back his hood and pulled down the mask bound about his lower face. He had dark hair, as almost all Aredorians did. Kind gray eyes gleamed above a nose sprinkled with freckles. He looked very young, only a few years older than she was. Unlike the rest of his band, he carried a scimitar. Summing up her courage, Kara asked him.

"Why do you have a Calorin sword?" Ian looked surprised at the sudden question, but answered.

"I tried using the broadsword, but wasn't very good with it. The captain had me try the scimitar. It's so much lighter and fluid feeling. He's teaching me, but I haven't quite mastered it yet," Ian admitted. "What about your blade? I've never seen one like it."

"It's called a rapier," Kara explained. "Our claymores were too heavy for me. The warrior who trained me found it and gave it tae me."

"You know, you're the first girl I've ever met to carry a weapon," Ian said. Kara laughed with him.

"My father always said I should've been a boy. I'm stubborn and wanted tae do whatever my brother did. It's gotten me intae trouble more than a few times," Kara said.

"We're here," Ian said. Kara stared in astonishment. Some force of nature had bent two pine trees to an angle at which they crossed each other. Ian dismounted and led his horse under the arch formed by the trees. Kara followed his example and came out the other side into a small clearing. Ian tethered his horse at the far end of the clearing. He watched Kara as she did the same.

She was tall for her age, slim and strong. Honey-brown hair was pulled back into a long braid. Some had escaped the braid and fell forward to frame an open face with green-blue eyes containing laughter ready to burst forth at any moment.

"I'm going to check our traps. You may as well come along," Ian said.

The first two snares were empty, and then they came to a small stream. Ian pulled at several hidden lines, flipping three fat trout up on to the bank. Resetting the lines, he turned to Kara.

"You ever gutted a fish?" he asked. Kara shook her head, and he pulled a knife from his belt and handed it to her. She took it, looking at the fish a little hesitantly. Ian grinned.

"Don't worry, I'm pretty sure they won't bite you," he said. Kara made a face at him and moved to pick a fish up. Still half alive, it flopped suddenly. Stifling a shriek, she jerked back. Ian tried in vain to stifle his laughter. Kara glared at him for a second and then began laughing. Splashing water at him she asked, "You going tae show me or not?"

Half an hour later, they left the stream and went back to the camp. Ian put the fish on a flat rock and built a fire. He began seasoning and cooking the fish as Kara picked blackberries from the bushes growing at the edge of camp.

Shadows lengthened as the sun began to set. Corin and his men arrived, and a short time later, they were joined by three more men. Kara was introduced to the new arrivals.

"We caught her telling off the captain in the village," Liam said.

"How'd Taysir take that?" one man asked with a grin. Corin laughed.

"You should have seen his face," he said.

"We found their outpost, Captain," the man said.

"Where?" Corin asked.

"Close to the border. It's fully armed and garrisoned. I'd say fifty soldiers. It's perfectly situated for striking into Braeton," he said.

"You think we could take it down?" Corin asked.

"Just us ten? Doubtful. But if we had another patrol with us, I think we could," the man said.

"It'd take too long for Martin to get here. We'll go early tomorrow morning and see if we can find a weakness," Corin said. Kara listened to this exchange, biting back questions. She wondered if she would be allowed to go along. The men were friendly enough but did not fully trust her. Ian tossed her an extra blanket as they bedded down for the night. She lay quietly watching the stars shine softly through the trees and listening to the quiet sounds of the sentry. Finally, she was lulled to sleep by the soft noises in the woods around them.

At dawn, the camp rose. Men moved about, saddling horses and drawing breakfast from their packs. Corin drew Kara aside.

"You'll come with us, but I have to know that you can keep quiet and take orders," he said.

"Yes, sir," Kara said.

"Good. Now, can you use a bow?" he asked.

"Aye, I can handle one, sir," she replied. Corin brought out a Calorin bow from a hidden place at the base of a tree. He handed her the bow and a full quiver and pointed to a large pinecone hanging from one of the pine trees.

"I know it's a small target, but do your best," he said as he positioned her across the clearing. Kara strung the bow and took aim. Sighting carefully, she released. The shaft sped across the clearing and pierced the cone.

"Now the one next to it," Corin said. Kara took aim at a much smaller cone. It also fell.

"Aye, you can handle a bow," Corin said. "Mount up!" he called. Kara settled the bow across her shoulder and mounted her horse. An hour's ride brought them to the Calorin outpost. Halting a short distance away, Corin left two men and Kara with the horses, and the rest slipped away to scout the fortress.

Corin and Liam circled and viewed the front of the small outpost. It was built from wood, and the walls were as tall as a man. They could see the movements of sentries through the loopholes cut into the walls. Two towers rose on either side of the stout gate. Calorins stood in the towers, watching the surrounding forest. The ground all around the outpost had been well cleared.

"They're learning," Liam said. "We won't be able to sneak up on them."

"We have to, or else Braeton goes down," Corin replied.

"Sure, and we were just thinking the same thing," a voice said behind them. Corin and Liam whirled around with swords drawn instantly. The stranger held up his hands.

"Don't be killing me just yet, lads. I have a feeling we might want tae talk," he said.

Corin eyed the stranger up and down. He was dressed in dark clothes. A green-and-black plaid cloak was thrown about his shoulders clasped by a silver brooch shaped like a stag's head. His left arm was bare and revealed markings. Two circles, one inside the other encompassed a *D* on his forearm. A stag reared majestically on his muscular upper arm.

"Who are you?" Corin asked.

"And I thought you would never ask," the stranger chuckled. "Dandin of Clan Dyson at your service." Corin and Liam sheathed their swords and introduced themselves. They knew they had nothing to fear from the clan leader.

"Call your men, Corin, and we can go somewhere safer tae talk," Dandin said. Liam whistled a signal, and within moments, they were joined by the rest of the patrol. Dandin turned and led them away from the fortress. Dandin eyed Corin curiously as they walked together. He didn't flinch when Karif flew in to perch on Corin's shoulder.

"So you're the one they're calling the Hawk?" Dandin said.

"That name seems to get around a bit," Corin said.

"We hear rumors of a man who leads a rebellion in the forest, determined tae drive the invader out. It's said wherever wolf howls or hawk cries, he appears," Dandin said.

"You seem well informed," Corin said.

"Never live in ignorance of your neighbors," Dandin replied. "We've been watching these Calorins for some time. It's pleased I am tae have met you now."

"How many men do you have with you?" Corin asked.

"About two score. I convinced my father tae let me watch the border and try and take down this outpost. It's too dangerous. The Calorins can sneak intae Braeton if we're not careful enough," Dandin said. With that, they arrived at the Braeton camp.

"Lads," Dandin announced, "I'd like you tae meet the men who've decided tae challenge the Calorin leopard." Introductions were made all around, and Corin and Liam joined Dandin and his captain in a large deerskin tent. Dandin produced a rough sketch of the Calorin outpost.

"How do you think we'll take it?" Brian, the captain, asked as Corin studied the sketch.

"We'd just get cut down trying to climb over," Corin said. "Unless we had a distraction."

"How big do you think, Captain?" Liam asked.

"I'm thinking the gates and these towers. We can fire the towers and knock on their gates a few times," Corin said.

"While the rest of us go over the back," Dandin finished.

"I think it could work. If we strike fast, we'll keep the element of surprise," Corin said.

"There's a great big oak that's gone and fallen not too far from here, my laird," Brian said.

"That'll do nicely," Dandin said. "See if we can find some smaller trees tae scale the back wall."

"Aye, laird," Brian said and left the tent. Dandin looked at Corin.

"I'll take half my men and attack the gates. You can take the other half, along with your men, and take the back. Make sure you let us in though. It's a fight I don't want tae miss," he said.

"Let me send my two best archers with you. They can take care of the towers and give us the signal," Corin said.

"Sounds grand. I'll go and tell the lads. They've been wanting a bit of trouble," Dandin said. He flashed an irrepressible grin and strode from the tent. Corin and Liam followed.

"I want Kael and Bran to go with Dandin. Once those towers are blazing, they can give us our signal," Corin said. As Liam went off to tell their men the plan, Corin found Kara.

"We're going to attack that outpost. I want you to stay well out the way, Kara," Corin said. He held up his hand to forestall any protest. "No, this fight could easily turn against us. I'm giving you an order, and I expect you to obey it," he said.

"Yes, sir," Kara submitted meekly.

Within an hour, the small force moved out, carrying with them three tree trunks. Kara remained behind along with the few men left to guard the camp. Corin and his men left their cloaks behind and moved their swords to their backs to allow for easier climbing. Corin and Dandin briefly clasped hands and wished each other luck, and then Corin led his men away through the forest. Dandin and his men crept forward, carrying the large oak tree. They halted a short distance away from the fortress and remained well hidden in the forest. Dandin watched as Bran and Kael kindled a small, smokeless fire. They wrapped several arrows in oil-soaked rags donated by clan members. Carefully setting these aside, they settled in to wait.

"You lads do this often?" Brian asked them curiously. A smile flitted across Bran's face.

"Attack outposts? Not usually," he said.

"We do a fair amount of ambushes and raids for supplies and weapons," Kael added.

"Sounds like a grand life," Dandin said. The men of Clan Dyson knew the ways of the forest and could appreciate the outlaws' stealth and cunning.

"Aye, lord, it is. Our captain knows what he's about. The Calorins are deathly afraid of the forest now," Kael said.

"But they've become smarter and more cautious. They've started travelling in greater numbers, which makes it more dangerous for us. But we trust the captain to come up with the best plan," Bran said.

"I've only known him for a few hours, but I'd gladly follow him intae battle any day," Dandin said. A curious cry went up; a hoarse birdcall ending in a screech.

"They're in position now," Bran said.

He and Kael fitted shafts to their bows and held them to the fire. Both shafts flew true, hitting near the top of the towers. They each loosed two more fire arrows as the sentries raised panicked shouts. Their next shots killed the sentries, allowing the flames to continue unchecked. Dandin signaled to his men. Sheltered under large wooden shields, they lifted the heavy battering ram. The Calorins threw ladders up against the walls, and standing on the upper rungs, they fired at the advancing men. When he gauged the enemy was sufficiently distracted by the ram pounding on the gates and the burning walls, Bran threw back his head and gave voice to the eerie wolf call. Then he and Kael turned their attention to the Calorin archers.

On the other side of the fortress, Corin heard the sound.

"That's us. Get those trees up against the walls," he ordered.

When they were well lodged against the wall, he loosened his scimitar in its sheath and scrambled up the nearest trunk. Pausing at the top, he glanced below. The back of the outpost was completely deserted. They were partially screened by a long building. He gave a sharp whistle and was quickly followed over the wall by the rest of his men. When they were all inside, weapons were drawn. Corin led the way around the building and gave another wolf call. The Calorins turned at the sight of the invaders and rushed to do battle.

Dandin halted the ram at the sounds of battle coming from inside the fortress. The blazing heat from the towers drove them back, and then with a great crash, one tower fell. Dandin ordered five men to make sure the fire did not spread to the surrounding forest, and then he directed one last assault on the weakened gate. They aimed their strength at the open corner of the gate. Under the weight of the ram, the still-burning gate was torn down. Dropping the ram, the men drew their claymores and, led by Dandin, threw themselves into the fray.

They came none too soon. Corin's men were outnumbered and had been forced back. Dandin and his warriors hit the Calorins hard from behind, turning the battle. It ended soon after. Those Calorins not dead threw down their weapons and surrendered. Under heavy guard, the prisoners were hurried out of the burning gates.

"The Calorins can bury their own," Corin said. "Let the fortress burn. It will take them longer to rebuild this way."

Dandin had lost seven men and more were wounded. Corin's small band had all survived though half went away bearing away wounds.

"Will you stay with us tonight, Corin? Tae celebrate and honor the dead," Dandin asked. Corin hesitated, looking at his men. A night's rest would do everyone good.

"Aye, we'd be glad to. Thank you," he answered.

"Grand," Dandin said.

By sundown, all that remained of the Calorin outpost was a smoking heap of timber. Dandin set his men to tying the prisoners together.

"You're to make your own way back to Lynwood Keep. Make sure you tell them that the Hawk sent you. Any other outposts will suffer the same fate," Corin told the Calorins.

"We'll be back no matter your threats," the Calorin captain replied. "Soon we will be more numerous than you can possibly imagine. As for him," he said nodding at Dandin, "He is marked for death for helping you. He and all his ragged band will suffer a traitor's fate!"

"He says you're a marked man and bound to die," Corin translated for Dandin. In answer, Dandin drew his claymore and laid the point against the man's chest.

"Tell him that if he ever shows his cowardly face here again, I'll not be as merciful. And tell him that the men of Clan Dyson do not fear death. We'll be waiting," he said quietly. Corin translated this to the nervous captive and then gave an order to his men. They drew their bows and aimed at the prisoners.

"Get going before we change our minds," Corin said. The prisoners stumbled off through the forest bound together in a line.

CHAPTER 8

Clan Dyson wrapped their dead in clean plaid cloaks and laid them on biers with their weapons. They would carry the fallen warriors back to their villages and bury them. As darkness fell completely, fires were lit and deer were roasted. Sweet cakes and breads were baked, and casks of dark frothing ale were broached. Men sat around the fires eating and drinking, relating many different tales of battles won and lost. Corin and Dandin sat together, watching their men and listening to the songs that were being sung. They sat in silence by the fire until one of Dandin's men began playing a haunting melody on his pipes.

"What is it?" Corin asked as the music filled the air.

"A lament," Dandin said. Then he began to sing softly.

> Where have they gone
> The men of Clan Dyson?
> We saw them ride out in the bright morn
> Fearless companions
> Sword brothers
> Forth they rode in the bright morn
> Tae face their mortal foe
> No news has come tae comfort those left behind
> What has become of them
> The warriors of the Stag?
> They met their enemy on the faraway plain
> The claymores flashed
> The bowstring sang
> They fought for doughty Laird and Clan
> No news has come

Where are they
The warriors of Clan Dyson?
For they fought and were slain
Tae return home tae the green woods never again.

"Harder than any battle is tae bury your men," Dandin said. "It goes deeper than any wound, and tae tell their families is worse than any torture."

"I'm afraid I'll find that out all too soon," Corin said. "We've been lucky so far."

"Aye, but from what your men tell me, luck has little tae do with it. They attribute it tae a rather cunning leader," Dandin said. Corin smiled faintly.

"If they really knew how much experience I've had, they'd change their minds," he said. Dandin saw, for perhaps the first time, how young his companion was.

"You've seem tae have done well so far," Dandin commented.

"I just have firsthand knowledge of how the Calorins move and fight. I spent three years fighting under a Calorin lord before I returned here," Corin explained.

"Returned? You were gone for while then?" Dandin asked. Corin merely nodded.

"Twelve years," he said.

"You're the lost prince? You were in Calorin for all those years then?" Dandin asked after a long moment. Corin nodded again, his jaw tightening. Dandin saw and understood what drove him against the Calorins.

"Most of my men know that I'm a prince. It's just that I was gone for so long and I've changed. That's why I didn't want to be anything other than a captain. I wasn't sure what to do. And now I have fifty men looking to me to do the best thing for them, and I'm afraid I'll let everyone down," Corin said. Dandin saw the uncertainty in his face.

"Don't underestimate yourself. You have everyone convinced otherwise," he said.

"My father used to say that if a commander showed any fear or uncertainty, his men wouldn't follow him. Fortunately, I have four extremely capable lieutenants that have been able to help me out. What would you do in my place, Dandin?" Corin asked.

"Trust my men and my instincts. Lleu put you here for a reason, and I've found that he usually knows what he's doing," Dandin answered after a moment.

"I hope so," Corin said softly. He hadn't confided his fear to anyone, not even to Martin. *Even if Emeth were here, I probably wouldn't have even told him,* Corin thought. But he felt he could trust the older, more experienced warrior beside him.

"When will you be leaving, Corin?" Dandin asked.

"Early tomorrow. We're due back at camp," Corin answered.

"Aye, and I'll have tae take a report back to my father," Dandin said. "I'll bid you good night then," With that, he strode off to see to the ordering of the sentries. Corin wrapped himself in his cloak by the fire. All around him men were doing the same, and soon sleep spread over the encampment.

"With your permission, my laird, I'd like tae keep an eye on the border," Dandin said the next morning. Corin noted his use of the title and smiled.

"Aye, gladly," he replied. "The Calorins will be back. They won't give up on Braeton easily."

"That's what I'm afraid of. I'm sending a message tae Clan Gunlon, and they'll watch the border tae the east. We'll be ready when they show their faces again," Dandin said. The mention of the other clan triggered something in Corin's memory.

"Lord Dandin, do you meet any of Clan Canich regularly?" he asked.

"Aye, they're our neighboring clan. Why do you ask?" Dandin questioned.

"If you could give a message to their lord for me. Tell him that his son, Aiden, is alive and doing well," Corin said.

"Sure, and he'll be glad tae hear it too, even though he doesn't show how much he misses the lad," Dandin said. "When did you see him?"

"We fought together in the south. He's the best warrior I've ever seen," Corin said.

"I'll be sure tae tell him then," Dandin said. "I think we'll be meeting again soon, Corin."

"There should always be a patrol in the area if you ever need anything," Corin said.

"Aye, and if Clan Dyson can aid you in any way, we'd be honored," Dandin returned. "Good luck tae you, Corin."

"Thanks, and to you, Dandin," Corin said, and then he and his men rode from the camp.

Kara rode toward the rear of the file. She found herself by Ian again.

"How long until we make it tae your camp?" she asked.

"We'll be there by nightfall," Ian answered. Kara grimaced at the thought of a whole day in the saddle, but it was not as tedious as she thought it would be. They met Martin's patrol around midmorning. Kara took an instant liking to the handsome, easygoing lieutenant. The men of the patrols conversed quietly as Corin and Martin exchanged reports. Ian introduced Kara to a young friend of his named Steffan. He explained Kara's story quickly.

"Well you don't have much farther to look for your brother," Steffan said. Excitement flared in Kara at these words, and she hardly listened to Ian telling Steffan about the battle. Shortly after, the two patrols parted and rode on. As the day continued, they avoided two large Calorin patrols on the main paths.

As Ian predicted, they reached the camp by sundown. They were greeted by Tristan and his men, who would leave the next morning. Corin explained Kara's presence to Tristan and gave him the more important news about the help they had received from the Braetons.

"One can never have too many friends. Balkor won't be too happy to hear that you met the clans," Tristan said.

"That's what I'm hoping. I'm worried though. Their captain hinted that Balkor might be expecting more troops," Corin said. Tristan rubbed his chin thoughtfully.

"Aye, that may be a problem," he said. "Trey is at Sentry Rocks. He might have picked up something."

"Kieran brought in his report yet?" Corin asked.

"Not yet, Captain. He should be in soon," Tristan said.

Kara stood shyly to one side. Ian showed her where she could stow her gear. As she finished untacking her gelding, a whistle went up, signaling someone's approach. Corin looked up expectantly as hoof beats sounded, and a lone rider cantered into camp. Kara bit back a cry as she saw the familiar figure. Kieran handed Corin a folded piece of paper and made his report. When he finished, Corin whispered something to him.

Kieran turned, and an astonished grin broke over his face when he saw Kara. He ran over to her, and she wrapped him in a fierce hug.

"What are you doing here?" Kieran asked.

"Looking for you," Kara answered.

"Lucky for you, I'm not hard tae find," Kieran laughed.

"I'm so glad you're safe!" Kara said to her twin brother. "What happened tae father?" Kieran's face fell at this question and suddenly Kara knew.

"No!" she whispered. Kieran only nodded miserably and held his sister as tears flowed down her face. He led her over to a secluded corner of the clearing where they sat and told each other what had happened since they had last seen each other.

"So what now?" Kara asked, watching the flames of the fire.

"I don't know, Kara. I feel like I need tae stay here," Kieran said.

"But I don't want tae leave you," Kara said.

"Me either," Kieran said. Then an idea began forming. "Maybe I can convince the captain tae let you stay for a while. It's too dangerous for you tae travel back home, or something like that," he said.

"Do you think he'll believe that?" Kara asked doubtfully.

"Well, it's partly true, and maybe I can get Liam tae help me tae convince him," Kieran said.

"Convince whom of what?" Ian asked as he walked up and handed food to both of them. They exchanged a look, and Ian was struck by how much they looked alike. They were the same height with the same honey-brown hair. Two pairs of mischievous eyes turned on him as they drew him into their plan.

Ian sat back after they told him. "You two are crazy" was all he said.

"Come on, Ian. She's my sister," Kieran said.

"Exactly. And if you wanted what was best for her, you'd send her home," Ian argued. Turning to Kara he said, "It's not a grand adventure out here. We could all be killed at any time, and you know that."

"I don't have tae fight," Kara said. "I can stay here at camp and help."

Ian relented a bit. He admired Kara's determination to try and stay with her brother.

"I'd try and get Martin on your side if you can," Ian said. "But in the end, you'll have to talk to the captain yourself."

"Good idea. Thanks, Ian," Kieran said gratefully, echoed by Kara.

Over the next few days, Kara made herself useful, gathering wood, caring for the horses, and helping with the cooking. Kieran left to bring back Tristan's first report. He would be gone at least two days. Kara watched him ride off down the path and gave a small sigh. She wanted to go with him, but she knew deep down that if she ever was allowed to stay, she would remain at camp. *I might as well get used to it,* she thought as she turned back to help Bran fletch arrows.

He was busy making new shafts for their longbows. Bran looked up as she sat next to him.

"Don't worry about your brother, missy. He'll blow back in before you know it," Bran said. Kara couldn't help but smile at the bowman's cheerful assurance. They had worked together for a few hours when Ian came up.

"I'm going fishing, Kara. You want to come?" he asked. Kara saw the mischievous twinkle in his eyes.

"Just as long as you don't let them attack me," she said as a smile tugged at her mouth.

"You have my word of honor," Ian replied, choking down a laugh.

"Oh, get out of here, both of you!" Bran said. Kara and Ian obediently ran off, laughing. Corin and Liam were sharpening their swords and watched them run by.

"What are you going to do with her, Captain?" Liam asked. Corin tested the edge of his scimitar.

"I don't know," he admitted. "She obviously wants to stay with her brother. I'll let her stay until we get back from our next run. I'll have whoever is here put her through some tests. If I let her stay, I have to know she can take care of herself," he said.

"You think she'll pass them?" Liam asked.

"Aye, I think she can," Corin smiled.

The day before they left on patrol again, Corin called Kara.

"I've decided that you can stay for now," he said. "I'll make a final decision when we come back in a few weeks. I still expect you to obey orders here."

"Yes, sir. I promise. Thank you!" Kara replied earnestly. After she was dismissed, she ran to find Kieran and give him the news.

"I'm going with them, for a few days at least," Kieran said. Kara's face fell. She would be alone at the camp with strangers. "Don't worry," he reassured her. "Martin and his patrol are coming in tonight. Just don't get caught in the tricks they play on each other."

Kara managed a smile. Any apprehension she still felt was dispelled when Martin's patrol rode in. Despite the bandages much in evidence, his men called out jovial greetings to their comrades. Martin remembered her and waved as he reported to Corin. That night, the usually quiet camp was filled with the good-natured joking and celebration for a safe return that occurred when the patrols met each other.

"Gavin and I are going hunting. You want to come along, Kara?" Martin asked a few days later. Kara was a little surprised, but readily accepted. Grabbing her bow, she followed the two men as they left the camp. Martin had deliberately picked Gavin to test Kara's knowledge and skills in the forest. Having grown up on the plains of Braeton, Kara was unfamiliar with some of the tracks and plants in the forest, but she was able to move quietly and stealthily through the woods. Gavin halted and studied fresh prints.

"Stag, sir. Shall we follow?" he asked. Martin nodded.

"Kara, see if you can show us where he is," Martin said.

Kara hesitated a moment, but a second glance at Martin showed that he was serious. She picked up the trail and moved after it as the men followed behind. They did not have far to go. Kara halted and pointed. The stag was grazing in between the trees ahead of them. With a smile, Martin indicated that she should try and bring it down. Slowly, Kara laid an arrow on her bow and took aim. Martin and Gavin did the same should she miss.

Her arrow took the stag high on the shoulder. As it tried to run away, Gavin sent another arrow crashing into its side. The deer staggered a few steps and then fell to the ground. Martin lowered his bow.

"Nice shot, Kara," he said.

"I missed my mark," Kara pointed out.

"True, but you're not used to that bow yet. Allow for some error at first. It was a good shot, all things considered," Gavin said, shouldering his bow as they went to retrieve the deer. Gavin and Martin brought the deer back to camp as Kara followed, covering their tracks.

"If you'll skin it, I'll cook dinner," Kara bargained.

"Fair enough," Martin laughed. "Steffan, get over here and help us!" he called. Most of the men pitched in throughout the afternoon as they cut the meat into thin strips and hung them over a low fire to dry.

Kara gathered potatoes, carrots, and various herbs as she heated water over the fire. An older warrior named Owain volunteered to help her. Gratefully, she accepted, and they chopped the vegetables and fresh meat for the stew. Kara found some flour and made biscuits, which she cooked on a flat rock over the fire and sweetened with wild honey. She was so busy that she didn't hear Kieran, just returned, sneak up behind her. She jumped as he grabbed her in a hug from behind.

"You're back!" she exclaimed as he released her.

"I smelled your biscuits cooking and hurried," he laughed. Kara punched his arm lightly.

"Lucky for you, I made plenty," she said. Martin came to get Kieran's report. They both deftly stole a biscuit, and Kieran dug into the pouch hanging from his shoulder before pulling out a piece of paper and handing it to Martin.

"Thank you, Kieran," Martin said as he opened it. After reading its contents he called, "Pack up, lads. Captain needs our help down at the rocks."

"When do we leave?" Gavin asked.

"Soon as we're ready and we eat," Martin replied. "Kara, you're coming with us too."

Within a short time, bags were filled and horses saddled. Gethin handed out food and doused the fire. Martin wrote a short note and left it where Trey would easily find it on his arrival.

"Where are we going?" Kara asked Owain as they rode.

"Sentry Rocks," the warrior answered. "Captain sent for us, which probably means a big patrol of Calorins, and we're the closest," he explained. Kara nodded in understanding.

Over the past two weeks, she had seen that the warband was held together by a system of message riders led by Kieran. He brought reports from the patrols to Corin and vice versa. Spies in the villages sent word of Calorin movements outside the forest. If any patrol was outnumbered, they would send to the nearest patrol for help. After months of the same routes, the patrol leaders knew instinctively who was closest.

They rode all night, only stopping briefly to rest the horses. By midmorning they reached Sentry Rocks and Corin's patrol. Before Darkan River flowed out of Dunham Forest, it split into a smaller river. This branching was flanked on either side by two huge rocks. The monolithic stones formed the boundary for a route run by the patrols. Upriver from the rocks was a shallow ford. Martin led his men across and on to a narrow deer track. They rode for an hour before they were met by Corin and his patrol.

"Well, Captain, what's the plan?" Martin asked.

"Bran and Kael were down at the port two days ago. Two ships are on their way in from Calorin," Corin said.

"More soldiers?" Martin asked grimly.

"Worse, they're Argusian mercenaries. They're fierce, savage warriors, and it'll easily double Balkor's fighting force," Corin answered.

"You fight them before, Captain?" Gavin asked.

"Aye, and I hoped I would never see them again," Corin replied.

"How are we getting rid of them?" Owain asked.

"Oh, you had to ask," Liam commented. The men smiled in anticipation. This usually meant the captain had been planning again.

"Mostly night attacks as they head toward Kingstown. We'll see if they're as superstitious as our Calorin friends," Corin said. "The ships docked this morning. We'll attack tonight."

CHAPTER 9

Corin and Martin stood at the edge of the forest watching the lights that marked the enemy's camp.

"I make it almost two hundred," Martin said. Corin nodded thoughtfully. Gavin and Liam led their horses up as the outlaws assembled.

"You all know the plan. Quick in and out, target the tents and picket lines. Make as much noise as you can to confuse them and be ready to get out of there on the signal," Corin said. Murmurs of assent came from the band. "Move out!" Corin ordered.

Sentries cried out warnings as they heard the rumble of hooves and saw the outlaws. Two guards ran into the camp but stumbled and fell as they were pierced by arrows. Argusians sprang from their tents, arming themselves only to meet the flashing swords of the outlaws. They tore through the encampment, slashing picket lines, scattering fires, and cutting down enemy soldiers. Martin and Bran grabbed torches from stands and fired two tents and then threw the burning brands into a loaded supply wagon. The eerie howl of a wolf cut the air, and suddenly, the outlaws were gone, leaving the Argusian encampment in disarray.

In the forest, the outlaws settled down for the night. Sentries were posted, and Corin called Kieran.

"I need you to ride tonight and bring Tristan here," Corin said. "Kara, do you think you can make it back to camp?" he asked. Kara thought carefully for a moment and then answered, "I think so, Captain."

"All right, ride back there. Trey should be there by now. Tell him to join us as soon as he can," Corin ordered.

"Yes, sir," Kara replied. She and Kieran mounted their horses and rode off together. After crossing the river, they parted ways. Waving farewell to each other, they galloped off into the forest.

"What were they?" the leader of the Argusian mercenaries asked the Calorin general with them.

"Aredorian rebels," General Kadar answered. "They hide in the forest, attacking any unsuspecting patrol. We call them the Hawk Flight."

"Hawk Flight?" Commander Jibril said questioningly.

"Their leader carries a hawk with him. They appear and disappear at will, almost as if they aren't human," Kadar said.

"Well, if your 'spirits' attack us tomorrow night, we'll be ready for them," Jibril said.

The outlaws watched the Argusian's progress all day. As night fell, the mercenaries began to set up camp. They drove their double-pointed spears into the ground around the encampment. Jibril set sentries to patrol around the inside of the barrier.

"We'll bring them out to us," Corin said as he watched the preparations.

"Once they're out of the camp, what's your plan?" Gavin asked. Corin looked to Martin.

"Did you see all those supply wagons last night?" he asked. A glimmer of a smile crossed Martin's face as he guessed Corin's plan.

"Aye, Captain. How would it be if, say, myself and a few others slipped in while the Argusians are off on a wild goose chase?" he asked.

"Who do you want?" Corin asked.

"Gavin, Kael, Huw, and Ian should do," Martin answered.

"Liam, you and Bran choose four men each. I want them going in as many different directions as possible," Corin ordered.

"Martin, they have some chariots with them. I want those disabled...permanently."

The sentries saw a movement in the darkness beyond the boundaries. Grabbing torches, they held them aloft, trying to see what it was. A hooded and cloaked figure stepped into the torchlight.

"Who are you?" the sentry asked. In answer, a hawk alighted on the figure's outstretched arm. Immediately, the sentries raised the alarm. Commander Jibril came riding up at the head of detachment of cavalry. Corin whistled, and Zephyr galloped up. Corin swung easily into the saddle as he heard Jibril order the pursuit. Sending Karif flying into the night sky, he gave the hawk cry. The howling of wolves answered him from the left and right. Liam and Bran were in position. He urged Zephyr on as the Argusians thundered after him.

Martin and his men circled around the camp. One by one, they quickly slid into the encampment. They could hear the sounds of pursuit as they made their way to the wagons. The camp was quiet; most of the Argusians had been deployed to chase the outlaws. Sliding under the wagons, they went to work.

Huw and Ian cut at the harnesses and lines. Kael loosened the fastenings of the axles. Martin and Gavin shaved the edges of the wheels down with their knives. Within a few minutes, all the wagons had been tampered with. They next turned their attention to the chariots the Argusians had brought with them. Martin inspected the light vehicles. They had seen the Argusians driving them throughout the day and were impressed with the skill with which the enemy handled them. He was reluctant to destroy the chariots, but now that he was closer, he could see how dangerous they were.

Light spears were stored on the sides within easy reach of the occupant. Razor-sharp blades were attached to the wheels and were meant to slice through oncoming infantry or cavalry. The outlaws again cut at the wheels, cutting at the axles so that when the wheels collapsed, the axle would break. Martin and Huw began weakening the floorboards. It took them longer to finish with the three chariots, but once they were finished, Martin was sure that they would never be operational again. Leaving them behind, the outlaws headed for the edge of camp. They had almost made it when they were seen. Within moments, they were surrounded.

"Steady, boys," Martin said as they drew their swords. "When I give the word, we go." His men gripped their blades as they readied themselves. "Now!" Martin yelled. Keeping tightly together, the outlaws cut through the line and out of the barrier toward their horses, hotly pursued by the Argusians.

Corin signaled his men to halt as they were joined by Bran and his men.

"Martin should be done by now," Bran said.

"Aye, let's get going. Owain, signal Liam," Corin said. Shortly after, Liam galloped up with his men in answer to Owain's signal.

"Let's go!" Liam gasped. "A lucky shot got Gethin in the arm."

"I'm fine, Captain," Gethin gritted out, but he swayed in the saddle.

"Bran and Liam, get going," Corin ordered as he saw the Argusians approaching. "All those with me, bows at the ready." His men quickly formed a line. "Two arrows each and then head for the forest," he said.

Bearing torches, the Argusians were easy targets for the outlaws. The front rank of the enemy went down under the aim of the Aredorians. The Argusian's ranks fell into confusion, which allowed the outlaws time to escape to the safety of the forest.

Martin and his men joined them shortly before reaching camp.

"Where's Ian?" Bran asked. Startled, Martin looked around. Ian was nowhere to be seen.

"He was right beside me when we got the horses," Kael said.

"And after?" Corin asked. Neither Gavin nor Huw could vouch for Ian's whereabouts.

"I don't like this, Corin. He could have been caught or injured," Martin said. Corin nodded grimly.

"Liam, take care of Gethin. The rest of you, form three groups. We're going to look for him," he said.

The first light of dawn crept over the horizon as the outlaws returned wearily to camp, emptyhanded.

"Corin, I'm sorry, it's my fault. I should've made sure that he was with us," Martin said. Corin wearily ran his hands through his hair.

"Tristan and Trey will get here soon. We'll make a plan before you start blaming yourself too hard," Corin said.

"Gethin's all right. He should be able to patrol again in a few days," Liam said.

"Good. How long do you think it will take them to get to Kingscastle?" Corin asked.

"Another day, maybe," Martin replied.

"Before you ask, I don't know what we're going to do," Corin said.

"Well, then sounds like we made it in time," Tristan said as he and Trey walked up.

"I never got a full story. Mind filling us in?" Trey asked. Corin outlined the events of the last two days.

"So if they've got Ian, we have to stop them before they get to Kingscastle," Tristan said.

"Aye. Only thing is, we're not sure where he is," Corin said.

"Let Trey and me go out and scout a bit. Fresh eyes, we might be able to pick something up," Tristan said. Corin nodded.

"Don't be gone too long," he said.

They were back in an hour with news.

"They've got him. I don't know what they've done, Corin, but he can hardly walk," Tristan reported.

"Balkor is supposed to meet them in the next village. They plan to execute him there," Trey said. "And General Kadar is with them."

Corin muttered a curse under his breath. Kadar was well known throughout Aredor for his cruelty. "Were you seen?" he asked. Tristan shook his head.

"It'll take them a while to get to the village. They seem to have some trouble with their wagons. Good work, by the way," he said to Martin.

"Aye, at the rate their going, it'll be dark before they get anywhere," Trey said. "The execution is set for tomorrow morning."

"Well, that gives us some time," Corin said. "Anyone know that village?" he asked. Two men stepped forward.

"Aye, sir. We were both raised in that village. What is it you need to know?" Huw asked.

Lord Balkor dismounted and strode into the house where Jibril and Kadar awaited him.

"Ah, Commander Jibril. An eventful journey, I hear," Balkor said. Jibril bowed.

"Yes, the rebels gave us trouble, but we got something out of it." He signaled to one of his men, and a bound and bloody young man was dragged forward. Balkor surveyed Ian dispassionately.

"Kadar, I'd recognize your handiwork anywhere. Did he talk?" he asked.

"Not yet, my lord," Kadar replied. Balkor went over to Ian and forced his head up.

"Still plenty of spirit," he said. Then switching to Rhyddan he spoke to Ian. "No rescue attempts yet. You know, I'm a little disappointed in your captain. Doesn't he care enough to fight through my mercenaries to free you?" he asked.

"He will, and when he does, he won't be hiding behind his soldiers like you," Ian answered defiantly. A spasm of anger flickered across Balkor's face.

"Make sure his last night is comfortable," he ordered Kadar. A cold smile crossed Kadar's face. Ian closed his eyes and steeled himself for what was to come.

"Trey and Martin, you'll get Ian out of there and take him to where Bran and Liam will have the horses. They'll have a small force to make sure you get away safely. Flynn, take ten archers and cover from the roofs. Tristan, you and I will provide the distraction," Corin said.

"How are we getting him out?" Trey asked.

"Huw and Aneiran are getting your uniforms now," Corin said.

"Here, I worked on this. It'll discolor your skin more permanently so you'll look like a Calorin. Don't worry, it'll wash right off," Liam reassured them as he produced a flask.

"We're taking him right up on to the scaffold, aren't we?" Martin asked.

"Yes, that's where Tristan and I come in. With Flynn and his boys, there should be enough confusion to get Ian out safely," Corin said. They reviewed the plan once again to make sure every man knew his part. "Get ready. We leave in an hour," Corin said.

"Is everything prepared?" Balkor asked.

"Yes, my lord. I've made sure the townspeople are assembled to watch the execution," Kadar answered.

"Good. This will discourage any further talk of rebellion," Balkor said.

Martin and Trey, disguised as Calorins, walked into the prison.

"We're here for the prisoner," Trey said in Calorin.

"The one to be executed?" the jailer laughed. "You'll have to carry him out most likely. Kadar was here most of the night."

Martin muttered something unintelligible under his breath.

"Well, he doesn't have far to go, does he?" Trey returned carelessly. The jailer laughed again.

"Right this way, boys," he said, leading them to a cell. "Let me know if he tries anything funny," he said, unlocking the door. Trey gave him a nod as Martin went in. Ian was slumped against the far wall. Kneeling beside him, Martin gently laid a hand on Ian's shoulder.

"Ian," Martin called softly. Ian's eyes opened, and he turned to face Martin. His face was bruised and bloody.

"Lieutenant? What…?" he said.

"We're getting you out of here. Can you walk?" Martin asked. Tears welled up in Ian's eyes as he shook his head.

"I'm not sure if I can. They hurt my leg," he said. Trey knelt by Martin.

"We'll help you. Come on, lad. Let's start by standing," he said. They slowly helped Ian stand, and holding firmly on to his arms, they helped him out.

Martin and Trey stopped before entering the town square. It was full of people and Calorin soldiers mixed with Argusian mercenaries. Martin took a quick glance around and caught a slight movement on a nearby roof.

"Looks like we're all in position," he said quietly to Trey.

"All right. Hold on Ian, it'll all be over soon," Trey said to Ian. He only nodded numbly, trembling with the effort of holding himself upright. As they pushed through the crowd to the scaffold, a woman caught sight of the prisoner.

"No, Ian, my son! No!" she cried trying to push her way toward him. A Calorin soldier grabbed her and held her back. Martin and Trey exchanged a grim look. The plan had to work now.

Balkor waved the crowd to silence as the two "Calorins" brought Ian up to the scaffold.

"Today, you are to witness the execution of one of the rebels who fights against my authority," Balkor said in Rhyddan. "Let this be an example to any who think that the so-called Hawk Flight can prevail against us. One by one, we will hunt them down and kill them all!"

"Then why don't you start with me?!" a voice cried. Heads turned to see the newcomer. He had a hood pulled over his features and sat astride a black stallion. A gray hawk perched on his shoulder. "Or are you too cowardly to go against a warrior who can fight back?" Corin called mockingly.

"Not so fast, Hawk! I have one of your men here!" Balkor replied.

"Do you?" Corin asked. Balkor turned around. The scaffold stood empty. Corin laughed.

"Would you like to try your luck with me?" he said.

"Get after him!" Balkor yelled, outraged. Soldiers ran towards Corin only to be met by arrows from Flynn and his men. Villagers fled in panic as Argusians marched forward. Corin gave a sharp whistle. Flynn and his men slid down from the roofs and took their place behind him.

"Two volleys then retreat," Corin ordered. He and Zephyr stood fearlessly as the enemy advanced on them.

"Fire!" Flynn called from behind him. The front rank of Argusians fell. Snapping shields in place, they deflected the second volley. Corin stared at Balkor. He longed to charge forward and avenge himself. He wheeled Zephyr sharply and cantered after his men. Balkor sent his men pouring after them.

"Ready, Tristan?" Corin shouted as he made it out of the village. Tristan and his ten men waited on their horses for Corin.

"Aye, Captain!" Tristan replied with a grin. "Get ready, lads. Here they come!"

Martin and Trey had dodged under the scaffold and pulled Ian with them when Corin appeared. Crouching under the scaffold, they waited until Balkor sent his troops after the outlaws. Martin took off his cloak and threw it around Ian as Trey cut his bonds. Ian drew the hood of the cloak over his head. Martin picked up a fallen scimitar and handed it to Ian.

"Just in case," he said. Helping Ian up, they walked through the square, which was still in a state of confusion. The crowd drew away from the drawn scimitars of the supposed Calorins. In the panic, no one noticed that one of them could hardly walk.

Safely out of sight from the square, Martin sheathed his sword and grabbed Ian, who was now on the verge of collapse. He half carried, half dragged Ian along. Trey hurried alongside them.

"Halt! Where are you three going?" a Calorin soldier called behind them. Trey turned and, confident in his disguise, replied to the leader of the patrol.

"Wounded soldier, we're taking him back to the barracks," he said.

"How did he get hurt?" the soldier asked.

"Arrow wound in the leg," M.artin replied in Calorin. The soldier looked suspiciously at Ian, supported by Martin.

"Hold on!" the soldier said. He threw back Ian's hood. "It's the outlaw!" he cried. Ian grabbed a knife from Martin's belt and stabbed the soldier. Seeing their leader fall, the patrol moved to attack.

"Martin, get Ian out of here! Bran's not too far off. I'll cover you!" Trey yelled.

Martin hurried Ian through the houses. Bran and his men saw them coming and moved to meet them. Liam pulled Ian up in front of him as Martin ran back to help Trey. He made it just in time as Trey was backed into a corner. He fought over to Trey's side, and together, they cut their way free.

"Go! Go!" Trey yelled as they came in sight of Bran and his men still waiting. Turning again, they fought off the front rank of Calorins. Bran remained with horses for them. Martin and Trey threw themselves on to the horses and galloped off after their retreating companions.

Corin ordered his men to fall back as the Argusians and Calorins pressed inexorably forward. The enemy soldiers were now using their own bows. An arrow zipped by Corin's head while another found its mark in the arm of the man next to him.

"Split up! Head back to the forest!" Corin shouted. Dodging more arrows, the outlaws turned and galloped out of range and back into the welcoming shelter of the forest.

Chapter 10

The campsite was sheltered by large rock outcroppings by Darkan River. Bran and his men were first to arrive. They were greeted by the few men who had remained behind. Gavin helped Ian down from in front of Liam and carried him to a small, dry cave. Liam followed to tend to Ian.

All morning groups of men trickled back into camp. Corin and Flynn were last to arrive. They had followed Balkor's force to make sure that the camp wouldn't be found. Martin and Trey, now washed and dressed in their own uniforms, sat with Tristan by the fire. Steffan took Zephyr from Corin, who then sat down beside them.

"The fearless leader of the Hawk Flight returns," Tristan said. Corin laughed as he unbuckled his scimitar.

"You heard that," he said.

"Everyone did," Trey said. "The lads like it."

"Well, I guess we have a name then," Corin said.

"It's a good name for Aredor's last warband," Martin said.

"The Calorins must think we're here to stay for a while if they've gone through the trouble of naming us," Corin said.

"Just as long as they don't bother us for the rest of the day," Martin said, stifling a yawn. "It's tiring work trying to save Trey from every angry Calorin."

"You didn't seem to have a better idea," Trey retorted as Corin and Tristan laughed.

"Still, you sounded pretty convincing," Martin said.

"Thanks, you weren't half bad yourself. I didn't think you knew Calorin," Trey said.

"I picked up a little here and there. And I did pay attention sometimes during lessons, contrary to popular opinion," Martin said.

"How's Ian doing?" Corin asked.

"Not so good. Liam's been in with him for a while," Tristan replied.

"We'll stay here for a few days then," Corin decided. "We could all use a rest."

It was early evening when Corin visited Ian.

"How are you feeling?" he asked. Ian pushed himself into a sitting position.

"All right, I guess, sir. Liam bandaged me up pretty well," Ian said.

"I'm sorry you had to go through that," Corin said.

"I didn't tell them anything," Ian said.

"Good man. Get some rest now, you still look awful," Corin said. Ian grinned a little crookedly.

"Captain?" he stopped Corin as he turned to leave. "Thanks for coming after me."

"You're welcome," Corin replied. "Sleep. That's an order."

"Yes, sir," Ian replied.

Over the next few days, Tristan and Martin tested Kara's skill with a sword, and Flynn supervised archery lessons.

"I think she'll do all right in a fight," Tristan reported to Corin. He knew that coming from Tristan, that was high praise, and then he turned to Flynn.

"She's better with the bow than some of the men," Flynn gave his verdict.

"I vote she stays just because she can cook," Martin said. Liam passed by at that moment.

"Aye, anything is better after two years of Trey's cooking," he called. Trey laughed sarcastically as he threw an apple core at Liam. Those within earshot smiled as their lieutenants and captain burst into laughter.

"All right then, she can stay. We could use another runner," Corin decided.

"What about her family, sir?" Flynn asked.

"I'm sure Dandin can get something to her relatives. They'll be wanting news of Kieran too," Corin said.

Trey and his patrol were last to leave. Martin and Tristan had already left to head back on patrol. Corin had ordered them to stay for two weeks on the same route, and then they would all return to the main camp. Corin and his men remained behind at the rocks, waiting for Ian to fully recover. Kieran took Kara on his message runs, teaching her the different routes to take. Twice they had to outrun Calorin patrols in the forest. The outlaws became used to seeing her and accepted her as one of the "lads." Under the care of Liam, Ian gradually recovered his strength. His leg healed seamlessly, and he could walk without trace of the injury. The two weeks drew to a close, and the Hawk Flight prepared to return.

Two hooded figures stole through the village in the pouring rain.

"It's that one, Captain," Ian said, pointing to a house across the street. Corin nodded and they quickly crossed the street. Ian knocked gently on the door. He pushed back his hood as a woman opened the door. She gave a small cry and gathered him in an embrace.

"Siana, what's wrong?" a man asked.

"It's Ian!" his mother answered. "Come inside quickly, both of you before you're seen." She shepherded them both inside. The man rose from the table to greet them.

"Ian?" he exclaimed. Ian crossed quickly over to greet his father.

"Father, this is our captain, Prince Corin," he said. Corin moved forward and clasped the father's proffered hand.

"Thank you, sir, for everything you've done," he said. Further talk was interrupted when an adjacent door was flung open, and several small figures tumbled out. Three young girls flung themselves on Ian, forcing him down into a chair. A young boy of about fifteen years followed more sedately. Corin and Ian's parents laughed as he tried to sort out the questions being thrown at him all at once. Siana laid her hand on Corin's arm.

"Thank you for bringing him here," she said.

"We thought it would be good for him to see you, especially after what happened," Corin said.

"Aye, we thought we had lost another son," Siana said. Her husband wrapped a comforting arm around her.

"Our oldest son was killed in the invasion," he said.

"I'm so sorry," Corin said. "I was asked if you could tell Catrin and Eilwen that Huw and Aneiran are alive and well."

Siana nodded with a smile.

"Now, I think I might have some news for you, sire," she said. "Only a few know this, but the princess Amaura is hiding in Kingscastle under Balkor's very nose!"

"How?" Corin asked.

"You wouldn't think to look for a princess among the castle servants, would you?" she asked. Corin laughed a little at the irony.

"My sister lives in Kingstown. Her daughter was sick, so I went to help her," Siana explained. "While I was there, the princess brought some food for the girl. My sister knew who she was and accidentally let it slip, but I haven't told anyone else."

"Thank you. It seems I'm now in your debt," Corin said. "But I'm afraid we need to go."

Farewells were said, and Corin and Ian slipped out into the rainy night and disappeared.

Kara took the oath of service before the entire Hawk Flight. Corin handed her a leather pouch similar to the one that Kieran carried. It contained parchment and ink that would serve her as a runner. Later, Martin gave her a hunting knife with a handle fashioned from the stag's antler complete with its own sheath. Her oath taking gave the outlaws a reason to celebrate. It was a simple affair out in the heart of the forest, but after months of patrolling and fighting, it seemed like a grand feast.

That night, Corin found Gavin.

"It'll be winter soon. We need a more sheltered place to make camp," Corin said.

"I think I know of a place, sir. We'll go tomorrow morning. It's not too far from here," Gavin said.

True to his word, Gavin rode out early the next morning with Corin, Trey, and Liam. The air was crisp and cool, and the trees were brilliantly colored in red, orange, and yellow hues. He led them toward the Darkan River as it curved through the middle of the forest. Finding a shallow ford, they crossed and turned upriver. They did not travel far before Gavin stopped.

"We're here," he said. He had brought them to the mouth of a cave situated a short distance from the riverbank. A small stream flowed from the cave and fed into the river. Gavin passed out the torches that he had brought along. Striking flint to steel, he lit the torches and entered the cave.

The interior of the cave was small and sandy. The stream rushed past coming from some source far underground in the caves. Gavin, however, was not interested in the stream. He walked to the back of the small cave. In the torchlight, Corin saw an irregular fissure in the wall. Gavin pressed through the opening, and after a moment's hesitation, the others followed. When they came out the other side, they found themselves standing in a large, dry cavern.

The ceiling was visible in the torchlight as they began to explore. Several smaller caves opened up from the main cavern.

Toward the back, the floor sloped down into another large room. As Liam walked around the main cave, his torch flickered, and he caught a breath of fresh air. Following the draft, he came to the back wall. Looking up, he saw an opening partially obscured by the bushes on the top of the caves. The wall inclined up toward the opening worn by rainwater flowing through the hole. Trey came over to join him. Wedging the torches into cracks in the wall, he boosted Liam toward the opening.

Liam scrambled the last few feet and heaved himself through the hole. He found himself standing on top of the caves. From there, he could see above the surrounding trees. To his left, the Darkan River flowed by, partially obscured by a thick belt of trees. Turning around, he saw a valley that had been formed when part of the caves had collapsed years ago. Immediately around him, the top of the caves were covered in thick bushes and small trees, providing plenty of cover.

Meanwhile, Corin, Gavin, and Trey had exited the caves and had walked around to find him. When he saw them, Liam descended quickly and easily from his vantage point and joined them.

"What do you think?" Corin asked.

"We'd all fit inside with plenty of room to spare. We have our own supply of running water as well," Trey said.

"I agree. We can have two entrances easily enough. There's a valley nearby where we can keep the horses," Liam said.

"Well then, I don't think we should waste any time," Corin said.

Over the next few days, the Hawk Flight moved into the caves. The smaller adjoining caves were used to store weapons and food supplies. The second cavern where the men slept and kept their own possessions was jokingly referred to as "the barracks." A curtain was hung over a small alcove for Kara. Steps were carved into the floor to give easier access between the two main caves. A sturdy ladder was constructed and placed by the hole in the ceiling for use of the sentries.

After the outlaws had settled in, the patrols went out again. Corin, Liam, and Bran went to Kingstown to test the truth of Siana's story.

CHAPTER
11

It was market day in Kingstown. Amaura hummed a tune as she left the castle. Once she passed the guards at the gates, she began swinging her basket. Two years ago, she never would have imagined that she would be buying food for the castle cooks. Pushing thoughts of her past life aside, she descended into the bustling marketplace. As she moved through the crowds, someone stumbled against her, almost knocking her over.

"Pardon, my lady," he murmured as he steadied her. Amaura stared after the dark-haired man as he moved off without a backward glance. She followed him and he led her into an alley behind a stall.

"Who are you and how do you know me?" she demanded.

"I'm here with someone who wanted to find you," he replied.

"You fought in the warband, didn't you?" she asked, vaguely recognizing him.

"I still do, my lady," he said.

"You mean the Hawk Flight? What are you doing here? It's too dangerous!" Amaura exclaimed. Bran merely smiled.

"Like I said, ma'am, we wanted to find you," he said.

"Who did?" she asked again. Bran gave a low whistle. A few moments later, they were joined by two more men. Amaura didn't know the darker-haired man, but the other looked strangely familiar. She watched him speak to the others for a few seconds, giving them some orders. Bran and Liam disappeared back into the town to see if they could find any more useful information.

Amaura found herself looking into the man's piercing blue eyes as he turned toward her, and suddenly she knew.

"Corin?" she whispered softly.

"Maurie," he used her nickname. Sobbing, she flung her arms around him.

"I knew! I knew you weren't dead!" she said. Corin held his sister gently.

"I missed you so much," he said. "You didn't give up on me?"

"No, you always took care of me. I just wouldn't believe you were gone. And now I can't believe you're here!" Amaura said, smiling through her tears.

"How are you doing?" he asked.

"Better now," she answered, drawing a deep breath. "Have you found anyone else?"

"Not yet. Amaura, we can get you out of here, right now. We have some friends in Clan Dyson. They could take you in," he said. Amaura thought for a moment.

"No, I'll stay here. I'm in the castle, maybe I can help you," she said. Corin smiled.

"You haven't changed much, have you?" he said.

"I've grown up," she said. "You're different than I remember. What happened?" she asked.

"It's a very long story. Maybe I'll tell you, one day when we're free again," he answered.

"Do you really think that will happen?" she asked hopefully.

"One day. Do you think you could do something for us?" he asked hesitantly. "It might get dangerous."

"I don't care. What do you need?" she asked.

"I need you to keep a lookout for any news of Father or Darrin. We need to find them," Corin said.

"I'll do my best," she promised. "But I should go. They'll begin to miss me soon." She gave Corin one last hug.

"You be careful," Corin said.

"I will. Be safe, Corin," she replied and then she was gone back to the castle while he returned to the forest.

As the weeks passed, the air grew colder and colder. Ice began crusting the streams and rivers. As the first snow began falling, the outlaws stayed close to the caves. The Calorins were still unused to the bitter winters of Aredor, so they seldom ventured out from their castles and keeps.

The outlaws set about making the caves more homelike. Rough tables and benches were built and set in the main cave. As captain of the Hawk Flight, Corin was quartered in one of the small rock chambers that opened off the main cavern. A natural ledge ran around the cave. It was there he kept his few belongings and slept on a pile of blankets and deer skins. The ledge also provided a perch for Karif, who hated being apart from Corin.

With Calorin movement lessened by the heavy snows, the Hawk Flight began roaming farther into Aredor, searching for any word on Darrin or the king and queen. By midwinter, they got it. Tristan brought Corin a piece of paper after coming in from a patrol.

"Rhys gave me this down in Carnedd. He said it came from someone in the castle," Tristan said. Corin scanned the paper.

"It's from Amaura. She says she's found Darrin," he said. A murmur ran through the men gathered in the cave.

"Does she say where?" Trey asked.

"No," Corin said, handing the paper to Trey.

"How do we know it's not some trick by Balkor? We'd walk right into a trap," Trey said as he read the short message.

"Well, I guess we pay Amaura a visit," Corin said.

A wagon rumbled slowly down the road toward Kingstown. Two young men sat in the back atop the sacks of grain.

"Do they always demand so much, Pryce?" Corin asked the old man who drove the cart. He and Trey had exchanged their uniforms for the rougher clothes of the villagers.

"Aye, my lord," Pryce replied. "If we do not deliver the correct amount, the Calorins come and take what they want by force."

"How often do these wagons go in?" Trey asked.

"Once every month, sir," Pryce said.

"Do you still have enough to eat in your village?" Corin asked.

"We live, sire," Pryce answered. "It's hardest on the little ones."

All talk ceased as they rolled up to the gates. The guards recognized Pryce and waved him through. Corin and Trey sat silently with heads bowed as if they were weary, subdued peasants. When they reached the castle, the steward came out to count the bags in the wagon.

"Unload it, and take it to the storeroom," he ordered when he finished the tally. Corin and Trey descended from the wagon and pulled bags of grain down. Slinging them over their shoulders, they followed a soldier to the storerooms.

Amaura was making her way from the kitchens to the courtyard when she stood aside to let two men pass by, burdened by heavy sacks. She stifled her surprise when Corin gave her a smile and a wink. She loitered in the hallway until they came back.

"What are you two doing here?" she whispered.

"You sent us the note?" Corin asked.

"Yes, he's in the dungeon here," she said.

"How did you find out?" Trey asked quietly.

"I overheard some guards talking about an important prisoner, so I managed to be the one to take food down to the cells and I saw him," Amaura said.

"Do you think you can safely get a message to him?" Corin asked.

"Yes, I think so. Are you going to get him out?" Amaura inquired.

"It's too dangerous right now with all the Calorins here. We'll make a move when spring arrives," Corin replied.

"Cor, someone's coming," Trey warned as footsteps sounded in the corridor behind them. Corin handed Amaura a slip of paper.

"For Darrin," he whispered and then they walked back to the courtyard where Pryce waited in the wagon.

The rest of the winter passed quietly. Corin began planning. They would need the best plan to get Darrin out of the heavily guarded Kingscastle. As the winter snows began to melt, Corin began sending the patrols out again. They brought back reports of hardship in the smaller villages. The winter and Calorins had been especially hard on them. The outlaws shared their supplies where they could and brought in fresh meat from the forest. The days finally grew warmer, and Corin began putting his plan into action.

CHAPTER 12

"You sure about this, Captain?" Liam asked.

"No," Corin replied with a grin. He stood in the small chamber, stripped to the waist, rubbing the paste into his skin. When he finished, his whole upper body, face, and hair were turned a dark brown. Liam sighed again and began handing Corin the rest of his uniform.

"And you're sure you're going in alone?" Liam asked as Corin finished fastening the last buckle on the uniform. Arming himself with weapons taken from their store, Corin stood ready. Liam had to admit that he looked the part. Martin pulled the curtain back and entered the room. He paused for a moment; Liam stood in the room with a Calorin.

"If I didn't know any better, Corin, I would've run you through," he said.

"Then this might work after all," Corin said.

"Seeing as this is more reckless than your usual plans, I hope so," Martin said. Liam voiced his agreement as he handed Corin a helmet.

"I guess I have a reputation to keep up," Corin laughed.

"Your horse is outside. The sooner you leave, the sooner you come back," Martin said. They made their way outside where Steffan held a bay stallion saddled and bridled. Corin donned the helmet and mounted.

"Right, with luck, I'll be back tomorrow afternoon with Darrin," he said.

"Be careful, Corin," Liam said. Throwing them a salute, Corin spurred his horse forward and made for the Lynwood Track. Late afternoon saw him riding through the gates of Kingscastle.

Corin strode down a corridor and descended the steps into the dungeons. No guards were in sight. Coming to the third cell, he stopped. The occupant of the cell looked up as he approached.

"What do you want?" he asked in Calorin.

"I want to get you out of here," Corin replied in Rhyddan. Darrin eyed him sharply.

"You're the one?" he asked.

"Aye, I'll be back later. Will you be able to ride?" Corin asked.

"If it means freedom, I'm strong enough to do anything," Darrin replied.

"Good. Be patient for now. I'll come back before dawn," Corin said. Darrin watched him leave. He had received a note midwinter telling him to watch for someone to come in the spring. Reluctantly, he settled back down. He had waited this long; he could wait until dawn.

Amaura was laying the fire in the great hall. She hardly looked up at the Calorin leaning against a nearby pillar.

"I think you'll need more kindling," he said softly in Rhyddan. Amaura recognized his voice.

"Corin?" she whispered.

"Yes" came the reply. Amaura stood as the fire sprang to life.

"Listen, Balkor is gone for a few days. I saw Darrin's sword in his chambers. I think I can get it out for you," she said quietly.

"Are you sure?" Corin asked. Amaura nodded.

"Do you think you can leave it in the stables?" Corin asked again.

"Yes. I'll get it during the late watch," Amaura said.

"Be careful, Maurie. Last stall on your left," he whispered.

"Good luck. Let Darrin know I'm safe," Amaura said before she walked away.

The torches flickered in the quiet hallway as Amaura stole through the sleeping castle. She halted at the foot of a staircase and listened for a moment. Hearing only the pounding of her heart, she stepped quietly up the stone stairs. She pushed open the door to Lord Balkor's chambers. She held her breath as it creaked open. Slipping inside, she walked over to the far wall where the sword hung.

Standing on tiptoes, she reached up and took it down. Wrapping her shawl around the sword, she left the chamber. As she reached the stairs again, she heard the footsteps of the guards. She looked around wildly for a place to hide. A tapestry hung nearby, sheltering a small alcove. She ducked behind it just in time. The guards paused for a few moments in the hallway before continuing on their patrol.

As soon as it was quiet again, Amaura left her hiding place and made for the stables. She exited the castle through the unguarded servant's quarters. She crossed the courtyard to the stables unseen and carried her precious bundle to the last stall. The bay stallion, freshly saddled and bridled, stood quietly in the stall. Exchanging her shawl for a blanket, she left the sword leaning against the wall of the stall.

Two hours before dawn, Corin entered the stables and quickly saddled his stallion and the horse next to it. Shouldering his pack, he left the stall.

"Bit early aren't you?" the prison guard asked as Corin entered the dungeons.

"I thought you might like to leave earlier," Corin answered.

"That I would, but I know my duties," the guard answered. Corin shrugged and went down the steps.

"Here, what's this?" he called. The guard ran to join him.

"What?" he asked.

"This cell's unlocked," Corin said. As the guard bent to check the lock, Corin sent his fist crashing down into the man's head. The soldier dropped unconscious to the ground. Corin relieved him of the keys and unlocked the door to Darrin's cell. Darrin stood to meet his rescuer as the door swung open. Corin opened his pack.

"Put these on," he said, handing clothes to Darrin. He quickly donned the Argusian uniform, casting away his old clothes. Corin went to the fallen guard and stripped him of his weapons. Tossing these to Darrin, he dragged the soldier into the cell, making sure he was securely bound and gagged. Corin relocked the cell.

Darrin had armed himself and was lacing up the boots also taken from the guard. Taking up a black scarf, he tied it around his nose and mouth and pulled on an Argusian helmet over all, effectively masking most of his features.

"Ready?" Corin asked. Darrin nodded and they left the dungeons. Reaching the top of the stairs, they came face-to-face with a pair of Calorin soldiers.

"Leaving the prisoner unguarded?" one asked. Darrin suddenly bent double and began coughing. Catching on, Corin reached out to steady him.

"My mate here suddenly took sick. I'm taking him to the infirmary, sir," Corin said.

"Sick with what?" the soldier asked suspiciously.

"Don't know, sir. I just hope it's not the plague," Corin said. At the mention of plague, the soldiers stepped back, and doubt creased their features as Darrin gave a groan.

"All right, but what about the prisoner?" the Calorin asked.

"Don't worry, sir. I'll be back as soon as I get him to the healer. The prisoner won't be going anywhere." He jangled the keys meaningfully. "Unless you want to take him to the infirmary so I can resume my duties, sir?" he added. Still taken with the thought of plague, the soldier shook his head vigorously.

"No, no, carry on," he said a little nervously, and he and his companion hurried off. As they disappeared around the corner, Darrin straightened up.

"Let's get out of here," he said.

"Aye, that was too close," Corin agreed.

The sky had begun to lighten as they made it to the stables. Corin saw a long object wrapped in cloth leaning against the wall and picked it up. Unwrapping the top, he saw the hilt of a broadsword. A wolf ran down the handle towards the carved pommel. Covering it again, he strapped it to his saddle. Once out of the stables, they mounted and rode to the main gate. The guards at the gate challenged them.

"I'm taking a message to Lynwood, sir," Corin replied.

"Are you crazy? Riding through that cursed forest alone?" the sentry asked.

"That's why they're sending an Argusian with me," Corin replied as if the sentry was stupid. The sentry took in his companion dressed in the flowing Argusian robes, face covered in the manner of the mercenaries. Still shaking his head at their foolishness, the sentry stood aside to let them pass. Corin returned the guard's salute as they rode through the gate. Restraining a wild urge to gallop away, Corin and Darrin rode slowly through the town. Once on the Lynwood Track, Corin set a quicker pace for the forest.

By late afternoon, they had reached the welcoming shelter of Dunham Forest, and Corin drew a sigh of relief. The journey had been quiet and quick after bluffing their way past two Calorin outposts on the road. Turning off the track, Corin led Darrin deeper into the safety of the forest. Halting at a stream deep in the forest, they dismounted to drink. Corin took off his helmet and threw it aside.

"We won't need these anymore," he said. Darrin gratefully did the same, and removed the mask covering his face.

"Where are we going exactly?" he asked.

"To rejoin the Hawk Flight," Corin answered. "It's not too far now." He could see that Darrin was exhausted. The journey had been hard on him after spending nearly three years in the confines of the dungeon. Mounting again, they continued on. Half an hour's riding brought them to the Darkan River, and Corin turned to the ford. Their progress was interrupted when a cloaked figure stepped out of the trees. Corin's horse reared in surprise, nearly unseating him. As he regained control of the stallion, Darrin rode up behind him.

"Trey! You could have said something!" Corin yelled.

"It's more fun this way. Anyway, it serves you right for sneaking off alone like that, *Captain*," Trey replied smugly.

"What was I supposed to do? If I didn't, half the warband would've insisted on coming!" Corin argued. Darrin couldn't help but laugh at Corin's indignant expression as his stallion still pranced nervously.

"Welcome back, sire," Trey said to Darrin.

"It's good to see you still alive, Trey," Darrin said. They were joined by more members of the warband.

"You made it back in one piece, Captain," Martin remarked, causing grins and chuckles from the men.

"Don't sound so surprised, Martin," Corin said laughingly as he dismounted.

"Here, Liam said to give this to you," Martin handed Corin some soap and a rough towel.

"Thanks, where is he?" Corin asked.

"He and some of the lads went to help Tristan transport some confiscated barrels of ale," Martin said with a grin. Fresh laughter greeted this comment. Darrin also dismounted and greeted Martin and the men he knew. Corin handed his horse to Gavin and, discarding his weapons, he headed off further downstream to wash the dye away.

"Well, sir, if you'll come with us, we'll get you some new clothes and some decent food," Martin said to Darrin. The prince nodded gratefully, still a little overwhelmed by the sudden turn of events. In the space of one day, he had gone from being a prisoner to being surrounded by the loyal outlaws after being rescued by their captain himself. Trey took Darrin's horse to the valley while Martin led Darrin inside the caves.

Corin knelt by the river and pulled off his tunic and shirt. Laying them aside with the mail coat and scimitar, he began washing. Kicking off his boots, he plunged into the river. A few minutes later, he hauled himself back on to the bank and let the late afternoon sun dry him. Tiredly, he closed his eyes as the warm spring sunlight played across his scarred back. He knew he couldn't stay long.

He felt nervous to finally meet his brother again. He had pushed aside any of those feelings during the escape, and now they came back full force. Would Darrin even recognize him? In truth, Corin had barely been able to replace his old memories of his brother with the man who now waited in the caves.

Mostly dry, he pulled his shirt and boots back on and gathered up the rest of his belongings and walked back to the caves. Pausing briefly, he whistled, and Karif dove from the sky in answer to his call. The hawk perched on his shoulder and gently butted his cheek. Corin reached up to stroke Karif's feathered chest.

"I missed you too, mate," Corin said softly.

Corin was in his chamber, dressing in his own uniform when a knock sounded. Pulling on his boots, he called, "Enter," and Darrin came in.

"I wanted to thank you properly for rescuing me," he said.

"Sorry it took so long to find you," Corin said, reaching for his leather tunic and lacing it up.

"Trey and Martin wouldn't tell me your name. They said you'd rather explain everything," Darrin said. He watched Corin buckle on his scimitar and knives. His face was turned away from Darrin, but something in his bearing was so familiar. The blonde hair, the blue eyes... *But no, it's impossible*, Darrin thought.

"Well, you got me out of more trouble than I care to remember when we were younger. I figured it was time I returned the favor," Corin said, turning to face him.

"I can't believe it!" Darrin said, recognition hitting him. "We thought you were dead. Corin, is it really you?"

"Yes, brother. It's me," Corin said. Darrin stared, a little dazed, at his brother. Then he shook himself and pulled Corin into a rough embrace.

"I thought I'd never see you again in this world!" Darrin said. Corin gave his old impish smile, and Darrin's heart lifted at the once-familiar sight.

"Well, you're stuck with me for a little while longer I guess," he said. "Talk about me, I'd given up long ago of meeting you again. Look at you, all grown up!"

Darrin's blue eyes matched Corin's that were snapping with laughter.

"And you! Somebody actually decided to trust you with weapons? And a captain as well?" Darrin said, grinning.

"You can blame Trey, Martin, and Liam for that one," Corin said. "And speaking of weapons, Amaura gave me this for you." He went to his packs, unwrapped the sword, and held it out to Darrin.

"Is she safe?" Darrin asked as he took his sword. Corin nodded. Darrin unsheathed his sword and swung it experimentally. Sheathing it with a sigh, he said, "It looks like it'll take me a while to get back to form. So what about you, Corin? You use a scimitar?" They sat down at the low camp table.

"Aye, it's what you learn in the south," Corin said.

"Calorin?" Darrin guessed. His brother nodded.

"That's where I've been, not exactly by my choosing either," Corin said. Darrin saw a guarded expression come over Corin's face as his eyes hardened at some memory. Darrin decided not to press him. His brother had always confided in him when he felt ready.

"You started the warband? From the little I was able to hear, it sounds as if you've been up to your old tricks," Darrin said.

"I made it back last year and found Martin, Trey, and Liam in the forest. Together, we started the fight," Corin replied. He was grateful that Darrin had changed the subject; he wasn't ready to tell his brother everything that had happened. "But enough about me, what did you do before the invasion?" he asked.

"Well, when you didn't come back, we tore the forest apart looking for any trace. But there was nothing. Everything got worse when we came home. All of us dealt with your disappearance differently. As for me, I threw myself into my studies and training, trying to stay busy. By the time I was twenty, Father made me a captain in the warband. My first battle was on the coast against the Raiders from Terminus. Then a few years later, the Calorins took us completely by surprise. Our forces were split. Father was in the mountains, so I took command. But by the time Father could rejoin us, it was too late. It was all over in a matter of months. And as for the last three years, not much happened that I care to remember," Darrin said.

"I know how that is," Corin agreed quietly. Then Gavin knocked.

"Captain, sire, reports have just come in," he said. Corin led Darrin out into the main cave where Kieran and Kara stood waiting. Recognizing Darrin as the prince they stood uncertain of whom to address until Corin signaled for them to begin.

"I went tae the port at Pentre, Captain. There's news that two new ships are expected within the week," Kieran said.

"More mercenaries?" Corin asked.

"No, sir. From what I gathered, they're coming from the Sultaan's army. Some important lord is expected as well, sir," Kieran answered.

"Anything else?" Corin said.

"No, sir, other than some big uproar about an important prisoner escaped," Kieran said with a grin.

"How careless of Balkor. I suppose he's blaming us?" Corin asked.

"Rather vehemently," Kieran said. Corin and Darrin chuckled at the description.

"All right, Kieran, you're dismissed," Corin said. Kara stepped forward, drawing papers from her pouch and handing them to Corin.

"Laird Dandin gave me these, sir. The Calorins are building two new outposts along the border. He says the clans would be happy tae dispose of them, sir," Kara said. Corin studied the papers. One was a rough sketch of the border, marking the positions of the new outposts. The other two detailed information about the garrisons. Corin passed them to Darrin.

"Do the Calorins know you have an alliance with the clans?" Darrin asked.

"Not for certain. Clan Dyson and Gunlon watch the border, but with our combined forces, we'd still be too few to drive the Calorins out," Corin answered Darrin's unspoken question.

"Laird Dandin did ask tae see you as soon as you could, sir. He said 'wee wooden buildings are one thing, but these blasted stone keeps will be the death of us,'" Kara said.

"How soon is he planning on moving against the outposts?" Corin asked.

"As soon as you can join him, sir," came the reply.

"Where does he want us to meet him?" Corin asked.

"The usual place, sir," Kara said. Darrin watched Corin as he studied the papers again, coming to a decision.

"Trey!" he called. Trey looked up from where he was sharpening his sword.

"What now, Captain?" he answered. Corin was unconcerned at the apparent disrespect in Trey's reply. Neither could resist a dig at the other whenever they got the chance.

"Have your men ready to ride with us tomorrow, we're going to visit Dandin," Corin replied.

"Good. Brian still owes me money," Trey said.

"Why? Did you cheat again?" Corin asked.

"As always," Trey replied, with a smirk.

"Anyone know where Martin is?" Corin asked.

"Trying to get some rest, but no! The cruel captain forbids it," Martin replied, entering from the side cave.

"Take your men out to Sentry Rocks in a few days. Stay a little longer than usual. I'll swing back through that way once we're done on the border. Trey will pick up the Lynwood route," Corin said.

"Fine," Martin replied, stifling a yawn.

"Gavin, make sure he actually goes with you," Corin said to Martin's second in command.

"Yes, sir," Gavin replied, grinning. Martin frowned to hide his own smile.

"Mutiny! After all this time, and I thought you were on my side, Gavin!" he replied as he left to return to his bunk.

Darrin couldn't help but smile at the informal but smooth way his brother seemed to run the warband.

Dinner was a wild affair as the outlaws celebrated the return of their prince. Corin related the story of the escape to cheers from his men. Darrin, seeing the men's admiration for his brother and in an attempt to learn more about him, slowly turned the conversation to the doings of the Hawk Flight. The lieutenants willingly obliged and, with help from the men in their patrols, recounted story after story of raids and ambushes on terrified Calorins. Most centered on the creativity of their captain. Fresh laughter greeted each new story, especially after Corin's wry comments on each.

"To hear the Calorins describe 'the Hawk,' he's no more than ten feet tall, has wings, emerges from trees, and shoots bolts of lightning at his enemies," Corin said.

"Lightning bolts? I think I remember where that one came from," Tristan said. "What did we use?"

"Burning javelins," Martin replied. "Corin stood in the middle of the path with Karif, while Llewellyn screamed his head off in the bushes. I think I missed with all my arrows. I was trying not to laugh and give it all away."

"Do you ever hit anything?" Trey asked innocently.

"You were trying not to laugh? I had a very good view of their faces," Corin said. "I made some very realistic choking, angry sounds."

"The Calorins were practically falling over themselves trying to get away," Tristan reminisced fondly.

"Come to think of it, I do remember hearing some very strange sounds and wondered what they were," Flynn put in. "It sounded like a dying animal."

Corin laughed. "Aye, Karif didn't think much of the whole affair," he said. The hawk ruffled his feathers haughtily from his perch on Corin's shoulder. "Still doesn't apparently," Corin said, catching the movement. Darrin chuckled. Corin had introduced the hawk to him as the "terror of Aredor," explaining how the bird's presence had given rise to their name.

After the meal concluded, Corin took Darrin outside the caves to the valley. He whistled, and a gray stallion separated itself from the herd and came toward them, its coat shining softly in the twilight. Corin slipped a halter over its head and handed the rope to Darrin.

"He's yours," he said. Darrin gently rubbed the horse's broad forehead.

"He have a name?" he asked.

"Not yet," Corin replied. "We took him on a raid of Calorin supply lines a few weeks ago."

A familiar nicker sounded, and Zephyr trotted up through the darkness. Corin stroked Zephyr's nose.

"You've gotten fatter in the last few days, Zephyr. Good thing we're leaving tomorrow, eh?" Corin said in Calorin.

"He's named for the west wind?" Darrin asked.

"Aye, he's carried me through a lot the past three years. He took me even though I was too late to save his first master," Corin said. Darrin heard a note of sadness in his voice. Zephyr gently butted Corin with his nose. "Look, Darrin, now that you're here, I'll turn over the command to you," Corin said.

"Why don't you keep it?" Darrin asked.

"It's your place by right, and you know more about leading a warband than I do," Corin replied.

"It doesn't seem like you've had too many problems so far," Darrin said. "Besides, this life is different from leading armies across open plains. I can learn from you."

"I won't hold the command over you," Corin argued. "I only took the command until we could find you or Father to take over. Before I came here, I had always been told what to do. I'd never commanded a warband before. It's mostly by luck and Lleu's help that we've survived so far."

"Don't sell yourself so short, Corin. You've done what none of us could do in the beginning, which is to effectively fight the Calorins," Darrin said. "Those men trust you and look to you as their captain, and I won't take that away from you. Since we can't agree on command, we'll share it and learn from each other. Agreed?"

"Sounds fair enough," Corin said. "Looks like you still have to talk some sense into me."

"Something I've missed having to do," Darrin said. Corin smiled.

"Me too, more than you know," he said as they turned the horses loose to rejoin the herd before heading back to the caves.

CHAPTER 13

Corin staggered through the forest behind his men. They had quickly ambushed a Calorin patrol. It turned into a fierce fight once the Calorins recovered from their initial shock. All his patrol had escaped unhurt except for him. Worse still, Corin had recognized the man who had wounded him.

———

"You all right, Ahmed?" Emeth asked. Ahmed stood on the forest path staring at the blood on his scimitar. With an effort, Ahmed met Emeth's concerned gaze. Seeing the haunted look in Ahmed's eyes, Emeth realized what must have happened. A cold feeling settled over him.

"Was it…?" he asked hesitantly. Ahmed nodded.

"Aye, he recognized me," he said.

"Shall we give chase, my lord Ismail?" Captain Taysir asked. Emeth spoke up suddenly.

"I advise against it, my lord. They could easily be waiting to attack us again," he said. To his relief, Ismail agreed, calling for a withdrawal back to Lynwood Keep.

———

Liam noticed that Corin was lagging behind. He hurried back toward him as Corin leaned against a tree. Liam reached out to steady Corin. Feeling him wince, Liam withdrew his hand and saw traces of blood on his palm. Liam moved Corin's cloak aside and saw a long cut across his back. Calling Bran to help support

Corin, Liam bandaged it as well as he could. Bran helped Corin along as they covered the remaining distance to the caves.

As the patrol came in sight of the caves, they passed through a small quiet clearing that contained three graves. The freshest held Steffan. Spears had been driven into the ground as markers with the names of the dead carved into the handles. The outlaws threw salutes to their dead comrades as they passed.

Darrin and Trey had come back to the caves earlier in the day. Darrin sat in the small cave, studying a map of the forest. He looked up in surprise as Bran came in, still supporting Corin. Liam came in quickly after them. Corin collapsed on to his bunk. Darrin saw the blood seeping through his leather tunic. Corin made no resistance as Darrin helped him take off the tunic and his weapons. Corin lay on his stomach as Liam pushed his shirt up and began treating the wound. Darrin saw for the first time the scars that crossed his brother's back. In the three months since Darrin had escaped, his brother had still not told him what had happened during the years he had been in Calorin.

Corin lay quietly while Liam bandaged the wound; his face was unreadable. Darrin waited until Liam left before pulling up the camp stool by Corin's bed.

"What happened out there?" he asked.

"A glimpse of a life before this one," Corin replied. Raising himself up on to his elbows, he pulled off the glove that covered his right palm. A hammer and a whip were crossed inside a circle. Darrin looked at the brand quietly.

"A slave, Darrin, that's what I was. You saw my scars. For eight years, Balkor worked me, beat me, and branded me. That's all I am," Corin said.

"You were gone for more than eight years," Darrin said.

"Another Calorin lord bought me and had me trained to fight. I served in his personal guard." Corin sat up slowly and pushed up his left sleeve showing the scars that the lion had left on his arm. "I got these protecting his son, Ismail," he said.

"What happened?" Darrin asked.

"Ambush. There was a lion, and I kept it from attacking Ismail. That's when my leg was hurt," Corin explained. Darrin had asked him before about his limp.

"And the one you couldn't protect?" Darrin asked gently. Corin looked down.

"Castimir, his younger brother." His hand strayed unconsciously to his side. "I was too late. I tried to make it over to him, but he was killed before I got there," he said.

"And this Ismail, is he the lord that now commands at Lynwood?" Darrin asked. Corin nodded.

"He has two of the Phoenix Guards with him. We were close friends when we fought together in Lord Rishdah's guard. That's whom I saw today," he said.

"How did you leave Calorin?" Darrin asked curiously.

"Rishdah gave me my freedom. I had sworn to protect him and his family because he had saved me from Balkor. After three years, he set me free. Before I left, he warned me that we might meet again, only on opposite ends of the sword. He was right," Corin said. "I don't know what to do now."

"We continue what we're doing. This struggle is against Balkor, not this Ismail. You will have to fight against your friends, but hopefully, it won't come down to the final blow," Darrin said.

Corin nodded again. He had hoped that Lord Rishdah would be kept away from Aredor. It seemed like a cruel twist of fate that sent Ismail, Ahmed, and Emeth to his country.

"For now, I'm relieving you of your duties for a few days at least," Darrin said. "No arguments, Corin. I am technically a commanding officer."

"Somehow, I think you're cheating," Corin said as he lay back down. Darrin smiled.

"Yes, I am," he said, leaving the cave.

Darrin left shortly after with Corin's patrol to go relieve Tristan's patrol watching the Lynwood Track. With the arrival of the fresh Calorin troops, the fighting had increased during the spring. The beginning of summer had brought no change. Upon their arrival, Lord Balkor sent Ismail to Lynwood Keep with a sizeable force and orders to engage the outlaws in the forest. Emeth and Ahmed dreaded every encounter, knowing they were fighting against their former comrade.

"I hate this! I wish the blasted Sultaan hadn't ordered us over here!" Emeth exclaimed, throwing himself on his bunk. He and Ahmed were alone in their room after returning from a foray with Ismail.

"What were we supposed to do? Refuse to go?" Ahmed asked, sitting on his bed. Emeth stood and began pacing restlessly.

"That would have turned out better than coming here," Emeth muttered. Ahmed sighed. Emeth had been increasingly moody since the encounter with Corin in the forest.

"It's all very well for you, but I feel like I'm betraying my own people just by being here," Emeth said. "Worse still, I feel like we're betraying *him!*"

"Emeth, we both knew this would happen when we were sent here," Ahmed said. "Just be grateful it wasn't you who struck the blow." Emeth saw the guilt in Ahmed's eyes. "Like it or not, we're enemies now," Ahmed said.

Ismail stood in the courtyard of the keep. A dispatch rider had just come in. He was severely wounded, and his letters had been taken. In his pouch was a gray hawk feather. Ismail took the feather and ordered a small force out to check the road for the outlaws. As soon as the troops left, he went to find Emeth and Ahmed.

"It's him, isn't it?" Ismail asked them. He saw from their expressions that he had guessed right. "How long have you two known?" he asked.

"A few weeks, my lord," Ahmed replied.

"Why didn't you tell me?" Ismail demanded.

"We thought it might be better if you didn't know, sir," Emeth said.

"Not know? The Hawk Flight roams the forest, leaving these," he said as he held up the feather. "Who else would be reckless enough to lead so few men against the Sultaan's finest troops?" Ismail said.

"What will you do now, sir?" Emeth asked.

"I don't know. But he saved my life, and I haven't forgotten my debt to him," Ismail said.

CHAPTER 14

"Captain, there's a large force of Argusians out. They're laying waste tae the villages along the forest," Kieran said breathlessly. He hadn't stopped until he made it back to the caves. Luckily, Corin was there with his patrol and Martin had just come back.

"How many and where?" Corin asked sharply.

"About thirty. They were headed north toward Tafarn village last I saw, sir. They're not moving fast, so it'll take them a while tae get there," Kieran said. Corin's men heard the report and stood awaiting orders. He began issuing commands. They began packing supplies and extra weapons. Since they were leaving the forest, all donned mail coats.

"Are you mad? Taking on thirty Argusians with ten men?" Martin asked as Corin packed provisions.

"Yes, we are, Martin. And if you and half you're patrol weren't hurt, you'd be going with us," Corin said. "Besides, someone has to stay and tell Darrin where we've gone," he said, grinning.

"That's not a comforting thought," Martin said.

"I want to take some of your men with me," Corin said.

"Good. I was going to send them with you anyway," Martin said.

"Tell them to pack extra provisions. We might be gone a while," Corin said. With that, he strode out to saddle Zephyr.

Tafarn village was located a few miles from the forest's edge and was close to the Braeton border. As Corin and his small force of fifteen men raced to cut off the marauding Argusians, they passed ruined barns, slaughtered livestock, and injured villagers. They were able to avoid the few Calorin patrols on the roads. As darkness closed in, they were still some distance from Tafarn.

Corin called a halt, and they made camp. The outlaws were on the move again shortly before dawn. The village looked quiet and peaceful in the faint light of morning. Corin sent Bran ahead to scout.

"They haven't been here yet, Captain," Bran reported when he came back.

"Take Kael and see if you can find any trace of them. We'll wait in the village," Corin ordered.

An hour later, Bran and Kael returned. Anxious villagers parted to let them through.

"They're coming, sir. Still marching slowly, and they've fired two more farms," Kael reported.

"How long?" Corin asked.

"About half an hour," Bran said. The village leader spoke up.

"What can we do to help, sir?" he asked.

"I want everyone inside, out of the way," Corin said. Mothers gathered their children and shepherded them inside. A few of the younger men came forward, armed with long knives and axes.

"We'll fight with you, sire," they said. Corin accepted their help and began positioning his men. Two more men found Corin.

"My name is Dylan, this is Marc. We both escaped from Lynwood when it fell. If you have arrows to spare, we can add two more bows," Dylan said. Corin took an extra quiver from his saddle.

"Arm yourselves and then find Bran. You can reinforce his position," Corin said, handing the arrows to Dylan. Ian handed another spare quiver to Marc. Shouldering the quivers, they saluted and hurried off to retrieve their hidden weapons.

The outlaws took up places behind houses and in the square. They did not have to wait long before the Argusians came into sight. Corin whistled softly and laid a shaft on his bow. All around, his men did the same. The Argusians were caught completely by surprise as the first flight of arrows landed in their ranks. A second flight quickly followed before they were able to raise their shields. Corin whistled again, and he and his men retreated into the square, still firing arrows at the charging Argusians. The two forces locked blades in the square with neither side giving any quarter.

Then a horn blared, and the Argusians retreated. Corin saw too late that they had set fire to several houses. Reluctantly, he let the enemy retreat and joined his men to put out the fires. Hours later, the Hawk Flight prepared to leave the village.

"Dylan!" Liam exclaimed, recognizing the warrior. "How'd you make it out of Lynwood alive?"

"Lieutenant!" Dylan returned, equally surprised. "A small group of us fought through to the back gate. But only Marc and I made it into the woods alive," he said.

"Is Marc here with you?" Liam asked.

"Yes, sir. If your captain will have us, we'll join you," Dylan said.

"I'd be glad to have you," Corin said, joining them.

"We have horses in the stable, sir. We managed to keep our swords and bows as well," Dylan said.

"Bring what you have and hurry before the trail goes cold," Corin said.

Within a short time, the patrol was mounted and ready to leave. Karif perched on Corin's shoulder as he led the men out of the village and in hot pursuit of the Argusians.

Kara spurred her gelding on faster as the Calorin patrol thundered close behind. By bad luck, they had seen her as she crossed a forest path. She tore through the forest, abandoning her route to the caves. Bowstrings twanged as arrows flew around her. They splashed through a stream, and Kara jumped her horse over a fallen log and left the track. Her heart pounding, she sped through the underbrush, trying to shake her pursuers. An arrow hit her in the leg, and she clung desperately to the saddle to stay on.

Turning Delyth to the left, she changed directions again. Surprised, the Calorins lost sight of her momentarily. Jumping down into a sheltered dell, she tumbled from the saddle. Sending her gelding cantering off, she crouched awkwardly in the shelter of the hollow. Kara heard shouts as the Calorins chased after the horse. Then she froze as voices sounded nearby. Not all her pursuers had gone after the decoy. They were coming in her direction. Taking the pouch from her shoulder, she hid it under the bushes. She stuck her knife in the ground beside the pouch. Kara turned and hobbled away as best she could. Sobbing for breath, she continued on as she heard the Calorins coming after her.

"Is Kara back yet?" Darrin asked as he came into the caves. Tristan shook his head.

"No, she was due back almost an hour ago," he said worriedly.

"She was coming from the Rocks, wasn't she?" Darrin asked.

"Yes, sir. I was about to take a patrol out to look for her," Tristan said.

It wasn't long before they found signs of the pursuit. Crossing the stream, they followed the path torn through the undergrowth. Darrin sent Iwan and Huw farther down the trail while he and Tristan rode into the dell. Tristan looked at the red streaks on the grass.

"Looks like she was hurt, sir," he said. Darrin saw a glint in the bushes. He pulled the knife from the ground and found the pouch.

"She kept this safe though," Darrin said.

"She tried to decoy them by sending Delyth off. From the looks of things, it didn't work," Tristan said.

"See where that trail goes," Darrin said. They followed the faint trail of blood and flattened grass.

"She didn't get far," Tristan said. "It looks like they took her to Lynwood, sir."

Ismail had been taken by surprise when he found that the outlaw they had captured was a young girl. As soon as they made it back to the safety of the keep, he ordered her put in a cell and had a physician tend to Kara's wounded leg.

Kara sat against the wall of the cell with her hands bound in front of her. Through the bars of the prison, she could see the guards glaring at her. Kara had never been so frightened in her life. *They'll realize I'm missing sooner or later*, she thought, trying to reassure herself. It wasn't comforting to know what would happen eventually. She began to breathe slowly and evenly, trying to steady her shaking hands.

A few hours later, two guards in red –and-black livery entered the dungeon. They helped her stand and escorted her to a private chamber where Ismail waited. After cutting her bonds, the guards withdrew. Ismail sat behind a desk littered with papers. He indicated that she should sit.

"How is your leg?" he asked in halting Rhyddan.

"It's fine," Kara replied shortly.

"Listen to me carefully. I do not want to hurt you, but that will happen if you do not answer our questions," Ismail said.

"I won't tell you anything about us," Kara said. Ismail shook his head.

"I admire your defiance, but it will be easier on you if you cooperate," he said. "What were you carrying? Letters? Orders to your warband?" he asked. Kara remained silent, staring down at the floor.

"I will not be the one continuing to ask you these questions," Ismail said. "General Kadar is on his way here as we speak." He saw the look of fear cross the girl's face.

"I don't care. I won't tell you anything," she repeated stubbornly.

"I won't be able to protect you from anything once he gets here," Ismail warned. Kara watched his face carefully.

"Why are you here?" she asked softly. "You don't want tae do it, do you?"

"I obey the Sultaan, and so I must obey Lord Balkor. Believe me when I say that I do not want to be here, but I must play the part," Ismail said.

He called his guards in and gave them orders. Kara was taken back to the dungeon by only one guard. Emeth watched the girl carefully. She was obviously frightened but was doing her best not to show it. Stopping suddenly in an empty corridor, he pushed up the sleeve on her left arm. Satisfied, he walked on with her. He thought it strange that she ran with the outlaws and, if he had his way, she would soon be back in the forest.

That night Emeth stood on the walls, carefully scanning the surrounding forest. His keen eyes soon found what they were looking for: a telltale rustle in the underbrush. Raising his bow, he loosed an arrow. It thudded into a tree. A sentry came running over.

"What happened?" he asked.

"I thought I saw one of the outlaws," Emeth replied. As he looked back, the arrow was gone. "If it was them, they're gone now," he said.

"Sire, Karif is here," Flynn said.

"What? Is Corin back?" Darrin asked, surprised.

"No, sir, but the hawk is outside," Flynn said. Darrin followed him out of the caves to where the gray hawk perched on a low branch. Darrin carefully extended his arm to the hawk. It normally did not allow anyone but Corin to handle it. Karif came down to perch on Darrin's arm. He saw a scrap of paper tied to its leg. Removing it, he handed it to Flynn to read.

"Captain says they'll be gone a few more days. The Argusians have picked up a bigger force and are leading them farther east. Once the enemy is taken care of, they'll head back, sir," Flynn reported.

"Thank you, Flynn," Darrin said.

"Will you send a message back, sir?' the archer asked. Karif shifted restlessly on Darrin's arm.

"No, he's anxious to get back," Darrin replied. "Take care of him, little friend," he whispered to the hawk before tossing it into the air. They stood for a moment, watching it wing its way east back to Corin. A movement in the darkening forest caught their attention, and Llewellyn strode toward them.

"This came from the castle walls, sire," Llewellyn said, handing the arrow to Darrin. "It's one of Kara's, and this was attached to it." He gave a scroll of paper to Darrin. Martin and Tristan joined them as they went back into the caves.

"What is it, sir?" Martin asked. Darrin glanced up from reading the paper.

"It seems we have a temporary ally in the keep. He wants to help get Kara out," Darrin said. "Two nights from now, there's a new moon. He says he'll wait on the west wall to get us in."

Martin took the message and looked it over.

"Looks like he's one of us," he said, pointing to a mark scrawled in the corner. Tristan studied it.

"It's a clan marking. Canich, I think," he said. The men stared at one another.

"What's a clan member doing in Lynwood with all those Calorins?" Flynn wondered.

"If he shot the arrow, then he saw where I was scouting, which is more than I can say for those Calorins," Llewellyn said.

"Do we trust it, sire?" Flynn asked.

"I'm not sure," Darrin answered. He regretted sending Karif back. He had a feeling that his brother might know something about this stranger. Tristan meanwhile had been looking at the note again.

"He doesn't say how many men to bring, he gives us two days, and he doesn't say that he can be trusted. It sounds safe so far," Tristan said. "Furthermore, he has the clan sign. He might be a traitor to his country, but he at least appears to have a conscience."

"How do you know Kara didn't say anything about the clans? They could've realized she was a Braeton," Martin objected. Tristan shrugged.

"I don't. But the fact that a clan member seems to be walking around unchallenged in the keep seems a bit unbelievable. I don't think even the Calorins could've come up with that one," he said.

"You're saying that we should trust him then?" Darrin asked.

"It's worth a try, sire," Tristan replied. When Trey returned from his patrol, he was quickly informed of the message. He agreed with his brother after reading the paper.

"Since I'm the one urging this plan, sire, let me go in. That way if it fails, it's my fault, and I'm the only one that gets caught," Tristan said. Reluctantly, Darrin agreed.

"All right, but we'll still have a few men waiting outside for you," he said. Once decided, they began planning to make sure that nothing went awry.

CHAPTER 15

Corin wiped his blade clean as best he could in the pouring rain. Seeing the riders coming towards his small band on the road, he gave a warning whistle. The foremost rider waved his hand.

"It's us, Captain!" Liam called.

"All accounted for, Liam?" Corin asked.

"Yes, sir. None escaped," Liam replied.

The Argusians had remained ahead of the outlaws until the night before. Early that morning, they had ambushed the Argusians on the road. Corin had divided his force in half to better pursue those that had escaped. Fighting on foot, the Argusians were disadvantaged against the mounted Aredorians. None had surrendered, and so none of the marauding force was left alive. Corin's men stood in the driving rain, bandaging their wounds as best they could. Corin tied off a bandage on his forearm as Karif came to perch sulkily on his shoulder while attempting to shake water from his feathers. The hawk had returned early the previous day after delivering the message. Ian brought Zephyr up for Corin. They were well east of Kingscastle and almost two days' ride from Dunham Forest. It would be a long, dangerous journey back.

Tristan and Darrin stood outside the walls of Lynwood Keep. Rain had fallen since early morning and showed no signs of abating. The walls had been deserted by the sentries who were trying to stay warm and dry and who only came out periodically to patrol the ramparts. Emeth waited on the parapet. He had laid aside the uniform of the Phoenix Guard and had donned the uniform of the garrison. Leaving behind his double swords, he instead buckled on a scimitar. Wrapped in a cloak, hood drawn up against the rain, he waited.

Tristan stepped forward and whistled softly. In answer, a rope was thrown over the battlements. Making sure his sword was loose in its sheath, Tristan took hold of the rope and began to climb. As he reached the top, Emeth reached down and helped him over.

"Up you come, mate," he said. Emeth began pulling the rope up, but Tristan stopped him.

"How do I know I can trust you?" he asked. Emeth unbuckled his vambrace and pushed his sleeve up. Tristan recognized the four-pointed star.

"I'm no Calorin," Emeth said. "I'm just looking out for a member of the clans."

"Why are you here?" Tristan demanded.

"That's a long story, and we don't have time. The guards will be coming out ontae the walls any minute. We need tae go," Emeth said.

"All right, let's make it fast," Tristan replied.

Emeth led him down the wall steps and across the courtyard into the keep. Once into the dungeons, they quickly overpowered the guards. Taking the keys, Emeth unlocked the cell. Kara lay huddled on her side in the corner. Seeing the dark figure looming over her, she started back in fear.

"Kara, it's only me," Tristan said, laying a hand on her forehead. She was feverish and shivering. In the dim light of the torches, he could see bruises on her face.

"I'm sorry, but Kadar got here yesterday," Emeth said. Tristan took off his cloak and wrapped it around Kara. She cried out softly as he lifted her and touched the raw wounds on her back.

"How are we getting out?" Tristan asked.

"The west gate. Let's get going before these two wake up," Emeth said indicating the guards. He replaced the keys as they left the dungeons.

Getting out was harder than it sounded. Guards patrolled the passages, which forced them to hide until the Calorins passed. Once outside, they quickly crossed the courtyard unnoticed. Emeth unbarred the gate and swung it open. The outlaws were waiting on the other side. Flynn took Kara from Tristan and carried her into the forest. Emeth handed another one of the men Kara's weapons that he had retrieved earlier that day.

"Wait!" Emeth said as Tristan made to follow his band. "A few years ago, I swore service tae Lord Ismail. For what it's worth, he didn't want tae hurt her. Even some of the lads thought it cowardly tae torture a girl, but that's right up Kadar's alley," Emeth said.

"Thank you," Tristan said.

"It's Aiden," Emeth said.

"Tristan," he replied, extending his hand. Emeth shook it firmly.

"Give this tae the Hawk for me?" he asked handing a piece of paper to Tristan.

"Sure, but one day, I want an explanation for everything," Tristan said. Emeth grinned.

"I'll see you get it. Best of luck tae you, Tristan," he said.

"And you, Aiden," Tristan replied before disappearing into the rainy night. Emeth bolted the gate and returned to the keep.

Emeth went to relieve Ahmed on guard duty. Ahmed noticed his hair was still damp.

"Where were you?" he asked.

"Unlike you Calorins, I actually enjoy the rain," Emeth said lightly. Ahmed nodded knowingly.

"You going to be all right once they find out?" he asked.

"Don't worry, I can talk the legs off a table if I have to," Emeth replied.

As the outlaws returned to the caves, Kieran ran up to them.

"Where is she? Is she all right?" he demanded.

"No, lad, she's not," Tristan said, drawing him aside. Darrin had Flynn carry Kara into the small cave and lay her on the blankets spread on the ledge.

"Do you know when Captain and Liam are coming back, sire?" Flynn asked worriedly. Darrin shook his head.

"Liam's the only one of us who really knows what he's doing around wounds and such. She needs a proper healer, sir," Flynn said.

"Sir, if I might suggest something?" Martin said.

"Anything," Darrin gestured for him to continue.

"My younger sister, Mera, if you remember, was well trained by the castle healer. She's in Gorwydd village not too far away. I could bring her here," Martin said.

"How soon can you be back?" Darrin asked.

"A few hours, sire," Martin replied. Darrin quickly gave his assent, and Martin rode off, leading a spare horse. Two hours of hard riding saw him at the edge of Dunham Forest, looking down at the village in the distance. Riding into the village, Martin left the horses standing and knocked on a door. A few minutes later, the door opened a crack.

"It's the middle of the night, what do you want?" a young woman asked.

"Mera, we need your help," Martin said. His sister flung the door open.

"Martin! What is it?" she asked.

"One of the warband is badly hurt. Liam's away with the captain, and we need an experienced healer," Martin explained. "I know it's dangerous for you if anyone found out…"

"No," Mera interrupted. "Let me get my things. How far is it?"

"I brought you a horse," Martin said as an answer.

Mera pulled on a pair of sturdy boots and threw a cloak over her dress. As she left the house, she slung a bag of supplies over her shoulder. As they rode, Martin explained further what had happened. Halfway to the caves, he blindfolded her and led her the rest of the way.

At the caves, only a few of the men were still awake. Darrin and Tristan sat at the table, waiting. Martin brought Mera in and took her to the small cave where Kara lay. Kieran sat beside his sister. Mera took off her wet cloak and rolled up her sleeves. Martin laid a comforting arm around Kieran and took him from the chamber as Mera pulled back the blanket covering Kara.

The rain had finally stopped. Corin and his patrol were still some distance from the forest when he called a halt. Night had fallen a few hours before. Liam rode up beside Corin.

"I've been talking with some of the men, sir, and we'd all rather just push on to the caves if that's all right," he said. Corin nodded.

"That's fine with me," he answered. "We should make it back by tomorrow morning then." He dropped back to ride beside Marc.

"How are you holding up?" he asked.

"I'll be fine, sir," Marc replied. The warrior had taken an Argusian knife through his arm. Liam had bandaged it thickly and fashioned a rough sling for him. But the long day's riding had begun to tell on Marc, and his wound began bleeding again. Liam rode close by, keeping an eye on Marc. Corin rode ahead again, taking his turn as an advance scout. Ignoring the pain, Marc rode on, keeping pace with the rest of the patrol.

Mera sat on the rough camp stool by the ledge where Kara lay. The young girl was still unconscious and fevered. Mera looked up as Martin came in.

"How is she?" he asked.

"The fever has gone down a little, and she's resting easier now," Mera replied. Martin blew a sigh of relief.

"You hungry? Some of the lads are up and getting breakfast," he said.

"Yes, I am. I didn't know I'd been here that long already," Mera said.

"Come on then. Kieran will sit with her," Martin said. Mera followed him out into the main cave. Room was made for her at the tables.

Breakfast was a simple: rashers of cooked deer meat, bread with wild berries, all washed down with cold stream water. Mera found that she knew some of the men, having treated injuries before and during the invasion.

"How is Kara?" Darrin asked.

"Much better, sire. I won't need to stay much longer," Mera said.

"I don't know if I can thank you enough for helping," Darrin said.

"No need. I'm glad I could help," Mera replied.

As the meal finished, the men began leaving to go about their duties. A sentry climbed down the ladder from the top of the caves into the cavern.

"My lord, the captain is back. They look to have made it back in one piece," the man said. They did not have to wait long before the patrol trooped in while shedding wet cloaks.

"I was almost dry, and then it started raining again," Bran complained, attempting to wipe mud from his boots. Owain flicked water at him.

"Stop moaning! I was completely washed away half an hour ago," he joked.

Corin was last to come in with Liam, who was helping Marc. Karif flew from Corin's shoulder and perched on a stone outcropping where he shook himself vigorously and began preening. Mera saw Liam help Marc sit down on a bench. Martin saw her glance, and knew she wouldn't be satisfied until she had helped.

"Come on, I'll introduce you. Liam looks like he could use some help," he said.

They went over to Liam, and Martin quickly explained the reason for Mera's presence. Liam readily accepted her help, and Mera began to unwind the bandage around Marc's arm. Marc leaned against the wall as she cut off his sleeve.

"You ready?" Liam asked.

"I never was much for stitches, but go ahead," Marc replied. Mera hastily crushed some herbs into a beaker of water and handed it to Marc as Liam began cleaning the wound again. Mera stitched as Liam held him steady. After they finished, Mera assisted Liam in caring for the other wounded men of the patrol.

When Corin came in, he went over to the table where Darrin still sat with Tristan, Trey, and Martin.

"You made it back," Trey said.

"Soaking wet and starving, but yes, we're back," Corin answered. Removing his cloak and weapons, he laid them on the table and sat down. He briefly gave a report, and in turn, Darrin told him what had happened while he was gone. Darrin brought out the note they had received.

"Recognize anything?" he asked, handing it to Corin. He saw the star sketched in the corner.

"It's a clan marking," he said. *Aiden must have risked much to help them,* he thought. Tristan told him what happened before he had left Lynwood.

"He wanted me to give you this. He seemed to know a little bit about you," Tristan said, handing Corin Emeth's letter. He silently read it and then looked up at them.

"I'm not getting out of this without an explanation, am I?" he asked. Darrin shook his head. Corin grinned ruefully.

"All right, let me eat while I tell you," he said. Food was brought for Corin, and while he ate he told them of how he and Emeth met, of their friendship, and of serving in the Phoenix Guard. He also told them about Ahmed and Ismail.

"Lord Rishdah and his family were strange to me. He took me in and showed me kindness. I couldn't believe that all Calorins weren't all as brutal as Balkor. Emeth, Ahmed, and I became close friends. We looked out for each other in every battle and fight we managed to get into. And now we're fighting each other," Corin finished.

"Did you fight a lot over there?" Tristan asked curiously.

"Yes. My first battle was on the Argusian border after the Sultaan declared war. We spent most of the year there in the desert, until the Sultaan made peace with the king of Argus. A few months later, he invaded here," Corin said. "The next two years, we fought against some rebellious lords in eastern Calorin."

"Did Emeth know about you?" Martin asked.

"Not at first. Neither of us used our real names. After we heard about the invasion, we found out about each other: a lost prince and a runaway chieftain's son," Corin said.

"He's a northerner. Won't he fall under suspicion when they find out that Kara is gone?" Darrin asked.

"Probably, but I wouldn't worry. We were up north in Qusay once. Lord Rishdah had to meet with the Sultaan. Emeth ran into some trouble with an angry, suspicious lord. He fed the lord a story of how he was banished from the northlands for killing some men and how he'd sooner kill himself before returning. We all almost believed him," Corin said.

Talk soon turned to other matters as scouts brought in reports of large Calorin patrols out in the forest. Darrin took Tristan and Trey with their men to waylay the Calorins. Martin would wait for a few hours before taking his sister back to the village.

Mera was checking on Kara again when Corin came quietly into the small room. He lay his weapons and pack on the ledge.

"How badly did they hurt her?" he asked.

"They just beat her. I don't think her body will take too long to recover, but I don't know what will happen when she wakes up," Mera replied somberly. "I didn't think the Calorins would be cruel enough to torture a young girl."

"Kadar is capable of anything," Corin replied bitterly. "I was afraid something like this would happen if she stayed, so it's partly my fault," he said.

"I think she knew the risks of riding out. You all do and you still go," Mera said. Corin nodded.

"You're not helping me feel better," he said. Mera suppressed a laugh.

"Let me look at your arm?" she asked, noticing the rough bandage on his forearm.

"It's fine really. Liam will take care of it later," Corin said.

"If I'm not mistaken, it's a recent wound, and Liam won't see it for a while," Mera said with a slight smile. Corin started to protest but stopped when he saw that she was determined to have her way. Sitting down at the low table, he pulled off his vambrace as Mera began to take off the bandage. Rolling up his sleeve, she began to wash the long jagged cut. After working for a few minutes in silence, she asked, "What's the south like? I heard you lived there for a time."

Corin was taken aback by the question, but he answered.

"It's flat. Grass plains as far as the eye can see. Each town and castle is like its own oasis. It looks lonely at first, but you get used to it after a while. I missed the mountains and trees most of all," he said.

"Are the people there all like Balkor?" she asked.

"Many of the lords are. They continually fight amongst themselves for more power. There are a few who will work with their people and rule justly. I was fortunate enough to serve under such a lord," Corin said.

"Why would they want to invade Aredor? We never did anything to them," Mera said.

"Power. If the Sultaan wanted to conquer the world, this is the easiest place to start. Controlling Aredor places him in the middle of the North. He could strike anywhere he wanted," Corin explained.

"So they are trying to completely subdue us so that there is no chance of their being overthrown once they turn to another country," Mera said.

"Exactly. But for now, we've been able to put the Sultaan's plans on hold," Corin smiled.

"I don't understand why men would want to conquer everyone else. Why can't we just be content with what we have?" she asked. Corin smiled again.

"It's always been that way. I've heard it said that men are at their best when waging war," he said. Mera tied off the bandage on his arm.

"It's strange that so many see honor and glory in battles and war, but I only see pain and suffering," she said and then looked away, a little embarrassed.

"There will always be a place for the sword, just as there is for the healer. We each have a place and duty in life," Corin said. Then he grinned. "You're making me sound quite profound."

Mera saw the twinkle in his eyes, and she returned the smile.

"Then I should go before you turn completely into a philosopher," she said.

Corin rolled his sleeve down and stood. Sweeping a low bow, he helped her stand.

"Talking so much, I almost forgot my manners," he joked. Mera laughed quietly. He took her outside where Martin was saddling horses to take her back to the village. Returning to the cave, Corin saw that Kara was sleeping peacefully. Lying down on Darrin's pallet on the opposite ledge, he wrapped a cloak around himself and fell asleep.

After a few hours, he awoke. The caves were quiet; Darrin and his men were still out. Rolling over, he saw that Kara was now awake and lying on her side. Karif perched on the ledge, and she was gently stroking the feathers on his neck.

"You found his soft spot," Corin said. Kara smiled crookedly.

"He came in when Liam did and decided tae keep me company I guess," she said.

"How are you feeling?" Corin asked, rising and walking over to her.

"Better, sir. Really hungry though. Lieutenant said he'd bring me something," she answered.

"I saw Delyth out in the valley. I didn't know if you knew that," Corin said. Kara brightened at the knowledge that her horse was unharmed. Liam came back in with a bowl of soup and some bread for Kara. She gingerly sat up and took the food.

"I'll have Kieran bring your pack in so you can change into some clean clothes," Liam said. Kara nodded gratefully. Her shirt and breeches were covered in dirt and grime from the dungeons.

Corin pulled on his leather tunic, laced it up, and then buckled on his weapons again.

"Going somewhere, Captain?" Liam inquired casually.

"Thought I'd go for a walk," Corin replied, equally casual.

"In the dark?" Liam raised an eyebrow.

"Yes," Corin grinned. "I won't be gone long. You're in charge." Liam shrugged hopelessly as Kara stifled a grin.

"Fine. Just try not to get yourself killed," Liam said.

"But everything is so much more fun that way," Corin laughed, whistling Karif to his shoulder.

The clouds had cleared to reveal a fiery sunset. Corin struck out in a northern direction towards Lynwood Keep. After days in the saddle, he was glad to stretch his legs. Striding easily, he would reach his destination in little over an hour.

CHAPTER

16

Emeth stood in a forest glade, gazing up at the stars peeking through the clouds. Ismail often sent his guards on errands. He had used that as an excuse to get out into the forest. Narak moved softly nearby, adding to the gentle noises of the forest around him. For the first time in a long while, he found himself thinking about his own forest home with his three brothers and of course, his father. Almost savagely, he pushed the memories away, not wishing to dwell too long on the past.

"Tell Ahmed that he needs to work on his aim," Corin said, stepping into the clearing. Emeth turned around.

"Gladly. Maybe he'll stop moping about it," Emeth said, smiling. They clasped hands, and he pulled Corin into a rough embrace.

"It's good tae see you again," Emeth said, reverting to Rhyddan.

"You too," Corin said. "Tell me, what brings you into this dangerous forest alone?" he asked.

"An errand for Ismail. I just haven't figured out what it is yet," Emeth said. Corin laughed.

"How are they doing?" he asked.

"Ahmed's doing all right, after I convinced him that he didn't kill you. Ismail is a little better," Emeth said. "Oh, I should tell you. Ismail has a son, born a few weeks before we left. Rishdah is the proudest grandfather you'll ever see."

Corin smiled. "What did they call him?" he asked.

"Castimir. It was Nadirah's idea," Emeth answered. They stood silently for a few moments and then Corin shook himself slightly.

"Did you get any trouble from Kadar?" he asked. Emeth grinned.

"Did I ever tell you that I was banished? Terrible story," he said.

"He believe you?" Corin asked.

"I think so. How is the girl, by the way?" Emeth asked in turn.

"She's doing better. Thanks to you, we got her out in time," Corin said.

"Listen, that's probably the last time I'll be able tae help," Emeth said. He shifted, a little embarrassed by what he was going to say. "I'm still held by oath tae protect Ismail, and I won't betray him. If it was anyone else, I would have come and joined you long ago, but I can't." He didn't meet Corin's gaze.

"I understand," Corin said quietly. "I wouldn't hurt any of them."

Emeth relaxed slightly. "I'm sorry," he said.

"We're pulled in different directions for now. I hope we may fight together soon," Corin said.

"As do I," Emeth replied, moving to Narak. "I need tae go before they send out a search party."

"Emeth, if you ever need help, follow the river until we find you," Corin said. Emeth mounted.

"Thanks. Be careful, Cor," he said.

"You too, Aiden," Corin replied. Raising a hand in farewell, he vanished into the forest.

The next morning, Darrin and his men returned victorious but subdued. Two fresh graves were dug in the clearing. Dylan and Marc replaced the two dead warriors in the patrols. The summer moved quickly on, and the two sides met in frequent skirmishes. Lord Balkor became increasingly angry at his commanders' inability to subdue the Hawk Flight. He began forming a new plan to draw the outlaws out of the protection of the forest where he could easily destroy them.

As the seasons began to change, Trey brought Ivor, who had word of this new plan, back to the caves. Riders were immediately sent out to recall all the patrols to the caves. A council of war was held in the main cavern.

"I and two other men from the village were taking the required supplies to Kingstown. I overheard some of the soldiers talking about Balkor's newest orders. They're going to burn the villages and kill everyone until the Hawk Flight is drawn out of the forest. He'll have an army waiting for you," Ivor said.

Darrin silenced the angry outbursts that ran through the caves.

"You are sure of this?" he asked Ivor. The warrior nodded.

"Yes, sire. Kadar is to lead the force. They will start at Caldor village in the morning," Ivor said. Darrin looked to Corin.

"It's dangerous. If we managed to fight our way out, Balkor will keep burning until every last one of us is dead," Corin said.

"And if we let the villagers die, then everything we've been fighting for dies as well," Martin protested.

"Balkor knows we don't want the villages to burn," Darrin said. "But we're severely outnumbered."

"With respect, sire, we've been outnumbered from the beginning, but we haven't backed down," Trey said. Darrin stood in silence for a few moments.

"I will go with whoever is willing," he said. Corin stepped forward.

"I'm willing, and I'll follow you to death and beyond, brother," he said. The men of his patrol rose and stood ready. Tristan faced Darrin.

"I'm going if only to ram my spear down Kadar's filthy throat before I die," he said. Loud cheers greeted his words as the remainder of the Hawk Flight rose. Martin and Trey stood by Tristan and Corin.

"Arm yourselves for battle, boys. We'll teach Balkor to fear our names," Darrin said.

Kadar was pleased. His men had surrounded Caldor, preventing any escape from the burning buildings. The villagers were panicking and were trying to find a way out. Kadar smiled thinly, enjoying their distress. His lieutenant rode up and pointed wordlessly at the distant tree line. Lines of horsemen emerged from the forest as the sun glinted off the tips of spears. Kadar's smile widened when he saw the outlaws. He had a hundred and fifty men under his command. The Aredorians would quickly fall.

Darrin stared down at the burning village and the Calorin army.

"Corin, you and Tristan take the left flank. Trey, circle the village and strike from the rear," Darrin said.

He raised his spear, and Corin and Tristan galloped off at the head of their men. Falling into battle formation, they leveled spears at the Calorins and raised the eerie wolf howl. Trey heard the cry and signaled his men. They rode off to the right to circle the enemy.

Corin and his men bit deep into the Calorin flank when Darrin raised his spear again. He and Martin's men urged their horses into an easy lope, gathering speed as they approached the unprotected right flank of the Calorins. Kadar was not prepared for the fury of the Aredorians as they swept through his men. The Calorins began to retreat under the onslaught. Then their lines broke, and they ran.

The Hawk Flight did not give chase. They had lost no men, but the ground was littered with Calorin dead. The surviving villagers stumbled out of the buildings. Corin rode up to Darrin.

"What now? Where do they go? Their homes are completely destroyed," he said.

Parents gathered up frightened children. An old woman wept as her house collapsed. Darrin dismounted and walked over to the people.

"You can't stay here. We can take you to another village or there is a valley hidden deep in the forest," he said. A man stepped forward.

"I will take my family to the forest. We will be safer there," he said. One by one, the other families decided to follow him to the hidden valley. Darrin chose several men, led by Gavin, to guide the families to Dunham.

They did not have long to wait before Kadar attacked another village. This time, the outlaws were driven back, but not before allowing time for the villagers to escape. Again, Darrin offered a place in the forest to the survivors. So it went through the fall with the Hawk Flight and Calorins clashing outside villages and in the open fields. Though greatly outnumbering the Hawk Flight and gaining reinforcements, Kadar's forces sustained heavy losses. The Aredorians fought on their own ground, and Darrin and Corin together came up with strategies to keep their warband from being overwhelmed. However, as the season passed, there was no sign of the attacks abating.

Trey and Martin stood looking at a paper nailed to a board outside the town hall.

"Who is it supposed to be, do you think?" Martin asked. Trey shrugged and leaned forward to better inspect the reward poster. The picture showed a man, face half obscured by a hood. A hawk was drawn on the figure's shoulder.

"It's hard to say really," Trey said. Corin joined them momentarily. Taking in the poster, he said, "I don't think it's me."

Martin shook his head. "No, the picture is much better looking," he said. Corin laughed.

"Two hundred gold crescents, not bad," Corin said.

"Think Balkor has that kind of money? Maybe we could get more for you," Trey said.

"It's possible. I think we could get three hundred at least," Martin returned. A mischievous smile spread across Trey's face. He tore down the notice and turned it over. Grabbing a charcoal stick, he began to sketch.

"How much could you get for a drunken tyrant?" he asked, holding up the completed drawing. Corin and Martin laughed helplessly. Trey had drawn a passable likeness of Balkor.

"Three hundred crescents!" Martin laughed, looking at the number written on the paper.

"You think I could get more?" Trey asked.

"I wouldn't press your luck," Corin said. Trey signed his name in the corner, "Just in case he wants to know," he said, and pinned it to the notice board using one of his arrows.

Darrin rode up with Tristan.

"Kadar's been sighted. The barricades in place?" he asked.

"Yes, we're ready," Corin answered. "All the villagers are out with whatever supplies they could carry."

"Marc should have them in the forest by now," Trey said.

"Good. Get to your positions. We don't have long to wait," Darrin said. They saluted and hurried off to take their places along the barricade.

Crouched behind the barricade, the outlaws were protected from the hails of Calorin arrows and javelins. Corin risked a glance over the barrier. The Calorins were getting ready to charge. He passed the word along the line on men stationed with him and then he ran to find Darrin. From where they stood, they could see the Calorins begin to spread out in an attempt to circle the town. Darrin nodded to Corin, who then took Zephyr's reins from Liam and vaulted into the saddle. Tristan and his men were likewise mounted. Darrin strode off to join the front line. Tristan and Corin waited until they heard the familiar wolf cry. Setting spurs to their steeds, they galloped off in different directions at the head of their men. Raising war cries, they rode head-on into the encircling flanks of the Calorin army. Darrin and the remaining men began pouring arrows into the center of the enemy force.

Kadar saw the mounted Hawk Flight begin to retreat under the press of his warriors. He rode forward, intending to oversee the destruction of the hated outlaw cavalry. Suddenly, he found himself confronted by Tristan. Kadar's guards had ridden ahead, and when he looked into Tristan's blazing eyes, his courage deserted him, and he fled. Snatching a spear from a surprised Calorin foot soldier, Tristan lashed his horse in quick pursuit, ignoring the call to rejoin the retreating Hawk Flight.

The outlaws made camp in Dunham Forest. Darrin sent Corin and his men on a quick foraging and scouting expedition while he went to greet the exiled villagers. Darrin had noticed Corin becoming more silent and restless over the past few days, and had tried to keep him busy. Any time he tried to broach the subject, Corin dismissed his questions abruptly. Darrin resolved to find the root of the problem that night, no matter what. Accompanied by Martin and two other men, he rode deeper into the forest. They were greeted by Marc and Llewellyn as they entered the small refugee camp. The townsfolk gathered around to greet their prince.

"Well, if it isn't young Martin. All accounts said you died on that plain."

Martin turned to confront the speaker. A tall, regal woman stood behind him. Streaks of gray ran through her jet-black hair. Although she was dressed simply, it didn't hide the authority she carried. Martin smiled and bowed.

"Your Majesty, I'm glad to see you alive and well," he said. Queen Elain of Aredor returned the smile.

"Thank you. It looks like this life agrees better with you than castle life did, what with all those young women chasing after you," she said. Martin laughed at her rather apt expression.

"Why do you think I was always begging Father to let me join the warband?" he said. Queen Elain laughed.

"As did your father before you. Anyone but you two would have let the attention go to your head," she said.

"There have always been more important and interesting things to do," Martin said. "In this instance, it is my solemn duty to present you to our commander." Sweeping another low bow, he proffered his arm and escorted her over to where Darrin stood.

"I will say one thing for you, you always did remember your manners," Queen Elain said.

"As always, you are too kind, Your Majesty," Martin replied. She smacked him lightly.

"You forget that your mother asked me to keep an eye on you before she died," she said.

"And you turned me into the charming person I am today," he returned. Queen Elain laughed.

Darrin caught sight of them and stood with a mixture of wonder and delight on his face. When Queen Elain saw Darrin, she gasped and her hand flew to her heart. She tenderly embraced her son, blinking back tears. Martin discreetly turned away and left them alone together. Mother and son talked, telling each other of all that had happened since they had last seen each other. Darrin made no mention of Corin, and the queen could give no information of the king's whereabouts.

"It's been almost four years since I last saw him," she said with a sigh.

Like Amaura, Queen Elain had fled into hiding as best as she could. At first she had been in the castle until some trustworthy servants had planned an escape. The plan had gone awry at the last moment, which forced Amaura to remain at Kingscastle while the queen and a maidservant were able to flee. Martin approached again.

"Sir, we'd best get moving if we want to get these families settled before dark and patrols are due back at camp," he said, shooting a meaningful glance at Darrin. The prince nodded and began issuing orders to the few men.

Some of the villagers chose to return to their homes; and three families, including the queen, decided to go to the hidden forest valley. Owain and Marc guided these families to the settlement and Darrin, Martin, and the two remaining men escorted the others back to the forest's edge.

Corin and his men arrived at camp before Darrin after commandeering a large supply train. Darrin found Corin sitting against a fallen tree, carving a piece of broken branch. Karif perched faithfully nearby on the massive trunk. Darrin sat next to him and Corin briefly acknowledged his presence.

"Where's Tristan?" Darrin asked. Corin shrugged.

"He took off after Kadar. No one's seen him since. Trey and Flynn have been out to look for him," Corin answered, continuing to carve.

I might as well get it over with, Darrin thought, and then he asked, "What's wrong, Cor?" As expected, he received no answer, but he was determined to wait Corin out. For a few moments, the only sound between them was the rasping of Corin's knife against the wood. Finally, "Balkor has an unlimited supply of men. He can afford to keep attacking the towns. We've lost five men and have no way of replacing them. We've been out here for almost a month and what's happened? Four villages burned to the ground, and to top it off, fifteen families that we have to provide for. Winter is coming on fast, and we haven't laid up any supplies for ourselves, let alone them!" Corin burst out. "This is completely hopeless! We might as well kill ourselves now and save Balkor the trouble," he muttered.

"Corin!" Darrin said sharply.

"You know it's true," Corin replied.

He is right, Darrin thought. He had been struggling to find a solution for days. There were many young children at the settlement who would need proper provisions over the winter. He also knew that they couldn't fight the Calorins out in the open forever, and there was no hope of reinforcements. Darrin was reluctant to bring the clans into the fight, for they might soon need all their warriors to defend against a Calorin invasion. This small band of warriors was Aredor's last hope.

"Corin, don't give up yet. We've lasted this long, we can survive a bit longer. There's always hope if you know how to look," Darrin said, rising and walking away.

A few hours later, a weary but triumphant Tristan rode into camp. He tossed a heavy, ornate scimitar to Darrin. Corin looked at the sword and then to Tristan.

"How?" he asked.

"In the back. He died like the coward he was," Tristan replied. "It took me a while to catch him, he ran so fast. I only needed to get close enough to use the spear."

Trey clapped his brother on the back.

"This should set Balkor's plans back a bit," Trey said.

"Hopefully," Tristan said. "With Kadar out of the way, the other generals will be fighting among themselves to get appointed to his position."

"So the army will be without a commander for a day at least," Corin said. Darrin looked carefully at him. It appeared that they had the same idea.

"Their main camp is set outside of Caldor. It wouldn't take us long to find them," Darrin said. The men around them began to grasp the implications of their statements. Trey, keen as ever for a fight, spoke first.

"When do we leave?" he asked.

"Three hours' time. We can try to catch them unaware before dawn," Darrin said. As the men left to prepare, Corin caught his brother's arm.

"I'm sorry for what I said before. It seems I was wrong. We have a chance to end this campaign sooner than I thought," he said.

"I don't blame you for anything you said. I myself have wondered how much longer we can last," Darrin said.

"I said I'd follow to death and beyond. I still hold to that," Corin said. "When the time comes, I'll be standing beside you."

"Thank you, brother," Darrin replied.

The outlaws ate a quick meal and then broke camp and rode out into the night. The Hawk Flight found the Calorins sooner than expected. The enemy force had withdrawn from the village but had not gone far without the guidance of Kadar. Full two hundred men were camped below. Watching the campfires of the Calorins, the two brothers formed a plan for the morning.

At dawn's first light, Darrin rode up and down the ordered ranks of the Hawk Flight.

"We are still severely outnumbered, but what we can do today will influence the remainder of this war. I only ask that you fight hard and true as befits the last warband of Aredor," Darrin said.

Corin tossed Karif into the sky. The gray hawk circled above them, shrieking his defiance. The warriors erupted with the time-honored war chant of Aredor. Strong as the mountains, lonely as the forest, steady as the plains, it rolled forth, echoing in the air and keeping time with the thunder of their horses' hooves. The Calorins rushed to defend themselves but were too late. In later years, the Aredorian warriors would try to describe that charge. At that moment, though sorely outnumbered, they were invincible. The warrior blood of the north flowed hot through their veins, and they could have conquered a kingdom.

Darrin and Corin fought side by side, and all fell before their shining blades. And together, they watched the Calorins, reduced to less than half their original force, flee. The Hawk Flight raised a great shout of triumph.

"Behold the wolf and the hawk of Aredor whom no man can stand against!" Martin cried, lifting his sword. Warriors raised swords in a salute, shouting their acclaim until the air echoed.

Then gathering their dead, the warband prepared to return to the forest. Balkor still controlled a sizeable army that could still easily overwhelm them. Upon returning to the caves, Kael, Owain, and a young man named Madoc were laid to rest beside their comrades in the silent forest glade. Spears into which their names were etched were thrust into the ground at the head of each grave. After a moment of silence, the warriors left the glade. Corin and Darrin were last to leave.

"Eleven graves. Eleven warriors gone to Lleu's halls beyond the stars. How will we replace them?" Corin asked quietly.

"We will find a way. Maybe there are others in hiding who will now have a chance to join us," Darrin replied. Corin smiled.

"Tell me, Darrin, do you ever lose hope?" he asked.

"As long as my brother stands by me, I won't ever lose hope," Darrin replied.

CHAPTER 17

A few days later, Darrin shook Corin awake. Muttering something that Darrin identified as Calorin, Corin came fully awake and rolled over.

"What?" he growled.

"Come on, lazy. All you've done the past two days is sleep," Darrin said.

"That's because some people actually need sleep," Corin replied.

"We're going to the settlement. There's someone I want you to meet," Darrin said.

Still grumbling, Corin rolled out of his pallet and dressed. Darrin waited patiently until he finished buckling on all of his weapons. As they left the cave, Corin knelt by the small stream at the entrance. Cupping water in his hands, he splashed it over his face as the cold water shocked him unerringly awake. Following Darrin to the valley, they caught and saddled their horses in the dim half-light of the morning. Karif flew up to perch on Corin's shoulder as they mounted. Darrin waved to the sentry as they rode out.

The settlement lay in the southwest region of Dunham Forest. It would be a few hours before they reached it. They rode in companionable silence along hidden forest trails. Karif flew off occasionally to chase small animals, but always returned to Corin. Midday saw them riding down into the valley. Young boys ran up to hold their horses, slightly in awe of the big stallions and their riders. Corin caught one staring openmouthed at him and Karif.

"Are you really the Hawk?" a boy asked him.

"Aye, I suppose I really am," Corin replied.

He gestured to the young boy to come forward. The boy did so hesitantly. Corin went down on one knee so that he looked directly at the boy. He clicked gently to Karif, and the hawk hopped down to his wrist. At his urging, the boy reached out and ran a finger down Karif's feathers. Corin moved the boy's hand to the side of the hawk's neck. The boys began laughing as Karif made small noises of enjoyment as he was stroked. Darrin grinned as he watched Corin talk with the children.

"Do you fight the Calorins all by yourself?" one asked.

"Not all the time. Sometimes he helps," Corin nodded to Darrin.

"No, silly," another boy chided. "He has a warband, huger than the king's!"

"Well, I don't know if it's huger than the king's. Maybe one day," Corin said. He stood as Karif cried out. Looking up, he saw the object of the hawk's focus. Karif spread his wings and flew from Corin's wrist in pursuit of a wood pigeon.

"Is he gone forever?" a boy of about five years asked.

"No, he'll be back soon. He got hungry," Corin explained. Then he had to field a dozen more questions about the hawk from the eager boys.

Darrin saw a young man nearby and spoke quietly to him for a moment; then the man hurried away. When Corin had finally answered all the children's questions, they ran off whooping excitedly to play a new game inspired by the outlaws.

Queen Elain followed her guide across the valley. She had been helping several other women bake bread when the young man arrived and told her that the prince wanted to speak to her. Stopping only to remove her apron, the queen stepped out briskly. As they came around the rough huts constructed by the refugees, she saw two men standing by their horses. One she knew to be Darrin, but the other was unfamiliar. She could not see his face, yet something tugged within her. Darrin said something to him causing a burst of laughter. As she heard the sound a memory flashed unbidden before her—a small boy, blonde like his father, with merriment sparkling in his deep blue eyes.

They turned toward her, and Corin stopped, uncertainty creasing his features. He looked to Darrin questioningly. His brother smiled and nodded once. Queen Elain watched breathlessly as Corin came slowly toward her in his long, limping stride. They stood in silence for a few moments, staring at one another. Then she gently laid a hand on his cheek and whispered, "Corin?"

"Mother" came the answer. Queen Elain threw her arms around her son in a fierce embrace, clutching tightly him as if she would never let go.

"My son!" she said, tears streaking her face. "I never hoped to see you here again!"

Corin didn't answer and just hugged her tightly. Corin carefully guarded his emotions, but Darrin could see that he was close to tears. Elain finally stepped back, still holding on to Corin.

"You've grown and changed so much," she said. Corin grinned in his familiar cocky way.

"You didn't think I'd stay twelve forever did you, Mother?" he asked. As Queen Elain laughed, she looked years younger.

"You know what I mean," she said. Seeing the ease with which he bore his weapons, she said, "You look to have become a fine warrior. I only wish your father was here to see you." Then she turned on Darrin. "Why didn't you tell me?" she demanded.

"Would you have believed me?" he teased. "I thought I'd surprise you both."

"Well, I suppose you can't stay long, but I'll see you fed before you go," she said. Corin and Darrin exchanged grins as they followed her over to a trestle table set out in the open air. Sitting obediently, they waited until she returned with meat pies and beakers of water.

As they ate, Elain gently pried the story out of Corin. Darrin already knew much of what he told, but Corin provided a few more details for his mother. As he finished, the queen wiped fresh tears from her eyes.

"Don't be ashamed of anything, Corin. You are stronger because of it," she said, taking his hand.

"Perhaps," Corin answered.

"I am proud of you, of both of you. Together, you help all of Aredor believe that we can be free again," Elain said.

"That may take years, Mother," Darrin warned.

"Today, a son returned to me. I believe anything is possible," Elain asserted.

All too soon, they had to leave. Embracing her sons one last time, the queen watched them ride from the valley, and Corin paused to let Karif alight on his outstretched arm.

With Kadar's death and the victory of the Hawk Flight, the attacks on the villages ceased. As news spread of the battle and the decrease of Calorin vigilance, those men brave enough moved to join the outlaws. At the beginning of winter, fifteen warriors had arrived. Most had been in hiding in the villages and had been unable to travel to the forest because of the Calorins. A few came from the settlement, mostly young men who wished to fight the Calorins who had destroyed their homes. All were welcomed into the warband.

That winter was an unusually mild one, which allowed the outlaws to continue striking at the enemy. The fighting continued, but with no end in sight. Corin and Darrin visited their mother a few more times as often as their duties would allow. A second spring arrived since the warband had formed. As warmth spread through the air, the outlaws could sense another change. Calorin patrols were not as frequent as they used to be, and Argusian mercenaries were rarely to be seen. The outlaws wondered at it but feared that Balkor was building up his army to attack again.

By midspring, Corin led his patrol out on a quick scouting expedition to gain any information on Balkor's movements. Leaving Liam in charge of the band in the forest, Corin took Ian with him into a town that housed a Calorin outpost. They left their horses hidden on the outskirts of the town and slipped inside. Corin grew uneasy. Whereas before, there had always been plenty of soldiers occupying the garrison, they saw only three in the square. Corin and Ian watched the barracks for over an hour and noted only a handful of Calorins go in and out.

"What's going on?" Corin muttered. "Even if Balkor was massing an army, he would leave this town heavily manned. It's too close to the forest."

"Maybe that's just it," Ian said. "There haven't been any new ships in months. Maybe these are the only men he can spare."

Corin looked at him quietly.

"If you're right, Darrin needs to know about this," he said. "Come on, let's get out of here."

But at that moment, luck turned against them. A Calorin soldier came running through the village. His shouts roused his comrades. Corin cursed.

"They found the horses. Run!" he said urgently. Together, Corin and Ian sprang up and ran for their horses. The soldiers saw them and ran to cut them off. Corin saw that they would soon be surrounded and drew his scimitar.

"Ian, run for it before we're completely caught. Get to the horses and ride for the forest. Don't stop for anything. I'll follow if I can," he said.

"But, Captain…!" Ian protested.

"Now!" Corin said harshly, shoving him away. Ian ran and heard the clash as Corin crossed blades with a soldier. He pushed on, shaking off a pursuing Calorin. Rounding a building, he found the horses. For a moment, he debated going back to find

Corin, but then a triumphant cry went up in Calorin, and he knew it was too late. Throwing himself on his horse, Ian galloped back to the forest.

Corin killed the first two soldiers to come at him, but he had been pushed back into a narrow alley between two houses. Soldiers advanced, carrying spears. Karif dove from the sky, shrieking angrily. He attacked one of the soldiers, causing a spear to fall. Corin knocked the other spear away and thrust with his scimitar. But before he could pull it free, another soldier jumped at him from the side. Corin was thrown forcefully against the wall. Painfully, he fell to the ground, only to find that he was surrounded with a spear pressed against his chest.

The Calorin captain eyed Karif flying angrily above and then looked to Corin.

"Well, if it isn't the Hawk himself," he sneered. His men raised a shout at finding their enemy powerless at their feet.

"Bind him. We leave at once. Lord Balkor will want to see him in person," he ordered.

The half mile back to the forest seemed to stretch on forever. Ian thundered into the camp. Practically falling off his horse, he lay on the ground with his legs refusing to support him. Liam crouched in front of him.

"Ian, what happened? Where's Corin?" he demanded. Ian sobbed for breath.

"They caught him!" he said. A groan ran through the men. Liam grabbed Ian's shoulders.

"Are you sure?" he asked. Ian nodded. Any doubt was erased when Karif swooped in, shrieking and hopping agitatedly.

"I ran like a coward, and I didn't go back!" Ian cried, close to tears. "I know what they'll do to him. He's as good as dead!"

Liam shook him.

"Ian, listen to me. We'll get him out. Get back on your horse. We're going to the caves."

CHAPTER 18

Corin rode in the midst of the Calorins. His hands were tightly bound behind him, and blood flowed from a cut on his cheek. The Calorin captain pushed on relentlessly, and by early afternoon, they rode into Kingstown. The portcullis clanged shut as they entered the castle, and the forbidding sound seemed to crush any hope of rescue. Corin was pulled off his horse, and Zephyr was led away rearing and fighting.

Corin's captors led him up the broad steps and through the great oaken doors of the castle. The great hall was dimly lit in comparison to the bright spring afternoon. As his eyes adjusted, Corin saw he was being brought up to the dais where Balkor sat in his father's throne. The Calorin lord came down eagerly to greet them. Lord Balkor eyed Corin but did not recognize him.

"What a pleasure! I have long wanted to meet the Hawk," Lord Balkor said in a smooth voice. Then he struck Corin savagely across the face.

"Don't flatter yourself. I never wanted to see you," Corin replied, spitting out blood. This time, one of the soldiers drove his spear butt hard into Corin's ribs. The captain held out all of Corin's weapons. Lord Balkor dismissed the long bow and the knives but took his scimitar. Unsheathing the blade, he inspected it carefully.

"This is the finest Calorin workmanship. Stolen most likely. And how did an outlaw learn to use it?" Lord Balkor asked. Corin did not answer even after several hard blows were given.

"My lord Balkor! I heard that a prisoner had been taken, and I came to congratulate you," an all-too-familiar voice said. Corin raised his head to see Ismail standing there, flanked by his guards. Any surprise they must have felt at seeing Corin was quickly masked behind impassive expressions.

"Yes, the cursed outlaws' leader himself," Lord Balkor said. Ismail again offered congratulations, forcing out the words.

"And now, perhaps you can help me, Lord Ismail," Balkor said. "How do you suppose he got this scimitar?" he asked, holding it out to Ismail.

Ismail took the scimitar and lifted it experimentally.

"This must have been a captain's sword, judging by the blade," he said. "A captain that he must have killed in order to obtain it."

"Yes, exactly. And now he shall pay for the offences he has committed against us and for his ill-advised rebellion," Lord Balkor said.

"We didn't ask for you and your pathetic Sultaan to invade! You don't care about the men you've lost, they were just pawns. You've never had any conscience!" Corin spat. Balkor stared into his blazing blue eyes.

"Let me see his right hand," he ordered. The soldiers untied Corin and held his arms firmly. Balkor cut off the glove covering Corin's palm.

"Well, well, if it isn't the slave boy. I think you remember how I've dealt with you in the past," Balkor sneered.

"You never broke me," Corin answered.

"Perhaps. But once again, you are under my power. Farid, bring the girl!" Balkor shouted at one of his generals. A few minutes later, Farid returned, leading Amaura by her arm.

"We caught her yesterday trying to pass information to the forest," Balkor said. "Her contact was killed, but before he died, he was kind enough to reveal that she is the princess."

Corin bit back a curse. Balkor would stop at nothing until he got information. Emeth clasped his hands tightly behind him, struggling to remain expressionless. Beside him, Ahmed stared fixedly at the floor. Whatever happened, they could not interfere.

"Now, boy, you will tell me everything, or she dies slowly before your eyes. Do not deceive me! You know what I'm capable of!" Balkor said.

"Corin, don't! I don't care what they do to me!" Amaura cried. Balkor hit her across the mouth.

"Don't underestimate me, boy!" he thundered. Amaura's eyes pleaded Corin not to betray his men. Corin was torn. He wanted to save his sister, but if he gave up his men, then Aredor would die. He had to choose.

"I'm sorry, Maurie," he whispered. Then he turned to face Balkor. "If we both die, so be it. But when we do, our secrets will remain safe," he said.

Lord Balkor was slightly taken aback his reply.

"Very well, you shall have your wish. You will both die together tomorrow at midday," he declared. As the guards began leading Corin and Amaura away, Ismail stirred.

"Wait!" he commanded. "Lord Balkor, it has occurred to me that it might be better not to kill the girl," he said.

"What do you mean?" Balkor asked.

"Executing them together makes them stronger, for in a way, they will have defeated you. The people will understand the execution of a rebel, but a princess will seem like a martyr. Let me take her to Calorin. A life of servitude weakens the resolve. Or better yet, marriage to a Calorin. For instance, my father would welcome a union between my brother Castimir and a princess," Ismail said.

Amaura saw a strange look cross Corin's face as he heard this. She had understood most of what was said, and cried out.

"I would rather die!"

Corin launched a tirade of Calorin at Balkor and Ismail. Despite the situation, Emeth hid a grin as he listened to Corin. He sincerely hoped that Amaura didn't understand much Calorin. When Lord Balkor saw the prisoners' reaction to Ismail's suggestion, a flash of understanding went through him, and he smiled maliciously.

"A fine idea, Lord Ismail. Yes, take the girl. I think you and I shall succeed together in finally subduing this land," he said. Ismail bowed.

"I look forward to it, my lord," he said. Ordering the soldiers to follow with Amaura, Ismail and his guards left the hall without a backward glance. Balkor turned to Corin.

"Farid, don't take him directly to the dungeons," he said. "Make sure it hurts." And he left. Farid saluted. Grabbing Corin he said, "You've caused me too much trouble. I'll make you suffer for it!"

Corin's eyes blazed dangerously.

"Try!" he spat.

Arriving at his chambers, Ismail dismissed the soldiers.

"Tell Lord Balkor that I will leave shortly. As soon as the girl is safely on her way to the ships, I will return to witness the execution," he told the captain. Once the door closed behind them, Emeth turned to Ismail.

"What are you playing at, sir?" he demanded.

"I'd like to know the same," Ahmed said.

"Repaying a debt, and I'm tired of playing along to Balkor's whims. Emeth, ask her how to get to the outlaws." Ismail pointed to Amaura.

"Follow the river until we find you." Corin's words flashed through Emeth's mind.

"No need, sir. I think I know," he stammered.

"Sir, what are we going to do?" Ahmed asked.

"Hamíd is in trouble, set to die. I refuse to let that happen. He'd do the same for any of us," Ismail replied. "Emeth, I'm not asking how you know the way, just make sure it's fast. Ahmed, saddle the horses. We don't have much time."

Silence reigned in the caves after Liam delivered the news. Darrin questioned Ian on what had happened. Ian also told him that the Calorin forces were severely diminished. Darrin sent Kara to bring Martin and his patrol back to caves. Not an hour later, Kieran rode in with news that Corin had been taken to Kingscastle.

"They've been spreading the news that they've caught the Hawk," Kieran said.

Darrin dismissed the men in order that he could talk in private with Trey, Tristan, and Martin.

"Any ideas?" Darrin asked.

"There are several ways we could get in, but how do we get out? You saw Ian and Kara after being their captives," Trey said.

"This won't be easy. The dungeons at Kingscastle aren't very accessible, and he'll be heavily guarded, if he's still alive at all," Darrin said. They all knew the somber truth of the statement. Balkor could have easily plunged a sword through Corin as soon as he learned his identity.

"But do you think Balkor would have killed him? He could decide to make a huge event out of an execution. I doubt he'd leave Corin very long in the dungeons," Tristan said.

"I don't see how that's supposed to help!" Martin said sharply. His face was creased with worry. The others understood his agitation.

"If they were right about the troops, then we should send a message to Dandin. With his help, we can retake Lynwood and hold it against Balkor," Darrin said. He sent for Kieran, who left shortly after. "Martin, follow with your patrol and meet Dandin."

"No!" came Martin's sharp refusal. "If you're going in after Corin, then I'm coming too. Or are you leaving him there to die while you try to retake the keep?" he asked. The challenge in his voice was unmistakable. Trey laid a restraining hand on Martin's arm, but he was shaken off. Darrin rose and faced Martin.

"We have a distinct advantage here. In retaking the keep, we take back part of Aredor. Corin would understand its importance," he said.

"I don't care about that blasted keep!" Martin shouted. "Every man out there owes him their life! I'm not going to let him die, and if you won't try and rescue him, then I'll go alone!"

"Do not think that I don't want to destroy Kingscastle to find him, but Corin would gladly give his life if it meant freedom from the Calorins!" Darrin answered. Martin was stopped from replying again when Llewellyn came in.

"Sire, you'd better come outside. There's something you need you see," he said. Darrin and the others hurried out of the caves. Standing in the early evening light and surrounded by wary outlaws, were Ismail, Ahmed, Emeth, and Amaura.

CHAPTER 19

Night had fallen by the time Corin was taken to the dungeon. Soldiers dragged him down the corridor and pushed him into the cell. Taking the chains that were fastened to the wall, they locked them around his wrists and left.

Corin slumped against the wall, bruised and battered. Farid and his men had contented themselves with spears and fists. He dimly twice remembered losing consciousness through the ordeal. Manacles clinked as he raised his arm and carefully wiped blood from his face with his sleeve. His ribs and left wrist throbbed unmercifully. The walls of the cell were made of iron bars, which gave it a cagelike appearance that Corin hated.

A small window near the ceiling allowed him a narrow view of the night sky. The last thing he saw before he lost consciousness again was a small, bright star.

"What are you doing here? How did you find us?" Darrin demanded. Emeth replied, "I'm the one who sent Corin the message. He told me where to find you in case I needed help. My master wanted to talk, so I brought him," he said.

Darrin turned to Ismail.

"What do you want?" he asked in Calorin. Ismail surprised him by replying in Rhyddan.

"I came first to bring your princess here. Second, because a man we both know is sentenced to die tomorrow and, I would stop it," he said.

"Why would you help the captain?" Trey asked.

"Because he saved my life by fighting off an attacking lion, and I swore to repay him. Now seems like the time," Ismail replied.

"You realize that you are betraying your lord by doing this?" Darrin asked. Ismail looked him in the eye.

"We have not received any more men since last spring because our Sultaan is dealing with an uprising on his southern borders. Many outposts stand deserted. Kingscastle is held by only seventy men. Our hold in this country is slim. We have lost many, many men. We do not belong here," Ismail said.

"It's true, Darrin. I was trying to get you a message when I got caught," Amaura said.

"You have risked a great deal in coming here," Darrin said. "I see why my brother respects you so much."

Emeth quietly translated for Ahmed.

"Do you agree with what Ismail's doing?" Emeth asked.

"I thought about it on the ride here. I think I do now. We each have our own country. I just want this to be over so that we can go home," Ahmed answered. "I just would have expected it more from Castimir."

Emeth agreed. "I hope this works and that Balkor never finds out. I'd hate to think about what might happen then," he said.

"It's a dangerous game to be sure, but Ismail's been putting on an act for Balkor since we got here. He can pull us through," Ahmed said.

"Aiden! You seem to get around a bit," Tristan said. Emeth grinned.

"Tristan! I hoped to see you here," he said.

"You still owe me a story, so I'll stick around for a bit," Tristan replied. He extended a hand to Ahmed, who hesitantly clasped it.

"Sorry, my Calorin is not the best, but you must be Ahmed," Tristan said in Calorin. "Corin told us a few stories about you two," he continued.

"Which ones?" Emeth asked curiously.

"An attack on the Argusian border. If I recall, the city was surrounded," Tristan said.

"Latharn! He probably didn't even mention what he did during the battle," Emeth exclaimed. "Ahmed, you can tell the story better than me." Prompted by Emeth, Ahmed related the entire story of the battle and the desperate sorties to break the siege. Tristan shook his head in wonder as the tale finished.

"What a fight! Your Lord Rishdah isn't short on nerve," he said. Further conversation was interrupted when Tristan was called to join Darrin.

"Martin and Trey will go back with Ismail. They can easily get into the castle. You two know what to do from there?" Darrin asked. Martin and Trey nodded. "Flynn, take Martin's patrol and join Clan Dyson at Lynwood. Have Dandin bring some of his men and meet the rest of us farther down the Track. We'll go to Kingscastle and stop the execution tomorrow," Darrin finished. "Understood?"

"Yes, sir," came the reply. Martin and Trey hurried to don Calorin uniforms. They fastened black masks about their lower face and donned helmets. Shortly thereafter, Ismail left to return to Kingscastle with two extra "guards."

"Kara, I want you to take Amaura to the settlement. I think you know which hut," Darrin said with a wink to Kara. A fresh horse was brought for Amaura.

"Make your way back as fast as you can, Kara. We might need you again," Darrin ordered. Kara saluted and led Amaura out into the night. Not long after, Flynn and his men rode out to meet Dandin and Clan Dyson.

Corin awoke before midnight. He carefully moved into a more comfortable position and tried to ignore a raging thirst and hunger.

"You look a little worse for the wear," a voice said, startling him. Another prisoner sat in the cell to his left. The shadows cast by the torches made it hard to see the man's face clearly.

"I've had better days," Corin answered, leaning against the wall. His fellow prisoner chuckled.

"So I take it you're one of the outlaws," he said.

"Aye, that I am. I ran into some bad luck this morning. Thought a dungeon might be a good place to wait for it to change," Corin said, smiling crookedly. The man laughed again.

"It might take a while. I've tried it for four years, and I still haven't gotten anywhere," he said.

"You been down here all this time?" Corin asked.

"I was captured near the mountains. The Calorins took Burkehead Tower by the border and stuck me there. From what I've heard, Clan Gunlon has been making some raids, so they brought me to this hole for safekeeping," the man said.

"Were you with the king when you were captured?" Corin asked, hope flaring in him for a moment.

"I guess you could say that I was. Here, see if you can reach this," he said, pushing a beaker through the bars. Corin managed to catch the rim and pull it towards him. Relief seeped through him as he heard the slosh of water. Raising it to his lips, he took a sip and rinsed the blood from his mouth. Corin took two more mouthfuls and then set the beaker down.

"You been on many campaigns?" the man asked, approving the way he rationed the water.

"I've been on a few. I traveled and fought for a while in the south. I've been back home two years now," Corin said.

"Probably didn't get the homecoming you expected," the man commented.

"No, I made it to the forest as fast as I could and met up with the beginnings of the Hawk Flight," Corin said.

"Who leads this Hawk Flight now?" the prisoner asked.

"Prince Darrin. He escaped early last year," Corin said. The man sighed in relief.

"Lleu be praised! That boy is still alive," he whispered. They lapsed into silence for a few minutes.

"I heard them call you 'the Hawk,' so you are no common soldier. Do you expect to be rescued?" the man asked.

"I don't know. We've discovered something important. If Darrin joins forces with the clans, he can end the war. I hope he's doing that instead of trying to get me out. Of course by tomorrow, it won't matter," Corin said.

"You don't seem afraid," he commented.

"I learned a long time ago to hide what I felt," Corin replied.

"You are willing to sacrifice yourself if Darrin chooses to retake Lynwood?" the man asked.

"If I can die and give Aredor her freedom back, I'd have done it a long time ago," Corin said. "I just wish I could die on a battlefield instead of a scaffold."

"Don't give up yet, there's still time," the prisoner said. Corin smiled.

"You're not the first to ever tell me that," he said. He wished he could see the man's face. There was something achingly familiar about the voice. Did he dare hope?

Despite the man's words, dawn came quickly as the sun's first rays peeked through the window. Heavy footsteps sounded in the corridor, and Balkor stood in front of the door. Two soldiers entered the cell, unchained Corin, and hauled him upright.

"I would have visited earlier, but I was preparing something for you," Balkor said. "I believe I might have to endure some sort of escape attempt before the execution. So in order to ensure your death, I made this." He held up a small dagger carefully. "The blade is covered with the venom of the adder that lives in the sands of Argus. It's been treated such that the victim will live for days before dying. Days racked with the worst pain ever imagined."

The soldiers held Corin tightly as he struggled to move away. Balkor folded down the collar of Corin's tunic, laid the blade against his neck, and cut.

"There is no antidote, so you see, I come out the victor no matter what happens. I also realized the resemblance between you and another friend of mine, and so I made some inquiries. The servants were full of good information." Balkor grabbed a torch and held it up so that the other prisoner was fully illuminated. "Remarkable! Celyn, I do believe I've found your long lost son. What? I can see he didn't tell you. How noble! Probably to escape telling you that he was my slave for years. I hope you got to know him again because he doesn't have much longer in this world!" Balkor said, laughing cruelly.

Corin fell to his hands and knees, trembling uncontrollably. He put his hand up to try and stop the bleeding cut on his neck. A bolt of pain shot through him, leaving him gasping for breath.

"Rest easy, Hawk!" Balkor laughed again, satisfied, as he left the dungeons. King Celyn moved closer to the bars.

"Corin!" he cried, helplessly watching his son. Corin crawled to the beaker of water. He drank some and then began coughing. Raising a hand to his mouth, he saw blood. Pain racked him, and he huddled on the ground until it subsided somewhat. Corin moved slowly towards his father. Celyn grabbed his hand through the bars.

"Steady, Corin," he said as another tremor racked Corin. "It'll pass, breathe slowly, it'll pass!"

"Father!" it was a relief to finally say the word. "It's getting worse!" Corin groaned, leaning against the bars. Celyn tightened his grip on Corin's hand.

"It's all right, son. I'm here."

Two hours before dawn, Martin and Trey went up to the battlements. They slowly walked the west wall. Trey heard the faint rasp of steel and whirled around, dirk in hand.

"Llewellyn! Put that oversized rabbit skinner up. It's us!" he exclaimed.

"Sorry, sir," Llewellyn grinned, sheathing his knife. "The sentries are taken care of. We're on the walls."

"Good. There are only five men in the guardhouse by the west gate," Martin said. Llewellyn leaned over the walls and gave a low whistle. Within minutes, four more men had climbed the ropes and stood on the wall.

"Any news on Lynwood yet?" Trey asked. Llewellyn shook his head.

"Not yet, we're expecting Kieran any time now. Have you seen the captain?" he asked.

"No," Martin said. "Let's get to the guardhouse. It won't be long now."

Morning sunlight streamed through the prison window. Corin sat carefully. It had been almost an hour since the last attack, and the pain had settled down to a steady throb. He didn't dare move for fear of triggering another spasm. He watched the sun beams play through the window. It was strange to think that soon he would never see it again. He had cheated death so many times before, but the end had finally come, and he hoped that he had earned a place in Lleu's hall.

King Celyn watched Corin. He had learned that the rest of his family was safe, but the only one he cared about now was Corin. With a sinking heart, he heard the soldiers enter the dungeon. Unexpectedly, one knelt by Corin and pulled his helmet and mask off to reveal very Aredorian features.

"Corin, are you all right?" Martin asked, looking at the bruises on his face.

"I'll be fine," Corin replied. Trey also removed his helmet and crouched by Martin.

"Can you use your scimitar? There will be fighting before today is done," Trey said.

"Lynwood Keep is ours again. The Hawk Flight and two score men of Clan Dyson are outside the castle waiting on the signal," Martin said.

"I'll do my best," Corin said. Trey grinned.

"Good, I went through no end of trouble to steal your scimitar back," he said. He and Martin pulled their masks and helmets back on as Corin tried to stand. He doubled over and began coughing. He wiped the blood away before Martin and Trey could see. Martin exchanged a concerned look with Trey.

"Corin?" he asked worriedly.

"I'm fine," Corin said, straightening up.

"Corin, are you sure?" King Celyn asked.

"I'm not giving in yet," Corin replied.

"King Celyn!" Martin exclaimed. Trey hurried to unlock the cell.

"Leave it for now," Celyn ordered. "I can't help you fight." Trey persisted and swung the door open. He tossed the king the keys and a dagger. "Just in case," he said.

Martin looped Corin's hands together behind his back and helped him from the cell.

A large scaffold had been erected in the middle of the courtyard. The main gates stood open, and a line of soldiers held the townspeople back. Ismail stood by Lord Balkor. Ahmed gripped his sword hilt nervously, and Emeth casually noted the number of guards on the walls. Corin gave them a small smile as he ascended the platform with Martin and Trey. An Argusian stood on the scaffold hefting a large ax.

"At last! Let today signal the end of the outlaws!" Lord Balkor proclaimed. His men raised a cheer, but the sound died on their lips as another cry rent the air. A wolf howled, wild and savage.

A figure stood on the walls above the main gates, broadsword in hand. The men on the walls turned, and Balkor saw that they held Aredorian longbows.

The quick rasp of steel brought his attention back to the scaffold. Martin and Trey had cast aside their helmets and had drawn their swords that they had hidden beneath their cloaks. Corin freed his hands, and Trey handed him his scimitar. That galvanized Balkor into action. At his commands, his soldiers drew their weapons and moved to attack. The outlaws on the walls drew their bows and fired into the Calorins below. Raising a war cry, Corin, Martin, and Trey jumped from the scaffold into the fight. Their cry was echoed by Tristan and Dandin leading their men in from the east gate. Darrin fought his way down the wall steps to join them.

The battle raged, and Balkor saw his men fall against the Northerners. He looked for a way to escape. The walls were choked with fighting, and any entrance to the castle was blocked. His eye lighted on the main gate. The people had fled, leaving the gate wide open. He cut his way towards it. A few more steps and he would be free!

"Balkor!" The sound halted him in his tracks. Unwillingly he turned and saw Corin thundering toward him. Confident he could overcome him, Balkor waited by the gates. Scimitars flashing, they clashed together, fury giving Corin the strength to fight. They strove against each other, neither losing nor gaining ground. Then Corin reeled back against the wall steps with blood pouring from a cut down his side.

He clung desperately to the steps to keep himself upright as pain washed over him.

"Can you feel the poison seeping through your veins? Eating away at you?" Balkor asked mockingly. "You cannot win."

"You always underestimated me!" Corin gritted. Pushing himself upright, he closed on Balkor again. Balkor was driven back. He swung his scimitar in an arc to bring down across Corin's neck. Corin ducked the blow, and then gathering his sword up, he gave a great cry and plunged it into Balkor. He dimly saw Balkor fall, and then he felt his strength failing. His scimitar clattered to the ground as pain enveloped him, and he fell into darkness.

Ismail handed his sword to Darrin. All around, the surviving Calorins threw their weapons to the ground and placed their hands on their heads in a gesture of surrender.

"Allow me tae be the first tae congratulate you on this victory," Dandin said.

"Thank you, but most of the credit goes to you," Darrin replied.

"Och, we're glad tae help. Some of Clan Gunlon should be arriving later," Dandin said.

"They'll be more than welcome," Darrin said gratefully. Under his orders, the prisoners were taken to the dungeons, and the servants willingly turned the great hall into a makeshift infirmary for the wounded. Darrin stopped Ian as he went by supporting a wounded soldier.

"Have you seen Corin?" he asked worriedly. Ian shook his head.

"No, sir," he said. Martin gave a strangled cry and pointed, but Darrin had already seen. He ran and knelt beside the crumpled figure lying by the gates.

He wiped blood from Corin's face as he held him. Corin's eyes flickered open.

"Corin! Hold still, brother, we'll get you patched up," Darin said.

"It's too late for me, I think. Balkor used a poison," Corin said hoarsely. "There's no cure. I don't have long."

"No! Corin, please! I don't want to lose you again!" Darrin said.

"I don't think I can fight it. Promise me you'll finish what we've started," Corin said.

"I promise, and I won't give up on you!" Darrin said fiercely. Corin managed a smile, but it was too late. He was dying, and he was frightened.

"You never have," he said then was overtaken by a bout of coughing. Darrin stared horrified at the blood as Corin lapsed into unconsciousness. Martin came up.

"They're bringing a stretcher. Liam will look after him as soon as he can," he said.

"Martin, take him to his old room," Darrin said. Martin nodded as he helped lay Corin on the stretcher. Tristan helped Darrin to stand.

"Where's Trey?" Darrin asked.

"Inside. Liam's working on him now." Tristan replied shortly.

"What happened?" Darrin asked.

"I found him against the wall, cut up pretty badly. The worst bit was pulling the spear out of his hip," Tristan said. Darrin looked around at the courtyard. There was still so much work to be done. He wished the day was over so he could sleep and forget for a little while.

CHAPTER 20

Mera made her way up to the castle accompanied by Kara. Darrin had sent Kara to find her early that morning. Now that the battle was safely over, Mera hurried to help with the wounded. Above the gate, the Calorin standard had been torn down and replaced with the banner of Aredor. A gray wolf ran proudly across the blue field. They paused for a moment to admire the sight and then passed through the gate. The courtyard and walls had been cleared, and sentries paced behind the battlements.

Kara took the horses to the stable while Mera went inside the castle. She found Liam bandaging the leg of a young clan member.

"Just start wherever you can," he told her.

The hall was filled with Calorins and Northerners alike. Mera saw a Calorin soldier with a splintered arrow in his chest. Going over to him, she began cleaning the wound. The hours passed slowly until all had finally been cared for.

"Can you help with one more?" Liam asked Mera. She nodded and he led her up the stairs and through a corridor to where Corin lay.

"It's the captain. Darrin said he'd been poisoned somehow. I'm afraid I don't know much about poisons. I bandaged what I could, but I was hoping you'd be able to help him," Liam said.

"I'll see what I can do," Mera said.

"Thanks," Liam said as he opened the door. "I'll get you whatever you need."

Mera drew back the blankets covering Corin. His side had been bandaged, but around it, she could see numerous bruises and welts. Her attention was distracted by a cut on his neck. It was swollen and discolored. She asked for hot water and clean cloths. While she waited, she sorted through her remaining herbs and powders. Corin lay unmoving on the bed, his breath coming in ragged gasps broken only by sudden bouts of coughing.

Mera prepared a poultice for the wound on his neck. His skin was hot and dry to the touch. She washed and rebandaged the other wounds he had sustained. Then she washed blood away from his face and neck, revealing more bruises and cuts. Mera worked tirelessly, preparing another poultice for his swollen left wrist. As she finished, she went to the windows and pushed them open. The forest was a distant line on the horizon. The setting sun caught at the windows, making them flash for a moment, and then it was gone.

Darrin sat with King Celyn, Martin, Tristan, and Dandin in a small council chamber. They were discussing how best to divide their forces. Castle Martel on the coast and the southern half of Aredor still lay in Calorin hands. A knock sounded, and the guard entered followed by a stranger.

He was a few years older than Dandin and carried himself with a confident air. Long fair hair was pulled back with a leather band, and he wore the armor of the clans—a leather tunic studded with steel plates. He carried a claymore under a purple plaid cloak. Like Dandin, his left arm remained bare and showed a rearing unicorn and a six-pointed star.

"Just in time! Lads, allow me tae introduce Colwyn, chief of Clan Gunlon," Dandin announced. Colwyn inclined his head.

"I brought three score men with me. We'd be glad tae help in any way," he said, his accent softer than Dandin's.

"Thank you," King Celyn replied. "I'm afraid our hospitality is limited right now."

"Och, not tae worry. With your permission, my laird, we'll camp on the plain outside," Colwyn said.

With the additional men, they were able to spread their forces more easily. As the council ended, Tristan left to go check on Trey. Dandin and Colwyn went to see to their men, and Martin left to oversee the changing sentries. Darrin and his father were left alone. For the first time that day, they were able to talk. Slowly the conversation turned to Corin. Celyn wanted to hear more about his son, and Darrin willingly obliged.

It was late when they left the chamber. Darrin went to Corin's room. Pushing the door open, he entered quietly. Liam sat in an armchair by the bed. Darrin dismissed him saying, "I'll stay for a while, Liam. Get some sleep. We leave tomorrow morning for the coast."

Liam nodded gratefully; he was exhausted.

"Don't stay too long, sire. You need rest as well," Liam said, leaving the room.

Darrin sat down in the chair, unbuckling his sword as he did. Corin lay still, laboring to breath. He was trapped in endless nightmares.

He saw again the scene of the ambush. He ran to Castimir. Too late; he saw the sword stab into the young man. Then to his horror, he saw it was his hand that held the sword. It faded, and the lion attacked, but he was powerless to move. Its claws raked his side…on and on it went, he could not escape.

Darrin woke at dawn. He had fallen asleep in the armchair. He stood stiffly, having remained in his mail coat since the battle. He belted his sword on again. Corin showed no change since the night before. A flutter of wings at the window announced the arrival of Karif. The hawk perched disconsolately on the windowsill. Darrin turned back to the bed. He hated to leave, for he knew that it was probably the last time he would see his brother alive. He reached out and gently clasped Corin's hand.

"Good-bye, brother," he whispered.

"He's dying, isn't he?" Martin asked, standing in the doorway. Darrin couldn't answer; his own anguished expression matched Martin's. Martin came forward and stood at the foot of the bed.

"I didn't think he would be taken away again so soon," he said, his voice catching as he looked down at his friend. Darrin laid a hand on Martin's shoulder.

"Come, it is time for us to leave," he said. Martin nodded, blinking back tears, and followed Darrin from the room.

Shortly after, the Hawk Flight rode from Kingscastle accompanied by Clan Dyson and Clan Gunlon. Kieran rode with them, and Kara again travelled to the forest to bring news to the settlement. As she rode through towns and farms, she spread the tidings of the victories, prompting celebrations among the people.

Queen Elain and Amaura insisted on travelling back with her immediately. Kara happily guided them back through the forest to their home. Amaura was only a few years her elder, and they kept lively conversation on the way. Kara welcomed her companionship after spending two years in the Hawk Flight. Queen Elain often joined in, sharing their laughter as they celebrated their newfound freedom.

The castle was quiet; only two score men remained to guard it. With Liam gone, Mera took charge of the wounded and directed the few healers that remained. She checked on Corin often, becoming more worried as the day progressed. She changed the poultice on his neck, hoping to draw out the poison. Instead, the wound became worse, and the skin around it turned red and inflamed. She tried various treatments but to no avail. She could see him become weaker and weaker. It tore at her heart to see him lie there so far removed from the confident, cheerful young man she had seen in the forest.

King Celyn greeted his wife and daughter at the gates in a joyful reunion.

"If Darrin's leading the warband, where's Corin?" Amaura asked. King Celyn's face fell as he explained what had happened. Queen Elain turned pale.

"Where is he?" she asked quietly. The three of them went to Corin's chamber. Mera met them at the door. Queen Elain crossed to the bed and sat down on the edge. Amaura stared at her brother and huddled in her father's arms, crying softly. Mera went to the queen.

"I'm so sorry!" she said, bursting into tears. "I've tried everything, but he's dying!"

Queen Elain rose and held Mera gently.

"It's not your fault that he's dying," she said gently. "You've done your best."

Mera dried her cheeks.

"With your permission, my lady, I'll keep trying," she said and left the room.

Corin lasted through the night and the next day. As night fell again, he struggled to breathe as the poison took its toll. Suddenly, his dreams shifted, and he was in a forest that he had seen once before.

A man walked toward him, a stranger. But when Corin saw him, he felt a sense of peace. The man was dressed in fine clothes and seemed to glow from within.

"Who are you?" Corin asked. The man smiled.

"A messenger of Lleu. He sent me from his halls to find you," he said.

"Is it time?" Corin asked.

"Yes and no" came the reply. "You are to go back. There is still much for you to do. It is not time for your journey to the halls beyond the heavens."

"How can I go back?" Corin asked bewildered.

"I will help," the messenger said. He reached out and touched Corin's neck. Corin felt the poison leave him, and he drew a deep, shuddering breath. The man withdrew his hand then gently touched Corin's palm.

"Thank you," Corin said. The man smiled again.

"Go, Corin!" he commanded.

Then the forest faded, and Corin awoke.

Mera was in the room with the king and queen and Amaura. As she prepared to change the bandage on Corin's neck again, she saw a change come over him. He stiffened slightly, and then the shadows of pain on his face passed, and he took a deep breath. Mera laid a hand on his forehead; the fever was gone. The others looked at her curiously, and then Corin shifted and slowly opened his eyes.

Mera quickly filled a beaker with water and helped him drink slowly. Queen Elain clasped her son's hand as tears of joy streamed down her cheeks. Mera removed the bandage over the cut. To her surprise, the skin was smooth and unbroken. All trace of the poison was gone. He gave her a tired smile.

"Hello again. I guess we can only meet when you're stitching me up," he said. Mera smiled.

"How do you feel?" she asked.

"Tired, but glad to be alive," he answered, his voice a little hoarse. "Where am I?"

"Home," Queen Elain answered.

When they left a few minutes later, Corin was already asleep.

CHAPTER 21

Castle Martel had been surrendered into northern hands. Reports came in from Martin and Colwyn that the port town by the Masian estuary was safely occupied. Aredor was freed from Calorin control.

The wolf standard flew from the battlements of the castle alongside the banner of Tristan and Trey's family. Their father had died in the invasion, making Tristan the lord of Castle Martel. The warband slept inside the protective walls of the castle as Tristan heard again the familiar sound of waves beating against the cliffs.

Darrin woke early the next morning. Going down to the main hall, he saw Tristan already awake and greeting Kara, who had just arrived.

"Kara, what are you doing here?" Darrin asked.

"I've a message for you, sire!" she said with barely controlled excitement. Darrin took the paper and unfolded it. After reading it, he collapsed into the nearest chair.

"Tris…Corin's alive!" he said. Tristan sighed in relief.

"Get back to Kingscastle and see him," he said. "Dandin and I can manage here."

Darrin needed no further urging. He gathered his saddlebags and prepared to ride again. He sent Kara down the coast to give the news to Martin.

Darrin was greeted on the castle steps by Amaura. She wore an apron and carried a basket full of linen.

"You look busy," Darrin said, hugging her.

"Aye, there's so much to do. I don't mind the work. It was either laundry or help rehang tapestries. I left Mother in charge of that," Amaura said. Darrin laughed.

"Where's Father?" he asked.

"Last I saw, checking the armory with Iwan. Oh, and Corin's still asleep. Mera expects him to finally wake up sometime this evening," Amaura said. Darrin in turn gave her the news of the recent events and then he left to go find the king and report.

Inside, the hall had been cleared. The wounded had been moved to beds in the barracks. Banners had been rehung behind the thrones. Rich, decorative tapestries had been hung on the walls between pillars. Darrin navigated the familiar hallways until he came to a room in one of the towers. The two guards opened to door to let him in. Ismail and his guards rose to greet Darrin.

"I never thanked you properly for what you did," Darrin said in Calorin.

"You're welcome," Ismail replied. "How is Corin? I knew what Balkor had done."

"He is past the worst," Darrin said.

"I am very glad to hear it. If I may ask, sir, what will happen to the prisoners here?" Ismail asked.

"We are provisioning your ships as we speak. Within a few days, you will all be taken to the coast to board the ships and return to Calorin," Darrin said.

"You show us great mercy," Ismail said.

"It's not in my nature to order the execution of hundreds of defenseless soldiers. With your return to Calorin, you will also carry a warning to the Sultaan against any return," Darrin said. Ismail nodded.

"You will make a great king one day," he said.

"Thank you. I hope I can," Darrin said. "I wish we could have met under different circumstances. I would like to know all of you better. Any friend of my brother is a friend of mine."

Before he left, Darrin spoke privately with Emeth.

"You are a Braeton. I can release you now if that is your wish," he said.

"I've been thinking about it, sire, but I'll stay where I am. I've one year left in service tae Lord Rishdah. Besides, when we get back tae Calorin, there might be trouble, and I'd rather see them safely through," Emeth said.

"Are you sure?" Darrin asked. Emeth nodded.

"It's only a year. When it ends, I might be ready tae finally come back home again. I just ask that you don't tell the clans about me. They don't know what I've been through, and in their eyes, I fight on the wrong side," he said. Darrin nodded in understanding.

He left the room and wound his way back to Corin's room. His brother was still asleep, so Darrin sat down on the window seat. Karif hopped closer to him on the windowsill. The hawk gently butted Darrin's hand, wanting to be stroked. He obliged, and the hawk closed his eyes in contentment.

"As much as I hate to, I'll have to report you for waking me up," Corin said. Darrin laughed and helped him sit up against the pillows.

"What's been happening the past few days?" Corin asked. Darrin related the arrival of the clans and the retaking of Aredor. Then he told Corin of Ismail's part in the events.

"The ships will leave in four days. As soon as the Calorins are safely gone, the clans will begin to leave, and we begin to rebuild the warbands," Darrin said.

"How many of the Hawk Flight did we lose?" Corin asked.

"Twelve dead, five were wounded badly. Thankfully, we already have more men coming in to join us," Darrin said. "How long until you're up?" he asked. Corin shrugged.

"Hopefully, nothing more than a week or two. I just look worse than I feel," he said. It was true. Bruises still covered his face and upper body. A long cut decorated his cheek, and his wrist still ached under the bandage, but under Mera's treatment, it would heal quickly. But most importantly, when Corin looked at his right palm, the brand was gone.

Before the Calorins were escorted to the coast, Ismail, Ahmed, and Emeth were allowed to visit Corin. They met in a private room where Corin thanked them for their involvement. Their friendship had been forged through war, and it would ever remain. By now, all three of them knew that Corin was prince of Aredor; but in their eyes, he would always be Hamíd, and he wanted it to stay that way. They bid a sad farewell to each other, for who knew when they would see each other again, if at all.

Three days later as they boarded the ships, Tristan handed Emeth an oddly shaped bundle. Emeth surreptitiously looked inside and saw the hilts of his swords as well as his companions' weapons.

"I'll be back," he said to Tristan.

"Be careful, Aiden," Tristan said, saying a short farewell to Ismail and Ahmed.

Two weeks later, Corin stood on the walls of Kingscastle, watching the sunset. There was a celebration of the victory and his recovery. He had slipped out of the castle for a few moments of quiet. As a prince, he was to have his own warband. He would retain command of the Hawk Flight and could choose replacements for the men he had lost from the new recruits pouring in.

Emeth would return in a year, and the Calorins would be back, he was certain. But this time, Aredor would be ready. He and the

Hawk Flight would patrol the forest and coast, ready and waiting to fight and defend their freedom again.

The End